# VARIED TRAITS

## A NOVEL

# PATRICK
# BROWN

# VARIED
# TRAITS

## A NOVEL

Varied Traits
Copyright @ 2015 by Patrick Brown

Published by
Peachtree Corners Press
Peachtree Corners, GA

ISBN: 978-0-9862549-0-1
Ebook ISBN: 978-0-9862549-1-8

Printed in the United States of America

Cover and Interior Design by GKS Creative

Library of Congress information on file with the Publisher

For Susan, Logan, and Madison,
who fill my days with laughter and love.

# 1

JOSEPH McINTOSH LEFT THE DEALERSHIP early on Friday. After a midday meet with his sales team, he'd had enough for one day. He rarely worked Saturdays and he was looking forward to being away from meetings, his sales team, and his older brother, Michael, until he returned to work on Monday. He had a pretty good idea how he was going to spend his Friday night too. It wasn't going to be a quiet night sipping wine with a nice girl; he didn't like wine and he didn't particularly like nice girls. He and Bud Sherman, another ex-jock whom he had met at the University of Georgia in the late 1990s when they both played football for the Bulldogs, had a big night planned touring some strip clubs, drinking liquor, and maybe doing a little coke and smoking some weed. At thirty-four, McIntosh still had some of his boyish good looks and wasn't lacking in charm and charisma—mostly he was full of shit, but that had certainly helped his career in car sales and sometimes came in handy with the fairer sex. At six feet, three inches and 240 pounds, he was about twenty pounds above his playing weight, and some of that former muscle was segueing into fat. His once wavy head full of brown hair was starting to thin, and to his surprise, he had plucked a few gray ones over the past year. The August sun was brutal this afternoon and the black asphalt was a mirror reflecting the heat from the bright Georgia sky. So he cranked the AC on high in his late-model Ford Expedition and headed north out of the dealership on Peachtree Industrial Boulevard. He crossed under 285 leaving Chamblee behind, and driving through Doraville towards his home in Peachtree Corners. Traffic was beginning to thicken, but he figured he would make it to his house off Spalding in good time. Within minutes, Joey pulled into his drive, admiring his freshly cut and manicured lawn. The zoysia sod got plenty of early morning sun and was mostly shaded from the late afternoon heat by the row of large cypress trees bordering the back of his property. A number of pink-flowered crepe myrtles looked stunning framing his driveway. Two Japanese maples and a big oak tree provided additional privacy to his house, which was well set back from the quiet street. He'd had the trim freshly painted the previous spring, as well as new windows installed throughout the house. His home, which he shared with his six-year-old black Lab, Herschel, was a well-maintained and attractive decorative stone home in this affluent northeast Atlanta neighborhood. He wheeled the Expedition around to the rear entry garage, hit the remote, and slid into the empty spot next to his spotless red Mustang GT500. He entered through the kitchen, which opened into a large, open, airy great room. He passed through the hall and opened the basement door where he was immediately greeted by Herschel.

"Hey, boy," he said while rubbing him behind his ears, all while the big dog was wagging his tail, which shook his whole backside. "Let's go outside."

He led Herschel down the carpeted stairs that led to a basement featuring a sixty-inch TV on the wall with surround sound, a sectional sofa, and a pool table, along with a kitchen and bar area. A full bath was at the back next to the basement door. Joey opened the door and

Herschel dashed out to do his business. Joey went to the bar and poured four fingers of Maker's Mark over ice into a cocktail glass, splashed in some club soda, and squeezed off a lemon in his drink. He finished it off in several slugs and poured another to sip on. He went back upstairs to the main level, and strolled past the two spare bedrooms into his spacious and lavishly furnished master. He peeled off his suit and tie and threw on some gym shorts and a tee shirt. He carried his drink and mobile phone back to the great room, flipped on ESPN, and kept an ear on SportsCenter while he keyed in Bud's contact on his iPhone.

Bud answered on the second ring. "Joey Mac! What the hell's going on, bro?"

"Hey, Bud, I'm thinking we can head out around eight tonight, get a bite to eat, and a few drinks at Shae's. Then maybe we can start down at Licorice or the Slick Kitty and work our way back towards Utopia. I wanna end up there. It's pretty close to the house and it's got the best looking ladies."

Licorice and the Slick Kitty were on Cheshire Bridge Road in the city of Atlanta, about fifteen miles or so from where McIntosh lived, and Utopia was in nearby Doraville. Joey had been in the VIP room with a particular dancer several times at Utopia, and he was ready to take it to the next level. He knew from experience that they used one of a couple "inns" along or just off the Boulevard that would be a short drive from the club.

"Utopia? Yeah, man. You got your eye on that tall chick, right?" Bud asked. "How much is she gonna set you back, bro?"

Joey responded, "I don't know. Worth every penny of it, though, I'm sure."

"What's her name again?"

"Her name is Velvet…'cause when you run your hand down her thigh it's like…well, velvet. She must use the cocoa butter," Joey laughed. "I think she's been dancing there for a while; tall, leggy, big naturals, and she's not like seventeen. You read me?"

"Hmmm. Go for it, dude. I like mine left on the burner a little longer," Bud stated. He preferred the black dancers and was especially particular to those with a full bush.

To each his own, thought Joey. "Okay, Bud. I'll see you in a few hours."

Joey clicked off, polished off his drink, let Herschel back in, and played with him until it was time to clean up.

Joey Mac showered, shaved, brushed his teeth, and rinsed. He dressed in black designer jeans, a gold Ralph Lauren polo, Gucci loafers sans socks, and added his gold Rolex to his left wrist and his 2002 SEC Championship ring to his left ring finger. A small key on his chain opened a lockbox in his closet. He removed $2000 in cash, a small baggie of weed, and a gram of cocaine. The lock-box was bolted to the frame behind the sheetrock in his bedroom closet. It contained $72,000 in cash, ¼ ounce of coke, 3 ounces of high-quality weed, and an ample supply of Vicodin and Percocet. It also housed an assortment of jewelry and other valuables. He knew he would need lots of money tonight. Bud Sherman wasn't exactly loaded, so Joey would probably foot most of the bill this evening, but he didn't mind. He had fun hanging with Bud, and Joey had done pretty well for himself. His father had started McIntosh Ford in the seventies and built a sprawling dealership. In the early 2000s, the elder McIntosh had turned the business over to his two sons to run, and then the old guy had quietly passed away several years ago. As sales manager and with a 50 percent stake in the dealership, Joey had invested well, been nimble between down markets, and had built himself an investment portfolio just slightly north of seven figures. He had just a few years left to pay on his house and, of course, he was always in a new Ford automobile that was paid for through the dealership. He had earned it. He worked hard and was good at his job. He made a nice salary, earned sales commission when he got out on the floor and moved cars himself, and split a portion of the profits with his brother. Joey lived large, but had no problem socking away moderately large sums of money each month for both short-term and long-term needs.

He locked the box, took Herschel to the basement and gave him food, and filled the big bowl of water he used when he wouldn't be home until the next morning. He checked the deadbolts, set the code for the security system, exited through the garage, and drove the Expedition out into the night.

# 2

MILLICENT IVEY WAS EXHAUSTED. Her day had begun at 6:30 am leading a high-octane aerobics class, followed by an hour and a half spent doing paperwork in her office at the Atlanta Rec Club on Ashford Dunwoody Road. From 9:30 to noon, she conducted an advanced gymnastics clinic for twelve-year-old girls whose mothers all thought their daughter was the next Mary Lou Retton. She'd had time for a quick bite at Jo's next to Blackburn Park before returning to teach another aerobics class followed by back-to-back one-hour private gymnastics lessons with eight-year-old girls whose mothers were *certain* that their daughters were the next Nadia Comaneci. The kids were great. The parents…not so much. At twenty-five, she was young for one of the ARC managers, but she had a strong resume that included a 3.8 GPA at the University of Alabama majoring in English lit with a minor in physical education. She was a four-year cheerleader and had won numerous medals as a floor and balance beam performer on the Crimson Tide women's gymnastics team.

She ended the day with a staff meeting, showered, and was ready to head home to rest her sore muscles and get some sleep before returning at 6:30 on Saturday. She loved her job, but the physical and mental demands were oftentimes draining. Mostly she worked with nice people, and the members were mostly fine people too. There were, however, exceptions. One of those exceptions was leering at her as she walked past the weight room towards the exit. A Neanderthal named Klaus, who had been coming a short time and apparently was a bouncer in some kind of club, always made it a point to stop his workout when she passed and present her with a mirthless grin that she found absolutely creepy. He was one of the muscle heads she was sure "juiced." The pimply rash on the back of his neck and aggressive manner seemed to confirm as much. She had tried to avoid him, but he seemed to have LoJack on her. When he got close enough, she was always grossed out by his bad teeth and some kind of funky aroma that came off him that was both gamey and feral. He was decidedly an unlovely creature. This time he stepped in her path.

"Hey, Milly," he croaked, "you looking hot, baby! We should hang out sometime."

She had figured this day was coming, but had partially blocked it from her mind. She made every effort to be courteous and professional. "Klaus, I'm on my way home. It's been a long day, okay?"

"Sure, Milly…but maybe you want some company later." He actually flexed his pectoral muscle as he said this.

The old standby, "let's just be friends," came to mind, but she wasn't even remotely interested in being this guy's friend. "I'll see you later, Klaus," she said instead, and stepped around him while getting a whiff of his unpleasant odor. He let her pass, but glared after her, clearly angered at being shined on.

Millicent stopped briefly at the front counter to check to see that the staff there had a printed schedule for Saturday's activities, then exited the building towards the large parking lot. She was looking forward to a hot bath—in spite of the recent shower—and maybe a glass of wine and a good night's sleep. Her late-model black Honda Civic was at the far end of the parking lot close to the street. The temperature had pushed into the mid-90s earlier in the day and with the humidity, it was like a sauna. She knew her black car, sitting in the sun since morning, would be a furnace when she got inside, and although Friday evening rush-hour traffic was thinning, Ashford Dunwoody was a long train of slow-moving cars. She was almost to her car when she glanced up to see a low-flying plane that had just departed from Peachtree-DeKalb Airport—probably some jetsetter off for a big weekend somewhere. The noise from the overhead plane and the traffic from Ashford Dunwoody were sufficiently loud that she never heard the approach from behind her. Her brain was just registering a rather familiar and unpleasant smell when her arm was grabbed roughly from behind.

# 3

SALEM REID SAT IN THE ARC PARKING LOT with the air conditioning running on MAX. He had missed his early morning run through Chamblee and Brookhaven because of some unexpected business concerns at his security/limo service located in Buckhead. He didn't relish the thought of running during rush-hour traffic, battling the smog, traffic, and noise from the cars and trucks moving down Peachtree. He would do about eight miles on the treadmill, grab a bite to eat at Pelligro's on Johnson Ferry, and catch the end of the Braves game at home. As he exited his Dodge Challenger, he saw the pretty girl who worked at the ARC walking to her car. He had admired her from a distance the few times he had seen her and was doing so again now. He was just about to turn towards the entrance when he noticed a big guy who looked like Shrek making a stealthy advance on the girl. He pulled his Glock 17 and holster from beneath the car seat and attached it on his belt under his shirt, threw his bag back into the car, hit the locks, and quickly maneuvered between cars separating him from the Hulk while staying low the whole way. The big guy looked menacing and was gaining on the girl with a look of bad intent. He grabbed the girl's arm and twisted, but before he could do any more harm, Reid surprised him by grabbing his left wrist and hand and pushing up, which caused the guy to go up on his toes. He released the girl, turned, and threw a wild right at Reid. Reid weaved beneath the punch and came out of his crouch while simultaneously delivering a hard straight left to the Hulk's ear. Reid kicked him behind the knees and sent him sprawling face down on the asphalt. He was on him in no time with his left knee positioned in the guy's back, while Reid's right leg and arm forced the man's right arm straight into the air placing tremendous pressure on his shoulder. Reid drove the Hulk's face into the asphalt with his free hand and then looked up at the stunned and frightened girl.

"You okay?" asked Reid.

"I think so," she replied.

"Okay. Take off. I got it from here."

The girl stood there staring at the spectacle. "Go," said Reid more forcefully.

The girl stared at Reid for another second or two and then quickly jumped in her car and raced for the exit.

"What's your name?" Salem Reid asked the guy.

"Fuck you," the guy snorted.

Reid bounced the guy's face off the asphalt and asked again, "Your name?"

"Klaus," muttered the guy.

"Okay, Klaus. Listen carefully. You don't lift here anymore. Never again. Find another place. We clear?"

"Clear," Klaus replied.

"Where's your car, Klaus?"

"A few rows over."

"What kind?"

"Gold Tundra."

Salem Reid spotted a gold Toyota truck several rows behind him. He dragged Klaus to his feet and pushed him towards his truck. Klaus held his right arm limply next to his body. His shoulder would be sore for a couple of days, and his face would have some road rash for a while, but he'd recover. Klaus removed his keys from his pocket, unlocked his truck, climbed in, and started the engine. As he drove away he gave Reid the finger, but Reid hardly noticed as he was committing to memory the truck's license plate number.

Salem Reid returned to his car and wrote down the tag number from the truck, replaced his gun, grabbed his bag, and headed for the building. Salem Reid didn't like bullies, especially ones who picked on girls.

———

Millicent was still shaking by the time she arrived home. She rented a small house near Keswick Park that had only a carport, no garage. At the moment, she wished she lived somewhere in a gated community. The encounter with Klaus had shaken her up pretty good. The subsequent rescue by the tall, good-looking guy with the short dark hair and ropy muscles had thrown her for a loop too. She knew him. Well, she didn't exactly know him—they had never spoken—but she had seen him several times over the past few months and heard a few of the girls who worked out there as well as a few of the staff talking about some "hot" guy named Salem. Millicent realized that she wasn't the only one who had found herself attracted to him. She discovered his last name was Reid and that he lived in Chamblee. She wasn't sure exactly where in Chamblee because when she was "stalking" him on the membership spreadsheet from the ARC's database, she hadn't proceeded as far as procuring his address. She had simply wanted to know his full name… and well, maybe his age.

Millicent entered her house, carefully locking the doors behind her. She went into the kitchen and poured herself a large glass of wine, and then plopped down in front of her computer to see if she could find out more about this Salem Reid. She accessed the company database—one of the perks of being a manager—and conducted her search. She found that he had an address on Malone between the Peachtrees and just north of Chamblee Tucker Road, not far from the Chamblee MARTA Station. She recorded his digits, took a long gulp of her wine, sat back, and tried to relax. She figured she owed this guy a thank you for helping her, but felt a little uneasy about just showing up at his home. She'd have to figure this out. She carried her wine to the bathroom, started a warm bath, used the toilet, brushed her teeth, and then climbed into the tub.

# 4

REID FINISHED HIS RUN, showered at the ARC, changed into faded Levi's, a black T-shirt, and black Nike running shoes. He dropped in at Pelligro's and decided to get a to-go order of pasta marinara with grilled chicken, some Italian bread, and a big Caesar salad with croutons and extra Parmesan cheese. He headed east on Johnson Ferry into Chamblee and north on Peachtree Industrial, then turned right onto Malone where he owned a fourth-story corner condo that had partial views of both Buckhead and the Dunwoody/Sandy Springs area. He parked next to his Explorer in the underground lot, entered the lobby, and took the stairs to his unit. He had purchased the spacious three-bedroom condo when he returned from Iraq after the second Gulf War. He had served in a special unit of the infantry that was highly skilled in hand combat and had earned an array of medals. He had left the army as a first sergeant and stayed on in Iraq to do security detail for a variety of corporate types and dignitaries who were involved in the rebuilding. He had earned a tidy sum of money that was mostly free from taxes, and when he returned to the states a few years later, he was able to mortgage the price of his condo, and start his security/limo service. His business now had three limousines, three full-time drivers, two part-time drivers, a dispatcher, and a secretary. He also employed a former member of his unit to help with the security work. Despite the recession, the business had thrived, and Reid was looking to add another limo and perhaps another driver and part-time office worker. He had furnished his condo very tastefully, yet in an understated fashion. He had some Pottery Barn furniture in the living room and dining room, and in the bedroom, he had some fashionable furniture that included a mahogany dresser and two nightstands, as well as a king-size four-poster bed. He had several flat-screen TVs placed strategically throughout his home, mostly because he liked to watch the Braves during baseball season and NFL RedZone in the fall. He moved to the kitchen and placed his food on the counter, grabbed his last Blue Moon from the refrigerator, and turned on the Braves game. He fixed himself a plate of food and parked himself in front of the TV. The Braves were batting in the top of the fourth in Cincinnati. Justin Upton had just plated Jason Heyward with a sacrifice fly and the Braves were up 8-0. He had just taken his first bite of his pasta when his cell phone buzzed. It was a trigger from an app he had on his phone indicating someone wanting to be buzzed in at the security gate. He muted the sound on the television and clicked his phone.

"Yes?" he asked.

"Umm…hi. This is kind of awkward. I'm the girl from the club that you…uh…helped out tonight. May I stop in to thank you?"

"I'm glad you're okay." He gave her his unit number, figuring that she already knew it since she had gotten this far, and clicked off.

Reid took a couple of pulls from his beer, removed his dishes from the living room, scraped the food he could back into the to-go container, and was just finishing these tasks when his doorbell rang.

Millicent Ivey stood before him. He had only seen her in passing from distances farther from how he now encountered her. She was short; he guessed maybe five feet, two inches. She wore green shorts that flattered her muscular build. She was thick through the thighs and hips, but firm and athletic. She wore a snug watermelon-colored tank top that showed off well-toned arms and a firm bosom. She wore sandals on her small, delicate feet. Her toenails were painted red, which matched the polish on her fingernails. She had shoulder-length black hair that she wore loose. On every other occasion he'd seen her, she'd had it tied back. It was thick and luxurious and Reid had to resist an urge to reach out and run his hands through it. Her skin was smooth and lightly tanned. She had a face that sported a sprinkling of freckles and bright green eyes. She hadn't carried a purse, but she had a smart-phone—a brand he didn't recognize—in one hand and a six-pack of Sam Adams in the other.

She broke the silence. "Hi. I'm Millicent Ivey…or Milly…either way. I really appreciate what you did for me tonight. I might have really been in trouble otherwise." She handed him the six-pack. "I hope you like beer. I…uh wasn't sure how to thank you. This seems insufficient."

She had a voice like southern honey, and her smile lit up her lovely face.

"Anyway, maybe I'll see you around at the club," she said.

"Do you like baseball?" Reid asked.

"Baseball?" she asked. "Sure, I like it okay. I enjoy sports in general I suppose." She didn't add that she thought this a very strange question.

"I'm watching the Braves game and was just about to eat some pasta I picked up from Pelligro's. Hungry?" Reid inquired.

He didn't wait for a reply. He opened the door wide and stepped back to let her enter. Millicent walked into the entryway and stopped. "I should be taking you to dinner, not the other way around."

"It's no big deal," he said. "Please join me. The Braves are up 8-0."

"You have a great place here, Salem," she said, as she took in the living room, dining room, and kitchen that all took up one very large, open, and bright area. Big windows on two sides of the living space led to a balcony with great views.

She helped him dish the pasta onto plates and they each had a bowl of salad; she passed on the croutons and the bread. He didn't. They carried their plates into the living room and the game was still muted. He left it that way. Reid sat on the love seat and Millicent took the sofa, so that they sat diagonally from each other. While they ate, she told him about her work at the ARC, her experiences at the University of Alabama, cheerleading, and about her participation on the gymnastics team. He discovered that she grew up in Huntsville, in the northern part of Alabama. She had a younger brother who was a junior at Tulane. Her parents still lived in the house she grew up in. Her dad worked as a foreman for a beer company in a factory just outside of Huntsville, and her mom taught middle school. She was close to both her parents and fond of her little brother. Her hope was to get experience at the ARC while she saved her money to start her own gymnastics academy. She told him about her little rented house in Keswick Park and that she might consider buying it in the future; she had some options on that through her original negotiations with her landlord.

She realized that she had been doing all the talking and that she knew very little about this man. What little she did know about him surrounded the violent events of the afternoon. For all she knew, she could be in the home of a crazy guy who enjoyed beating on people, but for reasons she could not explain, she felt calm and comfortable with this guy. Put simply, he put her at ease. He seemed polite, pleasant, confident, and comfortable in his own skin. He wasn't trying to impress her, which ironically she found impressive. He was tall, at least a foot taller than her. Lean through the waist, but heavy up top. His forearms had corded muscles that had probably come from more than just working out. He had short, very dark brown hair, piercing blue eyes, and handsome features. He looked like he was probably an athlete in school. She guessed maybe a wrestler.

"You don't say much," she chided him good-naturedly.

He smiled. "I like listening to you talk."

Millicent Ivey wasn't sure the last time she blushed, but it had been a while. She felt her face get warm and realized this guy was really affecting her. "Well…I can certainly do that. I just hope I'm not boring you."

"You're not," he said.

He realized the game was over. Jerome and Brian were doing the postgame on FSN. He was an avid baseball fan and took in the Braves as often as he could, which wasn't all that often lately. He didn't regret missing most of this game though; he had really enjoyed the evening listening to this pretty young woman's life story. He was a good listener and didn't feel the need to say much, either about himself or others.

They polished off their second beer, and Millicent grew quiet. She was curious about him, but wasn't sure how to proceed. Finally, she asked, "Can I ask you what you do for work?"

"I run a security and limo service," he answered.

Perhaps that explained how he had secured her from that monster earlier. "Where are you located?" she asked.

"In Buckhead on Piedmont. About a mile east of Peachtree Road."

As concisely as he could, he told her about his business and how he had gotten into this line of work. He told her about his tours of duty in Iraq and how he had stayed in that troubled country and served as a security officer after the war. He related how his experiences there had prepared him for this line of work. He avoided telling her about the atrocities he had witnessed, about the men he had killed both with weapons and with his own hands. He mentioned nothing about his background in wrestling, the martial arts, or the MMA fighting he'd medaled in while training with his special unit in the military. He said nothing about the firearms he owned and how he practiced at a shooting range in Sandy Springs three to four times a week, so that he could be prepared should the need arise while protecting his clients. He avoided going into detail about his clients. Some were great people who contributed great things to society whether they were corporate CEOs, entertainers, or sport celebrities. But it was a mixed bag, because others were thug rap stars, overpaid and pampered athletes, and entitled rich people whose wealth had been passed down to them over generations and had done little or nothing to attain their wealth themselves.

Silence fell over them again, but this time it was uncomfortable. They were at a crossroads and they both recognized it. Finally Millicent spoke, "Gosh! It's late. I'm sorry I stayed so long. I hope I didn't keep you from other plans tonight."

"I enjoyed being with you, Millicent," he said, looking directly at her and smiling pleasantly.

"Perhaps we could do it again," she said, and felt herself blushing again. Then she added quickly, "I could have you over to my place. It's only a mile or so from here."

"I'd like that," he said, and they both rose.

She helped him clean up the dishes and put away the leftovers. They placed the beer bottles in the recycle bin he kept inside of the pantry, and he walked her out and down the stairs to her car in the underground lot. They traded contact information and then she pressed the key fob to open her door. Before she got into her car, she pulled him down and kissed him on the cheek. He held her arms gently as she did, but then she leaned in again and kissed him on the lips. They shared a quick embrace and then she jumped in her car.

She rolled the window down and said, "Salem Reid, thank you so much for what you did for me today and thank you for a great evening."

He smiled and stepped back from her car. Millicent Ivey waved sweetly and headed home to sleep.

# 5

JOEY AND BUD HAD GRABBED A BURGER and fries at Shae's in Brookhaven while they sat at the bar and watched baseball and some meaningless preseason NFL games. They chatted up the girl tending bar and did some harmless flirting that usually got them a beer on the house or an extra stiff drink or two. She was a twenty-three-year-old math grad student from GSU named Kelli who looked good in the tight black jeans and the red tank top she sported. She had a moderate complexion and the Pi symbol tattooed on her right shoulder and the digits 3.14159 running down her left shoulder. Bud told her he liked her "figures" and she told him that she had a much more interesting "pie" that wasn't currently exposed. This cracked the guys up, so she poured them another beer without adding it to the tab. Then she leaned over and whispered something in Bud's ear. Her blond hair smelled like fresh peaches and fell against his face as she told him her secret. Bud took out his phone, punched in some numbers, and said he would put her "data" to good use.

Bud threw a credit card out, deciding he should be the "big shot" to cover the tab, and Joey added a generous tip in cash. They jumped in

Joey's big Expedition and Joey turned the ignition to cool the car. He dialed in some Zeppelin through the iPod port and they sat in Shae's parking lot and did a few bumps of coke.

"You coming back for some of that later, Bud?" Joey asked.

"I want to, man. See how the night goes. Might have to be another night. We'll see. She was pretty hot for a white girl."

"All right. You wanna ride with me to the Slick Kitty? You can pick up your car here later. We can hit Licorice after, so you can get your fix." The Licorice Club had predominately black dancers.

"Let's do it," Bud said.

The guys headed to Cheshire Bridge Road. Cheshire Bridge was widely considered to be a skuzzy, sleazy, and seedy thoroughfare. In part it was, but Cheshire Bridge was a road that led from 85 to Piedmont Road that had tons of character as well. Some long-established Atlanta restaurants like The Colonnade, Nino's, and Alfredo's were great places to eat and experience. The street also had a number of strip clubs, head shops, and lingerie places. The famed Tara Theater was located there also. It gave props to the fictional Tara Plantation where the O'Hara's from *Gone with the Wind* resided. It showcased indie films and it was considered a hip and eclectic place to see a movie. Actors and actresses from days gone by such as Greta Garbo and Charlie Chaplin had their pictures hanging in the lobby, which featured a checkerboard-tiled floor.

Their heads were buzzing good from the cocaine by the time they arrived at the Slick Kitty, so they added one more bump each, and tried to not sniff and rotate their jaws too much as they approached the entrance. They paid the $10 cover and entered into loud music and an already raucous crowd. The Slick Kitty had two stages and there were three naked girls dancing on each. Bud headed to the stage where a dark-skinned black, a Latina, and a redhead were twerking, gyrating, and working the pole respectively. The Latina had the greatest number of bills sticking out of her garter, but Bud might quickly change those dynamics as he found a table close to the black girl who was shaking her ample backside in the faces of a delighted young man and his girlfriend. The girlfriend was feeding a few bills into the woman's garter whose butt was only inches from her face, as the boyfriend remained seated and peered upwards, enthralled by the spectacle in front of him. The guys sat at a table next to the young couple and a scantily clad waitress laid siege to them immediately. Joey ordered a Maker's Mark and Bud had a Tanqueray and tonic. Their drinks arrived in no time and they were soon partying and hooting with the young couple, and Bud was stuffing bills into the black girl's garter left and right as she worked the two tables. Joey, being judicious, left a few bills in each of the girls' garters, getting a pretty smile from the redhead who, in Joey's estimation, had the cutest face. He guessed she was probably twenty-one or twenty-two and was still learning all the tricks of roping in the guys in order to drain their wallets. After a few more songs, the dancers rotated off the stage to work the crowd. The black dancer joined them at the tables that had now evolved into one big table of four. She introduced herself as Fanny—go figure—and chatted with the group mindlessly for a while until the boyfriend suggested a lap dance for his girlfriend. Fanny was happy to oblige and disrobed and stood over the panting girlfriend as Bud looked on drooling. Fanny was quite a talent. She stood over the young woman and worked her large breasts in her face before straddling her and grinding her crotch into the girlfriend's. In the end, Fanny gave the girl a long wet kiss while Bud announced loudly that he was indeed getting a boner. Next it was Bud's turn. He paid Fanny the agreed upon amount and she worked her magic on him. He groped her, caressed her, and rubbed her, pushing the envelope on the limits of interaction—at least outside of the VIP room. He was clearly worked up and having fun. The others in the party whooped and hollered, encouraging Bud's outrageous behavior. Fanny had to push Bud's hand away when on several occasions he got a little too close to the honey pot. But she was good-natured about it, and as the lap dance ended she proved her good nature by deftly groping Bud's erection as she slid off of his lap. The girlfriend, who had never taken her eyes off the spectacle announced—to uproarious laughter—that she too now had a boner! The group ordered another round of drinks, polished them off, and Joey Mac picked up the tab. The foursome decided to head to Club Licorice where Bud and the guy's girlfriend could have their pick of beautiful young black women to dance for them. They piled into Joey's Expedition and he gave everyone another bump of blow and then they wheeled down the street towards Licorice. Club Licorice was much more of the same except this time Bud found a thick-bodied beauty named Delilah who was all natural down below and now he was in love. The guy's girlfriend and Bud took a few turns alternating lap dances with Delilah, and talk began of joining her in the VIP room. Bud had a tactical problem, however. He was just about tapped on his credit card and needed it for drinks. He did not have enough cash for the VIP room, which could possibly range from $200 to $400 for the four of them.

Bud pulled Joey aside. "Hey, bro, I got to get this girl in a private room, but I'm a little light. Can you help a fella out?" he requested.

Joey had expected this at some point. Bud was his pal and they had a lot of fun together, but more and more Bud just seemed to expect Joey to fund his "nights out" whenever they ran together. Bud had never offered to pay Joey back the money he "borrowed." He knew Bud was struggling financially and to some extent wanted to help him out, but donating several hundred dollars to the cause almost every time was excessive. But Joey hated to break the momentum of the night for Bud and his new friends, so he acquiesced.

"Look, Bud, I got $200 you can take and do your thing. Maybe get the couple to pitch in. I'm gonna hit the road and stop in at Utopia, so get these guys to get you back to your car or get a cab or something. Okay?"

"Yeah, yeah," Bud said a little too impatiently, which further annoyed Joey.

Bud took the cash, smiled, and punched Joey on the shoulder a little too hard. "See you later, man," he said, and darted off to rejoin his group.

Joey went to the bar and ordered another Maker's Mark and watched some of the dancers while he polished off his drink. He had enjoyed Bud and the couple for awhile, but he had tired of it and wanted to get over to his side of town before he drank too much more. He slipped out of Club Licorice and headed for his Expedition. He didn't notice the big man with the hacked-up face, who had been hanging around the entrance and tailing him since Joey had left the Slick Kitty, shadowing him as he exited the club.

———

He climbed in his SUV and snorted a few more bumps of coke while listening to AC/DC through his iPod port. He was buzzed from the coke, and along with the alcohol he'd imbibed throughout the evening, he had a pretty good high going. But Joey knew he was fine to drive as long as he obeyed the traffic laws and didn't run into any bad luck with a cop on the road. It was just around midnight, which was a little early for the rare but possible roadblock. He headed towards 85 on Cheshire Bridge, being careful to stop at the caution lights, signaling whenever he made a lane change, and keeping right around the speed limit. He took 85N to 285W and quickly exited onto Peachtree Industrial. He exited a side street and curled around into the vast parking lot that surrounded Utopia. He didn't notice the pickup truck driven by a large guy that pulled in a few rows over. He used a mouth spray and checked himself in the rearview mirror, then locked his car, and headed towards the club. Inside, Utopia was as grand as ever. Lights and music, but especially the high-end dancers, created a buzz that was unmatched at other clubs in Joey's opinion. Many races were represented here, both in dancers and clientele: white, black, Latino, and Asian. There was also an exotic Middle Eastern girl who did some hybrid belly dance as part of her act.

Joey spotted Velvet right away. She was one of the taller girls and belonged to the minority who had not had breast augmentation. She had large breasts and they looked spectacular. She was blonde with a shapely figure; full hips that tapered to long lovely legs and delicate ankles. She had long arms and fingers and she was a rarity who could really dance and always looked graceful moving, whether on the dance floor or working the room. She was on the main stage now, completely naked with a wad of bills dangling from her garter. She was working a section of the stage where a bunch of young, rowdy guys were cheering and whooping for her. Guys that likely had limited funds because they were working part-time jobs while in college or just out of college with no real earning power yet. They were dressed in casual jeans, Old Navy polo shirts, and Rockport shoes. The kind of guys who would suffer their wallets running dry well before their energy ran out. They were the types who would try to pool their financial resources to get a half an hour with a girl in the VIP room, thinking maybe she would do something special for all of them.

Velvet spotted Joey as he sat at a high top a little bit off from the stage. He ordered an Absolut on the rocks and a Maker's Mark. She smiled prettily at him as she turned to give the young guys one more frontal view before her time was up. She stepped off the stage, put on her thong and top, kissed and pressed flesh with the boys, and to their dismay, strolled saucily over to Joey's high top. The drinks arrived as she did, and she kissed Joey on the cheek, sat down on the stool next to him, and took a sip of the drink he had ordered for her. She ran her foot along his leg and cooed, "I was hoping you'd show up here tonight, Joey Mac!"

"I told you I'd be back tonight. You look great, Velvet."

And mostly she did look great. He knew she was a little older than the average dancer at a club like this. He estimated that she was even possibly in her early thirties. With makeup, she was able to cover any small lines that might have been developing in her face, so she was quite striking in that regard. But while she seemed reasonably sober, he noticed that her eyes were a little droopier than he remembered from their first couple of encounters. He wondered if perhaps she was on something heavier than just alcohol, weed, or a little blow. She reached over and touched his hand. Then she started playing with his SEC Championship ring.

"My big college football stud," she said playfully. "Maybe you'll get me between the hedges one day, Joey Mac."

"The hedges might be a little prickly, but I'll take you wherever I can get you, Velvet," he replied.

"You can get me right now for a lap dance, on the house, Joey Mac. Just because you're my favorite."

She finished her drink and slowly pulled off her thong and top. She pressed close to him and he felt himself stir. He had been in a lot of clubs, been with a lot of dancers, one-night stands, and plenty of cheerleaders from college, but she had an effect on him like no other. He completely understood that she was a whore. In fact, he liked that about her. Joey Mac had never been interested in having one woman. He had screwed plenty of girls during high school and college, many on more than one or two occasions, but he had never had or wanted a girlfriend in the true sense. Girlfriends and wives wanted things. They wanted your undivided attention when you didn't want to give it. They wanted you to say sugary sweet things to them and wipe their tears when they were emotional. They demanded that you go pick apples with them at the fall festival or watch them try on shoes at Nordstrom when you wanted to be with your buddies watching the football game. If it lasted long enough, they'd need you to fix their toilet or help them put together a bookcase...some shit like that. Joey had no interest in these things, so more and more he had been happy to pay a whore. He didn't pay them for sex; that might be a misunderstanding that people had. He paid them to leave him alone once the sex was over and to have no expectations of him going forward. So he liked whores; preferred them over any other type of woman.

Velvet performed her lap dance with expertise. She was pure sex. It came out of every pore of her body and by the time she was finished, Joey was rock hard. She took her next turn on stage, and Joey tracked her moves. She collected solid tips, and had worked the stage and floor for about thirty minutes when Joey asked her for a private room performance.

He paid $250 for the hour and then he was escorted to the VIP room by one of the beefy bouncers who had gotten to know him a bit over the past several weeks.

"I'll make sure you two have some real privacy, Mr. McIntosh. Please let me know if I can get you a drink at any time. I'll be just inside the door behind the curtain," he said.

Joey slipped him a $50 bill and the bouncer thanked him for the generous tip. Joey made himself comfortable on the faux leather sofa and waited for Velvet. She arrived in about five minutes and quickly removed her garments. She gave Joey the royal treatment. She worked him with her hand and discreetly slipped on a condom for him. She worked him with her mouth for a while and slowly brought him to the point of climax. When he came, he came hard. She removed the condom and cleaned him up, and they sat for a bit relaxing, having a drink, and making idle chitchat.

Finally, Joey spoke up, "Velvet, I'd like to keep the night going with you, if you're agreeable to that."

She smiled and told him she would like that and that she needed to speak with some people to make arrangements. She left out any details about her security arrangement. She returned and explained that she would finish her shift at 2 am. She would need to shower and clean up, and that she would meet him at 3 am at the Peachtree Suites—a clean and fairly new no-frills hotel—which was located on the access road that ran parallel to PIB. He was required to secure the room and pay for the night. She would bring alcohol from the bar. The cost was $900 and she would be available to him until 8 am.

Joey exited the VIP room and decided to hang out at Utopia for a little bit before he made the short drive to the Peachtree Suites. At just before 2 am, Utopia was rocking. He noticed some commotion near the back stage and to his surprise, there sat Bud, the guy and his girlfriend from the Slick Kitty, and Kelli, the bartender from Shae's. Joey joined them, ordered another drink, and sat back to enjoy his friends having the time of their lives with a very attractive light-skinned black girl who was less curvaceous than the others they had partied with earlier, but was still fairly well put together. As she turned to face them, Joey wasn't surprised to discover that Bud had managed to find yet another girl who was unshaven. The girlfriend was pretty drunk by now, and was making some rather lewd suggestions to the black dancer, who didn't seem to mind as long as she kept collecting tips. Kelli was the most sober, and she seemed to be having fun, but was latched on to Bud pretty good, perhaps thinking she could prevent him from having other ideas about how the night might turn out.

As Joey got up to say his goodbyes, Bud stumbled after him. "Joey Mac, bro…do you think you could spot me another $100? I gotta get this chick in the back room before the night ends."

Joey was a little pissed at the request. "No, man. The well has run dry for the night, Bud. Take Kelli home and show her a good time. She's all about you, dude."

Joey left Bud standing there, and as he turned his back on his friend, he didn't see the hostile glare that Bud was giving him.

# 6

JOEY HOPPED INTO HIS EXPEDITION and drove the short distance to the Peachtree Suites. He paid $99 in cash for the room and was told that he could check out at noon on Saturday. The kid at the desk said that checkout was at 11, but that the maids wouldn't get to the room until about 2 or 3 in the afternoon.

He winked at Joey and said, "We get a lot of late nighters here, so we let them sleep in."

Joey thanked him and texted the room number to the phone number that had been provided to him at Utopia. He assumed it was a disposable phone that someone other than the dancers monitored. He did not receive a text in return.

———

Velvet showered after her shift, blew dry her long blonde hair, applied makeup, and lightly sprayed herself with perfume. She was a bit nervous and twitchy because she was getting close to needing another fix.

She didn't want to admit to herself that she was becoming addicted to heroin. The man who ran both the Slick Kitty and Utopia as well as a club near the airport was called Oscar. She didn't know his last name. He was behind the scenes, and rumored to be mobbed up. There were managers and bouncers who took care of the daily grind, but Oscar was definitely in charge, and never questioned. Oscar would supply the girls with drugs, but insisted on administering the doses, so that he kept them from getting too stoned to work. She was afraid of him; he had black eyes that seemed dead to her. He was short, shorter than her, but powerfully built. He had a pitted face and a scar that ran from his left eye down his cheek, and curved slightly before stopping an inch from his mouth. Presumably from a knife fight. It was rumored that he was good with a knife and that the guy who had cut his face did not survive. It was further rumored that he once sliced up a dancer in New Jersey when she displeased him. She didn't want to displease him, but she was working up the nerve to ask him for a small dose of smack to loosen her up a bit. She walked down the hall to a room next to the back exit and knocked on the door.

A gravelly voice quietly said, "Come in."

Oscar sat on a plush leather sofa. He had a bottle of water on the coffee table in front of him. He was picking his teeth with a toothpick. A TV was on across from him, but the sound was muted. A big ugly guy who was vaguely familiar to her was standing in the corner, and she noticed his face was scraped up—perhaps from some recent altercation. Perhaps he had displeased Oscar and gotten off easy. There was a faint unpleasant smell in the room that she couldn't place.

Oscar stared at her for a moment, then said, "Sit," much in the way one would command a dog.

Velvet sat on the couch next to Oscar. "Tonight is the night. I need you to take care of this issue for me, Velvet. Are you up for the task? You seem a little…drawn," he said.

"I'm fine, Oscar, maybe a little fix would help, though."

"No. After." He handed her a Percocet. "This will tide you over until you satisfactorily complete the task," he said in his gravelly, accented yet cultured voice. She took the pill and he handed her the water bottle from the coffee table. "My assistant will drive you now. He will see to your needs afterwards."

———

Velvet left Utopia through the back exit where a gold Toyota Tundra sat parked, ready to take her on the short drive. She walked around the back of the truck oblivious to the license plate, which was covered in mud and illegible. She got in the passenger side and noticed the funky smell from Oscar's lounge had followed her. She glanced over at the guy who was heaving his bulk into the driver's seat, and he was leering at her. He grinned and showed her bad teeth. She was glad it would only be a short drive to the Suites.

Her driver repeated her instructions during the short drive and explained that he would be waiting close by for her, and would follow her out later. They wheeled into the Peachtree Suites parking lot, and she exited the truck. The big guy parked in a discreet location where he could keep an eye on the room and parking lot.

It was about five minutes past 3 am when Velvet knocked on the door to Suite 114. Joey opened the door for her. He had taken about twenty minutes to shower quickly, brush his teeth, and dry his hair. He was moderately refreshed and still had some energy despite how much he had drank. He had smoked a small amount of weed to mellow him out before she had arrived and the room still had a faint smell of cannabis. He let her in and she set her large Vera Bradley bag on the floor next to the bed. The suite had a bed, dresser, Sony flat screen, a small refrigerator, and the usual desk enclave with ports for phones and computers. The bathroom was at the rear of the room. The blinds were drawn and Joey had turned a bedside light on low. The room was clean and the smell of disinfectant was vaguely noticeable beneath the musky aroma from the marijuana.

Velvet looked beautiful to him. She was dressed in very skimpy and tight purple shorts with a white lace blouse that showed her cleavage, and pumps that were shorter in the heel than the ones she wore on stage. Her blond hair was hanging loose.

"You are lovely," he told her, and quickly added, "in case no one has mentioned that to you yet today."

Velvet smiled and thanked him for the compliment. "Joey, will you see if you can find an ice machine outside? I'll make you a drink," she said as she produced a pint of Maker's Mark from her bag.

Joey put the key in his pocket, grabbed a small bucket, and walked outside to locate the ice machine. He returned within minutes with the ice and Velvet poured him a little whiskey and water over the ice.

He took a sip and said, "Just right. Thanks."

Velvet stepped into the bathroom and closed the door. He heard the toilet flush followed by running water. She exited the bathroom totally naked with her hair piled on top of her head. She helped Joey out of his clothes, pulled back the bed covering, and gently pushed him back on the king-sized bed. She reached in her bag for some oil and rubbed a small amount on his cock. He moaned appreciatively and sprang to life. She toyed with him for a short while, and then placed a condom over his penis and started working him yet again with her mouth. She could sense him getting close to orgasm, so she removed him from her mouth, and asked him how he liked it.

Joey's intuition told him that going down on a hooker was probably a little risky, but since she had used a condom on him twice that evening, he felt that it was worth taking the risk. He wanted to enjoy her completely, and he hoped that she got off on him administering to her orally. In fact, he really hoped she dug it.

He pushed her back on the bed and grabbed the backs of her thighs and pushed her legs into the air. He went to work and she seemed to enjoy it. She moaned and writhed, but for all he knew it could have been an act…he couldn't be sure. After all, it was her job to pretend that she was all into the guys who were all into her.

After a bit, he came up and she was smiling at him. He rolled over and placed her on top. He slid easily into her and she moaned loudly. Within moments, she whispered in his ear that she was cumming, and then he came too. Hard and furious.

They lay there spent and a little sweaty, but after a couple of minutes, Velvet quietly got up, grabbed her bag, and went into the bathroom. Joey lay there with mixed emotions like he usually did right after sex. It had been excellent, but he always felt a little regret and a bit chagrined after sex with a hooker. Even if she was a high-class hooker, she was still a hooker. But to him, this beat the alternative of a regular girl. He had never been interested in love. He had loved his dad for sure. He loved his mom, of course, but saw her only occasionally. He loved his dog, Herschel, but there were few others he could truly say he loved.

Velvet came out of the bathroom still naked. She asked Joey if he wanted another drink, and he said he would love one. He asked her if she wanted to smoke a little weed, but she declined. Joey took a couple of hits from his one-hitter that usually supplied him with more like three or four hits. He lay back on the bed and closed his eyes, enjoying the buzz from the weed. Maybe he could rest a little and have another round with Velvet in an hour or so.

———

Velvet poured Maker's Mark into Joey's glass and went into the bathroom to add a splash of water. She hated herself for what she would do next, but she feared Oscar and this was what she had been instructed to do. Velvet dropped a "roofie" into his drink. Rohypnol or Flunitrazepam was the formal drug name for "roofies," and was in the benzodiazepine family and acted as a sedative that was frequently used as a date rape drug. Joey would be knocked out until the late morning or early afternoon with the quantity she had supplied. Despite her own need to get a fix and make a living doing what she did, she felt awful because she had grown to like Joey. She seldom had an orgasm with guys who paid her for sex, but he had caused her to climax. But it wasn't just that. He was nice. He treated her like a lady and not like a whore. She realized that after this she would not be able to see him again and that he would hate her. She was deeply troubled by this, but saw no way out other than to proceed.

She came out of the bathroom and handed Joey his drink. He took a gulp and set it down and pulled her to him. He kissed her breasts and she let him. He kissed her on her forehead and told her how much fun he was having with her.

"Finish your drink," she said. "Maybe we can go for round two if you can get it up again, big boy."

He laughed, and said, "That's never been a problem, baby. Count on it!"

He took his time finishing his drink, and as he emptied his glass he felt an intense sluggishness creep over him. He got up and went into the bathroom naked. He splashed cold water on his face, and noticed he was having trouble keeping his arms raised. He toweled off as best he could, and returned to the bed. Suddenly sex was the furthest thing from his mind. He thought maybe he could sleep for an hour and try again with Velvet in a little while before the sun came up and dampened the mood. Then the lights went out, and his life as he knew it was about to change dramatically.

# 7

VELVET FOLLOWED HER INSTRUCTIONS to the letter. She dressed quickly and packed her belongings. She rinsed Joey's cocktail glass and placed it in her bag. She soaped her hand and removed his SEC Championship ring from his finger. She had to work it off slowly, but it came off pretty easily. She grabbed his gold Rolex off the night table, and located his wallet and keys. She left his phone. A tear rolled down her cheek. She wondered how she had gotten herself jammed up like this. It would have been easier if this guy had been a creep, but he wasn't a creep at all. She gathered up all his clothes and placed them in her bag. She left his Gucci loafers on the floor. She walked to the door, then turned back to look at Joey sleeping soundly in the bed.

She ran over to him, bent down, kissed him full on the lips, and said, "I'm so sorry, Joey Mac."

She wanted to cry, but she pulled herself together. She glanced once more at the man lying in the bed, then turned and exited the suite. She located Joey's Expedition and triggered the key fob. She climbed in and started the vehicle. She made only a slight adjustment to the seat and mirrors. She located Joey's driver's license and punched the address into the GPS on her phone. The phone told her that the destination was 3.7 miles. She took Peachtree Corners Circle to Holcomb Bridge, then turned onto Spalding Drive. She turned off Spalding onto Joey's street and slipped into his driveway. She pulled back and around, and opened the garage with the remote attached to the visor. She left the garage door open and waited a few minutes as instructed. A few minutes later, the big man appeared at her window. Though she was expecting him, she was nonetheless startled and repulsed by his appearance. She exited the SUV and followed the man to the door. He gloved up and pressed the button on the wall to lower the garage door. He took the keys from Velvet and opened the door. The alarm began to chime and he located the pad and keyed in the code that Oscar had provided. He ignored the barking dog in the basement. The alarm beeped once and then was silent. He told Velvet to sit on the sofa in the great room while he tended to his business. He located the master and went directly to the closet. He found the lockbox just where he had been told it would be located and used the small key on the keychain to open it. He removed the $72,000 in cash, the jewelry that consisted of a few more expensive timepieces, a few rings, and several thick gold chains and bracelets. He left the cocaine and weed that he was told might be there because those were his instructions. He found a nice supply of Vicodin and Percocet that nobody had mentioned, so he helped himself to the pills.

He returned to the great room and found Velvet sitting right where he had left her.

"Okay," he said. "You did your job…the boss will be pleased." Then he added, "I have a little something for you. We will do it here."

Velvet was too shaken by the events of the last few hours to think everything through for herself, and she badly needed a fix. She could think of nothing else. The big man produced a kit, and prepared a dose of very potent and little cut heroin. He filled the syringe and knelt before her. She placed her foot on the man's knee, and he located an area between her toes that would receive the injection satisfactorily. He pulled up about twice the amount in volume of what she normally received and proceeded to inject her with the drug. The effect was almost immediate. She sighed heavily and made a few other strange sounds that were somewhere between a moan and a shriek. She lay back into the sofa and the world began to swim. She had pleasant thoughts of her evening with Joey, then she thought of her mom and dad, and of Bella, the cute Irish setter puppy her parents had given her on her ninth birthday. Her final thought was a bittersweet one of a young man she had known long ago; a young man who had touched her heart like no other. Then she was gone.

The big man placed the syringe, spoon, and lighter in her hands momentarily, then dropped them between the sofa and her bag on the floor. Then he opened Velvet's bag and removed the Rolex watch, which retailed for close to thirty grand. He opened Joey's wallet and removed $500 leaving $676 in the billfold and tossing it back into her bag. He took the glass from the suite, but left Joey's ring in Velvet's bag too. All of the contents he had looted from Joey's house fit snuggly in his large backpack, with the exception of $5,000 from the lockbox that he placed inside of her bag also. He exited the house, opened the garage door, then closed it, and quickly scooted out, taking a high step at the opening to avoid triggering the door to re-open. It was about 5:30 am when he left the house. He texted Oscar and started walking. He crossed Spalding into another neighborhood and continued to walk. Soon a Ford Flex pulled up alongside of him and stopped. He quickly got in and the Flex sped off towards an alternate exit and then was gone. Oscar delivered Klaus Vormer to the area where he had left his Toyota; it was a short walk through the woods from Joey's house. Oscar relieved him of the backpack he had provided to carry the loot, and the Flex continued at a moderate speed out to Peachtree Parkway. Oscar headed south towards the club to examine his new treasure. Joey McIntosh had been looted for close to $100,000.

# 8

IT TOOK REID A LITTLE LONGER than normal to get to sleep Friday night, but once he dozed off he slept soundly for six hours and awoke Saturday morning before dawn. He grabbed a granola bar and some fruit and washed it down with cool water. He threw on his running shoes, shorts, and tee shirt and ran to Blackburn Park. He stopped in a flat, secluded area near the woods and performed several martial arts routines called Hokeis—more art than martial, focusing on balance, stamina, and body control. Then he did five sets of fifty push-ups, varying the placement of his hands on the ground to work different muscles. He followed this with crunches and leg raises to strengthen his core and to keep his stomach flat. Reid then ran back to his condo and worked out on the speed and heavy bag. One of his spare rooms was full of equipment that he used to practice chops, kicks, and punches. With these drills, he practiced and maintained speed, accuracy, and power. He also had a hard wooden post stuck into a cement block that had rope tied near the top that he punched regularly to toughen his hands. He and his security partner, Ian Callahan, met once a week either in a park, or in the makeshift gym that was fitted with a mat in the garage area of Reid's business on Piedmont to spar, grapple, and practice their hand-to-hand combat techniques.

Reid finished his training, then showered and dressed in jeans and a red polo shirt. He wore a casual pair of black Cole Haan shoes. He had planned to spend the early part of the day grocery shopping and running a few errands. As he was gathering his wallet, keys, and phone, he noticed that he had a text message from Millicent.

Milly: "Good Morning. Thx again for a fun evening! I saw you running this morning on my way to work."

Reid: "Hungry?"

Milly: "Starving. Free from 10:30–12."

Reid: "Meet at IHOP in Chamblee Plaza at 10:30?"

Milly: "Sounds great! See you then."

Millicent added a smiley face at the end of her text.

It was 9:15, so he thought he could make it to the Costco in Brookhaven and return in time to meet Millicent at IHOP by 10:30. He hustled down to Brookhaven, purchased eggs, cheese, coconut milk, fruit, chicken, salmon, corn, granola bars, water, beer, and a few other items. He was able to drop off his supply and race down to Chamblee Plaza, arriving just a few minutes before 10:30. Millicent had already arrived, and was sitting at a booth in the middle of the restaurant.

"Hi," she said perkily, her green eyes sparkling.

"Hey," he replied, as he slipped into the booth across from her, "how's your day going?"

"Better than yesterday, for sure. I'll have to learn to be on the lookout from now on, Salem. I forget sometimes that there are some bad people out there."

"Do you keep mace in your purse? That might be a good idea."

"No. I never have. Maybe I should consider it."

The waitress arrived and they both ordered whole grain pancakes with a side of fruit. They added a side of bacon to split. Millicent chatted about her morning at the ARC and told him she had to return at 12, but that she was finished at 3 pm and didn't return to work until Monday. She had planned on spending parts of the rest of the weekend painting some wicker furniture in her house that needed some sprucing, and doing a little yard work. She asked about his weekend.

"I have a job at 9 pm tonight," he told her.

An aging comedian needed limo service from his hotel to the Fabulous Fox Theater where he was performing a ninety-minute routine. The guy liked to use Southeast Security, the name of Reid's company, when he came to Atlanta. He had been assaulted by a guy throwing tomatoes at him a few years back when he came through the hotel lobby, and since then he had used Reid's services. Apparently, the guy took offense to a joke in the comedian's routine about overweight people. No surprise to discover that the assailant's wife was a 300-pound woman who had battled weight problems since she was young.

When Millicent asked specifically what joke had set the guy off, Reid suggested that a nice young lady like herself might take offense to the comedian's off-color joke.

"Come on, Salem," she encouraged, "I can take an off-color joke. I'm not a prude, after all."

Reluctantly, Reid told her the joke. "How does a guy know when his wife's too fat?"

She smiled. "I gotta hear this."

"When she sits on his face, and he can't hear the phone ring."

Millicent Ivey laughed so loudly that several people from nearby tables glanced over to see what the commotion was.

"You have a great laugh," said Reid. "Remind me to tell you more dirty jokes."

They finished their brunch, and she said that she still had a little time to walk through old Chamblee if he was interested.

Reid and Millicent walked up Broad Street and browsed some of the antique shops along the way. They were content to window shop mostly, but entered one store in particular that had some beautiful old mahogany glass bookcases, china cabinets, and dining tables. Towards the back of the shop, they found some old hardcover classics from authors like Faulkner, Hemingway, and Salinger. They also found more recent books from popular writers like Stephen King, Jonathan Kellerman, Robert Crais, and Michael Connelly. Some of the books had slightly yellowed pages, but were otherwise in good condition and many could be purchased for as little as $3. Millicent was an avid reader and took an interest. Since she didn't have much cash on her, she said that she would come back on another day and take advantage of some of these great deals.

They left the antique shop and headed back down Broad Street towards their cars. It was a beautiful morning; the sun was warm but the humidity was low and there was a light breeze. Millicent walked closely to Reid and brushed against him several times. Then she boldly reached out and took his hand. She was pleased that when she did, he gave her hand a little squeeze that confirmed that he was happy to be walking hand in hand with this lovely girl on a pretty August day in Georgia. He smiled at her and she beamed…carefully trying not to blush again.

They continued in silence, then dashed across Peachtree Industrial at the light, hand in hand. He walked her to her car, and as she reached the driver's side door, she turned and curled into him, squeezing him tightly. He was surprised at her strength. She buried her head into his chest for a moment, then pulled back slightly to look up at him. This time she didn't have to initiate the next move. He brushed her lips with his; gently at first but it quickly evolved into a passionate kiss. They lost themselves momentarily, but gradually recovered.

"How about I make dinner for you on Sunday night at my house?" she asked. "Do you like spaghetti?"

"I like spaghetti," he replied. "Mostly I just like being with you."

She got on her toes and they kissed again, this time exploring. She had full lips, straight white teeth, and an adventurous, yet not intruding tongue that she used deftly. He found himself stirred by her, and suddenly wished that they could both blow off everything they had to do that day and spend it together. But neither could, so they resolved to look forward to Sunday evening and make the best of it then.

They said their goodbyes and decided on 5:30 Sunday evening for dinner. She said she'd text her address later tonight. He held her car door for her, and she sped off to finish her day at the club.

Reid decided to return to the antique store and buy the hardcover edition of *Catcher in the Rye* for Millicent and present it to her on Sunday evening as a gift. She had seemed to have the most interest in the Salinger novel. As he exited the shop, he was considering heading down to his office in Buckhead to check on his staff and troubleshoot any problems that had arisen since he had left yesterday afternoon. While he didn't have anything pressing until that evening with the comedian, he could possibly get ahead on a few things and tie up some loose ends. But his phone rang and then everything changed.

# 9

JOEY McINTOSH SLOWLY CAME TO EARLY on Saturday afternoon. His head throbbed and his mouth tasted like someone had
crammed an old shoe in it. For several minutes, he simply laid there
in the motel bed, unsure of where he was, what he'd done, and why
he felt the way he did. He knew he'd been out drinking and partying,
but he had never had this much confusion subsequent to a crazy night
out. Sure, he'd been hungover and sick before, but he could never recall
being this dazed. Had there been a girl? Where had they met? Why
wasn't he at home? It was like amnesia; he simply couldn't get his fac-
ulties together to determine what had occurred. What day was this?

He stared at the ceiling feeling extremely sluggish and achy. He must
have laid there for thirty minutes before he stumbled to the bathroom.
He urinated and started the shower. He climbed in and soaked himself,
running lukewarm water over his aching body. He washed and sham-
pooed his hair, climbed from the shower and toweled himself off. He
brushed his teeth several times and still had serious cotton mouth. He
removed a plastic cup from its protective wrapper and slugged water
until his stomach began to slosh. He took off his towel and hunted

for his clothes. His clothes were missing. This was *not* good. Then he started looking for his other possessions. He still had his phone and his Gucci loafers were on the floor by the bed. His wallet and keys, however, were missing. He pulled the curtain to look outside, but the sun nearly blinded him. He slowly adjusted himself to the light and peaked again through the drapes. His SUV was not in the lot. He wrapped the towel around himself and checked his iPhone. He had placed it on the port in the suite so it was fully charged. He had no missed calls, voicemails, or text messages. He noted that it was 12:36 pm. He sat down and made himself think about his predicament. He would need a ride home. But who to call? This was a bit embarrassing, and he would need some discretion. Bud came to mind first, but when he dialed his number the call went straight to voicemail. He wouldn't call his brother. He'd either get smug silence from him, or possibly even a lecture. He didn't need that. Calling one of his neighbors was not desirable either, so Joey scrolled through his contact list until he landed on a name from the past. A guy he had been friends with years ago when they played high school baseball together. They had drifted apart since then, running into each other occasionally over the years, but Joey had kept his number in his contacts because he knew that he was a solid guy. He was gonna need a solid guy, so he clicked the contact and Salem Reid answered on the second ring.

"Yes."

"Salem, it's Joey McIntosh from Dunwoody High School," Joey croaked, realizing the strain in his voice. "I need your help, man."

"Joey. It's been a while. What's the trouble?"

"I need a ride from The Peachtree Suites on the PIB access road to my house in Peachtree Corners. I live off of Spalding."

"What's the room number?"

That was how he remembered Salem Reid. He didn't ask too many questions, just got right to solving a problem.

"Room 114."

"Be there in ten."

"Uh…Salem?" Joey said tentatively, "I'm gonna need some clothes."

"Be there in twenty," he corrected and clicked off.

Reid drove directly to a nearby church that had a budget store and bought some large polyester tan slacks and an Old Navy polo shirt off the rack…XL. He paid $13 for the clothing and sped north on Peachtree Industrial Boulevard to see about his old friend.

# 10

IT MAY HAVE BEEN NINE MONTHS or even a year since Reid had last seen Joey and then it was usually just them bumping into one another. Reid sometimes took his old Ford Explorer that had belonged to his dad and had been purchased years ago at McIntosh Ford to the dealer for service. He had needed a fuel pump for the car sometime back, and he had taken it to McIntosh for repairs. He had poked his head into Joey's office and said hello. Joey looked a lot different today. His face was pinched and drawn and he looked a little dazed. He also looked heavier and his hair may have thinned a bit. He opened the door of 114 to let Reid enter, but stood behind the door because he was wrapped only in a small hotel towel.

Reid tossed a plastic bag containing the budget store clothes to Joey as he came through the door. Joey reacted slowly and the clothes fell out of the bag onto the floor.

Joey picked up the shirt and pants. "Thanks, Salem. Thanks for coming."

Reid said nothing, but nodded at his old pal.

Joey went to the bathroom and put on the clothes. The pants fit well, but the shirt was a little snug. He came out of the bathroom and threw on the Gucci loafers. Reid had to stifle a grin. Joey looked like a clown.

Joey pocketed his phone and left the key card on the night table. They left room 114 and jumped into Reid's car and made the short drive to Joey's house. They pulled around back and immediately heard Herschel barking. Joey figured he might have a mess to clean up in his basement; Herschel may have had to go by now. Joey used a keypad outside of his garage and opened the garage door. He was happy to see his Expedition sitting in the garage next to his Mustang exactly where it belonged, but he had not expected it to be here. In fact, he was terribly confused how it had gotten here.

"Look, Salem, apparently I had a rough night last night. I'm not sure what happened to me, or why I was at the hotel and how my car got here. I'm embarrassed and more than a little spooked," he said. "This just doesn't happen to me. My head is really foggy and I can't figure this out."

"Let's go inside and maybe get you some coffee. Do you have any?" Reid inquired.

"Yeah. Maybe that's a good idea. Do you mind hanging with me until I can sort it out?"

The dog began barking again. "I need to see to my dog. He hasn't been out since last night."

They walked through the garage and entered the house. The first thing Reid noticed was that the security pad was silent, but he didn't mention this to Joey. Then they both simultaneously noticed the tall blond girl lying awkwardly on the sofa in the great room, and it all came rushing back to Joey.

He didn't immediately understand why or how Velvet had gotten into his house, but it didn't take him long to figure it out. He approached her to wake her up but as he got closer, he noticed a decaying stench and the girl's color looked wrong; she was grayish blue. He stopped a good ten feet from her.

Salem Reid pulled his Glock from his holster and told Joey to wait outside and not to touch anything. Joey hesitated, but then did as he was told. He looked like he might cry.

Reid quickly cleared the main level and grabbed a hand towel from the kitchen before approaching the basement. He used the towel to open the basement door. A black Lab was at the top of the stairs when Reid opened it and the dog barked and whined, but didn't attack.

"Easy boy," said Reid to the dog and held his left hand out to him.

The dog sniffed his hand, barked once more, and then ran down the stairs. Reid followed carefully with his head on a swivel as he descended the stairs. He used the towel to unlock and open the back door, and the big Lab ran outside where Joey stood in the backyard near the gate to the fence leading to the driveway. Herschel did his business then ran to Joey, who got down on his knees and hugged his dog all while issuing apologies to him about the neglect.

Reid cleared the basement and told Joey to come back inside and reminded him not to touch anything.

He explained to Joey that the master closet was open and that a lockbox was open as well and that there was coke and weed in the box, but nothing else. He asked Joey if there was anything else illegal in the home he should know about before the police were summoned.

"Oh shit," said Joey. "I can't believe this is happening."

Reid grabbed Joey firmly by the shoulders. "Listen very carefully. Get the drugs, any paraphernalia, and anything illegal and put it in a bag and bring it to me, NOW!"

Joey scampered into the kitchen, grabbed a thirteen-gallon white trash bag from beneath the kitchen counter and headed to his room. He came back with the drugs and was white as a ghost.

"I'm missing about sixty or seventy grand in cash, Salem, watches and jewelry too."

"You can't worry about that right now," he told Joey. "I'm trying to keep you out of jail. Follow along and trust me."

———

Reid opened a disposable phone and made a call. He recited an address to the person on the other end, and finished by saying, "Get here very fast. Park on the street one block west of the address I gave you and locate a white trash bag along the cypress trees. You know what to do after that."

"What are you doing with the drugs? Why don't we just flush them?" asked Joey.

"No. They leave residue in the toilet and pipes. With a corpse in the house, it's likely a crime scene. Your place is going to be combed over thoroughly."

At this point, their attention turned to the dead woman on the couch. Reid found a long thin spatula and tongs in a basket in the kitchen and carried them with him to the sofa. The stench was getting a little ripe. Reid glanced at his watch and noted that it was 1:25pm. He looked down at the girl. He could tell that she had a fine body, but her blond hair was loose and hanging over her face. He gently tried to lift her arm with the towel and noted that rigor mortis had set in. Usually at this stage the person had been dead between three and twelve hours. That put the time of death between 1:30 am and about 10:30 this morning. He examined the Vera Bradley bag lying on the floor and saw that its contents included men's clothing, condoms, a man's wallet, and a roll of $100 bills that looked to total between $4,000 and $5,000. Using the spatula, he splayed the contents and saw some personal female items, and a smaller Vera Bradley bag that was partially unzipped. It contained wads of cash—mostly in small bills. He noticed a small Vera Bradley wallet at the bottom of the bag. He turned his attention back to the girl. He didn't see any obvious wounds and there was no blood on or around her. Her short pants were slightly wet at the crotch; she had probably passed urine at death or shortly after dying. He turned back to the bag. Joey Mac stood close watching and saying nothing. He moved the bag slightly by hooking the straps with the spatula and spotted a syringe on the floor. A discolored spoon lay next to the syringe that sat on top of a baggie, which contained white powder. He replaced the bag near the syringe, spoon, and powder, and once again turned his attention to the girl. He used the spatula to push her hair off her face. It was difficult, so he used the tongs. He finally got the hair pushed back from her face and stopped dead in his tracks. He knew her. She was older now, but still very pretty. He had not seen her for many years, but a face like that you didn't forget. Her name was Sarah Lindstrom and they had been an item many years ago.

# 11

REID EXHALED DEEPLY AND LOOKED at his watch. It was 1:40 pm. They had been in the house for about twenty to twenty-five minutes. He needed to call the police. Unexplained gaps in time could cause lots of problems. But first he wanted to examine the contents of Sarah's bag a little closer. He used the tongs to extract her wallet and using both kitchen utensils, he was able to open her billfold. He found a Georgia driver's license that put her at thirty-two years of age. The name on the license was indeed Sarah's, with an address in Alpharetta. He used the utensils to fold up the wallet and returned it to her bag. He stepped back and placed the utensils and towel in the bag with the drugs. He added the disposable phone. He went through the basement and out the back door. He went through the gate at the back of the fence and placed the bag at the edge of the middle cypress tree. He glanced up and saw Ian Callahan scrambling through the woods. He didn't acknowledge Ian, but turned and retreated to the house. He pulled out his iPhone and dialed 911. Then he and Joey Mac sat at the kitchen table and waited. It was 1:45 pm.

While they waited for the police, Joey began to have some clarity. He explained to Reid the events leading up to the phone call just over an hour ago. He told him how he had met Velvet, or Sarah, as he knew her in death. He told him the complete truth because he realized he would need help from his old friend. He now believed that he'd been given a Mickey or something similar that explained the disorientation he'd had upon waking. He believed that she had knocked him out, stolen his vehicle, and come to his house using information from his missing wallet, which he knew was in her bag. He had wanted to remove his property, but Reid insisted that they not touch anything before the police arrived. It now seemed clear to Joey that she had looted him and then shot up heroin in his house, but had overdosed in the process. Reid realized that Joey was putting some pieces together, but he must still be foggy because he was missing some things. For instance, Joey claimed to have a lot of money stashed in his house, but Sarah's bag only contained a fraction of that. He said he was missing jewelry that was not in the bag. Where had it gone? Perhaps some of this confusion would get cleared up during the police investigation, but these inconsistencies were troubling. Or, what if Joey was mistaken or confused about what was in his house? He'd been drinking, doing drugs, running with prostitutes, and he'd been given a knockout drug. What was fancied and what was real? Reid was also curious about the security alarm. Had it been set? If it had been set by Joey, then who had disarmed it? Had he given Sarah his code? Surely he wasn't that stupid, but maybe she had gotten it from him somehow without him knowing. But how? There were many unanswered questions, and Joey was distraught about many things at the moment. This would take some time to clear up. Reid considered asking Joey some of these questions, but even had he decided to do so, time had run out. The first squad car had arrived.

Two uniformed police officers announced their presence, and cautiously entered Joey's home through the open garage door that led into the kitchen. Both had the straps to their weapons unclasped and their hands rested on their firearms. Reid told the officers that he was armed and that his permit was in his wallet. They took his gun and permit and waited for the second squad car to arrive. When the other team arrived, the first group of officers secured the house and the corpse that had once been Sarah Lindstrom. The other group took Reid and Joey to separate squad cars and asked them some basic questions while they waited for the detectives to arrive. Soon the medical examiners arrived and after the criminalists worked the scene, the body was removed. The lead detective, Derwin Larribee, questioned both Reid and Joey extensively. To Reid's surprise, the police were viewing this as a robbery and accidental overdose, but advised both Reid and Joey to be available for further questions, and strongly suggested that if either were to leave town, that it would be wise to contact the Westside Detective Bureau before leaving the metro area.

Reid wanted to ask Larribee about the inconsistencies in the missing cash, but to do so would reveal that they knew what was in Sarah Lindstrom's bag. If the large difference in the cash was a concern of the detective's, he was not showing that concern. Perhaps he was dismissing Joey's claims as untrue. After all, how many people keep sixty to seventy grand in cash inside their homes? Few wealthy people even kept that kind of cash on hand, and most of those who did were criminals.

Reid needed to get with Joey and begin sorting through all of this. Reid's gun and magazine were returned to him separately, and he was told he was free to go. The house would be a crime scene until late Saturday night or perhaps as early as Sunday morning. The investigation team was still finishing up both inside and outside of the house. So Joey Mac could not stay at his house. Under police supervision, he was allowed to pack a bag of clothes and sundries, collect his dog and food for the dog, and leave the house. His car needed to stay on the premises as well. Reid offered to let Joey stay overnight at his house. He wanted to ask him some more questions and try to dial in this sordid ordeal a little better.

They left the house in Reid's Challenger, and Joey was distraught that the first stop Reid made was at the Peachtree Suites.

"What are we doing here?" asked Joey.

"Just wait here," he responded, and walked into the office. A young woman of perhaps twenty or so was behind the desk.

Reid got right to it. "Do you have surveillance video for the property; if so, how long do you keep the video?"

She eyed him suspiciously, and said, "I've already spoken with the police. Are you the police?"

"No," Reid admitted. "But I'm investigating an incident that involved some folks staying here last night. I'm hoping that you can help me."

"Why do I want to help you?" she asked.

"Look, I just want to know about surveillance capabilities. How about helping me out?"

"I already gave a video to the police. Maybe you should talk to them," she said.

"So you do have a video," he said. "How long is the loop?" He slid a $50 bill onto the counter, keeping a finger on it the whole time.

She shrugged, and said, "It tapes over every twenty-four hours, beginning at midnight." She looked around and behind her. "Maybe I could make a copy for you, but it'll take a little more coaxing."

He produced another $50 bill, but kept his fingers on both bills.

"How long?" Reid asked.

"Give me an hour, $50 now and $50 later," she replied.

"Done," he said and slid one of the bills to her.

Reid drove Joey to his condo in Chamblee. They didn't speak on the ride. Reid figured he'd drop Joey at his house, take a shower, shave, and change into clothes he would wear tonight for the security job. Then he would return to the suites and get the video. It was 5:45 pm, so he would need to keep moving to fit everything in.

He got Joey settled in the spare bedroom and they got Herschel set up in the kitchen. He got cleaned up and left his condo. As he was making the drive to the Peachtree Suites to collect the video, Reid had time to reflect on Sarah. He was saddened by her death. It had been fifteen years or so since he had last seen her, but she had been a part of his life. They had met when he was a senior at Dunwoody High School and she was a sophomore at Lakeside. They had attended a football game at North DeKalb Stadium where their two schools had matched up. He was seventeen and she was fifteen, both of them just a few months shy of their next birthdays. During halftime, she had been standing behind him in line at the concession stand. Lots of people were lined up to get coffee or hot chocolate on that cool night in late October. She had been only wearing a tee shirt; at almost sixteen, she had been anxious to show off her considerable assets, but as the night wore on, she had become miserably cold. Reid had dressed warmly, wearing a long-sleeve shirt with a sleeveless sweatshirt over it. He had wisely grabbed his baseball letter jacket as he left the house and had been plenty warm. As she stood there shaking, Reid peeled off his jacket and asked her if she wanted to borrow it. She smiled saucily at him, thanked him, and tossed her long blonde hair on him as he draped the jacket on her. They had introduced themselves to each other and chatted while they waited in the line for their warm drinks. He had been surprised that this gorgeous, tall, leggy, big-chested girl was only in tenth grade. She had looked to be perhaps in college, and she had a worldliness about her that defied her age. He bought them both a hot chocolate and she commented that since she was now wearing a Dunwoody jacket, that she would join him in that section of the stadium. She hooked her arm in his and accompanied him back to where he'd been sitting with his friends. By late in the third quarter of the football game, Reid and Sarah had managed to get under a large bedspread that some wise soul had brought to the game. The spread had managed to cover six people sitting closely together trying to stay warm. Reid was on the far end with Sarah just inside of him. She had snuggled closely to him and he'd been intoxicated by her. She looked great, smelled great, and had a sexuality about her that he'd yet to experience with any girl...even the senior girls that were his own age.

She had nuzzled his ear some, and they had shared a kiss as they sat watching the game. Halfway through the fourth quarter, she had run her hand near his groin, sending an electric shock through his body. She had whispered in his ear that they should leave the game early and find a secluded place to "park." He hadn't hesitated. He had owned a Ford Taurus SHO back then, so he guided her to his car and they drove to Silver Lake. The lake was in an area near Brookhaven in a neighborhood behind Oglethorpe University. Inman Drive was a long, winding road that had little secluded areas above the lake where kids pulled off into the woods to smoke dope, drink beer, and make out. She'd produced a small bottle of Peppermint Schnapps from her boot and they took turns taking swigs. He was running the heat, so it was warming up in the car. The windows had steamed up and now the two of them were warm and buzzed. Without warning, she reached over, undid his belt and jeans and went down on him. Soon they were both naked. Reid had not been a virgin, but he had never been with anyone quite like this girl. She was loud and wild; the sex was intense and they kept at it for over an hour. She bit him, clawed him, scratched him, and pulled his hair. He didn't mind. He had never experienced pleasure like this before. They rested briefly and then they were at it again. They were two feral animals in heat. There was nothing tender about the sex; it was pure physical desire. She bit him hard on the shoulder, leaving teeth marks and drawing blood. He didn't care; he could not get enough of her and she could not get enough of him. They worked each other over for close to another hour and finally their energy tapered. They dozed for a while and then Reid roused himself. It was past midnight and he needed to get home. He guessed that he would need to drive her to Embry Hills. He noticed that his gas tank was nearly empty, so he woke her. They shared more Schnapps and then he asked

her where she lived. She explained that she was supposed to be spending the night with a friend whom she had ditched at the game when
she'd met him. She instructed him to take her to her friend's house.
Her friend's parents were out of town and the girl's older sister who
was in her mid-twenties was the adult in charge. He stopped to get $10
worth of fuel and then headed for Embry Hills.

Reid drove north to Ashford Dunwoody Road where he took 285
east to Chamblee Tucker. She directed him to a blue collar, but well-
kept neighborhood about a mile inside the Perimeter. As he approached
a small brick home from the 1950s, he killed the lights. He rolled to a
stop in front of the home and quickly shut off the engine. She jumped
out quickly and ran to the driver's side door. Reid figured she'd kiss
him goodnight and arrange to meet him again, but she had hauled
him from the vehicle and placed her finger to her lips to silence him.
She led him through a gated fence off the driveway into the backyard
as they quietly tiptoed to a sliding glass door. The door was unlocked
and she pulled him through into a makeshift den. She pushed him into
a small room sparsely furnished with a twin bed and a small table with
a lamp on it next to the bed. She closed the door and locked it, and
immediately laid siege to him again. Her thirst for sex was immense,
and they had yet another frenzied coupling. This time she managed to
stay mostly quiet, but where volume was lacking she made up for in
passion. Then they slept and when Reid awoke, it was 4:30 am Saturday morning. Sarah was sound asleep. He quietly picked up his jacket
off the floor and gently placed it over her. He slipped out of the house,
through the backyard, and out into the street. He got into his car and
rolled down the street a block before turning on his lights.

As he exited the neighborhood and headed for home, he hoped his
dad would be asleep when he arrived at his house in Dunwoody. His
father was past waiting up for him; Reid had avoided trouble mostly
during his youth, and at almost eighteen years of age, his dad trusted
him. But he had never stayed out this late before without permission,

and he hadn't wanted to worry or disappoint his father. His dad had had enough worry and disappointment. Reid had lost his mom to cancer four years prior, and it was just he and his dad in the house now. His father had tried to be strong for his only son, and had succeeded mostly, but Reid was mature enough now to recognize that his dad was sad and lonely. He sensed that on some days he was simply going through the motions, just to provide for his son. But when he arrived home, his dad was sitting in the den staring at a TV that he wasn't really watching. He had acknowledged Reid when he walked in with a nod, risen, and clicked off the TV. Then he walked over to his son, hugged him fiercely without uttering a word, holding him for a long moment, then turning slowly and shuffling off to bed.

———

The next afternoon, Reid had been outside raking leaves when his dad had hollered from the house that he had a call. He hoped it was Sarah. He wasn't disappointed. She had found his name and phone number written on the label inside of his jacket as he had hoped. She wanted to know if she could see him again on Saturday night. Thus began a whirlwind relationship that would change his life forever.

He discovered that this girl, while an average student at best, was clever and resourceful and also a rascal. It wasn't beyond her to visit neighborhoods and knock on doors and collect money for the Spanish Club or Junior Civitan from unsuspecting husbands and fathers. The cash that she collected actually went to fund a hotel room, beer, and sometimes a little weed for an outrageous party on a weekend night. Sarah wasn't evil, but she was self-absorbed and manipulative. She had learned that she could easily use her good looks to get her way with most men and also more than a few women. Her mom and dad were nice enough people, but they had two grown children who were out on their own, and her parents had grown tired and weary. Sarah had come as a surprise when her mom was in her mid-forties, and they had gradually just allowed their youngest child to operate with little supervision. Sarah was crafty enough to stay out of trouble, or at least deflect it elsewhere when required, so she ran the streets with impunity. On the surface, Sarah and Reid had been a handsome couple. But she was a handful constantly, and he recognized early on that they operated from a different code of ethics. So their relationship was cracked and flawed and filled with conflict except for the sex. The sex was tremendously satisfying for them both; it was the glue that held them together up until the following August when it all unraveled in a hurry.

Reid had received a partial scholarship to play baseball at Georgia Southern in Statesboro. The university was a three-hour drive from Atlanta, so it was close enough for them to try to make it work. But days before he departed for school, she had done something that alarmed him sufficiently enough for him to break it off. He knew that she had deceived people out of money to pay for her adventurous lifestyle, but he'd only suspected that she'd stolen money. So when she had bragged about ripping off a friend's parents for almost $300, he had balked. When he discovered that she had used the money to abort his child that she'd been carrying without consulting him, he was unable to forgive her. During the fall, she had surprised him on two occasions by dropping in on him at college in Statesboro. He'd even given in the second time and slept with her. He had stopped short of rekindling the relationship though and told her that she shouldn't come back again. She had shed some tears. It was the only time he had seen her cry. Her parting words to him were to tell him that she loved him. It was the only time she had ever spoken those words to him, and the final time they had spoken. Reid had spent a year at Georgia Southern majoring in criminal justice, and serving as a super utility player as a freshman on the Eagles' baseball team. When he came home from school that summer, he had no contact with Sarah. Then his father had gotten very ill from a rare liver disease and died within weeks. Distraught, angered, and with limited resources, Reid had sold his father's home, quit school, and joined the army. He spent a few years on base at Fort Bragg, and then spent most of the next six years in Iraq. He returned a hardened and experienced war veteran and started his business. The next time he saw Sarah Lindstrom, she was lying dead on Joey Mac's sofa.

# 12

REID PULLED INTO THE PEACHTREE SUITES around 6:30 to
retrieve the security video. A couple was checking in, so he lingered
outside the office lobby until they departed, and then without
fanfare entered the lobby and swapped the disc with the girl for an
additional $50. As he sped away from the parking lot, he keyed in
a call to his old friend, Tenise Jackson. They had grown up together
after her family moved from a housing project in southeast Atlanta
to Dunwoody when her shrewd, yet uneducated father was able to
set up a successful handyman business in the area following a stint as
a janitor in the Dunwoody elementary school that Reid attended in
his youth. Despite her being a year younger than Reid, the two had
become fast friends when she was in fourth grade. After moving to the
new suburban school, the slight, slender, and shy Tenise was routinely
picked on by some of the kids in the neighborhood for being the new
kid. The fact that she was a rare black face in the upper middle-class
neighborhood unfortunately may have played a part in the abuse as
well. Reid and one of his friends had issued a beating to the three guys
who had instigated it, and neither they, nor anyone else ever picked

on the girl again. He discovered that she could play baseball as well as most of the boys in the neighborhood, and although slight, was a bit of a tomboy and preferred the company of boys over girls. So the two had hung out a lot, especially in the summer, playing stickball in the cul-de-sac and a game they made up on the side of her house called "fast pitch." Tenise was now a thirty-three-year-old senior detective on the Gwinnett County police force.

She answered her phone on the first ring. "Detective Jackson."

"It's Reid," he said. She had always called him Reid because she had trouble with words starting with the letter "S" as a child.

"Reid, oh man! You always manage to find trouble, don't you?"

"We need to talk," he said.

"So talk," she responded.

"In person," he replied. "Joey McIntosh is staying at my house. Can you get here later tonight? Are you still on the second shift?"

"Joey might be in some trouble, I hear," Tenise said. "I get off around 11:30. Where do you wanna meet?"

"Let's make it 12:30 at my house. You need the number?"

Reid gave her his address. She had been to his condo once or twice, but it had been a while.

"I have a job tonight, but I should be done by midnight and back to my house by 12:30. I'll text if I'm running late," he said.

They disconnected and Reid headed to Buckhead to retrieve a limo and head to the hotel to pick up the comedian. He thought that very little about his day had been funny.

# 13

REID MET IAN CALLAHAN AT HIS BUSINESS in Buckhead. Southeast Security was located on Piedmont Avenue just a little less than a mile east of Peachtree. Buckhead is a ritzy, wealthy area in North Atlanta that is filled with fine homes including the governor's mansion, which is located on West Paces Ferry. The high-rise financial district lent itself to the need of many high-end towering hotels. Some of Atlanta's finest restaurants were located in the area including Bone's, Atlanta Fish Market, Bistro Niko, and the Capital Grille to name a few. Before the Super Bowl murder saga involving Ravens' linebacker, Ray Lewis, Buckhead was a raucous party district where college types and young adults would drink, dance, and party to live music until the wee hours of the morning. But over the past dozen years or so, Buckhead had undergone a change in image. There were still bars and nightclubs and plenty to do if you were into the party scene, but many of the clubs had been razed and construction had been ongoing for years to re-establish the district as a "Beverly Hills light" area that consisted of top-of-the-line jewelry and clothing stores and other popular retail outlets.

Southeast Security was in a one-story brick structure built sometime around the middle of the twentieth century. It had plate glass windows in the front that were reinforced with a film that would not allow the glass to shatter if someone tried to break in. The entry door led to a clean and spacious lobby equipped with all of the modern bells and whistles of today's technology. A large receptionist's desk was in the middle of the floor and a dispatcher's table that was really more like a booth or kiosk was located to the left. To the right was a smaller desk for the office assistant. Directly behind the receptionist's desk was a sturdy wooden door that led to a hall that had four equal-sized offices along the corridor. Reid occupied one of the offices and Ian used the one across the hall from him. A third office was used by the three limo drivers and was equipped with several computers, printers, and ports to recharge phones, tablets, and other devices the drivers would need on the job. The fourth was a catch-all. It was for storage and spare office equipment, but it did contain a desk and computer in case someone needed it. A door at the end of the hall led into a large warehouse area where restrooms were located just inside to the left. There were three roll doors in the back that were motorized and could be keyed by remote to allow access for the limos, two of which were parked inside the warehouse. The other was currently out on a job. Reid found Ian in his office. He entered, closed the door, and sat across from him. He filled him in on what had happened with Joey Mac. He explained his own involvement as concisely as he could. Ian was one of Reid's closest friends. They had fought in Iraq together. Ian had been a member of the special unit with Reid that had fiercely engaged the enemy. They had saved each other's lives on several occasions and shared a bond that few men could claim. Ian had returned to the states at the same time as Reid, but had come back a bit lost and bewildered. Reid offered Ian an opportunity in his fledgling company, which had been a godsend for the tall, rangy, rawboned Irishman. He had truly been floundering until Reid had extended the offer to join him.

"I'm likely going to need more of your help on this, Ian," Reid explained.

"I'm on it. No problem," Ian replied. "Whatever you need me to do. I have the package secure. Just let me know what you want me to do with it."

Reid nodded and said nothing for a few moments. Then he finally spoke, "Let's get the comedian. I may need to cut out early. I'll get Julie to pick me up if required. I'm meeting with Tenise after midnight."

Julie ran the office and she would be available to pick up Reid at the Fox, or preferably the hotel, and bring him back to the office if needed.

The pair pulled the limo out of the warehouse and drove down the narrow lane alongside the left side of the building that was the exit. Another lane flanked the building on the right for entry. They headed west on Piedmont and turned north on Peachtree, then made a quick turn into the Ritz Carlton hotel where the comedian was staying. They extracted him from his room on the eighteenth floor and escorted him through the lobby without incident. Ian drove and Reid rode in the back with the comedian down Peachtree to the Fox. The drive to the Fox took about twenty minutes in Saturday night traffic. The comedian was a friendly and pleasant guy who was excited about the upcoming NFL season. He talked about his fantasy football league and which players he hoped to draft. Reid made a few comments here and there, but mostly let the guy talk.

They reached the Fox Theatre and drove past it, taking a right on Ponce de Leon. They parked the limo along Ponce and escorted the comedian through the service door with no problems. Reid returned to the limo and Ian stayed with the guy inside.

Back at the car, Reid checked his texts and noticed he had a message from Millicent. She had provided her address in Keswick Park and confirmed their dinner date for 5:30 on Sunday. He hoped he could put the developments of today aside for a while and enjoy the company of this fine young woman on Sunday. She had, without a doubt, been the bright spot of his day. It would take some effort on his part, he knew. He had seldom thought of Sarah as the years had gone by, but to say she had never crossed his mind would be a lie. And now she had re-entered his life by the events of her own death. At 10:40, his phone buzzed and Ian told him they would be exiting the building at 10:45. Reid locked the limo and stood outside the exit, surveying the crowd. He noticed a few fans lingering who had come out of the side exits, but saw nothing suspicious. At 10:45 exactly, Ian came through the door closely followed by the comedian. Reid fell in behind them and a little to the side. A middle-aged woman approached holding a program and pen. A few other attendees noticed the commotion and joined the small circle of people. Ian and Reid deftly and with practiced expertise were able to keep anyone from getting within arm's length of the guy, all while allowing his fans to pass their programs to him to be signed. They allowed about five minutes of this and then whisked the guy into the limo and drove off. They drove him back to his hotel in Buckhead where he met up with an attractive woman named Lily, who appeared to be in her mid-thirties, in the hotel lobby where they proceeded to have drinks in the spacious lounge. A trio played jazz and swing music and the guy and his lady were soon showing off some nifty moves on the dance floor. The guy seemed to be having a good time dancing with his lady friend. A smattering of folks recognized him and asked for autographs…mostly on cocktail napkins. But he was eating it up and having a great time. When it got close to midnight, Reid begged off, confident that the comedian was secure with only Ian attending to him and had Julie pick him up outside. They made the quick drive to the office and he jumped in his car and headed north to his condo in Chamblee. He arrived at 12:25 and noticed Tenise Jackson in his rear-view mirror filing in close behind him. She was right on time.

# 14

REID LED TENISE UP THE STAIRS into his home. The building was equipped with an elevator, but Reid rarely used it. Joey Mac was sitting at the kitchen table bathed, dressed in shorts and a polo, hair combed and composed. He had a half-full bottle of spring water on the table in front of him. He had spent the day talking to his lawyer, talking to his brother and partner at McIntosh Ford, and organizing his thoughts about what had occurred in the past thirty hours. He had taken Herschel for a lengthy walk in Keswick Park and the dog was now dozing on the floor next to him.

Reid got fresh bottles of water for everyone. He wasted no time. He got Joey to go over everything for Tenise. She listened without interrupting. When he finished, Reid jumped in. "There are some things bothering me, Joey…mostly your security alarm. Was it armed when you left on Friday?"

Joey considered this. "Yes. I always arm it and I remember doing so. Why?"

"It was disarmed when we arrived at your house earlier yesterday. We didn't disarm it. That begs the question: Who did?" Reid said.

"I hadn't thought of that," Joey said.

"Did you give Sarah the code, Joey?"

"I absolutely did not. My house or where I lived never came up in conversation. She had to have gotten my address from my driver's license, but that doesn't explain the alarm being disarmed."

Reid said nothing.

Tenise chimed in. "Look guys, Larribee is a bit of a jerk. He's also lazy and if a case seems to be clear cut, he'll close it and not dig too deep. I admit he lacks some drive and creativity. He's not my favorite guy. But Joey, you were out drinking, probably doing some drugs, right? And you were with a prostitute that possibly had ways of manipulating you without you knowing it. Maybe you did forget to set your alarm. The girl rips you off and decides to get high in your nice home. She figures she'll drive off in your car and dump it and move on to another club. She figures you're probably too vulnerable to pursue her anyway. She's probably protected by thugs anyhow and figures she's safe from retribution."

"Joey says he's missing about sixty to seventy grand in cash, Tenise. He had on a gold Rolex at the hotel that wasn't in her bag," Reid said. Then he added, "Yeah, I checked before the cops got there. He's missing a lot that's unaccounted for."

"Shit, Reid. You didn't just tell me you went through her bag," she said, and shook her head. "I guess I shouldn't be surprised though." She turned to Joey, and said, "Who the fuck keeps seventy grand in their house, fool?"

"Me. It's missing, Tenise. I'm not confused about this."

Reid said out loud for the first time what he believed happened. "I think someone else is involved. Sarah didn't act alone. Joey, I need to know everyone who had your security code. When I walked into your house with you, the first thing I noticed was your alarm pad, and that it wasn't armed. I do security. I see these things. At that point, we didn't realize that someone was in your house, so I found it strange that it wasn't chiming. Of course, if it was armed as you swear it was, then someone disarmed it. They had the code, and you're certain that you didn't give it to Sarah. So how did Sarah get it? Was she with someone else who knew it? How did that person know it? I think you were set up. You were hanging with her at Utopia on a number of occasions and someone preyed on you. The alarm not being armed, the missing cash and jewelry, yet the police see Sarah as the lone perpetrator… it doesn't add up. It seems odd that Sarah would shoot heroin in his house, Tenise, without someone there to drive her away. Perhaps she was on drugs, but according to Joey, she was fairly lucid during the evening. It's very suspicious. I can't believe she would OD in his house on her own. I think it was facilitated by someone. She was murdered. I think she was forced, coerced, or manipulated into rolling Joey. So who…and why?"

Tenise exhaled deeply. "Okay. I'll talk to Larribee. I'll look into a few things, but it's not my case.

"Joey, make a list of everyone who had your security code. Everyone: maid, neighbors, family…any maintenance people," Reid repeated.

"Okay. Is that everything for now?" asked Tenise.

"No," Reid said, "let's watch a video."

———

The three of them crowded into Reid's converted office and Reid threw in the disc. Joey guided them as best he could about likely times that there would have been activity outside the room or in the parking lot. Reid started at 2:15 am and soon they saw Joey arrive in his Expedition and park. He entered and then there was no activity until just after 3 am. Reid watched without reaction as his girlfriend from fifteen years prior exited a Toyota pickup truck. The video had no color so the color of the truck could not be determined, nor could they make out the driver. But Sarah was clear upon exit. She walked directly to room

114 and entered. Reid froze the video as the truck pulled away from the door. The plate numbers would have been legible, but there was mud covering most of the number. He made out what looked to be a six for the first digit, but the remaining digits were covered. Moments later they saw Joey exit and quickly return with ice in a bucket. Then they sped up the video until they saw Sarah exit the suite and climb into Joey's Expedition. Within thirty seconds, Sarah drove smoothly from the parking lot. They searched the video of the parking lot several times, playing and replaying it, but could see no one follow her. The video confirmed little that they didn't know.

"Convenient that the plate was covered in mud," Reid said.

"Look, Reid," Tenise said, "there could be something to that, or maybe it's nothing. It's thin, very thin. And what does it prove? It looks like she got a friend to drop her off to do a trick, that's all. But I'll keep an eye on it. I'll do this for you. Sarah was never my favorite person; I'm not gonna play games with you about that, but if she was murdered—and right now I gotta tell you that I don't think she was—then I'll get involved in this one way or another. Okay?"

Reid said nothing. He had wanted to ask her to check the license plate number on Klaus's Tundra that he had recorded on Friday; he was planning to ask her to look into this guy before the events of Saturday morning, but now he could not. If it turned out Klaus was involved in this in some way and she got caught sniffing around it, it would jeopardize her career. It was very unlikely that red flags would be raised had she run a plate on some guy who wasn't involved in an investigation, but the odds of it being noticed greatly increased now that he could possibly be linked to a death—even if she was unconvinced at this point. He was not willing to place her in that predicament. Not to mention the fact that it could eliminate options for him in how he would ultimately deal with Klaus should the police continue to label this as an overdose. Reid would need to find an alternative to running the plate. He had an idea how he might do this.

He walked Tenise to her car. Before she left, she asked him, "Do you really believe that Joey had seventy grand in cash in his house? People don't do that, Reid. They keep money in the bank. Even $5,000 is a lot."

"I believe him. Why would he lie about that? Joey may party a bit too much, but he's pretty together otherwise. Some guys like a lot of cash. I'm sure he has his reasons…you don't use credit cards to buy hookers and drugs. He seems to like both, so while it may not be reasonable that he'd have that much cash, it is believable."

She softened. "I'm sorry for what happened, Reid, this really sucks. Get some sleep. I'll call you either tomorrow or Monday and let you know where we are with this."

"If you're willing, some confirmation on the contents of her bag would be helpful. I saw a lot, but not everything."

She gave him a grave look, but smiled and then hugged him tight. "Get some sleep, Reid."

Then she climbed in her car and drove away.

———

When Reid came back inside, Joey was waiting for him. "Salem, man…I don't know what to say. This is so crazy. I never knew this girl had been your girlfriend years ago. So, I'm really sorry about what happened to her—for her especially, but for you too. I guess by our senior year you and I didn't hang that much outside of baseball, so I guess I never met her. I want you to know that I liked her, beyond the obvious things. She had a sweet side to her that many of these girls really don't. I wanna think that deep down she was okay. I appreciate you doing all this for me…or for her, or whatever. I'd like to help. I think I need to help. Let me help with this. I got some time now. I talked to my brother, Michael, today and he's asked me to keep a low profile around the store for now and I may need to take a leave of absence depending on how badly the media portrays me on this one. He thinks I'm baggage. It's gonna cost me some money, but I'll be okay. I didn't piss everything away."

"I'm going to find who did this to her, Joey," Reid said, and walked to his bedroom and closed the door.

# 15

REID SLEPT UNTIL 7 AM ON SUNDAY. It was two in the morning when he had finally drifted off to sleep. He slept soundly and awoke moderately refreshed. He and Joey grabbed breakfast at the nearby Waffle House, and then he ran six miles. He returned and did abdominal exercises for his core and followed with 250 push-ups in sets of fifty. Next he worked out on his speed and heavy bag. Joey joined him and told him that Larribee had contacted him, and that he would meet him at his home at noon to turn his property back over to him. He would need to sign a few forms and they had a few follow-ups for him. It seemed Joey had been cleared. The police had the same video Reid had shown Joey and Tenise. It was obvious that Joey was in room 114 from 2:20 am until after noon on Saturday and could not have been at his home when Sarah had died. No one had really believed that anyway. They had, however, taken a urine sample from Joey because of his claim of having been given a knockout drug. That had been confirmed. Unfortunately for Joey, the urine test also revealed the presence of cocaine, THC, and he'd had a blood alcohol level of 0.235. He was likely going to have a little trouble with that.

Reid drove Joey to his house in Peachtree Corners and returned to Chamblee by 1 pm. He ran up the stairs to his condo to grab the book he'd purchased for Millicent, and then back down two flights to the second floor. He knocked on his neighbor's door. The door opened and Raymond Strickland stood before him. Raymond was dressed in blue capri pants, a yellow silk shirt unbuttoned halfway down his torso, and house slippers. He had a blue-and-white polka dot ascot wrapped around his neck. "Salem Reid, to what do I owe this unexpected pleasure?" he chirped. "Please come in!" He actually batted his eyes.

"Hey Ray," Reid said, and stepped inside Raymond's spiffy two-bedroom condo that was decorated to the nines.

He had met Raymond at a condo association party several years ago and they had become—if not friends exactly, at least friendly acquaintances. Raymond had been there with his then boyfriend, Roberto. Roberto was a young Latino who Raymond had fallen for and lavished with gifts, money, and exotic trips only to be jilted by the young rogue in favor of a competitive body builder from Los Angeles. The problem was that Roberto and his new flame had ripped off Raymond of some of his fine china, some silver, and a very nice Tiffany lamp. Reid had recovered these items for Raymond, whom he'd had compassion for when he realized how hurt and heartbroken this guy had been, and Ray had helped out Reid once or twice with some very useful information. Ray was a high-level employee at the Georgia DMV.

Reid didn't really enjoy most parties, but he had learned that instead of social networking, he could spend his time at these get togethers by building business contacts. Raymond turned out to be a bright, friendly, and funny guy who had been of valuable assistance. He hoped he would again, but it usually had a price.

"I saw you with two different girls the past two nights, Salem. Sit down and tell Raymond all about them. Tell me everything, dear! Omit nothing!" he squawked.

"Look Ray, I need some help. I wonder if you'd be willing to run a plate for me. It should come up as a guy named Klaus. The plate number should be 647 ZUB," Reid told him.

"Hmmm. I might be able to help. You're not going to give Raymond any juicy details are you—either about your love life or why you need this guy's info?"

"I need a current address for him, Ray," Reid responded.

Despite Ray's flamboyance, Reid had learned that he was very discreet when it came to matters of a more serious nature. He could count on him to keep his mouth shut and leave no trail in regards to his search.

"Well how about a trade, Salem?"

"What is it, Ray?" Reid asked.

"Well, my friend Tito got slapped around by a guy the other day at a bar in midtown. Some homophobe was actually drinking at Galileo's on Juniper and started saying some ugly, rude things to Tito about being a faggot and about the way he was dressed and all. Well, Tito stood up to him and told him to fuck off. Then the guy punched poor Tito right in his mouth. I think maybe someone should talk to him. His name is William North and I have an address for him. Don't ask me how I got it, Salem!" he cackled and shrieked with delight at his own wit.

"Get me the stats on this plate, and I'll see what I can do, Ray," Reid said.

"Well, Salem Reid, is there anything else?" Raymond inquired.

"Yeah Ray, there is. Can you gift wrap this for me?" Reid handed Ray the book. "It's for the girl you saw Friday night," he explained.

Ray took the book to the dining room table and left briefly, returning with a box of supplies. He wrapped the book with expertise and handed it back to Reid.

"Look, I even put a pretty pink bow on it for you!"

"Thanks a lot, Ray," Reid said and walked out the door.

# 16

OSCAR VILLANUEVA STAYED in a modest neighborhood in a modest, unspectacular home off Beaver Ruin Road in Norcross. The neighborhood was mostly Mexican and Guatemalan, so he blended in just fine. He was a mix of Salvadoran and Guatemalan, but most people simply mistook him for Mexican. Unlike other Guatemalans, Oscar did not mind. He preferred to be as anonymous as possible. It didn't bother him a bit if people were confused about his ethnicity. He drove a two-year-old blue Ford Flex instead of a BMW, Benz, or Cadillac. All of this served his purpose. Oscar was a fairly wealthy man, but no one would ever know this. He didn't want anyone to know of his wealth. He had "friends" in New York and New Jersey who backed his enterprise loosely, but he was essentially his own boss as long as he paid a reasonable "tribute" and kept a low profile. He had developed a lucrative drug operation selling heroin. The girls made him a considerable sum as well, both in the clubs and serving the club clientele in the VIP rooms and doing tricks at a few nearby hotels. Of course, the girls and their security ate into his profits a bit, but he was able to get some of the dancers hooked on heroin and he either sold them drugs for a tidy profit, or bartered with them in various ways to make up for it. But his new operation was very lucrative. He had developed a new source who got him into some wealthy homes that had scored big. In the past, he had rolled a few johns and followed up by looting their homes using the dancers who were willing to be prostitutes—he didn't push too much there. Eventually, many of the dancers would come around on that score when they realized they could double their take compared to what they made shaking their asses on stage for businessmen and frat boys. But now, with his new source, he was striking very large, but none as large as he had struck with that ex-football star from UGA. And he had killed two birds with one stone.

Velvet had become a problem. It had been a risk with her. She had been different from the usual girl. He could get many of them using smack, make them purchase it exclusively from him, and keep them in line subsequently, all while they were making him money on stage and in the back rooms. He had tried that with Velvet, but she had resisted. Then several months ago, she had badly sprained an ankle while trying a new dance move. She had been in remarkable pain. The club kept some marginal medical personnel on staff who were willing to do some unethical things a little outside the lines if the price was right. They had provided the obvious treatment for her with ice, compression, and having her elevate the leg. Then Oscar had persuaded one of these people to treat her by giving her an injection to help with the pain. They had started her on heroin under the guise of giving her a "pain medication." Since she was trusting of the staff, she never suspected that they had duped her until she was using the drug regularly. In fact, they had always administered the drug to her. She didn't even know how to go about doing it herself. Eventually, she had figured out what they had done to her and angrily confronted the "doctor." She had started making noises about wanting to seek treatment. She had been unable to kick it on her own. The "doctor" let Oscar know that they had a problem.

Oscar had no intention of getting treatment for her, but he had met with her and suggested that he would, in fact, get her some help. But she would need to help him with a matter first. Quite coincidently and to his good fortune, his new source had marked the ex-jock who had frequented two of his clubs off and on for years. He had instructed Velvet to befriend this guy and do some extra things for him to keep him coming back. If all went well, he would help her get off the heroin. She had been a great dancer over the past several years dancing at his clubs. She brought in plenty of money, and had been agreeable to prostitution. But she was getting a little old, and he had to admit that getting her addicted to drugs had backfired. And now she was complaining about her situation and there were rumors that she talked to some of the other dancers she'd been close to about her predicament. He also did not want her seeking treatment on her own. He knew this might make him vulnerable if she talked. He had slit the throats of two prostitutes back in New Jersey years ago, but that was part of the reason he had fled to the south. He did not want to repeat that process. None of this was good. She needed to be dealt with. No whore was going to issue an ultimatum to Oscar Villanueva.

So he had brainstormed a scheme, and gotten that big freak of a bouncer to assist him. The bouncer wasn't too smart, but he could follow directions well, and after trying him on some smaller "ventures" over the past few months, Oscar decided to use him for his big score.

Oscar always tried to insulate himself and stay in the background these days. Plus, he figured that there was a good chance that the police would view her death as an overdose…and after all, she was a whore. These things happened to whores all the time. He was pleased with his brilliant plan and was sure it would succeed.

On Saturday morning, he had returned to his modest home with his score. He had $67,000 in cash, and a Rolex watch, which he thought was beautiful. He had agreed to pay his source 20 percent of the take, but figured to pay closer to 15 percent as he'd done in the past. There had been no questions asked, but he didn't want to risk losing the source by being too greedy. He would still have over $50,000 in cash plus all the jewelry after the payment. He was considering keeping the Rolex for himself and wearing it, but was contemplating whether that would be wise. If he did keep it for himself, he would need to be careful of when and where he wore it. He estimated that he could sell it for $15,000 to $20,000, should he decide to go that route. The other jewelry and timepieces would likely fetch an additional $20,000. He would have liked to have taken the Expedition or the Mustang in the garage, but that would have alerted the police to something else entirely. He figured that they would possibly come by the clubs where Velvet danced asking some questions, but that would likely not be a problem. He intended to lie low for a few days anyway, and had told the big bouncer to do the same. He had paid Klaus $2,500 for the job. So now he was planning to meet his source later on either Sunday or Monday and make the payment of approximately $15,000.

He still had several marks left to hit that his source had provided in the area and hopefully he'd be given another list soon. He was confident that they would continue a financially rewarding enterprise for some time. Oscar Villanueva was a very happy man on this fine Sunday.

# 17

ON SATURDAY MORNING, Klaus Vormer had driven straight to the seedy Atlantic Motor Lodge hotel on Cheshire Bridge Road, for which he'd paid for a room with cash in advance on Thursday afternoon. He had been told by Oscar not to return to his Doraville apartment until Tuesday morning. Oscar had said he should be okay by then, but would let him know on Monday evening if everything was good. Klaus liked the room okay. He had gone ahead and gotten the room for a week since the weekly rate turned out to be $40 per night; he would actually save money by doing it this way. He'd kicked back and watched some TV on Saturday evening and then walked a few blocks to a sandwich shop to eat. As he walked back to his room at the Motor Lodge, he was approached by a street hooker who offered to suck his dick for the price of $35. He took her in the room, but her dick sucking technique didn't please him. So he held her down with his considerable strength and sodomized her. He covered her mouth when she tried to scream and then she had tried biting him, so he smacked her hard on the back of her head with his other hand. He enjoyed her useless fight and this aroused him greatly. By the time he finished with her, she had become subdued and withdrawn. He could hear her weeping softly after he'd soiled her and pulled out. His penis was only a little bloody though. He enjoyed the sight of that too and thought it possible he might become erect again. He left her lying face down on the bed. She was probably in her late thirties, but maybe she was a little younger. It was hard to tell with street whores. She didn't look too bad yet, but she was way past her prime. Her teeth were okay, not great, but okay. Like a lot of hookers, her legs and ass were still looking pretty good, but her tits sagged a bit and were only average sized. Klaus thought he might try her again in the same position, but he wanted a few minutes to recuperate.

The street hooker finally got up and walked gingerly past him without saying anything and went into the bathroom. He glanced at her purse on the floor and picked it up. She had no wallet or ID, but she had about $150 clasped with a rubber band. He placed it back in her purse. She had a pack of Marlboro Light cigarettes and at the bottom was a small paper bag. Inside the bag was a pipe, a lighter, and what appeared to be crystal meth. There was a zippered compartment on the inside and there was something heavy in there. He unzipped it and smiled. He removed a pair of handcuffs; the keys were in the lock. He placed them under the bed. He heard water running and then the toilet flush. When she came out, he leered at her. She brushed her hair back off her face and exhaled. He could see she'd been crying.

"Can I have my purse?" she asked.

"Sure," he said, and tossed it towards her stomach.

She reached to catch it, and as she did, he sprung and hit her hard on her jawline just beneath her ear. She collapsed to the floor. He picked her up with ease and placed her on the bed. She was alive, but the knockout punch had served its purpose. He retrieved a washcloth from the bathroom and moistened it slightly and placed it in her mouth. He picked up the handcuffs from under the bed and handcuffed her hands behind her back. He set the keys on the TV stand behind him. He got a glass of water and threw it on her face. She slowly came to and he was pleased to see that the look in her eyes was total fright when she realized what was happening. He chuckled and grinned at her. She tried to kick him, but he slipped the kick, grabbed her, and threw her face down on the bed. He was erect again, so he forced himself inside of her torn and bleeding rectum. He used all his force, punishing her, pulling her hair, and calling her bitch and slut.

He soiled her again and fell on top of her, winded. He rested a bit in this position and then stood up. He picked her up off the bed and tossed her in the closet like a forgotten pair of shoes, and then he closed the door on her.

Klaus slept late on Sunday and treated himself to some excellent fried chicken at the famous Colonnade restaurant that sat just a block away from the Motor Lodge. He felt good. He had slept deeply and dreamlessly after his encounter with the street hooker. He had a pocket full of money. The bouncer job paid decent, but he'd wanted more. He wanted to be able to hook up with some of the good-looking dancers at the clubs, but they always shined him on; much the way that short bitch at the ARC had. He would make her pay somehow, and he was also gonna make that prick who had interfered and given him the road rash on his face pay too. Now he was in with Oscar and he would have all the money and pussy he wanted. Prime pussy, not skuzzy low-rent hookers like the one he currently had in the closet back at the Motor Lodge. Although every time he thought about his encounter with her, he couldn't avoid an erection. But it would soon be different. Being one of Oscar's guys would elevate him in the respect factor, and the girls would be begging him for his big dick. Oscar told him that he'd have more jobs like this one if he performed well. He had performed well and he was going to be a rich guy. He had made $2,500 for about three hours of work. It was easy work, too. Risky, but easy.

# 18

BUD SHERMAN WAS STILL PISSED at Joey Mac. Joey was wealthy and had more money than Bud would ever see. Bud felt his friend had been stingy on Friday night by withholding the funds Bud had wanted to use to get that dusky chick with the big bush in the back room. He and Joey went way back to college, had played football together, and still chased women together regularly. Hell, Bud thought, I even take care of Herschel for him sometimes when he's out of town. He'd never been paid for it, so he felt entitled to have Joey throw some good fortune his way from time to time.

Bud hadn't been home since Friday. He didn't have much of a home. He lived in a one-bedroom apartment off PIB in the southernmost section of Duluth. He was tired of living in that rat hole, but he'd had trouble keeping a job. He once had a decent position with UPS as a driver, but he'd screwed that up with a DUI several years back. Since then, he'd worked for a sports radio station, but that didn't pay well, so he had quit. He'd tried construction, but since the recession, work had not been steady and he hated doing hard labor anyway. He had been collecting unemployment for the last four months, but now he had something brewing that, although it was a bit sketchy, should give him a big payoff soon. But he hoped it came through very quickly or he'd be out on his ass. The rent was due last week, and he hadn't paid it yet. His credit card was tapped out and he could barely afford to make the minimum payment. But here was rich Joey who couldn't even set him up for a few bills at the end of the evening on Friday…or Saturday by then, he guessed. Maybe he could stay with Kelli for a while. They had been hitting it off good since Friday night. They had spent the whole weekend together, much of it in bed, and she had been a lot of fun. She seemed to really dig him and she'd funded their weekend together since early Saturday morning. She had plenty of alcohol in the house and they'd smoked some weed. Since Labor Day was tomorrow, she told him they could spend one more day together before she had to return to classes during the day and bartending during the evening. He was trying to figure out a way he could stay a little longer when his phone buzzed. It was Joey Mac, of all people. He let it go to voicemail and pulled Kelli into the bedroom for some more activity. At least she wasn't holding out on him.

# 19

SALEM REID HAD SEVERAL HOURS before his dinner date at Millicent's. He was trying to clear his head, so that he could enjoy the evening with her, and temporarily put the events of the last twenty-four hours out of his mind. He had a maid who cleaned his home, but she came only once a month and only did the kitchen, bathrooms, and mopped the hardwoods. So he wiped the dust off of some of his furniture with a damp rag and cleaned up his place a bit. Next, he drove to Jimmy Carter Blvd. and had his car detailed at the car wash. He returned home and had time for another quick shower, brushed his teeth, flossed, rinsed, and shaved. He dressed in faded jeans, a green Banana Republic short-sleeve button down, and his Cole Haan shoes. By the time he finished, it was nearly 5:30, so he grabbed the box with the book in it, hopped in his car, and drove to Keswick Park.

Millicent lived just off Keswick Drive in a small, well-kept cottage. The lawn was fescue and in decent shape, and had a pretty maple tree sitting in the middle of it. The tree was large and provided shade and probably kept enough direct sunlight off the lawn that prevented the cold weather grass from turning brown in the summer heat. The house was white with blue shutters. Three white steps led to the little porch that had a white decking, balusters, and railing. The covered porch had a freshly painted wicker chair towards the corner and a little table that was unpainted next to it. An unpainted footrest sat in front of the chair. A small ceiling fan was creating a little breeze that, along with the shade, would make this little porch a fabulous place to relax on a late summer evening.

Millicent Ivey opened the door for him. She looked stunning! She wore red shorts and a white sleeveless blouse that complemented her toned athletic body perfectly. She wore her luxurious black hair down again and her green eyes danced in the sunlight that shone through the leaves of the maple tree behind them. She had sparkling diamond studs set in platinum in her ears, and a shiny silver ring on her right ring finger. She had on simple, yet elegant, white sandals that showcased her delicate feet. Her nails were done in red. And once again, when she smiled, it lit up his world. He caught the aroma of the spaghetti she was making and it smelled wonderful. He smiled for her and handed her the gift-wrapped box.

"Open it," he said.

"You bought me a gift?"

"A little something I thought you might like. Open it," he repeated.

She carefully pulled the bow and ribbon off like many women do, and opened the box. Her smile grew even larger.

"How did you know that this one was my favorite?" she asked, and punched him gently on his arm. "This is perfect, Salem Reid."

Then she curled into his arms and squeezed him tightly. They kissed and then kissed again.

"Come on in. Dinner is almost ready."

Her little home was neat, tidy, and organized. She had cute paintings of dogs and cats and rustic settings on canvas hanging from her walls. There were little potted plants scattered around the living room. A comfy looking sofa sat in the middle with a coffee table in front of it. She had a small table with a covering over it where a twenty-six-inch TV sat. The Braves were playing on FSN; she had tuned it in for him but muted the sound. There was a bookcase by the window that was loaded with hardcover fiction. Many were classics like Twain and Dickens. She had the *Complete Sherlock Holmes* by Conan Doyle and many others. She found a space and added the Salinger novel, then changed her mind and set it flat on the coffee table, so that she could look at it.

The kitchen had a small white dinette with four chairs around it. It was a little cluttered with her current work, but was otherwise a tidy and functional area. A small hallway led to a powder room and a bedroom a little farther on at the back of the house.

"I need to stir the sauce and make the pasta. There's bread in the oven; it should be done in a few minutes."

He moved in behind her as she stood at the stove and wrapped his arms around her from the back. He bent and kissed her neck as she momentarily bent her head back to give him access. She smelled wonderful. She dipped the wooden spoon into the sauce and brought out a taste for him. She blew on it for him and then stuck it in his mouth.

"Delicious," he said. Then he added, "So is the sauce."

She raised her eyebrows at him, then smiled and said, "Get a beer out of the fridge if you want. I have wine, tea, and bottled water…whatever you want."

He grabbed a Sam Adams for them both, removed the bottle tops, and gave one to her. They clinked bottles and drank.

Dinner was outstanding. He hadn't had a meal like that in some time, and he told her how great a cook she was.

She smiled sweetly and thanked him. They finished and he helped with the dishes and then helped her clean up the kitchen. They each grabbed another beer and sat together on the sofa. The Braves were in the sixth inning; she turned up the sound for him so he could watch and listen. She asked him some questions about what was going on in the game and this is when she discovered how to get him to talk. He explained in great detail every aspect of the game. Why a pitcher didn't want to just throw strikes, but wanted to hit certain spots that may only be close to strikes. He explained that the best pitches were those that looked to a hitter like it would be a strike, but ended up off the plate. His job was to fool the hitter or at least keep him off balance. He explained a hit-and-run situation; why it was used, what counts were best for using it. He explained bunting, footwork for middle infielders, base-stealing situations, and why he believed "small ball"—moving runners over, hitting sac fly balls, and doing all the little things right—was a much better game than the power game that involved nothing more than sitting back and waiting for the home run. He may have gone on like this for hours, but she stopped him by climbing up in his lap and kissing him fiercely. She was warm and passionate. She probed him with her tongue and nibbled his ears. She pressed his head into her bosom and he kissed her exposed cleavage. She sighed audibly. He used his hand to cup her breast outside of her shirt and she moaned when he ran his fingers lightly over her hard nipples. They kissed more, then she climbed off his lap and grabbed his wrists. She pulled him up from the sofa and led him to her bedroom. Her bed was a queen. She had a patterned spread with a dust ruffle and matching decorative pillows. She pushed them aside and pulled him down on top of her. They kissed more and fondled each other. Then he pulled her up. They undressed one another as they continued kissing and touching. He removed her blouse and bra. She was gorgeous. Not large and not small, but firm and evenly proportioned. Her nipples were engorged and he took them into his mouth. Her skin was warm and smooth. She pulled his shirt off and ran her hands along his chest. She noticed a scar running down his left side that was rippled and puckered. It had come from shrapnel in Iraq and was six or seven inches long. She ran her hand over it, then slid her hands down to his waist, and pulled his belt loose. She pulled off his pants and boxers. He was rigid with desire. He knelt and removed her shorts. She was wearing a thong from Victoria's Secret that caused him to catch his breath. He slowly pulled it down over her strong and muscular legs, admiring her athletic beauty as he did. He kissed her navel, and ran his tongue down her tummy towards her crotch. She moaned louder and gently ran her hands through his hair. He carefully guided her down on the bed. She was warm and moist. Her musky aroma was sweet and wonderful. He probed her for her sensitive spots. He brushed lightly at first and then with greater force. She became more audible and he alternated back and forth with a light touch and then a heavier one. She responded by forcing her pelvis into him. And then she stiffened and quivered and let out a louder moan. He continued for just a little longer, then she pulled him up and on to her. They kissed again and explored each other, both taking their time. Their breathing had become more labored in anticipation of what was next. When he entered her, she was even more audible, but not quite loud. They worked very slowly at first, kissing and touching while they moved to a matching rhythm, gradually speeding up until once again she stiffened and quivered. She grabbed his head in both her hands and spoke in his ear.

"Salem, I'm cumming, I'm cumming!"

It was only seconds before he followed with an explosion of his own that rivaled the intensity of his youth.

They lay there, breathless and sweating. Darkness had settled in outside and they could hear crickets and a few cicadas. They didn't speak, but she soon rolled over and put her head on his chest. Her hair smelled magnificent. She ran her fingernails along his side, not so lightly that it tickled but not so rough that it scratched. Just right. He explored her body again with his hands. She was soft and curvy where a woman should be, but hard and firm in other places. He marveled at her...and the strength and vigor she had during sex. She was very strong; he liked that about her. He didn't feel like he might break her.

She was surprised when he broke the silence. "I guess we should discuss baseball more often."

She giggled and jabbed him in the side, and he grabbed both her wrists and tickled her ribs. They wrestled a bit and he became aroused by her strength and athleticism. And then he was inside of her again. This time their lovemaking was deliberate. He moved her around, and she responded as if she knew just what he wanted. They fit well and worked well together. They experimented and explored deeper than they had before. Then she came. It took him a little longer this time, but he soon got there and it was every bit as thrilling as the first time.

———

After they cleaned themselves up, Reid suggested that they finish painting the wicker furniture. So she got out a tarp and supplies and they set to work. She didn't want to risk getting paint on the clothes she'd been wearing, so she painted wearing only her thong, and he wore only his boxers. Together, it took them close to an hour and a half to complete. They cleaned up and put away the supplies.

He glanced at the clock on her microwave and said, "It's getting late."

"No you don't, Salem Reid," she said, and pushed him to the living room floor. In no time, they were naked again, and she climbed on top. They took it very slow this time, and again experimented. When they finished, she stayed on top of him and hugged him closely.

Then she said, "Can you stay the night?"

"Okay. But I have some business in the morning." Then he added, "Do you work tomorrow?" It was Labor Day and he couldn't remember if she had it off.

"I go in after noon, and work until 6," she said.

They heated up the leftovers from dinner, and it was almost as delicious as it had been earlier that night. They cleaned up the dishes and then showered together. She gave him a spare toothbrush and they both cleaned their teeth. They were both very tired from the excitement of the evening. They climbed into bed and she rolled on her side facing away from him. He fit his midsection into her ample buttocks and they both fell fast asleep.

Sometime before dawn, Reid woke from a disturbing dream. He rarely dreamed, and when he did, he usually remembered few details of his dreams. But this one had been vivid. He was riding on the Scream Machine Rollercoaster at Six Flags near Atlanta. Only two people were on the coaster. He was one of the riders and he was in the last car. He was eighteen and still in high school. A sixteen-year-old Sarah was in the front car and she had turned around, smiled, and waved as they had ascended the big hill at the beginning of the ride. Then they descended the first big hill and back up the next one and the coaster slowed. She turned again, but this time she had a tentative smile, like she was a little uncertain about riding this rollercoaster. There was something a little off with her face too, perhaps a little pinched. Then they were off on the next hill, and he could only see the back of her head. The next time she turned she was not smiling and one of her eyes was drooping and unfocused. Now he wanted to get to her and help her, but he could not. He tried to climb out of his seat, but when he did, the coaster would take off again and throw him back into the car. The ride ended and he jumped out. She turned to him, but her lovely face had completely disappeared. There was nothing there but her blond hair blowing in the breeze. Her body was still there, but as he ran to her, she completely vanished. He heard her voice from above and he looked up. He caught a glimpse of the thirty-two-year-old prostitute she had become and then she was gone.

Reid quietly rose from the bed. Millicent was breathing deeply, not quite a snore. He grabbed his clothes from the floor and moved to the living room where he quietly dressed. The microwave clock told him it was 5:28. Light would not come for another hour. He found a pen and a scrap of paper in the kitchen and left a brief note that he placed on top of the book he had gotten for her. It read: "You are beautiful and I adore you. —Salem" He left her house, locking the knob on the door and pulling it shut.

# 20

REID DROVE QUICKLY TO HIS HOUSE, grabbed a granola bar and some juice, then washed up a bit and brushed his teeth. He checked the address that he'd placed in his GPS the day before and headed to some apartments on Ashford Dunwoody Road just north of Perimeter Mall. William North lived on the third floor of a nicely maintained complex in a gated community. Reid parked to the side, then simply followed the next car in through the gate. He drove to North's building and spotted his car. Reid had discovered that North worked at a nearby country club and that he did not have Labor Day off. It was forecast to be a decent day and there would be a lot of people golfing today. Reid parked a few buildings over and then walked to a wooded area along the edge of the property, which was thick with pine trees. He would easily be able to see North when he exited his building, if he was indeed home and had not slept at a girlfriend's or buddy's house. He waited only twenty minutes before he saw a man exit the apartment into the dark morning. Reid met him before he reached his car and blocked his path.

"William North?" Reid inquired.

"Yeah? Who are you?"

"You need to answer for Tito."

"Who?"

"Tito," Reid replied patiently.

"Who the fuck is Tito?" asked North.

"He's a gay man that you punched at Galileo's."

North chuckled. "So? I don't like fags, dude."

"I don't like you," Reid said, and before the guy could respond, Reid had landed a lightning quick straight left to North's mouth.

He followed it with a right elbow to the guy's left cheekbone just below his eye. The eye would be black and swollen for days. North landed on his butt and started to get up but Reid landed a swift front kick to his forehead that snapped the guy's head back. He stayed down this time.

Reid bent and grabbed the guy's left wrist with his right hand and worked his left arm over the top of North's shoulder and snaked it through and grabbed his own right wrist. The Kimura armlock was persuasive. He pulled the guy over on his side and knelt over him. He had tremendous pressure on the guy's shoulder. He squeezed tightly so that if the guy tried to move, the slightest twist would cause him great pain and perhaps a trip to an orthopedic surgeon.

"Look, William, it's gonna go down like this. You're going to Galileo's tonight and you're going to find Tito and apologize. Also, take him some flowers, you hear? I'm going to follow up, and if you don't make it right with Tito, I'll come back and rip your arm off. Clear?" He added a little pressure to North's shoulder as he spoke.

"Clear," North grunted.

Reid released him and walked back to his car. He got in and headed to Southeast Security. He wanted to get some tracking devices.

———

Reid drove south on Ashford Dunwoody inside the Perimeter and took it all the way to Peachtree Road. Traffic was light due to the holiday. He took Peachtree Road to Piedmont and was at his business in no time. The late summer sun was rising above the horizon; it would be a warm day. He parked in front and entered the building. He went to his office, checked some emails, and looked at the day's schedule. Ian had two separate security details today, and there were seven limo services setup. Two would be longer term and five would not take much time. Not a bad day. He would be able to leave all of this to his crew and deal with the details of the weekend without being missed too much. He went to the storage office and located a couple of spot tracking devices. He placed new lithium batteries inside each one. He checked his watch. It was 7:30. He texted Millicent: "Coffee?"

He didn't immediately hear back from her, so he guessed she was still asleep. He stopped at Dunkin' Donuts across from the Brookhaven MARTA Station, purchased two coffees, and grabbed some cream and sugar in case she wanted some. He always drank his black. He drove back towards her house and while he was stopped at the intersection of Johnson Ferry and Peachtree Industrial, he noticed she had texted back: "Yes! Come back, I miss you."

He pulled into her drive a few minutes later and she met him at the door in a pair of gym shorts and a sports bra. He handed her coffee to her and she pulled him down for a kiss. It was a splendid kiss and he felt a wave of electricity run through him.

"Thanks for the coffee, it's great. But the note you left was even better." They kissed again. "Want some breakfast?" she asked when they finally came up for air.

"Maybe a little something. Can I help?" he inquired.

"No. I like cooking for you," she said. Then she winked and added, "It's worked out well so far."

He sat at the kitchen table and admired her from the back as she made omelets for them both. She placed some toast in the toaster and when it popped up, golden brown, she brought the food to the table. She poured them both some apple juice and they began to eat. The omelet contained cheddar cheese, red and green peppers, and some diced ham. She had cooked it perfectly and it was delicious. She insisted on cleaning up the dishes while he relaxed, so he admired her again, but from the side this time as she stood at the sink.

She glanced over and said, "What?"

"Just admiring your ass," he said.

She smiled and jutted her butt towards him. "You like?"

"Yes I do," he replied.

She finished the dishes and without warning, peeled off her shorts and sports bra and straddled him on the chair. They made love again right there in Millicent's kitchen.

After satisfying one another, she said, "My morning is off to a great start!"

She needed to leave for work in about an hour, and he was anxious to get rolling on his agenda for the day. She walked him out, and as he passed her little black Honda, he pulled his Chap Stick from his pocket and it fell from his fingers. It rolled directly under her car, so he shrugged and dropped to fish for his lip balm. As he did, he secured the activated tracking device, which he'd cupped in his hand, under her car.

He popped up, held up his Chap Stick, and grinned.

"Klutz," Millicent said.

They kissed goodbye and he told her he would call her later that night.

Reid jumped in his Challenger and drove away. Millicent Ivey stood smiling and waving from her driveway.

# 21

REID HAD BEEN CONSIDERING the tracking device on her car since Saturday afternoon after their brunch at the IHOP. It was unsettling to him to have to sneak under her car and put the device on there, but he didn't like the alternatives. Had he asked her to allow him to do so, he figured she would have resisted and maybe even angered. What would he say?

"Look, Millicent, after the incident at the ARC I was concerned about you, but now I have some other reasons to be even more concerned. You see, this girl I dated in high school possibly overdosed but was more likely murdered in the home of an old teammate of mine at DHS. I'm investigating it, and oh by the way, this Klaus character is possibly involved in her death."

So he decided that this was the best course of action to take, and he had no compunction whatsoever about being a little underhanded to protect a smart, kind, and lovely young lady whom he admired and was becoming extremely fond of.

He drove to his house and used his computer to locate an address and phone number for Sarah's parents. It looked like they still lived in the same home off Chamblee Tucker Road inside of the Perimeter in Embry Hills.

He sat for a moment and composed himself, then he dialed the number. A woman whose voice he didn't recognize answered.

"Hello. Lindstrom residence," she said. She sounded to be younger than Sarah's mom, who would have to be around seventy-five years old now.

He glanced at his watch. It was just before noon.

"Good morning, my name is Salem Reid. I was hoping to contact Mrs. Lindstrom."

There was hesitation on the other end. Finally, the woman said, "Salem? Are you the boy that Sarah ran with in high school?"

"Yes, ma'am," he said, and noted that she'd used the expression "ran with" instead of "boyfriend" or "the guy she dated."

"This is Stephanie, her sister. I think we met once or twice, years ago. I guess you know about Sarah. Please call me Stephanie," she said.

"Yes, Stephanie. I know. I would like to come by your parents' house and pay my respects. Do you think that would be okay?"

"I think my mother would really appreciate seeing you. She still talks about you from time to time. My dad is a little distant, though, Salem. He's been ill and he and Sarah weren't particularly close in recent years, but losing his baby girl must be just killing him." She sniffled a little when she said this last part.

"I understand. Would this afternoon be a good time?" he asked.

"Hang on and I'll check with Mom." She put the phone down and he heard subdued voices in the background, but he could not determine what was said.

She came back on the line a few minutes later. "Salem?"

"I'm still here, Stephanie."

"She asked if you could come around two. My dad takes a nap after lunch. She thinks that might be the best time. Okay?"

"I'll see you at two. Thank you."

He clicked off and called Joey Mac.

Joey answered after several rings. "Hey, Salem."

"Hey Joey, did you get the names for me?'

"Yeah, I got a list here, hang on." Reid heard some papers shuffle and Joey said, "Okay. Bud Sherman has it, or had it rather. I changed it today. I just got off the phone with ADT."

He paused and then continued, "Consuelo Valdez is my maid. She had it. My next-door neighbor, Walt Vickery, is an older gentleman who watched my house when I was out of town and took care of Herschel for me once or twice. Dalton and Devin Dewey had it. Remember them from high school? They have a plumbing business and I gave it to them when my water heater blew last winter. They came in and fixed it while I was at work. And my brother and his family also have taken care of Herschel when I've been out of town, so they have it. That's it, Salem."

"Okay. How about making a more detailed list? Don't email or text it. I'll come by in twenty minutes and pick it up. You'll be there?" he asked.

"Yeah. I'll be here, man."

"Okay. I need any contact information that you have: phone numbers and addresses…emails too if you have them."

"See you in twenty, Salem."

———

Reid figured he had time to get to Joey's and pick up the detailed list and then he could scope out the area around Peachtree Corners Circle and see if anything struck him. He'd need to become the person in the pickup truck. Where would he have waited on Sarah, so that he could follow her to Joey's house? He was going on the hypothesis that the person in the truck would not want the hotel or the Expedition out of his sight. Therefore, waiting at or near Joey's house, or waiting for a text or phone call seemed unlikely. He would sit somewhere en route that was secluded and he would watch the hotel. He would glide in behind her as she passed and then follow her. He would park a block or two away and then approach on foot. It was probably between four and five in the morning when this occurred. This would be the best time because the fewest cars were on the road and most people in the surrounding neighborhoods would be asleep.

As he pulled into Joey's driveway, he noted how secluded his property was. It was almost certain that any neighbor who'd witnessed the Expedition pull into the driveway and around the back and out of sight would not even blink an eye. Joey was out late a lot, and it was his car pulling into the drive after all. This, of course, was assuming that the guy executed the plan as he would have himself. During his brief encounter with Klaus at the ARC, he thought that the guy seemed a bit dumb…and that was being charitable. So that furthered his belief that there were smarter people behind this and Klaus was just a lackey.

But he knew if he could locate the guy, he and Ian and perhaps his old pal, Petey Ward, could put a tail on him that might just lead to the boss. Once Joey gave him the list of people who had his code, a few on that list may need to be tailed too.

Joey met him at the garage and let him in the house. He handed Reid the list. "What else can I do, Salem?"

"Whatever I have you do, you tell no one about it. We have to be clear on this."

"I won't say a word to anyone. You can count on me," replied Joey.

"I want you to ride down the southeast corridor of Peachtree Corners Circle, over around JR's. Start close to there and move north. See how many business, shops, stores, and restaurants have video cameras. Make another list. Don't talk to anyone about what you're doing. I'll get the list from you later today or tomorrow. Be thorough."

"Okay. Have you seen the *AJC*?" Joey asked.

"No. I was going to pick one up, but I haven't yet. How bad is it?"

"Here, take a look." Joey produced the Monday morning *Atlanta Journal-Constitution* and handed it to Reid.

The story read:

Sarah Lindstrom, 32, of Alpharetta, a strip club dancer who went by the stage name "Velvet," was found dead early Saturday in the Peachtree Corners home of former UGA star, Joey McIntosh. The Gwinnett Medical Examiner's office concluded that Lindstrom died from an apparent overdose of heroin. A Gwinnett police spokesperson said that Lindstrom had drugged the former Bulldog with the date rape drug Rohypnol, AKA "roofie," at a local hotel, rolled him, and stole his vehicle that was later found at his home. Police said that $5,000 was found in her bag that allegedly belonged to McIntosh along with his SEC Championship ring. They believe that she injected heroin at his home subsequent to robbing him, and she died shortly after. The ME suggested that three times the lethal dose of heroin was found in her body. McIntosh has been cleared of any wrongdoing in connection with her death, but he faces unrelated drug charges that stem from a urinalysis that showed concentrated levels of cocaine and marijuana in his system.

Lindstrom was a graduate of Lakeside High School, in Atlanta, Georgia. She had worked briefly in modeling prior to becoming a dancer at various clubs in metro Atlanta. She had most recently been employed at Utopia, an upscale dance club in Doraville. She had previously danced at the Slick Kitty and Split Tails dance clubs, both located in northeast Atlanta. She was described as hard working and pleasant by the staff and other dancers at Utopia, all of whom declined to give their names for this article. Services for Lindstrom will be held on Wednesday, September 3rd, at Patterson's in Brookhaven.

———

Reid dropped the paper on the kitchen table and said nothing for a moment.

Joey said, "I talked with my lawyer, and he thinks we can work around most of the charges, but my brother is embarrassed and concerned about how the notoriety will affect our business."

Joey didn't add that Michael, his brother, may actually benefit by this since Joey's rather substantial salary would not be paid to him during his leave of absence. This was an agreement that the two had made when they absorbed the business from their father together. Joey would continue to receive proceeds from the profit the company made, but in addition to lost salary, he would also not receive sales commission on cars he normally sold. His commission was double that of the average salesperson.

"Okay, Joey," Reid said. "Let's get moving on the video canvas. I'll call you later and we can see what you came up with."

They both got in their vehicles and headed over to the area of Peachtree Corners Circle that they had discussed. Joey got to work weaving in and out of the businesses along the street, looking for outside video cameras that would potentially pick up road traffic. Reid had decided on his ride up earlier that a business park across PIB from the hotel might have been a desirable location for the pickup truck driver to keep an eye on things. It was en route too, so it made sense to be on the western side of the boulevard in order to make it up to Peachtree Corners Circle as Sarah approached, and easily fall in behind her as she passed. He drove down into the business park. There was little activity because of the holiday. He drove to the far eastern end of the parking lot and realized that this was a perfect spot. It sat low from Peachtree Corners Circle and had some areas that were treelined for adequate cover to the north, but sat above PIB to the west. The lot had a bird's eye view of the hotel room that Sarah and Joey had used. It was maybe 175 yards away. It was an ideal location to watch the front of the hotel. Reid slowly drove his vehicle around looking for video cameras attached to the outside of the businesses. He spotted one camera that was towards the far end of the building from where he guessed the truck might have parked. It was a possibility, he supposed, that the camera could have picked up something, but whether he could get the video from them and what its recording capacity would be added more variables. He checked the sign above the door and saw that the suite that had the video camera was called Precious Medals. He Googled it on his phone and discovered that they were a wholesale outfit that made designer, high-end awards, trophies, and engraved plates. They actually used gold, silver, and platinum to make their products, hence the security camera, Reid figured. Their website showed that they were open Monday through Friday, from 8 am to 5:30 pm. There was a flashing graphic going across the screen that read: "Closed Monday, September 1st for Labor Day." He clicked on the "contact us" tab and a screen showed a phone number and contact names of Bernard and Karen Lowenstein. Reid entered this information into his contacts on his iPhone.

He glanced at his phone and saw that it was 1:35. He would need about twenty minutes to get to Sarah's parents' house. He drove through the far end of the parking lot and back, but noticed nothing else that would be helpful, so he exited the business park and jumped on PIB south to 285. He took 285 east to Chamblee Tucker Road and drove inside the Perimeter towards his old girlfriend's neighborhood.

# 22

MICHAEL McINTOSH SPENT HIS MORNING on Labor Day playing nine holes of golf at Country Club of the South. CCS was one
of the most fashionable neighborhoods in metro Atlanta. It was home
to many sports celebrities as well as pop and rock stars. He lived
in one of the "point" homes in CCS. Point because of where the
decimal was located in the price of the home. His home was valued
at $1.4 million and he loved living in the area. Like his brother, he
drove a Ford Expedition, but that wasn't quite good enough for his
wife Claire. She had to have the big black Navigator with all the
bells and whistles. He was, of course, able to make a reasonable trade
with a Lincoln Mercury dealer for the car, but it had actually cost
him a little money. She was always costing him money. She had just
recently had her second breast augmentation. He loved her large
breasts, but he hadn't seen the need to have them redone after only
seven years. He thought they still looked great, but she had decided
that she wanted them a little bigger. This had just set him back
$10,000. She had wanted a beach home in Destin, Florida, too. He
had given in to her after an evening when they had gotten a little

tipsy drinking sangria following a double's tennis match, and she had gotten particularly randy with him. He had figured they could rent the place to help pay for it, but she would have none of that. She wanted complete access to the beach cottage whenever she desired, so he had no way to offset the expenses for the home. The expenses were considerable too. Maintenance, utilities, landscaping, and property taxes just to name a few. Their teenage daughter was in private school also, and the tuition was approaching $20,000 a year. So now, on Monday afternoon sitting in his office at McIntosh Ford, he was going over his finances and feeling a little glum. Despite his considerable compensation, money was very tight at the moment. And now, on top of all of that was this sordid affair his younger brother was involved in. He had demanded that Joey take a leave of absence. Of course, he had said a prayer for his depraved brother while attending the big Presbyterian church near his neighborhood during services on Sunday, but mostly he had been embarrassed and ashamed of him. Now he had to navigate the dealership without his partner; he didn't want this tawdry ordeal affecting business, and he would see that it didn't. He knew his brother loved the nightlife. He knew Joey was a drinker and a womanizer, but he hadn't expected this to happen. Fortunately, the write-up that had appeared in the paper was on page seven of the A section of the *AJC*, and it was a small article. But still, it was disconcerting to have this disruption in his life.

Jared Marlow appeared at his door. Jared was the assistant sales manager. He would be able to fill in to some degree for Joey. The silver lining he supposed was that Jared would come considerably cheaper than Joey.

"Hey Jared, come in and have a seat," Michael said.

"Yes, sir, I hope everything is okay, Mr. McIntosh," Jared said.

"Well Jared, I just wanted to let you know that Joey will be on a leave of absence for a spell. I suppose by now the news has gone around the dealership," Michael said.

"People know about the trouble he got in over the weekend, yes. I'm very sorry, sir, but you know that you can count on me to do whatever needs to be done. Will I be running the sales meetings?" Jared asked.

Jared was a little too ambitious sometimes and it was showing here. Michael proceeded cautiously. "We can do it together for now. Let's ease into this without upsetting the applecart too much, Jared," he said.

Jared seemed a little disappointed with the vague answer. "Yes, sir. But if you need me to take it over at some point, I believe I'm ready for the challenge. I've been working closely with Joey and I know the ropes, sir," he responded.

"Thanks, Jared. Now go sell some cars, okay?"

"Yes, sir, and thank you for speaking with me about this. Please let Joey know I'm thinking of him and I hope he can return to work as soon as possible," Jared said, laying it on.

"I sure will, Jared."

Jared departed and Michael sat for a moment lost in thought. Then he dialed his wife and told her it would be late in the evening when he returned home, and she should make dinner plans without him. Of course, when she made dinner plans it usually cost him money.

# 23

MILLICENT IVEY WAS A LITTLE TENDER TODAY, so she was glad that she had only a low-impact aerobics class to teach. Of course, every time she made a quick or labored movement, she noticed the soreness and smiled and thought of Reid. She knew that she had become quickly infatuated with him, and that was unusual for her. Sure, she'd had plenty of boyfriends, and had enjoyed a two-year relationship with a nice guy in college. At one time she thought that she may have been in love with him, but towards the end of their junior year at Alabama it had started to fizzle. She felt as if she'd finally run up on a very special guy in Salem Reid. She couldn't get enough of him and all she could think about was figuring a way to hook up with him again and again ever since he had saved her from that creep on Friday. She was pretty sure that he wanted to as well, but she didn't want to appear to be the needy or cloying type. He had said he would call, so maybe he was thinking the same way as her. She hoped so. Since moving to Atlanta almost two years ago, she had dated several guys and even had a rather disappointing sexual encounter with a guy who played guitar in a band she had seen in a club in town. She had regretted sleeping with him but her friend Jill, a co-worker from the ARC, had known the guys in the band and Jill had been dating the drummer at the time. The drummer and the guitarist had been roommates. When they all ended up back at the musicians' apartment in Virginia Highlands and Jill and her drummer boyfriend wandered off to his bedroom, Millicent had decided to be adventurous and fool around with this guy. One thing led to another and then they were in bed. He had been attentive, but only to his own needs and she had been left dissatisfied and unfulfilled. She had left the apartment abruptly and taken a cab home. After that incident, she had been reluctant to date. Jill had set her up with a couple of different guys who were both nice enough, but her heart hadn't been in it, so neither had lasted past a third date.

All of this had been close to a year ago, so maybe she was trying to catch up with Reid. He was the opposite of all the guys she had been around since college. He was thoughtful and attentive; the book he had bought for her had really touched her heart. It truly was the thought that counted. She doubted that he had done the fancy wrap job, but man, if he had, then he really was some kind of a special guy! He was very handsome, fit, and strong. She knew he was tough, but he wasn't mean or aggressive. He didn't boast or show off, and he was polite to everyone he encountered unless they gave him reason not to be. Yeah, she thought and laughed, over a long weekend I've managed to get real caught up in this guy. She was happy, though. She was happier than she had been in a long time, and she knew that Salem Reid was a big part of that.

She had been a little uneasy this morning when she awoke, and he had vanished. She had gotten up and checked around her house for him, but when she looked outside and saw that his car wasn't in her driveway, she knew he was gone. Truthfully, she had panicked a little. Had he gotten a night of marathon sex and simply left her behind? So she had sat on her sofa thinking she might cry, when she saw his note:

"You are beautiful and I adore you. —Salem"

Then she remembered him telling her last night that he had business in the morning. And when he texted about bringing coffee, she had been terribly relieved, and just a little bit ashamed of herself for being so paranoid.

She thought about texting him, or even "sexting" him, but she decided not to. She wasn't seventeen anymore and he was probably busy. So she contented herself that he would call her this evening as he said he would.

"Damn!" she thought. "What is wrong with me?" She giggled audibly enough that her friend Jill, who was standing at her office door, asked, "Really? What's up with you, girl?"

Millicent smiled up at her friend. "Just laughing at something funny."

"Do you care to share with your bestie?" asked Jill.

Jill Cramer was a tall, slightly lanky young woman. She wore her long dark brown hair in pigtails almost all the time, whether she was working at the ARC or out on the town. Millicent had seen her hair loose on only two occasions. Once when they attended a colleague's wedding together and another time when she had just showered at Millicent's house. She had pretty ice blue eyes and an ever so slightly bent nose that had a pierced loop through it. She almost always wore short shorts with long white-and-red striped socks pulled up to her knees. When she walked, she bent forward a little and glided, giving the appearance that she was on roller skates. She reminded Millicent of one of those roller derby girls she had seen on the classic TV stations from the seventies. She had small but perky breasts, long limbs, and long lovely fingers with nails she painted in various colors. She had a sundial tattooed on her left wrist, where she wore a Swatch watch. She wore an assortment of bangles on her right wrist. Most guys thought that she was cute as hell, and more than a few girls did too. Jill was not shy about announcing that she would occasionally swing that way if the mood struck her.

"Share what, Jill?" Millicent asked, knowing she wouldn't get out of this.

"What's with the glow and the giggling? Who is he?"

Millicent glared at her friend, then burst out laughing. "Am I that obvious?"

"YES! And who?"

So Millicent Ivey described the events of the weekend to her friend starting with Friday afternoon in the parking lot and ending with this morning. She really tried to tell it tastefully, but Jill's facial reactions throughout the story made Millicent feel like she was telling some lurid tale.

"OMG, girl, you did not!" exclaimed Jill. Then she said, "Salem Reid? OOOOOHHHHH girl, I can't believe you bagged that hottie!"

"Gosh Jill, you make it sound so crass," Millicent said.

"Crass ass, Mil," she retorted.

"He's a nice guy," said Millicent.

Jill looked at her friend and could see she was really smitten with this guy. She softened and said, "So, a damsel in distress, huh?"

"I guess so," Millicent said a bit too sulkily, and then they both cracked up.

Jill stood up and as she glided out of the room said, "Guess I won't be seeing much of you for a while, bestie!"

# 24

REID PULLED UP TO SARAH'S OLD HOUSE where her parents still lived. It was a brick ranch built in the fifties. The house had a few steps that led up to a small front cement porch with an iron railing on both sides of the steps and surrounding the porch. Reid knocked on the door. He heard footsteps slowly coming towards him. Patsy Lindstrom stood erect in the doorway. A slight melancholy smile reached her lips, but her eyes danced a little with pleasure at seeing Reid again. He had never spent much time around either of Sarah's parents. When he would arrive to pick Sarah up back in the day, she would rush out of the house and jump in his car before he ever had a chance to turn off the motor. He had probably only been in their house a half dozen times during the time he dated Sarah, and usually only for brief encounters. He had eaten dinner once at their house for Easter during his senior year. It was probably the only time he had engaged in any kind of conversation with her parents. Her mom had seemed to like him, but her dad had been indifferent. Sarah had seemed a little distant during the meal, as if she were uncomfortable in this setting. Reid believed that having him to dinner had not been

Sarah's idea. Later that night when they had found a place to be alone, he had been surprised to discover that it was one of the rare occasions when she seemed uninterested in sex. She had been quiet and sullen, another rarity for her.

"Salem," Patsy said in a sweet southern drawl, "look at you. You are every bit as handsome as I remember. Please come in."

Patsy Lindstrom was about seventy-five years old, but she could have been sixty. She was still quite striking. One could easily see where Sarah had gotten her beauty. Her hair was blond and cut to her shoulders in a conservative but fashionable style. She still sported a decent figure, and she moved with grace.

"You look great, Mrs. Lindstrom. Thank you for seeing me."

She led him into a small, neat living room. A dated but comfortable looking sofa sat along the far wall. It may have been the same sofa from fifteen years prior, but he could not be certain. A worn chair sat in the corner of the paneled room with a small medical oxygen tank next to it. Presumably it was for the sickly Mr. Lindstrom who was apparently down for his afternoon nap. Next to the chair along the wall was a table with a number of framed photographs on it. There were pictures of the Lindstrom's older children, pictures of grandchildren he assumed, and one of them was a picture of him and Sarah attending his senior prom at DHS. She was breathtaking. There had been a picture just like it in his father's house. Reid had taken it down and put it in a box when he had come home from college at Christmas during his freshman year. His father had watched him do it, and had said nothing about it. It was probably still in that same box, either in storage or possibly on a shelf in a closet in his home.

"Please have a seat, Salem. Can I get you a beverage?" she asked.

"No, ma'am. I'm fine, thank you," he said.

They sat on the sofa together and she took his hands. "Just look at you," she repeated. Then she asked, "Are you married?"

"No, ma'am," he said.

He told her about his job and a little bit about his two tours in Iraq, and then how he'd stayed over there to do security work for several years. Perhaps he had said this to make a point that he'd been either out of the state on an army base or out of the country for the nine or ten years following his breakup with her daughter.

"I didn't realize that you are a war veteran, Salem. Thank you for your service to our country."

"Yes, ma'am," he replied.

"Are you seeing anyone special, honey?" she asked.

He figured she would get around to this. He might have been vague or even misleading with his answer, but his short time with Millicent had been precious to him, and out of respect for her he said, "Yes, Mrs. Lindstrom. I've recently met a young lady I'm quite fond of."

"I'm so glad," she said simply and it seemed as if she meant it. Then she fell silent, and Reid took the opportunity to plunge into the reason for his visit.

"Mrs. Lindstrom, I'm terribly sorry for you and Mr. Lindstrom in regards to Sarah," he said.

"Yes. Thank you, Salem." She hesitated as she composed herself. "Her father and I...well, it was always difficult with Sarah. She was always wild and we were getting older by the time she was a teenager. We couldn't control her. We knew if we demanded that she behave differently that we would lose her. So, Bill and I agreed that we would just love her the best we could and hoped she would grow out of it." She hesitated again, then she said, "Were you aware of what she did for a living, Salem?"

"I hadn't spoken with Sarah in fifteen years. I knew nothing about her life until just recently."

"I knew she danced and I suppose that some of those girls are prostitutes too. I didn't know that for certain about Sarah, but I wasn't totally shocked when I learned," she said. "I was surprised about the drugs though. Sarah and her father weren't close, but she and I would talk frequently and I would see her from time to time. She didn't seem like a drug addict to me. Was she into drugs when the two of you were an item, Salem?"

"No. She drank a little, but no more than most of the kids," he said. "What did the police tell you about all of this, Mrs. Lindstrom?"

"Pretty much what was in the paper." She sniffled, then pulled herself together again and continued, "She was, uh…turning a trick with this former football player from the University of Georgia whom she associated with at Utopia, and drugged him and stole his car. They said she robbed his house and overdosed while inside."

"So they haven't said anything about foul play to you? Did they question you or go to her home in Alpharetta?"

"Detective Larribee said that there had been a rash of robberies in the area, but nothing that indicated the involvement of dancers. They did go to Sarah's apartment and looked through some of her things to see if there was a connection to these other crimes. My understanding is that there is no evidence to suggest that she was involved in any other crimes. Oh, Salem, this is all so sordid!" she blurted abruptly.

"Mrs. Lindstrom, I need to tell you some things. Please listen carefully and then I'll have some more questions," he said.

He told her how Joey Mac had called him early Saturday afternoon, how the two had been teammates on the DHS baseball team. He explained how they had found her and how it didn't quite add up to him the way the police believed. He gave her an abbreviated and gentler version of his hypothesis that he had given to Tenise Jackson.

"I plan to follow through on this, Mrs. Lindstrom. I'm going to find out what really happened in Joey McIntosh's house early Saturday and who was behind it," he told her.

"Salem, I can't believe you are the one who found her. I had no idea. This is all so bizarre!" she said.

"I'd like to speak with her friends. Do you know anyone she may have been close to?" he inquired.

"She spoke of a girl named Janice and maybe a Lara too, but I didn't know them or how she knew them. I assumed that they were girls she worked with."

"Did she ever mention a man named Klaus?" he asked.

"No," she said, "I don't recall that name."

"What about her home? Are you responsible for her belongings?" he asked.

"I have a key to her apartment. I've never been there, but I have the address. We will have to clear it out I suppose. The police have released it to us. My daughter, Stephanie, is here to help; she can stay for about a week. She's going to help me go through her things and deal with all the details after the funeral on Wednesday. Will you attend the service, Salem? I would like for you to be there," she added.

"Yes, ma'am," he said. Then he asked her, "How would you feel about me helping you with her apartment? I'd like to make sure the police didn't overlook anything."

She surprised him with a smile and said, "Why that's a splendid idea, Salem."

"I'd like to start tomorrow, ma'am, before the funeral on Wednesday. Are you willing to do that? I can pick you up at your convenience," he offered.

"I'll have Stephanie stay with her father. Let's say 2 pm; the same as today."

"Okay. Thank you."

"No. Thank you, Salem."

He rose and she surprised him with a gripping hug, and then Reid left Patsy Lindstrom to sort through the things he had told her.

# 25

KLAUS WAS JUST FINISHING his sub sandwich when his phone buzzed. The caller ID said that the origin was unknown. He answered on the second ring.

"Hello?"

"I have another job for you tonight. You may return to your apartment tomorrow," Oscar told him.

"Okay," said Klaus.

"The job will be done between 3 and 4 am," Oscar told him. "Meet me at 1 am exactly at Utopia. Come to the back door and knock twice, pause, and then knock twice again. I will give you the instructions then. You will make $1,300."

"Okay," Klaus said, and hung up.

This was less money than the last job, but still a good payment for a few hours of work. Maybe he would pocket a little something extra that Oscar would never know about too.

He would do the job and return to his apartment briefly to stash some of his cash and get some fresh clothes. He'd been wearing the same dirty jeans and shirt since Saturday. He might shower while he was at his place too. The street hooker was secure in the closet. He had gone by a hardware store after his dinner at The Colonnade on Sunday and bought some rope, duct tape, and a machete. He had enjoyed running the sharp edge of the big knife over the whore's tits, and along her inner thighs, drawing just a little blood here and there. He had used the rope to tie her spread eagle on the bed, securing the rope under the bed on the metal frame. He had stood naked over her with an erection while he tortured and abused her. She had tried to scream, but the washcloth secured by the duct tape had muffled any noise from her quite sufficiently. When his excitement could no longer be contained, he had masturbated and ejaculated on her face.

He had wiped his jizz off her face, and then allowed her a little chicken he'd brought from The Colonnade. He gave her a little water and then allowed her to smoke a small amount of meth. He kept the machete on her the whole time, and he warned her that if she made any noises that he would slice her in two. Then he gagged her, bound her legs, handcuffed her again, and shoved her back in the closet. She had been in there overnight while he slept peacefully. He had checked on her Monday morning and provided a little water for her and allowed her to pee. She had urinated only a little, so he knew he'd need to supply her with more water going forward.

He finished his part of the sandwich and wrapped a small portion for the hooker. He wanted to have another "episode" with her before he ventured out tonight. He hoped she would try to scream again when he stroked her with the blade. It made him very horny.

# 26

REID GLANCED AT HIS WATCH as he headed west on 285. It was 3:45. He called Joey.

"Any luck with the videos?" Reid asked.

"I found several places: a Quick Trip, a few businesses on both sides of the road, and a place in that little strip center before you get to apartment row on the south side of the road. It's a sports bar. I've made a list, and was able to get the addresses and numbers for each. Only the Quick Trip and the sports bar are open today."

"Good, Joey. I need to eat. Meet me at Chipotle in the Forum so I can get your list. Give me about ten minutes," Reid said.

The Forum was an upscale development on Peachtree Parkway that had evolved into the city center of Peachtree Corners. Peachtree Corners was the newest and largest city in Gwinnett County. It had once been an unincorporated area of Norcross, but the citizenry of the affluent area wanted to control their own zoning and property interests, so they had moved to form their own city. They had a mayor and city council, but police and fire services were provided by the county. The Forum was a large outdoor mall with shops, restaurants, and clothing stores, but it was also home to doctors' and dentists' offices, as well as a brokerage firm that had a nice corner space over the Trader Joe's. The property was lavishly landscaped year-round, and was a popular meeting place for teenagers who sat near the Roundabout and played guitars, drank Starbucks coffee, and socialized with their friends.

Reid and Joey met at Chipotle and both ordered a veggie burrito and sweet tea. Joey handed Reid the list, then they both got to work on their giant burritos.

After they had eaten most of their food, Reid asked Joey, "Were you aware of any dancers from Utopia who were friends with Sarah?"

"There was a girl named Destiny who she seemed chummy with, but I doubt that's her real name."

"Describe her."

"She's shorter than Sarah by several inches I would say. She has thick brown hair a little past her shoulders. I think she's a little bigger through the hips than Sarah, but a bit smaller up top. She's pretty tanned, more so than Sarah, and she has full lips and a tattoo on her hand. I'm not sure what it is though, and I don't remember which hand," Joey answered.

"What about eye color?"

"I really don't know, Salem. I'm sorry I can't tell you more."

"You did well, Joey. It helps."

"Are you going to the club?" Joey asked.

"I might," he responded.

He left Joey at Chipotle and headed back towards Chamblee. By the time he arrived home, it was close to 5 pm. Millicent got off at six and he'd told her he would call. He figured that he could organize his lists and plan his schedule for Tuesday. It would be a busy day. He planned to start at Precious Medals, and then maybe check out some of the people and places on both lists that Joey had made for him. He hoped to hear back from Ray by noon tomorrow and Tenise as well. Once he filtered through the information that they would hopefully provide, he would figure out how to integrate it into his schedule. He decided he had done everything he could do on this until Tuesday, so he made a couple of phone calls to set up a fun evening with Millicent.

He reasoned that since traffic would not be too bad because of the holiday, he would get in a quick sprint to Blackburn Park and back. By the time he returned it was almost 6:30, so he called Millicent.

She answered on the third ring, "Hey, Salem," she said sweetly.

"Hey," he said, "I made plans for us tonight. Why don't you pack a bag?"

"Aren't you bold, Salem Reid?"

"Yeah," he replied simply.

She laughed and said she'd like that and asked if she needed to bring anything else. He told her that she did not, and he suggested that she arrive by 7:15. He pumped out five sets of fifty push-ups, and then he jumped in the shower. He shaved and cleaned his teeth, flossed, and rinsed. He dressed in Banana Republic slacks and a Ralph Lauren polo. He wore his Cole Haan shoes and a Movado watch.

Millicent arrived wearing a knee-length sundress, pumps, and a pretty silver chain around her neck and matching ring on her right index finger. She wore silver loop earrings as well. She was mouth-wateringly beautiful. She carried a large patterned bag, but he figured she'd need a change of clothes for the morning.

They drove down Chamblee Tucker to Buford Highway and went north into Doraville. She raised her eyebrows when he pulled into the foot massage parlor. "You're gonna love it," he said, and got out of the car and went around the front to let her out.

"I've never had a foot massage, Salem. Have you done this before?" she asked. She seemed a little uncertain.

"All the time."

"Really?" she was truly surprised.

They went in and he was amused at how tentative she seemed. The parlor was extremely clean, softly lit, and had relaxing Asian music playing in the background. They were greeted and taken to a private room where they reclined in big, cozy chairs that practically swallowed up Millicent. They were offered green tea or water. They both chose tea and then were instructed by the staff to remove their shoes and soak their feet in the very warm water that had been brought in and set on the floor between the chair and footrest. They had a small table between them, so he reached over and took her hand as they soaked. Soon two attractive young Asians, both females, came in and pulled the water baskets back and placed their feet on top of the ottoman.

"Sit back and relax. It's great, you'll see," he told her.

She did as he suggested and the girls went to work on them. They oiled up their left feet first, and massaged them deeply. Then the two Asian girls worked each toe with practiced expertise.

Millicent began to relax and smiled big at Salem. "Oh my gosh, this is wonderful!" she said.

"Uh huh."

She was a little taken aback when they began slapping her foot back and forth, but it felt good, so she relaxed again. She was again caught off guard when they took sticks and swatted at her foot, but it felt really nice too, and by the time they started on her right foot, she had become a believer.

When they finished with their feet, they had them turn around in their chairs so their heads were on the towel-covered ottoman and their feet were up on the back of the chair. The Asian girls worked their heads, necks, and shoulders. Then the girls focused on their ears and faces. By the time the massage was over, Millicent commented that she was as relaxed as she could ever remember being.

Reid paid for the service and tipped the girls generously.

In the car Millicent was beaming. "Wow," she said. "Just WOW!"

"I hope you're hungry. Do you like Cuban?" he asked.

"I've never had Cuban food, believe it or not, but I've decided to trust your judgment completely tonight, Salem Reid!"

He took her to Mojito's in downtown Norcross. The place was crowded and the live Cuban music was loud and spirited. They got a table in the middle of the narrow dining room near the stage. They ordered Vaca Frita and Salmon Tropicale. The orders came with white rice and black beans, tostones, and plantains. They had Cuban coffee and Millicent tried a mojito that she thought was delicious. Both were decent dancers, so they got up a few times and Reid swung her around to the delight of a middle-aged couple at the next table. After dinner, he took her for a stroll through Lillian Webb Park. Then they walked hand in hand back to his car and drove back to Chamblee. He bought her ice cream at a little place along the MARTA tracks across from Vintage Pizza. He kissed her in the moonlight on a perfect late summer evening in the South, and then he drove her to his place and made love to her in his bedroom, leaving the balcony doors open so that the breeze and city sounds blew in from outside. It had been a spectacular evening.

# 27

REID AWOKE AT 6 AM after a dreamless night. Millicent stirred but kept sleeping. He figured he'd wake her in twenty minutes or so. He went to the kitchen and started coffee, then jumped in the shower. When he emerged from the bathroom, she was sitting groggily on the edge of the bed. She smiled at him when he came into the room dressed and looking fully awake.

"I made some coffee. I have granola bars and juice. I could make you some peanut butter toast if you like," he told her.

"I'll just have a granola bar and coffee," she said, and pulled herself up from the bed.

She had told him last night that she'd need to leave a little after 7 am. She had a 7:30 class to teach and wanted to be at the ARC by 7:10.

Reid was normally an early riser and he was anxious to get started on his busy day, so it was convenient that she needed to get to work. Nevertheless, he marveled at how pretty she looked even before she'd showered, brushed her hair, or had fully awakened. She was "pretty as a peach," as his mom used to say.

They had enough time to have coffee together in his kitchen and he let her know then that it could be a few days before he could get together with her again because he had a full slate during the front end of the week. He promised to call her by Thursday. She smiled and said maybe she'd take her friend, Jill, to get a "foot job" at the Asian parlor, and they both laughed at her joke. They shared a long kiss and then he walked her down to the underground lot where she had left her car. They kissed again, and then she took off.

Reid left his house shortly after 7:30 and headed to Precious Medals in Peachtree Corners. Morning traffic was a bear on the Tuesday after the holiday, but the worst of it was heading south on the boulevard and he was going north. He made it to Precious Medals about ten minutes before they opened. A ten-year-old Mercedes Benz was parked in front of the store. It looked to be in great condition, as if it were well maintained and well cared for. He parked facing out on the opposite side from the building, but in front of the store, so they could see him approach. He waited until he saw a woman unlock the door, and then he locked his car and headed towards the shop. A chime dinged pleasantly as he entered and a well-preserved woman in her early fifties looked up and smiled at him.

"Good morning," she said. "How can I help you?"

She had a northeastern accent. She was moderately tall and thin with blonde hair from a bottle. She was dressed and made up sharply and she was decorated with an assortment of jewelry that, unlike her hair, didn't look fake.

"Good morning, ma'am," Reid said.

He looked around at what he guessed was considered a showroom. It had plates, trophies, and awards sitting on platforms as well as hanging from the walls. There were also display cases showing off their impressive wares. The showroom was neat and clean and lit brightly with overhead tracking lights. He noticed a hallway towards the back, which presumably led to a warehouse and possibly their offices. The woman stood behind a glass display counter where a sleek computer and credit card terminal sat at the corner.

"My name is Salem Reid, and I work as a security officer for Southeast Security. I have what may be a strange request for you. Are you Karen Lowenstein, by chance?"

"Yes. I'm Karen."

The smile was gone and a look of curious concern had replaced it.

Reid continued, "Perhaps you're aware of an incident that involved a man getting robbed by a strip club dancer across the street at the Peachtree Suites. I am looking into the incident and I'm hoping you might be willing to help me."

Reid had decided that honesty was the best policy in this case. "I'm not the police and you are under no obligation to help me. I'm simply requesting your assistance," he added.

"I see. I was not aware of the incident, and I'm not sure how I could possibly help. When did this happen?"

Before he could answer, she held up her hand. "I'd like to bring my husband into this conversation, please."

She walked into the hallway and shouted, "BERNIE!! Come out here. There is a young man asking questions about a robbery across the street at the suites."

Bernie Lowenstein ambled out a few moments later. He was about the same height as his wife and a little stooped. He had a massive head full of curly dark hair sprinkled with gray. He wore slacks, a monogrammed pale blue shirt, and a cashmere sweater vest over his shirt. He had reading glasses hanging from his neck.

Reid introduced himself and explained again the same thing he had told Karen, and then added, "I think the woman who rolled the man in the suites possibly had an accomplice. I think it quite possible that he sat in the parking lot along the pines at the far end of your lot. I saw that you have a security camera, and I wondered if you might be willing to help me. I'm thinking perhaps you may have captured something useful that would help this man recover his property," Reid finished.

"Are the police looking into this?" Bernie asked.

Reid chose his words carefully. "I can't speak for the police. But they're not here and I am," he said. "The man who was robbed is an acquaintance of mine and I'm investigating this matter for him."

Karen Lowenstein asked, "Are you a private investigator?"

"No, ma'am, I'm not, but in my field sometimes I'm asked to check into incidents like this," he told her.

"When did this crime take place?" Bernie chimed in.

"Early Saturday morning. I'm interested in video from early last Saturday morning from a little before 3 am and maybe as late as 5:30 that morning. What kind of capacity does your security camera have?"

Karen and Bernard Lowenstein shared a look. Bernie spoke, "Young man, give us a few minutes in private. Please have a seat."

He pointed to a chrome-framed bench covered in blue faux leather next to a water cooler and one of those trendy coffeemakers.

The Lowensteins moved into the hallway and just out of earshot. They were gone for several minutes and then they returned.

"We will help you, son," said Bernie. "Have a cup of coffee and I'll see what I can find from Saturday morning."

Reid waited on the bench patiently. A customer entered and Karen took an order from him for an engraved gold plate he was purchasing for his elderly parents who were celebrating their fiftieth wedding anniversary. Twenty minutes later Bernie poked his head out from the hall.

"I think I may have something for you. Come on back."

Reid entered a spacious office off the hallway; it was carpeted, well lit, and tastefully decorated with cherry and mahogany office furniture. A big desk sat in the middle of the room with another sleek computer system in the center. Bernie had Reid pull up a chair and he booted up a video that was remarkably clear. It had a time stamp of 3:11 am on Saturday. The video showed a panoramic view of the entire parking lot. It was black and white, but the clarity was quite good. A pickup truck entered the lot and parked next to the treeline, and just below a retaining wall. It was perfectly shielded from the road above. There were shrubs bordering the edge of the lot looking towards the boulevard, but the truck sat high enough that it would give perfect views of the front of the hotel. Reid could not make out the driver; it was simply too far away.

"Can this image be enlarged?" he asked Bernie.

"A little, but I think the truck is too far away to make out the driver."

He created a still and Reid could see a bulky shadow in the driver's seat, but couldn't make out the features well enough to say that it was Klaus. But he was almost sure it was now, and he felt his adrenaline spike a bit. He now had some evidence supporting his theory of what occurred early Saturday morning. "There's more," Bernie added.

He forwarded the video to 4:28 am. The truck backed out of the spot and headed straight down the lot towards Precious Medals, slowly at first. The shadowy figure was clearly a large man now, but his head was turned facing the boulevard and away from the camera. But as he passed the door he sped up and straightened to watch in front of him, and Reid caught a brief glimpse of the ugly snarling face of the man he'd seen at the ARC on Friday night. Klaus. It wasn't absolute proof that Klaus had been to Joey's house that morning with Sarah, but it was close enough for Reid. Bingo! The day was off to a productive start.

# 28

REID THANKED THE LOWENSTEINS. They had broken the ice for him, but he knew he had a long ways to go. But he felt now like he was making some progress. They copied a disc for him and he left Precious Medals. He exited the business park and headed west on Peachtree Corners Circle. He pulled into the little strip center where the sports bar was located. It was 9 am, so they were closed, but he saw the camera mounted on the edge of the roof. He got out of his car and walked to the window, cupped his hands and peered inside. The bar had the big screens typical of such a place, a long bar spanning most of the far wall, and maybe twenty or so high tables with stools around them in the center of the room. Some booths were located on the sides for more private dining…or drinking as the case may be. There were memorabilia, jerseys, banners, and pennants hanging from the walls and rafters above the bar. Reid noted that it was very heavy in red and black inside. Obviously the bar owner was loyal to the Georgia Bulldogs. Perhaps this person was an alumnus or maybe even played sports at the university. This might make it easier to coax some footage from them if they, in fact, had the capacity to produce a video. Reid thought it would be nice to see the Expedition pass with the Toyota following, but after seeing the images from Precious Medals, it had become of lesser importance. As he climbed back in his car, his phone buzzed. It was Raymond Strickland.

"Well hello, Salem," he chirped.

"Ray."

"Oh! Aren't you excited to hear from me? Don't be so dull, Mr. Reid!"

"What have you got for me?" Reid asked.

"Buy me lunch at the Buckhead Diner. 11:30. Raymond has lots of interesting tidbits for you!"

"Okay, Ray. I can do that." He clicked off and his phone buzzed again almost immediately. It was Tenise Jackson.

"Hi, Tenise," he said.

"Reid. Listen up. I shouldn't be doing this; in fact, I'm not if you get my drift. This conversation never occurred."

Reid didn't respond.

Tenise continued, "Sarah's bag contained exactly $5,000 in $100 bills tied with one of those money bands you get at the bank. Black jeans and a gold Ralph Lauren polo shirt. A 2002 SEC Championship ring. Joey's wallet, which contained $676 in cash. Condoms. Cash in a little purse, mostly in fives and ones, but a few twenties too. A couple of tampons. Oral hygiene products: toothpaste, floss, mouthwash, and a toothbrush. Some Kleenex. Her wallet was in there too. Larribee let me go through it. She had some cash, a driver's license, credit cards, a pharmacy card, and a retail bookstore card. And lastly—and this may surprise you—but there was one of those little plastic picture holders that's a helluva lot less common for people to carry around these days. You know, since most people carry all their pics on their phone. Well, lo and behold, there is one of the two of you in there. On the back, it says Prom '99. There were several other pictures too. Maybe a nephew or something. A picture of an older woman, probably her mom. There was one of an Irish setter too. Larribee was clueless about the photo of you, I think. It doesn't matter anyway, but I thought you'd wanna know."

Reid asked, "Did he follow up with the driver of the Toyota?"

"He did, Reid. He went to Utopia. Nobody knows anyone that drives a Toyota Tundra pickup, or at least if they do, no one is saying so. It doesn't mean anything anyway, Reid. Somebody dropped her off. It's a dead end."

Reid was silent for a moment. He believed someone at Utopia knew who drove the pickup, but was afraid to say.

"Okay. Thanks, Tenise."

"You're not gonna let this go, are you, Reid?"

He said nothing.

"Stay out of trouble, my friend," she said, and clicked off.

So that was it. They doubted Joey's assertions about the large amount of cash. Tenise was dismissing Reid's intuition that there was much more to this than met the eye. Of course, Tenise didn't know about Klaus and Reid's run-in with him, and he hadn't told her about the video from Precious Medals. He knew it proved nothing, but it would likely raise her eyebrows and perhaps persuade her towards his point of view. Information that she could put her hands on might be useful to him, but he didn't want her involved in a way that would limit his actions. The police weren't going to pursue this. That was clear. But he would follow it to the gates of hell.

# 29

AFTER KLAUS ENTERTAINED HIMSELF with the street hooker late Monday evening, he drove to Utopia and waited in the parking lot of a nearby restaurant. A few minutes before 1 am on Tuesday morning, he went to the back exit and knocked as instructed. Oscar let him in without a word and took him into his private lounge. He gave him an address and directions. He explained what he would find inside the home and where those items would possibly be. His source had indicated that the family was on vacation in Florida. The family chose to go to the beach the week of Labor Day since they could avoid the big crowds that way. Conveniently, their two middle school-aged children were home schooled and they had flexibility as to when they vacationed that public or private school children did not.

The home was in a ritzy subdivision off Mt. Vernon Road in Sandy Springs. The neighborhood did not have a gated entry and this particular home had no security system.

Klaus parked on a secluded path that ran along the swim and tennis club. He hauled the empty backpack from his truck and strolled through the woods to the back of the home that he would soon invade.

He jimmied a basement window and entered through the back. He quickly located a valuable coin collection that was on display in one of the children's bedrooms. He broke the locked display case and emptied its contents. He moved to the master and combed through drawers where he located a woman's jewelry box with several fine pieces in it, including a diamond-studded tennis bracelet, a sapphire ring, and some diamond earrings that he guessed might be around one karat each. He found $2,500 in an athletic sock tucked near the back of a man's dresser drawer. He then focused on the dining room where he found some valuable silverware. He headed into a study that had a new Dell laptop. He unplugged it from the power strip and loaded the computer and adapter into the backpack.

He had been in the home for close to forty-five minutes. It was time to leave. He strolled back out the way he had come in, and walked to the edge of the woods. He texted Oscar and waited patiently for five minutes until he saw Oscar glide down the hill with his lights off. He tossed the backpack inside the Flex, and then he walked the edge of the woods to his truck. He had pocketed $500 of the cash he had taken from the sock and turned all the other items and the remaining $2,000 over to Oscar.

Klaus drove out of the subdivision calmly, but his adrenaline was roaring. He decided that instead of heading to his apartment now, he would go back to the Atlantic Motor Lodge and engage in a little sport with the street hooker. Once his energy waned, he might head to his place in Doraville and take a good nap. He thought it best to wait until the Tuesday morning rush-hour traffic died down. Maybe around mid-morning, he'd make the drive to his apartment. He had made over $4,000 working with Oscar in the course of four days. That was damn good money, he thought.

———

Oscar carried his loot back to his house. He had taken his considerable sum from the ex-Bulldog and put it in storage. The storage company he used had twenty-four-hour surveillance and security alarms. He did not have security at his home. Why would he? He had presented himself as a man of modest means. He had rented a small storage area in an unspectacular Norcross location off Jimmy Carter Boulevard. He had placed some old useless furniture in the space and taped stacks of money in unobtrusive places in, under, and around the furniture. He had roughly $650,000 in cash in there. In addition to that, he had close to $200,000 in jewels and other valuables he had yet to fence in an old box that sat in the corner of the storage area. He had placed some old junk on top of the box to conceal the treasure and make the contents look like ordinary clutter. He knew that the chances were very slim that the box or its contents would ever be inspected by anyone other than himself, but he did not like to take chances.

He kept a little at his house. He had a hidden storage space behind a panel in the master closet where he kept between five and ten thousand dollars. And of course, he had held onto the nice Rolex. He hadn't been able to part with it yet.

He had met Monday evening with his source and given them $15,000. He would meet with the source again soon to pay the percentage for this last score. His source would quite likely provide Oscar with another job.

Oscar estimated that this job would get him between $15,000 and $20,000, so he would give the source around $3,000. He thought that he would do two or three more jobs in the next couple of weeks and then slow it down a bit. No need to get greedy, he thought and laughed.

# 30

CONSUELO VALDEZ WAS GLAD to be in America. She had come from Mexico illegally twelve years ago when she was just fifteen years old. She had crossed into Arizona with two older brothers, and she had settled in Atlanta several years later. She had learned English well enough that she could speak it conversationally, and she could read and write it even better. She had gotten on with an older Puerto Rican woman who had given her a job as a housekeeper in the north metro area of Atlanta. The old woman had died a few years later, and Consuelo had managed to pick up her clientele and enlarge her services. She cleaned six days a week and on Sunday mornings, she would put her business card in little baggies with rocks in them, so that they wouldn't blow away, and throw them in driveways next to the Sunday paper. This had been her best advertisement technique. It had worked significantly better than referrals or the mailers that some of the more sophisticated services used.

She was a diligent housekeeper. She cleaned thoroughly and didn't cut corners. She kept her appointments. She had a young Salvadoran who helped her four times a week and an older black woman who cleaned houses three times a week with her. They were both good at their jobs and she was glad to have them.

Consuelo had become a documented worker in the U.S. during this process, and she filed taxes and withheld the appropriate sums from her employees' paychecks. But she was a thief. She had no compunction about picking up loose change or crumpled bills found under a bed or in the laundry and putting the money in her pocket. She was amazed that some people were so careless with money. If there was a $1.50 in change on a dresser, she would take seventy-five cents and leave the rest. No one ever noticed. She had learned where to look for the abandoned loose change and the forgotten paper money. She usually pocketed over $100 a week doing this. She had saved the money separately and over a two-year period had gathered enough to purchase a four-year-old Honda CR-V.

There was one house where she had never put this process to practice though. She had been cleaning for Mr. Villanueva for over a year now. She liked him very much. He always seemed to be at the house when she cleaned, and he would smile at her and ask about her day. He usually insisted that she "sit for a moment" and chat. They would speak in Spanish and he would flirt with her a bit. She had never been clear on what he did for a living. But he seemed, at least in her mind, to be successful. He was older than she was. She guessed that he was in his forties, but he was thick and strong and handsome too, she thought. He had a big scar on his face, but she didn't mind. She thought it made him look rugged. She cleaned his home every Wednesday and he had always paid cash. He tipped her generously every visit too. A few months back she had decided to experiment with him a bit. It was June and she had started wearing very short skirts to his home. She would bend over to clean a table or move a rug, so that he could get a glimpse of her thong-clad curvaceous backside. She had a decent body and enjoyed showing it off to him. Then one day in July, it had happened. He moved in behind her and caressed her bottom. One thing led to another and they were naked and having sex in his kitchen. It had been nice. She had begun fantasizing about Oscar Villanueva being a stepping stone to get her out of the life as a housemaid. She had even spent the night at his home on Monday evening for the first time. She felt as if the two of them were heading towards a mutually beneficial relationship.

# 31

REID POPPED INTO HIS PLACE OF BUSINESS to check on things briefly before meeting with Ray at the nearby Buckhead Diner at 11:30. Julie told him that they were busy, but everything was under control. He had a few phone messages that he returned and he was catching up on emails when Ian knocked on his door.

Reid waved him in and had him close the door.

"I may need you some on Wednesday during the day. I have a funeral to go to and I might need a tail on a guy. You clear for that?" he asked.

"Should be," Ian said.

"Okay. Thanks. We may have some night work coming up soon too. Stay ready," Reid added.

"Sure thing, Salem. Let me know and I'm there."

"I know you are. Thanks."

Ian got up and Reid finished his emails and walked to the lobby to see Julie.

"I'm gonna be in and out for a few days. You and Ian hold it together," he told her.

"Sure, Salem." She looked at him inquisitively, but he offered no more.

"Thanks, Julie," he said, and walked out the door.

He drove northwest on Piedmont to the Buckhead Diner. He valeted and met Ray, who had reserved a table for them. The Buckhead Diner is a popular restaurant on Piedmont that caters to an affluent clientele. Celebrities of all types were often seen having lunch or dinner at the slick and eclectic establishment. The food and service were both excellent and the diner had become an Atlanta icon over the past twenty-five years.

Salem sat across from Ray.

"Hey Ray," he said.

"Heeeyyyyy Salem," Ray mimicked.

Before they could say anything else, a waiter appeared and took their drink orders. They both ordered the Arnold Palmer, a mix of tea and lemonade.

The waiter scurried off to fetch the drinks and Salem said, "Thanks for doing this."

"Well first, Tito says 'thank you very much, Salem.' He received a very nice apology from a rather beaten and battered young man yesterday and a beautiful bouquet of flowers from him too. Tito took a picture and sent it to me. Look!" he said.

Ray produced an iPhone picture that showed a slight young man holding the bouquet that William North had been told to purchase.

"That's great, Ray. What have you got for me?" Reid asked.

"Oh, you are absolutely no fun sometimes, Salem," Ray said, but before he could continue the waiter returned with their drinks.

Ray ordered a seared tuna salad and Reid chose the salmon BLT. After the waiter left to place the orders, Ray handed Reid a manila envelope.

Reid opened it. Ronald Klausen Vormer was last listed at a Chestnut Drive address in the south end of Doraville. It was inside the Perimeter and sat between 85 and Buford Highway. It was a scruffy area of apartments, duplexes, and small homes. He owned a 2006 Toyota Tundra. He hadn't paid his latest tags. They were four months overdue. Ray had pulled two other recent addresses also: one in northeast Atlanta and one in Decatur. The packet that Ray handed him was a little thicker than Reid expected. The next page was a "sheet" on Klaus. Reid looked up at Ray admiringly. Ray had picked up on the fact that this was serious business. Ray had used at least a few contacts of his own to pull some strings.

Ronald Klausen Vormer had been arrested a number of times as an adult. At eighteen, he'd been arrested on misdemeanor Peeping Tom charges and a year later on a more serious sexual assault charge. He spent six months in the DeKalb County jail along with a fine and probation for the assault. At twenty-one, he received a suspended sentence for petty theft and was again placed on probation. There was a smattering of other misdemeanors, but nothing in the last three years.

Ray had produced some mug shots as well, and a variety of other pages that Reid only scanned at the moment. Ray had also provided a history on the guy, which Reid read. He had gone to Stoney Brook High School in Mableton in Cobb County where he'd dropped out in his junior year. He was currently employed as a doorman at the Slick Kitty just down the road from where they were dining. There was a picture of his latest driver's license too. Vormer was six feet, four inches and weighed in at 240. Brown on brown. He did not wear corrective eyewear according to the information provided. He was not an organ donor.

The food arrived and it was very good. Reid continued to leaf through the pages Ray had given him while he ate. He learned a lot. Ray had been very helpful indeed. He was anxious to finish eating and get out of there. He had work to do, but he figured he should at least go through the motions of trying to socialize with Ray a little. The guy had gone out on a limb for him and he appreciated it.

Reid put down the package and said, "So Ray, have you spotted any celebrities in here?"

"Not today. I did see Elton John in here a few weeks ago. I love his music, but I just can't take his looks! Salem, I swear to God, he looks like my chubby Aunt Betty. That man should never wear shorts out in public!" Ray said.

Reid laughed dutifully and asked, "That's it?"

"Well, Salem, if Sir Elton John is not enough I've also seen Mick Jagger in here, but that was years ago. I am almost positive I saw Beyoncé in here a while back. Well, Salem, if I was a straight man I would chew her up. She just looks delicious. Don't you think so?"

"Sure I do, Ray."

"So tell me about this cute little dish I saw at your place last night."

"You're like one of those old women who lives alone in a neighborhood and knows everybody's business, Ray. A watchdog."

"Uh-uh. I don't know your business 'cause you won't tell me. Now tell me," Ray said.

"Her name is Millicent and she works at the ARC. I met her there. We've been hanging out."

"Naked?" Ray quipped.

Reid stared at his neighbor and tried not to laugh, but said nothing.

"Well, I know she spent the night, so I'm thinking y'all got naked. That's good, Salem. She's a very pretty girl."

"She sure is, Ray," he said.

Ray beamed a little and pursed his lips in a smile, and before he could say anything else, the waiter came with the check. Reid picked it up and laid cash and a generous tip on the table.

"I gotta get going, Ray. Thanks again. You've been a big help."

"Okay, Salem. Go catch a bad guy."

# 32

REID DROVE SOUTH ON PIEDMONT fighting the lunch hour traffic. He turned onto Cheshire Bridge and drove past The Colonnade restaurant and then he passed the Atlantic Motor Lodge where the street hooker was imprisoned. He jumped on 85 north and exited Chamblee Tucker and took DeKalb Tech Parkway to Chestnut. He drove past the apartments that Klaus lived in and parked in a food mart just beyond the complex. He took his sunglasses and grabbed a Yankees baseball hat, binoculars, and a windbreaker from his trunk. He hopped a fence behind the food mart and walked through the woods that were heavy with pines. The floor of the woods was covered with pine straw that was popular in landscaped lawns along the north side of Atlanta. He went down a little incline and hopped over a creek that was about three feet wide. He saw the clearing in front of him and got a glimpse of the apartments. His iPhone GPS led him towards the apartment building address he had for Klaus. He guessed that the apartments were built sometime during the Johnson Administration and little had been done to them since. They were worn and deteriorated. The roofs had missing shingles, the paint on the shutters was flaking, and there was essentially no landscaping. Weeds popped through the cracks in the asphalt. Reid was pleased to see that although Klaus's building was in back of the complex, it was next to the heavily wooded area where he'd come in. A gold Toyota Tundra was parked three spaces from the woods. He was maybe thirty feet away. He moved back towards the front of the complex to get a frontal view of the property. He located Klaus's number using the binoculars. He lived in the corner building on the second floor. There was one window on the side of the building, and two flanking the front door. All the drapes were closed. He panned down to the truck and located the license plate. Dirt covered much of it, but some had fallen off and he could make out the 6 and part of the 4 at the beginning and most of the B at the end.

He stayed about ten feet deep into the edge of the woods and watched the building for twenty minutes. He heard a baby crying in the distance somewhere towards the front of the complex, but otherwise saw nothing and heard little else. He then backtracked towards the rear of the complex, so he was on the other side of Klaus's unit. Another group of units faced out on the backside. He moved through the woods to a point where he could not be viewed from Klaus's window and walked out into the parking lot, moving at a purposeful pace; not too fast, but not too slow. He hugged the side of the building and moved to the front corner just below the chipped iron railing that enclosed Klaus's porch. There was no activity. He glanced behind him. He bent down and untied his shoe, and then he removed the tracking device from his windbreaker pocket and proceeded casually out into the parking lot. As he approached the Tundra, he glanced in his periphery and saw no activity anywhere in the building. He stopped directly behind the truck and kneeled to retie his shoe. When he finished with his shoe, he reached his left hand under the back of the Tundra and quickly mounted the tracking device under the bumper. He stood casually and walked at a steady pace to the far end of the building away from Klaus's unit. He quickened his pace once he got around the corner and circled the building. He walked straight into the woods at the same location from where he'd emerged just minutes before. He plunged about fifteen feet into the woods and moved back towards the front of the complex to the point where he had a good view of Klaus's unit and the Tundra. He checked the app on his phone and received the coordinates from the device. It was working just fine. He watched the building for another twenty minutes, but the only activity he saw was a heavyset black woman drive an old Corolla into the lot and park facing the building in front of the one where Klaus lived. She opened the back door on the passenger side and a little girl about six or seven emerged from the backseat. The woman fussed briefly at the child, grabbed her arm a little too gruffly, and hauled her upstairs into their apartment. Reid glanced at his watch. It was 1:40. He had just enough time to walk back to his car and make the ten-minute drive to the Lindstrom home. He had a date with Patsy Lindstrom.

# 33

REID CALLED IAN FROM THE CAR as he hopped on Chamblee Tucker and headed east past 85.

"I have a device on the Tundra," he said, and gave him the data. "I'm going to be tied up for several hours, so if this guy moves, I want you to follow."

"I'm on it, Salem," he said, and clicked off.

Salem Reid arrived at the Lindstroms' just before 2 pm. He was greeted at the door by Stephanie Lindstrom Maclin. She wore shorts and a tank top, and looked to be in her early forties. She was average height and athletic looking, like maybe she played a lot of tennis. She had great legs, and a nice tan. There was some resemblance to Sarah, and though Stephanie would be considered an attractive woman, she was nowhere near the knockout Sarah had been. She greeted Reid warmly, "Hello. You must be Salem. It's nice to see you again." She held out her hand and Reid shook it. She had a warm, dry hand and a firm grip. "Thank you for doing this for Mom. Please come in."

Reid entered the living room he'd visited less than twenty-four hours ago. This time though, Mr. Lindstrom sat in the chair next to the oxygen tank. The tank's regulator was open and a long clear tube snaked up the arm of the chair before splitting and attaching just below Mr. Lindstrom's nose.

"Good afternoon, sir," Reid said.

The old man nodded grimly but didn't speak. Stephanie smiled apologetically at Reid and said to her father, "Dad, are you ready to lie down for a while?"

The old man slightly inclined his head, and she went to his side and helped him with the tubes, turned off the tank regulator, and pulled him to his feet. He moved slowly, but he was able to navigate through the hallway without too much assistance. Patsy Lindstrom met them in the hallway, spoke briefly to her husband and daughter, and then moved into the living room and greeted Reid.

"Hello, Salem. It's so very nice of you to do this for me. Thank you so much."

"No problem, ma'am. Thanks for allowing me to tag along."

She grabbed her purse and she and Reid walked out the door and headed to his car.

As they settled into the seats she explained, "Steph is up from Orlando to help out. I think I mentioned yesterday that she can stay for a week, but she may extend it to ten days. I'll know better when I see what's involved at Sarah's place."

She grew quiet for a moment; perhaps she was uneasy about going into her dead daughter's home for the first time and uncertain as to what would be revealed. A tear rolled down her cheek, but she remained silent.

After a few minutes Patsy Lindstrom spoke again, "Sarah was helping out financially with her father's medical bills. Medicare covers the majority of the expenses, but there is plenty that is not covered. She was giving money to me to help out. She gave me $2,000 in early August and it's almost used up. Steph's husband is well off I suppose, but I could never ask him for money. My son makes a decent living out in Colorado, but he doesn't have a lot extra. I'm embarrassed and ashamed that I was taking money from Sarah, but I didn't know what else to do, Salem. Bill has been sick, but he's not dumb; he knew money was coming from somewhere to pay for the extra bills. I think he suspected it was coming from her; if so, it must be absolutely crushing him."

Reid didn't know what to say, so he said nothing. This shed new light on aspects of Sarah's character, however, and it made him feel a little better about her despite her involvement in the crimes of early Saturday morning.

They had taken the Perimeter to 400 north and exited onto Mansell Road. They traveled east to Haynes Bridge Road where Sarah's apartment complex sat just off Haynes Bridge, a little south of North Point Parkway. She had lived in a new and luxurious complex on the first floor in a two-bedroom apartment next to the pool and clubhouse. The grounds were immaculate and the landscaping pristine. They parked and entered her apartment.

The home was neat and clean with only a few signs of the police having been there. Sarah had chosen a matching cream-colored sofa and love seat for her spacious living room. Small burgundy pillows were ornamental on the furniture. An elegant glass coffee table matched an end table that sat at the corner between the love seat and sofa. There were coasters, a few knick-knacks, and a *Glamour* magazine on the coffee table. A small Tiffany lamp adorned the end table. A romance novel was on a little shelf below where the lamp sat. It had a bookmark at page ninety-eight. The dining room was an extension of the living room; it was spacious too. A glass-top table sat in the center under a chandelier. Four high-backed chairs sat symmetrically around it. She had added a metal stand with glass shelves that sat along the dining room wall. It looked like something she may have picked up at a specialty store like Bed, Bath and Beyond. She had a few vases and wine glasses sitting on the middle shelf and an empty wine bottle with a fake yellow flower poking out of the top of the bottle on the top shelf. A Pier 1 basket of plastic flowers was on the lowest shelf. The kitchen was clean and uncluttered. A coffeemaker, grinder, and toaster sat on the counter near the refrigerator. A small wine rack held a few bottles of wine and a knife set was positioned in a corner next to the stove. She had only a few pictures on the walls. They were tasteful prints of things like street cafes and other similar urban landscapes. There was nothing personal except for the novel and the magazine on the coffee table.

"It looks almost like a fancy hotel, Salem, not someone's home," Patsy Lindstrom said. "It's so...so clinical."

Reid said nothing. He opened her refrigerator. Ten spring water bottles sat cooling in her fridge; water that she would never drink. There was a six-pack of light beer with only one beer missing from the case. A half-gallon of low-fat milk was in the door along with some grapefruit juice. There were five or six Granny Smith apples in a grocery produce bag on a shelf and a to-go box from a local bar and grill that was half full with angel hair pasta marinara topped with grilled chicken. The freezer had a few frozen dinners and other low-fat, low-carb pre-packaged meals. There was a liter of vodka, a large bag of gourmet coffee beans, and a few Velcro ice wraps commonly used for sports injuries on the shelf.

The pantry contained things like cereal, bread, and reduced fat peanut butter. There was a box of low-fat snack crackers and some granola bars too.

Before they moved down the hall towards the bedrooms, they opened the shades in the living space. The sun rushed in and lit up the area, making it feel a little bit warmer and homier. Along the hallway, the first door on the left was a full bathroom. It had a door on the right side leading to the spare bedroom that was farther down the hall. On the right side was the master bedroom. It was large and tastefully decorated with a queen sleigh bed, a dresser, chest of drawers, a nightstand, and a credenza sporting a forty-inch TV. A DVD player sat on the shelf below the TV. A Comcast digital cable box sat near the TV. A little compartment between the shelves held DVD workout videos that were popular with the fitness crowd. She had a nice mahogany desk that matched her other bedroom furniture. A laptop sat in the middle with a small printer sitting near the back corner of the desk. There was a folded-up yoga mat next to the desk on the floor along with some eight-pound dumbbells. She had some live plants scattered around the room that looked a little thirsty.

"I would like to examine some things in here, Mrs. Lindstrom. I want to see if I can understand what was going on in her life prior to her death. Personal items and the things she saved on her computer might be revealing. Is it okay?"

"Okay," she said simply.

Reid saw that her computer had been turned off, so he turned it on and while it booted, he moved to her nightstand. Mrs. Lindstrom had gone to Sarah's closet and opened the French doors that led to a spacious walk-in closet. Reid opened the top drawer of her nightstand. It was filled with books; mostly romance novels in paperback. He opened the lower drawer. This drawer was more cluttered. He found three more paperbacks; he guessed that they were an overflow from the other drawer and perhaps more recent. A few skimpy nightgowns were folded neatly in one corner. He opened the drawer a little further and found a Jack Rabbit vibrator and some lubricant towards the back laying on a towel. He made a mental note to suggest that Stephanie could dispense of it rather than Mrs. Lindstrom. On the bottom of the drawer was what appeared to be a decent size photo album. He opened it. It contained plenty of photos, but it was more of a scrapbook than an album. She had some pictures with her family from when she was a small child. She was maybe six or seven. Stephanie and her brother were teenagers; they seemed to dote on her. Everyone, including her father, was smiling and happy. It looked to be a family outing at Stone Mountain Park. You could see the engraving of Jefferson Davis, Robert

E. Lee, and Stonewall Jackson behind them. There was a picture of an Irish setter puppy; Bella was written on the back. Another picture of the dog showed Bella to be full grown. Sarah was pictured with her and she had probably been eleven or twelve at the time. She was still fairly innocent looking, but there was an aura of something older and more mature in her eyes. She had a look of something sad and wistful.

He continued through the scrapbook. There were more family photos from when she was young, but there was only one from her teenage years. It was a photo of the wedding party from her sister's nuptials. Sarah was maybe fourteen and had already blossomed into the beautiful woman she would become. Stephanie Lindstrom was only the second prettiest girl in the picture. Sarah was by far the most beautiful. She looked fabulous despite the ugly bridesmaid's dress. The other women in the picture didn't even come close to pulling that off. Reid wondered how the older girls, and Stephanie for that matter, felt about Sarah stealing the show.

Next he found a report card of hers from eighth grade. She had made two A's, three B's and a C. Maybe those had been a real achievement for her. He knew she wasn't a good student when they dated; she had just managed to squeak through her sophomore year. The eighth grade report card showed the two A's in math and economics. The C had been in grammar/composition. Perhaps this had been her best report card during her school years. Next, he saw that she had saved some pictures she had drawn of various animals over the years. They were pretty average, but one of a squirrel was particularly good.

Towards the back were maybe three or four yellowed newspaper clippings. They were folded over, so he gingerly pulled them out and unfolded them. And for the second time in three days a woman he hadn't seen in fifteen years caused him to stop dead in his tracks. The first was a small clipping from the back of the *AJC* sports section. It had a small article from March of 2000. The headline said **Reid hits walk-off homer for Eagles**. It was an article about his first career homerun during his freshman year at college. He had gotten significant playing time because he played well at both middle infield positions. He had pinch hit in the sixth inning for the starting second baseman because the coach wanted a righty/lefty matchup. Reid had flied to left in his first at bat, but had homered in the ninth to win the game. He had broken off contact with her about five months prior to when this had occurred. Nevertheless, she had taken a pink highlighter and drawn a heart over his name. He felt a lump in his throat and moved to the next article. This one was from April of 2000. He had hit his second and final homer of his college career. She had drawn the same pink heart around his name. The other two articles were from his senior year at Dunwoody High School during the time they had been together. One had a picture of him in his uniform. She had drawn numerous pink hearts circling his face. The last clipping was from a game when he'd gone 5 for 5, driving in 6 runs in a lopsided victory over Marist. He replaced the clippings and turned to the last page in the scrapbook. The picture he had seen yesterday in the Lindstrom house from his senior prom was the sole item on this page. She had cut the photo so that there was significant white border at the bottom. She had written in ink: "I love you forever and always. You are the only one."

He replaced the book and closed the drawer. Mrs. Lindstrom was saying something, but he didn't hear. He stood up and said, "Excuse me, ma'am, did you say something?"

She had been taking items from Sarah's closet and making two piles on the bed. One presumably for give away and a much smaller pile that she wanted to keep.

"I said, I think this belongs to you."

She was holding his DHS baseball letter jacket he had given to Sarah on that chilly October evening fifteen years ago. He walked over and she handed it to him. His name on the tag and his phone number had faded and blurred. It was not legible. But the jacket was in good shape. He held it to his nose and made out a faint aroma of perfume. It was late summer in Atlanta, so she had probably not worn the jacket in many months, but he thought maybe she had worn it as late as last spring.

"Okay. Thank you," he said. His head was spinning.

"She loved you, Salem. I think you should know that. She never talked about it, but a mother knows. She had boyfriends after you, but it was different. I don't think she ever felt that away about a boy again. I hope it's not upsetting to you that I say this. I just think you would want to know."

"Okay," he said again.

He needed to move on. He had come to learn something to help his investigation. Though learning that her feelings for him were stronger than he had ever realized touched him profoundly, it wouldn't help the investigation.

Patsy Lindstrom left the room and then returned with several large garbage bags. She started placing clothes in them. Reid helped her until the bed was clear, and then he went into Sarah's bathroom. He went through her medicine cabinet and the bathroom counter as well as the drawer and cabinets under the sink. He found nothing unusual. She had typical OTC medications and ointments. There were deodorants and perfumes, shampoos and soaps. She had a container of birth control pills, spare toothbrushes, toothpaste, mouthwash, and floss. Her bathroom was as neat and tidy as the rest of her apartment.

He exited the bathroom and crossed the room to her desk. He sat and wiggled the external mouse she had connected to her laptop. The screen came alive. He clicked on the Internet Explorer option. First, he checked her URL history to see which websites she visited most often. She had a number of sites in the drop-down menu. Apparently she had a Facebook page. It was listed about eight sites down. He brought up the page. She had stored her user ID and password, so it went directly to her news feed. He clicked on "Sarah" on the blue tab at the top of the page and her timeline appeared. She had last posted in mid-May, over three months ago. She had posted several times a month dating back a few years before then. Her last post was a picture from Disneyworld in Orlando. She had visited her sister and gone with Steph and her two nephews to the amusement park. She was gorgeous as usual, but had dressed conservatively and appropriately for an afternoon at Disney. She was all smiles as she knelt between two handsome grade school boys with an arm around each. Her hair was tied in a ponytail and she wore medium-length shorts and a plain purple tee shirt. She had Nike running shoes on her feet. Her caption read: "At Disney with my Boyz." She had several likes from all females and two comments. He clicked on her "Friends" page and saw that she had only forty-two Facebook friends. Her profile picture was pretty, but not suggestive. He went back to her "Friends" page. She had thirty female friends and twelve who were males. Nothing odd jumped out at him when he surveyed her male friends, but he took a scrap of paper from her desk and wrote down all of their names. He scanned the women for a Destiny or Janice. He didn't find a Destiny, but clicked on a Janice Cooley and the page changed to her timeline. A striking woman with full lips and thick, dark brown hair graced the screen. She was easily pretty enough to be a strip club dancer. She had a great tan. Her profile provided a birthday that put her at twenty-eight years old. She was much more active than Sarah on Facebook with regular postings. He looked through her photos and found several of her and Sarah together. They had been to Seaside in the panhandle of Florida between Panama City Beach and Destin. They had tropical drinks in their hands and both looked like a slice of heaven in their skimpy bikinis. Sarah was at least four inches taller and she was slimmer than Janice. The posting was from early April. So Destiny and Janice Cooley were very likely the same person. He clicked back to Sarah's page and searched her female friends for a Lara or Laura. He found a nice-looking twenty-nine-year-old black woman named Lara Brooks. He scrolled through her photos. He had to go back almost a year, but another beach picture showed Sarah with Lara. They were dressed in shorts and sweatshirts. The darker sand made Reid think they had visited the Atlantic on this trip. He found a few more pictures of the pair and saw that they were at Tybee Island, Georgia. Tybee is a charming beach town about ten or twelve miles east of Savannah. He researched to see if Lara and Janice were friends. They were. Janice's page indicated that she currently lived in Johns Creek and Lara in Sandy Springs. Lara had routinely posted every few days on Facebook, but had abruptly stopped posting around the same time that Sarah had. He made some more notes on the scrap paper and then exited Facebook.

The most recent website that Sarah had visited was a well-known brokerage firm. Her username was stored but not her password. He sifted through her desk and found nothing that looked like password information. Maybe he'd get lucky. Financial institutions usually required alphanumeric passwords and sometimes special characters. People were prone to use birthdays, kids' names, nicknames, or maybe the name of a pet. He consulted Sarah's mom.

"I remember that Sarah has a December birthday, but I don't remember the date."

"December 9th. Why do you ask?" she inquired.

"I'm trying to crack her password. I'm trying to log into some financial websites she frequented. Why don't you join me?" Reid answered, as he vacated the chair and knelt next to it so that she could sit.

She watched as he tried several options. He figured he would have five attempts and then be locked out for at least twenty-four hours. He'd probably need to answer security questions too if he wanted to get back in. Not a good option. On the fourth attempt, he typed $12Bella0981, a combination of her birthday, her dog's name, and money. He waited a few moments and then the browser logged him in. He wrote her password on the scrap paper.

Patsy Lindstrom was impressed.

"Very clever, Salem," she said.

"Luck," was all he replied.

Her portfolio page loaded. Sarah Lindstrom had done quite well for herself. She owned some Google, Apple, and Home Depot stocks that had all done spectacularly since purchase. She had an IRA in an aggressive growth fund, and money equally distributed in three remaining funds that were conservative, moderate, and aggressive. She either knew her stuff or had been advised well. Her investments at the brokerage firm totaled $378,942.13. He opened the bottom drawer of her desk again and took notice of several investment guides including a copy of *Investing for Dummies* that was tattered and worn and dog-eared. He logged out of the brokerage firm's site and logged into her banking website. Again, her username was stored but not the password. He typed in the same password he'd used on the previous site. The page loaded without a hitch. She had a linked money market and checking account. The money market drew about 1% and the balance was just north of $20,000. The checking account had close to $11,000. Her net worth was over $400,000. This was quite a sum for a thirty-two-year-old single woman who did not come from a wealthy family. This begged the question: Was this the type of woman who would become addicted to heroin? There was no indication of drug abuse, or even drug use for that matter, in her apartment. Recent Facebook pictures showed a robust, lively young woman who did not look strung out on drugs. She had been thoughtful and disciplined enough to invest her money, and was helping out her elderly parents. He knew drugs could take over in a hurry, but in his mind, it simply didn't add up.

Patsy Lindstrom sat there stunned.

"Mrs. Lindstrom, your daughter did very well for herself. I hope you can take some pride in that."

"I never knew she had that kind of money, Salem," she said, overstating the obvious.

He closed the banking site and looked at her hard drive. She stored her files on the C drive in a directory called "My Documents" under a folder called "Sarah."

He scanned the files and saw "Will" towards the bottom. He opened it. Sarah had downloaded an online "last will" kit and filled it out and procured the necessary witnesses and signatures. She had a scanned file that showed Patsy and William Lindstrom as her primary beneficiary and her sister Stephanie as the secondary. Mrs. Lindstrom crossed her chest with both hands upon seeing this and inhaled deeply.

"Are you aware of Sarah's wishes for burial?" he asked her.

"No. Is that information on her computer?" she asked incredulously.

Reid pulled up her medical POA and printed it out. He printed the will and her financial POA as well.

"You will want to secure an estate lawyer to help you with this, ma'am. It may cost you a few grand, but I think you can afford it now. I can recommend one if you like. Maybe you can get out a little cheaper."

"Yes. Please. I'm going to need some guidance with all of this."

They spent another hour packing things up and placing some items in his car. They included Sarah's laptop as one of those items. Patsy Lindstrom needed to use the restroom before departing, so Reid waited in the living room. He picked up the Nora Roberts novel that Sarah had been reading and fanned the pages to where it was bookmarked. She had been on page 98. The bookmark was a three-by-five note card with nothing written on it. He fanned the pages again trying to locate 98 when a small piece of bathroom tissue fell out. It read: L 7-416-6124. He put the bathroom tissue in his pocket. Patsy Lindstrom emerged from the restroom a minute later and together they exited Sarah's apartment. It was after 6 pm.

# 34

REID DROVE SARAH'S MOM to her house in Embry Hills and helped unload her daughter's belongings. She thanked him and he said he would see her at the service in Brookhaven tomorrow. He called Joey.

"Hello?" Joey answered.

"Go to the sports bar on Peachtree Corners Circle and make some friends. It's Bulldog nation. I'll be there in thirty," he said, and clicked off.

———

Reid called Tenise Jackson. "Reid. You don't give up."

"No," he said. "What about Sarah's car?"

She sighed heavily. "It was parked at Utopia and impounded."

"Was anything suspicious found?" he asked. "Any signs of drugs?"

"Not in her car, no," she replied. "Her parents have been notified that they can claim it."

"Her apartment?"

"No signs of drugs there either."

"That doesn't bother you?"

She exhaled.

"Actually, yes. It does bother me a little. I was surprised. Her fingerprints were on the syringe and spoon found at Joey's house, though. Maybe she just shot the stuff in work-related environments, Reid." She sounded uncertain. "Look, Reid, a lot bothers me about this. I don't like loose ends and I admit there are more than a few here. But all cases have loose ends. We rarely get the whole story, so we do the best we can."

"Larribee does the best he can?" Reid asked.

"Once again, Reid, Sarah was a hooker. She drugged Joey and ripped him off. Then she's found dead from a heroin overdose inside his house. What are we supposed to think, she's Mother Teresa?" Tenise said. Then she added, "I think at the end of the day, most detectives would view this the way Larribee did. The brass accepted it. They are not going to waste any more time and manpower on this, Reid."

He shifted gears.

"Anything else in her house seem off? I assume her computer was checked thoroughly."

"She had the usual stuff in her house and on the computer; nothing out of the ordinary."

He fished deeper.

"You've kept my connection to Sarah on the low?"

"Yes. Your only connection is that you drove Joey home on Saturday and the two of you discovered her body. That's it."

"Thanks for talking to me, Tenise," he said, and hung up.

———

Reid met Joey at the sports bar on Peachtree Corners Circle. Joey was sitting at the bar talking it up and smiling with a fortyish female bartender. He had a beer sitting in front of him, but it was untouched. Reid sat next to him and ordered a beer of his own. Then the bartender moved to the opposite end of the bar to serve a couple of guys who had just sat down.

"Her name is Jody. She co-owns the bar with her brother. They both went to UGA."

"She know you played there?" Reid asked.

Joey tapped his SEC Championship ring on the bar and grimaced.

"I really don't wanna be wearing this, but I thought it might help." He shrugged and continued, "She saw it and asked about it. She figured out who I am." He nodded as she headed back down the bar.

Reid took a swig from his beer mug. It was cold and tasted good after a long day. Jody stopped in front of Joey and smiled at him.

"We'd love to have a signed jersey put up on the wall from the great Joey Mac."

Jody was a bit weathered, but had probably been attractive fifteen or twenty years ago. Reid thought she looked like a smoker and that she probably spent too much time in the sun. Her too-tanned face was lined around her mouth and eyes. Maybe she was a heavy drinker too.

"Jody, I could get you one today if you want. But could I ask a favor from you?"

Jody reached her hand over and placed it on Joey Mac's hand where he wore the ring. "What's that, darling?" she said with a big grin, and Joey had to stifle a shudder.

"Well Jody, it's kinda awkward. You see, I think my girlfriend's been cheating on me. If I find out she is, I think I'm gonna have to dump her."

Jody turned serious. "She was in here?"

"No. I don't think so. It's like this, Jody...I was out of town last Friday and Saturday on business and she was using my SUV. She works at a club until 3 or 4 am. A neighbor said there was a Toyota Tundra parked near my house early Saturday. This guy I'm suspicious of drives a truck like that. I'm guessing he followed her home to my house, for crying out loud!" Joey said convincingly.

"That's awful," Jody said sympathetically, then added, "but I'm not sure how I can help."

Joey ploughed in. "I saw you have a security camera outside. She would have driven right past here, probably sometime between 4:30 and 5 in the morning. I really need to find out," he added, with a bit of a whine.

Jody bit. She seemed very excited to be included in this sordid affair. "The camera rolls over every twenty-four hours, but it stores each twenty-four-hour period on our computer for seven days. I can probably help," she said conspiratorially.

"Kenny!" she hollered and a tall slender guy of about twenty-five, with about a week's worth of facial hair, came slinking out through a red and black curtain behind the bar.

"Yeah, Jody, what's up?" Kenny said.

"Watch the bar for a bit," she said to Kenny, and then she turned to Joey. "Give me a few minutes to locate the feed and then you can come back and watch it. What about your friend?" she asked, pointing to Reid, who had yet to utter a word.

"This is my neighbor. I'm hoping he can recognize the truck."

"Okay. That's fine," she said. She gave Joey a wink and a smile and headed behind the curtain.

Reid looked down at Joey's untouched beer and swapped it with his own half-full mug. He took a big swig and then another. Then they sat and waited.

Ten minutes passed before Jody returned to the bar and waved the guys back. They entered an area that was too big to be called a store-room, but it was too small to be a warehouse. It had a cement floor and a dock door was open to the back alley. The room had a big walk-in refrigerator and boxes and crates of various beers and liquors were stacked around the space. Just a few paces inside the area sat a desk with a computer on it. She told Joey to have a seat in front of the monitor while she and Reid flanked him. Jody bent down over Joey Mac and brushed him with her breast. Up close like this, he got a whiff of nicotine. She cued the video. The time stamp showed 4:36 am on Saturday. They watched in slow motion as Joey's Expedition rolled by. They could make out Sarah pretty well in his SUV. Salem Reid felt the lump in his throat for the second time that day. Within seconds, a gold Toyota Tundra cruised past with a clear image of Ronald Klausen Vormer in the driver's seat.

"Boy! She sure is a fool. That guy's uglier than a load of stumps! I'd dump her for sure, Joey," she said, as she reached across him again to stop the video and once more brushed him blatantly with her breast.

Joey stood and said, "I'll go get that jersey for you, Jody."

He decided he'd give her a signed football too. He felt like a turd for what he had done.

She gave them a disc with the video from the security camera and they thanked her and left.

# 35

REID CALLED IAN CALLAHAN when he reached his car.

"He's definitely our guy. Has he moved?"

"No. I have a security job at 9. Do you want it or are you coming here?"

Reid glanced at his watch. It was almost 8 pm. "I'll be there at 8:30. Does that work?"

"That's fine," Ian said and disconnected.

Reid hadn't eaten and he was hungry. He drove up to Holcomb Bridge Road and took a right. He whipped into a sandwich shop and bought subs for Ian and himself. Holcomb Bridge ran into Jimmy Carter and Reid took it up to PIB. He drove south to 285 and went east to 85 south then jumped on Chamblee Tucker and over to Chestnut and parked at the food mart. He gathered everything he would need for his mission and put it in a duffel bag. He added the food and several bottles of water. He jumped the fence, ran through the woods in the dark, jumped the creek, and found Ian just where Reid had been stationed earlier that day. It was 8:20. He gave Ian his sub and a bottle of water.

"When's your security detail over?" he asked Ian.

"Probably around midnight."

"Okay. If this guy moves tonight, we need to both be on him."

"Got it, Salem," Ian responded.

They dug into their sandwiches. They finished in about ten minutes and Ian took off.

The lighting was dim around Klaus's building, but he could make out his front door okay and the truck even better. He sat and waited; he was tired but years of training had taught him how to stay alert. He could sit motionless all night if needed. But that did not happen.

———

Klaus exited his apartment just before 1 am and got into his truck. Reid dashed through the woods and made it to his car about four minutes later. He found the app on his phone and tracked the Tundra. Klaus was heading north on 85. Klaus took 85 north to 285 west to PIB. He quickly exited PIB and drove to a restaurant parking lot near Utopia and parked. Reid found a spot about 100 yards away, but he had a clear view through a moderately crowded parking lot for a Wednesday morning at 1 am.

Reid used his binoculars and located Klaus. He was just sitting in his truck with the window down doing nothing. Reid put the binoculars down, but would raise them again and check on Klaus every few minutes. The crowd at Utopia was starting to thin, so he was concerned about becoming more exposed, but he figured he was okay for the moment. He texted Ian and told him of his location. Twenty minutes later, Ian texted the message: "Here."

They waited patiently and just before 2 am Klaus drove down from the restaurant parking lot and moved behind Utopia. Reid started his car and moved to a space between Utopia and a sports bar that sat adjacent to the strip club. He got out of his car and moved to the corner of the building. The Tundra was parked at the back door. Klaus had climbed out and was standing at the door as if waiting to be admitted. Reid saw the door open outward towards his position, so he could not see who opened it. He went back to his car and drove around the sports bar through the parking lot making a 270-degree rotation, so that he'd be on the other side. He still did not see Ian or his car but knew he was close. Ten minutes later, the door opened and Klaus exited. He saw no one else at the door. Klaus fired up the truck and drove off. The detection device on his truck would come in handy. It would be very difficult to put a tail on Klaus without being spotted during the wee hours of the morning.

The tracking device showed Klaus heading north on PIB. Reid stayed back about a half-mile and Ian another quarter mile behind Reid. Klaus passed through Peachtree Corners and continued into Berkeley Lake. He turned on South Berkeley Lake Road and continued for another mile. He drove along a secluded, wooded road just east of the lake and stopped. Reid parked about two blocks east and phoned Ian. "Stay in your car and trail him if he takes off. I'll track him on foot. My guess is he's out of the car and on the move."

Reid was dressed in the windbreaker and Yankees hat. He wore dark cargo pants and Nike running shoes. He spotted Klaus with the binoculars. The big hulking man stood motionless at the street corner behind a tree examining the landscape. After several minutes, he scooted east towards Reid, then abruptly shot into a driveway that was long, curved, and mostly obscured from the street. Klaus was carrying what looked to be a flat backpack. Reid shot into the yard on the far side of the house. The home was large and sat high on a hill. The lawn was pristine; it was likely professionally landscaped. The house was a big white affair with some kind of high-end siding like hardy plank. Klaus went to the back of the house off a turnaround in the long drive on the west side of the house. Reid shadowed him on the east side. As he approached the back of the house, he noticed that there was a pool with a fence that measured about five feet high. He watched as Klaus opened the gate and walked up the back stairs to a door that entered what was probably a utility room off the kitchen. Klaus simply kicked in the door and entered. Reid did not hear an alarm sound, nor had he noticed any security system signs in the yard. About a half hour passed and then Klaus exited with a bulking backpack. He worked his way down the west side of the house and Reid again shadowed him on the east side. But Klaus did not head towards his truck. He walked a bit west towards the far end of the lake staying in the shadows as much as possible. There was no traffic and it was very quiet. Reid stayed with him as close as possible and then he saw it. An SUV that looked like a toaster on wheels sitting off the road near and just above the southern tip of the small lake. He thought perhaps it was a dark-colored Ford Flex. He stopped under a large bush and watched Klaus approach the vehicle. The car moved as Klaus entered but the lights didn't come on. He tracked the car and it appeared to be circling back under the lake. Then it suddenly stopped at the wooded road southeast of the lake and Klaus exited.

Reid called Ian. "A dark Ford Flex at the southeast corner of the lake. Approach it with your lights off and follow at a distance."

"Got it, Salem," he said, and clicked off.

Reid raced back to his car and slipped out of the side street onto South Berkeley and raced up to PIB.

He called Ian. "Talk to me."

"I'm on the Flex about 100 yards back on PIB at South Old Peachtree," Ian said. They were only a half-mile in front of him.

"Okay, Ian. I'm gonna take the Flex, you stay with Klaus. He's probably just behind me."

Reid sped up and soon saw Ian ahead. Ian moved to the right-hand lane and eased back. Reid now had the Flex in his sight. There were only a few other cars on the road. One was between Reid and the Flex, so he tried to keep it positioned there. Just before 285, the Flex exited onto the access road. Reid followed about seventy-five yards behind. Luckily, the light was green at the intersection below and the Flex turned left. Reid was able to pace him without being obvious, and when the Flex turned into the strip club, Reid continued straight ahead. He drove another 100 yards and turned into a big hardware store parking lot. Conveniently, the far entrance was obscured from the strip club. Reid turned out his lights and circled back through the lot until he could see the club in the distance. He grabbed his binoculars from the back seat and surveyed the area. He located the Flex just as a short, heavily built man with a dark complexion exited the vehicle and walked briskly towards the back door. He carried a bulky backpack. He used two separate keys to unlock the rear door to the club and entered. Reid tried to make out the plate on the Flex, but the distance was too great. He considered driving through the parking lot of the club to get a closer look, but he thought it too risky. He didn't want this guy spooked. He had accomplished a lot during the day, so he decided to get to his house and grab several hours of sleep before the rising sun that was only a few hours away brought on another busy day.

# 36

AFTER LOOTING THE HOUSE in Berkeley Lake and delivering the stolen goods to Oscar, Klaus decided to go into North Atlanta and have another go at the street hooker. She had become weaker and more despondent each day. He gave her water and a little food periodically, but he wondered if it was enough. Every few days he would let her smoke some of the crystal meth too. It was just enough to keep her from Jonesing too much. She had gotten a little gross also, having not bathed in four or five days. He had purchased some wet wipes and cleaned her up a little. He had delighted when he used them on her torn and battered rectum and she had tried to scream. Of course, with the gag in her mouth, the screams were barely audible. She was growing hair under her arms and on her legs too. It had grown fast and was more than just a little stubble. He discovered that the hair growing under her arms had turned him on. When he fucked her ass and tortured her, he liked holding her arms up so that he could look at her hairy pits. He would continue with her for a few more days probably, and then he supposed he would likely kill her.

Traffic was light on this early Wednesday morning, and he was clueless that he'd been watched and tailed for the past fifteen hours. He was caught up in the newfound control and power he had been able to exert. The money had thrilled him too. He would be a rich and powerful guy just like Oscar soon. He had just received another $1,300 for his assignment this morning and had pocketed another $300 that Oscar hadn't known about.

He pulled into the Motor Lodge and, moments later, Ian Callahan cruised at a moderate speed past him on Cheshire Bridge Road. Callahan proceeded down the street for two blocks, then doubled back, turned off his lights, and slid slowly into the lot next door. He moved quickly and quietly on foot into the Motor Lodge lot and got a glimpse of Klaus climbing from his Tundra. Klaus had parked in the very back of the lot across from the second and smaller building. Ian's location was protected from detection nicely. He had slid in behind the registration office; the wooded and weeded area behind it was a perfect location to be shielded from most vantage points.

Ian watched Klaus go into a room on the first floor in the very last unit. So what was Klaus doing here? Ian had figured the guy in the Flex was the boss, or at least a boss of some sort in this rip-off scheme. Was there another participant involved who was staying in this seedy hotel room? That seemed unlikely. So Ian Callahan got as comfortable as possible in his setting and watched the room where the big nasty guy had entered.

Ian saw dim lighting appear shortly after Klaus entered the room. So if there was another person in the room, they probably had been sleeping. Therefore, whoever it was probably wasn't an associate in terms of the rip-off scheme. The chances of it being someone who Klaus would show deference to would be remote as well. Maybe he had some skuzzy girlfriend or buddy he was hanging out with who was unrelated to the prior events of the early morning. He continued to watch. The room seemed still for a bit, and then suddenly there was deflection of light that continued for a while. The movement of the light ceased for a bit and then started again. It seemed to Ian that the movement was quick and active at times and then it would slow again. After an hour or so, the lights suddenly went out. He watched for a bit and when they didn't come on again, Ian decided that Klaus was sleeping and that he would take the opportunity to do the same.

# 37

REID HAD GOTTEN TO SLEEP just before five on Wednesday morning and had awakened at nine. He saw that he had a text from Millicent. It was one of those emoticons that young women always seemed to be adding to their texts. It was a simple heart on the screen. It made him smile but he was uncertain how to reply to it, so he texted back: "The feeling is mutual." She responded with another emoticon. This time it was a smiley face, so he texted her back that he would catch up with her as soon as he could.

He was glad to hear from her; he had been thinking about her, of course, but he had forced himself to unclutter his mind and focus on the task at hand. That was finding the truth about what went down inside of Joey's home on Saturday morning. There was absolutely no question in his mind about who was involved; it was obvious now. Klaus for sure, and the dark, stocky guy driving the Ford Flex was likely behind it. He was obviously some kind of boss at Utopia, so that linked him to Sarah as well. His impulse was to take Klaus down immediately, but he needed to think it through. Was there something or somebody else that Klaus could lead him to? He wasn't sure. He knew some things about the mysterious Flex driver, but not enough. He wanted to talk to Sarah's friends. Perhaps Janice Cooley or Lara Brooks could shed some light on the man. He called Ian.

"Salem. I have some news," Ian said.

"Okay. What?"

"Klaus shacked up at the Atlantic Motor Lodge last night." He explained what he had witnessed and his thoughts on what he'd seen. "He's still there, or at least his truck is. I took off about a half hour after the lights went out."

"Interesting. Okay. I got the funeral in a while, and I hope I can talk to the girls who were friends with Sarah. I think we should meet later. I have some ideas and I think we may need Petey."

Petey Ward was a big, crusty middle-aged former Marine who had fought in Grenada and the first Gulf War. He was a decorated war veteran and he had become a good friend to Reid and Ian over the years. Petey and Reid had met when Reid was a freshman in college. Reid had helped Petey's daughter out of a jam during a frat party at Georgia Southern. A couple of guys were attempting to sexually assault the girl and Reid had interceded. The frat boys both ended up hospitalized, but the girl had been okay. She had called her dad and told him about it, and he had come down right away. As far as Petey was concerned, Reid had saved his daughter's life. Reid had thought that a gross exaggeration, but had appreciated the sentiment.

Reid disconnected with Ian and called Petey.

"Hey, son, how the hell are you?" Petey thundered.

Reid gave him a rundown on the events of the past several days.

When he finished, Petey said, "Damn, son, you always manage to stumble into shit, don't you?"

"I'd like your help if you're willing, Petey," Reid said.

"Of course. Tell me what you need," Petey said, and Reid told him what that would be.

Reid showered and cooked himself some scrambled eggs and toast. He ate a couple of granola bars and some fruit too. He wasn't sure when he'd get to eat again, so he took advantage while he could. He downed two cups of coffee and then brushed his teeth and rinsed with mouthwash. He located his dark suit and somber tie in his closet, and dressed slowly. He had about twenty minutes before he would need to leave. The funeral home was only a short drive from his condo straight down Peachtree.

Reid flipped on the MLB Network and checked up on the divisional races. The Braves had dropped a number of games behind the Nationals and now were looking to just stay alive in the wild card race. The Braves had solid pitching and defense, but struggled to score runs. Reid guessed that, similar to the past few seasons, even if the Braves got into the postseason, they would not go deep into the playoffs.

He checked his watch and decided to take off for Patterson's Funeral Home. Patterson's was a stone's throw from Oglethorpe University and not far from where Reid and Sarah had experienced their first sexual encounter together. The irony was not lost on him that she had brought them both back full circle from the beginning.

The parking lot was only about half full, so he made the short walk onto the side portico and into the building. Patterson's was a nice place as far as funeral homes go, and the staff was appropriately solemn and respectful. He walked the long corridor into the chapel and took a seat about halfway down the row of pews on the right side. Soft music was playing low, but otherwise the chapel was quiet. Reid glanced around the room. It was spacious. He figured you could probably cram close to 300 people in, but he guessed that fewer than fifty people had come to say goodbye to Sarah. He found this incredibly sad. He spotted the Lindstroms. Stephanie and Patsy flanked Bill Lindstrom near the front. He had his head bowed, but Reid wondered if he was praying or if life had just thrown him too many blows for a sick old man to endure. Reid noticed that the majority of people gathered were middle-aged or elderly, and therefore more likely to be friends of Sarah's parents. Then, just as the minister was walking out to begin the service, Reid saw three attractive women move into the chapel and slip into a pew directly across the aisle from him. He recognized Janice Cooley immediately; she was just as stunning in person as she was on her Facebook timeline. Reid didn't recognize the other two girls, but he would bet that they were dancers at one of the clubs where Sarah had danced. One of the girls had short, dark hair and the other was a blonde with long flowing locks. Lara Brooks was not in attendance. The minister began by reading some scripture and saying some prayers. Reid watched the congregants carefully, but he noticed no one suspicious. He didn't think it likely that Sarah's managers or bouncers from the club would attend, and he certainly didn't expect the Flex driver to show up. But one never knew, so Reid kept his eyes open and stayed very alert.

Reid saw that there was no casket, but an urn was sitting on a table surrounded by flowers and a framed picture of Sarah that he had never seen before. She looked beautiful as usual, but seeing her reduced to ashes affected Reid dramatically. It was so final.

When the service ended, the minister announced that there would be a reception in the fellowship hall of the neighboring church. Reid greeted the Lindstroms and Sarah's mom asked him to stand with her as Stephanie took a red-eyed Mr. Lindstrom to one of the parlor rooms where he could sit and grieve without any onlookers.

Reid was impressed with Patsy Lindstrom. He stayed by her side as she stood erect, looking everyone in the eye. She briefly shook hands and shared a few words with a line of friends and family. She managed to smile some. She would save her tears for later. As the line neared the end, Janice Cooley approached and paid her respects to Sarah's mom.

"Mrs. Lindstrom," she said, "I'm Janice, a close friend of Sarah's. I'm so sorry about Sarah. I want you to know how much I loved her."

"It's nice to meet you, Janice," Patsy Lindstrom said as the two women shook hands. "Sarah spoke of you fondly. Thank you so much for coming."

Janice glanced at Salem and blinked as if she was seeing him for the first time despite him having never left Sarah's mom during the procession.

She glanced back at Patsy Lindstrom and said, "We had such fun times at the beach together. We tried to go two or three times a year. I...I will miss her so much," Janice sniffled.

Sarah's mom changed the subject.

"Will you be joining us next door for the reception? I hope to see you there."

"Yes. I can come for a little while. Thank you." She shook Mrs. Lindstrom's hand again, smiled weakly, and turned away.

———

Reid walked with Sarah's family to the church next door. He had retrieved a wheelchair for Sarah's dad from the trunk of the Crown Victoria the Lindstroms had driven for the past twelve years. Once they had navigated the curb, Reid opened the chair and helped Mr. Lindstrom into it. Reid offered to push him and the ladies accepted his offer. They got into the hall and Reid at once noticed the wonderful aroma of home-cooked food. A few of Patsy Lindstrom's blue-haired friends had gotten together and offered to cook for the attendees of the reception. A long line of tables all covered in white tablecloths were pushed together with an unbelievable array of food. Great southern recipes prepared with the experienced and loving touch of these grandmotherly types occupied nearly every inch of the space: fried chicken, fried okra, macaroni and cheese. Green beans cooked in sausage. There was sliced watermelon, homemade peach and blackberry cobblers. He saw sliced ham, biscuits and gravy, and corn on the cob. It was incredible, and it lightened the mood as most everyone smiled and remarked on the display of food before them. It was an excellent touch on a solemn day. People began to socialize while they ate, and Reid found himself wishing he had not eaten so much at breakfast. He still managed to sample the fried chicken, okra, and macaroni and cheese. He saw Janice sitting alone in a corner checking her phone, so he loaded up two plates with cobbler, one of each kind, and walked towards her. He was almost to her when she popped her head up quickly. He had startled her. He held out the cobblers.

"Peach or blackberry?" he asked. And then he added, "Maybe you'd like to try some of each."

She stared at him a second too long. He sat down leaving a chair between them. He set both plates on the empty chair.

"Did your companions leave?" he asked.

She nodded, but remained silent.

"My name is Salem," he said, and put out his hand.

She hesitated and took his hand. Her hand was a little damp as if she was nervous.

"Salem Reid," she said. "Oh my God! I thought that was you."

He picked up the peach cobbler and handed it to her, but she shook her head hastily as if she was agitated and couldn't be bothered with making culinary decisions. So he dug in. He sat back and crossed his legs and chewed the delicious cobbler.

"You should try some," he said. "It's the best I've ever had."

She laughed in spite of herself.

"I don't want any pie," she said, but the smile stayed on her face. "She always told me how handsome you were."

She shook her head and lost the smile.

"You were her best friend," he said, more as a statement than a question.

She nodded and a tear rolled down her cheek.

"We were close."

"Then help me find who did this to her," he said.

She looked up with fear in her eyes and he knew he'd struck a nerve.

"She overdosed," she said unconvincingly, and he knew she didn't believe it.

"Talk to me, Janice. Don't be afraid. I can help," he said to her.

"Oh my God, I'm so afraid," she said, and wrung her hands. More tears rolled down her face.

"Janice, please? Let's do this for Sarah," he told her.

She sobbed and a blue-haired lady glanced over at them disapprovingly. Reid reached out and gently touched Janice's shoulder.

"Tell me," he said.

"I can't! He'll kill me."

And then she was up and dashing across the room towards the exit. He moved quickly after her and caught up with her outside. She had made it to the funeral home parking lot.

"Janice," he said, and took her arm, "tell me who's behind this."

"No," she shouted at him.

She broke free and ran to her car. She drove a baby Benz. It looked fairly new. She fumbled for her keys, but Reid didn't pursue her. She got her car unlocked and furtively glanced back at Reid as if he would chase her down. She got in and quickly peeled out of her parking space, nearly hitting an old Buick parked across the aisle. He noticed a white Lexus fall in behind her, the driver's long blonde hair blowing in the late summer breeze. He got a good look at her plate as she departed. He committed the tag number to memory as she sped out of the parking lot and headed north towards Chamblee.

# 38

REID WENT HOME AND CHANGED CLOTHES. He checked on Klaus; the Tundra was still parked at the Atlantic Motor Lodge. It was 3:30 pm. He punched in the number he thought belonged to Lara Brooks. Maybe she would talk to him. The phone rang and went into an automated voice message recording: "770-416-6124 is not available. Please leave a message at the sound of the tone."

Reid recorded a message. He stated his name and asked Lara to call him.

He worked out in his training room. He punched and kicked bags for over an hour, working up a good lather. He did some abdominal work and then pumped out 180 push-ups in three sets of 60. He showered and made some coffee. After his coffee, he texted Joey and Ian telling them to meet him at Jo's near Blackburn Park at 6:30. Then he called Petey and told him over the phone where they were meeting.

Ian was the last to arrive at Jo's. He was running a few minutes late. He was the only one coming north from Buckhead in the worst of the evening traffic. Reid and Joey both ordered a salmon filet sandwich, Ian had fish tacos, and Petey ate a burger. Reid filled everyone in on what he had learned over the last twenty-four hours. It had been a lot. He focused especially on his conversation with Janice and how she had seemed frightened to the point of fearing for her life. He felt that he needed to move fast before something terrible happened again. He wanted to protect her, but she had hastened to get away from him as if he were poison.

"Petey, I need a car and a couple of drops," Reid said, and Petey nodded.

Petey Ward had a body shop on Buford Highway in northeast Atlanta. He also had a few mechanics on hand and they would strip parts from totaled cars and rebuild and sell them. Petey always had a few anonymous cars on hand.

Reid had used them before. Plates for these specialty cars were valid but usually for other cars that were exact makes and models. Hartsfield-Jackson Airport was the busiest airport in the U.S. and a great place to borrow a plate for a few days. Reid preferred nondescript models and colors like dark-blue, beige, or champagne Accords, Camrys, or Civics. They were a dime a dozen.

Petey had non-traceable guns too. Reid was one of the very few people he would loan one out to.

"I have a few things to tie up, and then I want to hit Utopia tomorrow night and see if we can find this guy who drives the Flex. Joey, are you in or out on this? Either way it's okay," Reid said.

"I'll go. I guess we're not paying the cover." It might have been funny in a less tense situation, but no one laughed at his joke.

Ian took off for a security job he had at Centre Stage Theater in midtown. A new pop rock star, Vance Fite, was making a big splash, especially with teenage girls. It had gotten a little weird a few times for him when he played his hometown, so he had taken to hiring Southeast Security for before, during, and after the show. Ian had joked with Reid that if the music business didn't work out for Vance, they could hire him to work security. He was a big, strong rocker with a background in martial arts. And he was smart too. Ian liked his music though, and he said it was doubtful that Vance Fite wouldn't make it big. The guy actually had talent and he was getting noticed.

Petey took off a few minutes later. He wanted to get started on gathering all of the items together for Reid. He told him before departing that he'd have a car ready for him to pick up by this evening, but the other items wouldn't be available until tomorrow.

Before leaving Jo's, Reid checked the device app on his phone and discovered that Klaus was no longer at the Motor Lodge. He was going north on 85, possibly towards his apartment. He looked at Joey.

"Let's take a trip to Cheshire Bridge Road. Klaus is on the move. Let's see what's going on in that room of his. Follow me."

———

Reid took Ashford Dunwoody to Peachtree where it dumped out close to Patterson's Funeral Home. The parking lot was full this evening, suggesting viewings in the parlors and maybe even an evening service in the chapel. He drove a little over a mile and jumped on North Druid Hills over to 85, then took it south to Cheshire Bridge. He navigated the evening traffic, but it was still thick, and it took over ten minutes to get to the Motor Lodge after exiting the interstate. Darkness was settling in over the city as they both wheeled into the lot. Reid drove to the back building where Ian had located Klaus's room and Joey followed.

Reid checked the tracker on Klaus's Tundra again; he was in Doraville near his home. He parked in a space in front of the room adjacent to Klaus's and Joey parked a few spaces over. He reached into the backseat and removed his lock picks from the duffel bag. He was not an expert lock picker, but he was adequate. Reid and Joey got out of their vehicles and moved quietly to the corner unit.

# 39

ELIZABETH HARRIGAN KNEW she was going to die. She had been bound and gagged and kept mostly in a closet for days; she wasn't sure how many. Her brain was misfiring and she felt feverish and achy. But time spent in the closet gagged and bound was preferable to what that monster had done to her every time he had dragged her out. He had sodomized her numerous times; the pain had been unbearable, but she had been unable to scream. She could smell the decay on herself, but worse, she could smell the monster. He had been foul and his scent on her was a constant reminder of her predicament. She was barely lucid now, but she was coherent enough to know that she was malnourished and dehydrated. The monster had fed her sparingly at first, but had stopped at some point. She wasn't sure exactly when. She had lost track of time and days. The withdrawal from the meth had been awful too. She had craved it at first, but to her surprise, he had let her smoke a bit. Then he'd given her the drug again to keep her from tweaking too badly. But she was tweaking now. Besides being terribly ill from the abuse she had taken, she had escalated feelings of emptiness and craving. Her skin itched and she felt as if bugs were crawling over her body. She knew she had become an addict, but it had only developed recently. She thought that maybe she could survive the Jonesing for the drug, but she doubted she would survive the monster. He would kill her soon; she could sense it and now she was convinced that death would only come as relief.

As she lay in the closet for days, she'd had periods when she had reviewed her life. Ending up in a seedy hotel in this horrible condition, of course, hadn't been the plan. She had grown up in a middle-class neighborhood near Brookhaven and attended Cross Keys High School. She hadn't been a great student, making C's and a smattering of B's in basic courses. She had been a pretty girl, though, and had made the cheerleading squad for football during her sophomore, junior, and senior years. She had dated a second string football player who was in many of her classes, but even more academically challenged than she was. Brian had liked to party and goof off with his friends, but she had discovered sex as a way to get him to pay more attention to her. She found that she enjoyed the sex to some extent, but she rarely achieved orgasm with him. She thought maybe she could if he had been interested in helping her do so, but mostly he'd been only interested in his own pleasure. His pleasure usually happened quickly too. She went to the high school parties like most teenagers, and drank sometimes and had tried weed on a couple of occasions. Marijuana wasn't really her "thing" though, so she only drank at parties, and only when she was with Brian. She wasn't sure what her "thing" was. She had no hobbies or interests for the most part. If she had been good at something, maybe it had been gardening. She had helped her mom fix up their modest backyard when she was a teenager. Then one day her dad, a mean alcoholic, arrived home drunk and ripped up the flower beds and mums they had planted. He told her that he wasn't going to have a bunch of sissy flowers in his yard. She had cried herself to sleep that night. She had really enjoyed the experience of creating the garden and had been even more satisfied by how pretty it had looked upon completion. She compensated for her disappointment by creating drawings of flowered landscapes after that, and even won a second place award in a school art contest in her junior year.

Somehow, she had ended up marrying Brian a few years after graduating from high school. She had tried again with gardening at their small and unspectacular rented house in North Atlanta. But it had mostly gone unnoticed by him until, like her father, he had come home drunk one day from his job as a mechanic and told her that she should stop trying to make a silk purse out of a sow's ear. She had cried herself to sleep again that night and vowed never to garden again.

Then they had tried to have a baby, but she didn't get pregnant. They kept trying for several years. She took herbs and read fertility books; they couldn't afford to try expensive medical solutions. The money he made at the auto repair service station barely covered their living expenses and his beer and wings requirements. She made just a little over minimum wage as an office assistant in one of those strip mall tax preparation outfits.

Then one day in the third week of April at the conclusion of the busy tax season, she had been given a paid day off by her boss. She had cleaned up the house, taken a bubble bath, washed her hair, applied enough makeup to look as pretty as she could, and polished her nails. Then she had prepared lasagna for her husband for dinner. She called his workplace and let him know that she was making dinner and that he should drive straight home after work to eat. Three hours after his expected arrival, he had come home drunk, dirty, and smelly. He got straight into the sack, without showering, on the clean sheets she had just put on the bed. He told her on his way to the bedroom that she could cover the food and place it in the fridge. He might eat some of the lasagna the following day. He never touched it.

Two months after that incident he came home from work, gave her a disapproving look while shaking his head at her, packed a few things in a bag, and left.

All he had said to her on the way out was, "I want a divorce. I'm leaving."

She saw him once again in court and that was it.

She became very frightened. She knew that she had limited skills. They had credit card bills nearing the limit and they were overdue on the rent. They had barely survived financially together. There was no way she could survive alone. Her father had died in a car collision shortly after she had gotten out of high school, and her mom was poor. She was living solely on her dad's social security.

Liza had ended up renting a small room in a house off Lavista Road from a woman who was a religious fanatic, but had been otherwise kind. She had endured the "sermonizing" and "scripture reading" that this batty woman had practically forced upon her, but the financial cost to live there had been quite reasonable.

At this point in her life she had been with the tax firm for over six years; she had gotten steady raises and was doing okay, but she wanted to be able to at least rent her own apartment and get away from the Holy Roller. A few of her coworkers invited her to a bar after work one evening and that's where she met Lenny. Lenny was a halfway decent looking guy, but a bit on the cheesy side. She didn't see the cheese, but she thought he looked pretty good. Besides, a guy was giving her some attention and she had been starved for affection. She went to his apartment that evening and had sex with him. She enjoyed it very much. It had been the best sex she'd ever had up to that point. After a few weeks, Lenny said he would love to have a video of her masturbating and asked her if she would do that for him. The video ended up on a pay site on the Internet without her knowledge. Then one night they were sipping a little wine and she had gotten a bit tipsy; she wasn't much of a drinker, but she had enjoyed drinking with Lenny more and more. He convinced her that the two of them could make a lot of money if she'd be willing to have sex with other men…and maybe some women too. She wanted to make him happy and she had learned to like the sex, so she agreed. Lenny set it up. He had the johns rent a cheap motel room at the Piedmont Arms. Lenny would show up and collect the money and wait outside. They usually charged about $200 for an hour. Sometimes they settled for $175 on a slow night, but often received as much as $250. Lenny took 60 percent and Liza took 40. Liza had finally made enough money to get her own place, but now that she was hooked up with Lenny, she thought they could live together. He decided that was an excellent idea. They rented a two-bedroom apartment together off Monroe Drive. The smaller bedroom was hers, of course, and was setup with video equipment. Lenny would film Liza having sex with a variety of men, women, and sometimes both men and women together. He was making very good money on his porn website and they both made money when she performed tricks at the Piedmont Arms. Liza had paid off all of her bills and had saved $11,000 of her own money. She felt like she was rich.

This arrangement went along real well for about a year. Then one evening, Lenny had arranged for Liza to do a trick for a swarthy Middle Eastern guy who had purchased Liza once before. The Middle Eastern guy had snorted cocaine and smoked weed in the room at the Piedmont Arms with Liza. Liza had participated in the cocaine snorting, but had passed on the weed. Marijuana still was not her "thing." She had come to enjoy cocaine, and sometimes crack, ever since Lenny had turned her on to it shortly after he got her turning tricks.

The Middle Eastern guy had problems maintaining an erection during his time with Liza. This probably was due more to the drugs than Liza's sexual prowess, but the Middle Eastern guy became angry and belligerent. He smacked Liza around a bit, and knocked her out cold. Then he exited the room, located Lenny, and demanded a refund. When Lenny refused, the Middle Eastern guy pulled a gun and shot Lenny right between the eyes. Liza was alone again.

———

Without Lenny in the picture, she wasn't sure how to proceed. He had handled all the business arrangements and secured the johns for tricks. She wanted to keep the apartment, but without Lenny, it would be tough. She didn't trick for a while at first, but with the two-bedroom apartment and her crack and cocaine habit, she went through her savings very quickly. Her once "ripe" and desirable body was starting to change a bit too. Her breasts had begun to sag a little and she was getting lines in her face. The drugs and subpar nutrition had given her an unhealthy hue. She needed money; that would solve her problems, so she returned to the street to try to drum up a little business on her own. But things were different. She found herself giving blow jobs in alleys for $40, or simply trading favors for drugs. She had one guy trade her crystal meth for sex. The meth took over pretty quickly. In the course of six weeks, she had lost her apartment and was living in the Piedmont Arms for $185 a week. And now, at thirty-three years old, she was gagged, bound, and dying in a seedy hotel on Cheshire Bridge Road.

# 40

REID APPROACHED THE DOOR SLOWLY and carefully. He had instructed Joey to stay back a few paces until he was sure that the room was empty. He reached the window and tried to see inside, but the blinds were drawn tight and there was no light coming from inside the room. He checked the door and saw that the old motel still used key locks and not the swipe cards now common in most modern hotels. He quietly worked the lock. Reid spent several minutes manipulating the tumblers while Joey served both as a lookout for the curious onlooker and as a cover for Reid. It took close to five minutes, but Reid was able to get the door unlocked. He held the knob with his left hand and removed his Glock with his right. He crouched low and pushed the door open. He reached in quickly with his left and found the switch. A dim light flooded the empty room and Reid entered. The stench was overwhelming. He held his Glock in front of him and slowly and methodically cleared the room. Then he checked the bathroom. It was empty, but the toilet was vile with dried urine stains on the seat and a brown ring inside the bowl. The tile in the shower stall was cracked and corroded. There was black mold on the ceiling above the shower. The bathroom smelled worse than the bedroom. Joey had entered the unit and closed the door. Reid came back into the room; he kept his firearm in his right hand, but held it down along his leg. He started opening drawers and looking under the bed for anything that might prove useful to the investigation. In a drawer by the nightstand, he spotted a small metal key. He placed it in his pocket. There was debris in the room. Fast food bags and wrappers were strewn about, and empty drink cups were sitting on the dresser and nightstand. There were wet wipes in and around a small trash can next to the dresser. Some of them appeared to be caked with dried blood.

Reid looked around the room again. It was a pigsty. He had checked everything but the closet. The closet door was the variety that had two doors with knobs on them. When you pulled the knob, the door opened outward and folded in on itself. He was reluctant to just fling the door open. He motioned Joey to pull the near one open. Reid raised his gun and moved again into a crouch directly across from the door. Joey quickly pulled the closet door open. Neither initially saw anything. Then they heard a faint muffled cry, and simultaneously they glanced down and saw a bound and gagged woman lying naked on the closet floor. The closet was long and narrow and she was stretched out along the length of it. Her hair was stringy, damp, and dirty. A washcloth was crammed in her mouth with duct tape wrapped completely around her head. Her legs were tied together snuggly with rope. She was lying diagonally on her side and propped against the closet wall. Both arms were bent behind her back. Joey bent down to get a better look while Reid positioned himself towards the front door, keeping his gun extended with both hands as he checked every crevice of the closet. When he was sure that only the woman was in the closet, he holstered his weapon and maneuvered to help Joey, who was gently lifting and pulling the woman out and onto the bed. Reid rolled her on her side and saw that handcuffs were clasped to her wrists. He removed the small metal key from his pocket and tried it in the lock. It was a perfect fit. Reid removed the cuffs and Joey was busy trying to get the rope untied and untangled. Reid produced a Swiss Army knife from his pocket and cut the duct tape where it centered over the washcloth and pulled the gag from her mouth. The woman's eyelids fluttered and she was breathing in slow, shallow breaths. Her pale skin was on fire. She had a couple of abscesses on her face. One was near her mouth. She appeared to be bleeding from her rectum, vagina, or maybe both.

"I'm going to the car to get my bag. Stay with her, Joey," Reid said, and bolted from the room.

Joey went into the bathroom to search for a clean towel he could use to clean her up. The only towels he saw were soiled and had been flung to the corner of the dirty bathroom floor. He went back to her and waited for Reid. Joey stroked her head and held her hand.

"Hang in there, darling. We're going to help you," he said.

Her eyes fluttered again and she labored to say something, but Joey gently placed two of his fingers over her dried and crusted lips.

"Don't try to talk," he said.

Reid returned with his bag. He removed a bottle of water and handed it to Joey.

"Just a little bit," he instructed, as he took out a first aid kit and removed a sterile gauze pad.

"Pour water on it and try to clean her up some," he told Joey. She had green mucous running from her nose. "Start with her mouth and nose."

Joey cleaned her face the best he could. He looked over at his friend. Reid was pulling a tee shirt and shorts from his duffel.

They took more sterile gauze from the first aid kit and tried to clean her torso and legs. Her rectum and vagina they would leave to the medical staff at the hospital. They were pretty certain that the scaly white crust on and around her breasts and stomach was dried semen. She had numerous small cuts all over her body as if she'd been poked with a sharp object just enough to draw blood. A few of the cuts looked infected. The guys maneuvered her into Reid's gym shorts. They were much too large, so they used a piece of the duct tape they had removed from her face to secure them on her. The tee shirt was huge on her, but it covered her body sufficiently.

"Carry her to my car, Joey. I'll open the back. Give her small doses of water if she'll take it."

They got her into the back seat and Joey climbed in behind her. She fell over into him, so he cradled her with his left arm as she laid her head on his shoulder. He wrapped his right arm around her in a gentle bear hug. She had seemed mostly incoherent in the room, but now that they had moved her a bit and she was upright, she seemed to be marginally responsive. She began to sob. The sob turned into a sickly cough. Joey hugged her firmly and promised her everything would be okay.

They peeled out of the lot and Reid navigated onto Piedmont and then cut through Ansley Golf Course over to Peachtree where he turned north towards Piedmont Hospital.

"You were down here with a friend and we found this girl on the street, naked and abused. You brought her here for help. Say that. That's all."

"Okay Salem. I'll figure it out," Joey replied.

"Good. I'll check with you in a bit. Take good care of her. She should make it," Reid said, as he pulled up to the emergency room at Piedmont Hospital and dropped them off.

He watched Joey carry her to the door and inside the building. Then he took off to get a car at Petey Ward's.

––––––––––

Reid drove fast to Buford Highway and arrived at Petey's shop in twelve minutes. He traded his car for a six-year-old, smoke-colored Honda Accord. It was a perfectly anonymous car. He knew that Petey had taken care of the plates. He grabbed his duffel from the Challenger and tossed it into the trunk of the Accord. He checked the app on his phone and saw the Tundra was still parked at Klaus's apartment. He decided to go by his condo in Chamblee and dress in appropriate clothes for the work he would need to do this evening. Then he would pay Klaus a visit.

———

Klaus left his apartment about the same time Reid was heading towards his condo. He had come home to retrieve one of two large blue tarps he had purchased from the hardware store. He had bought more duct tape too. He knew he'd have to end the fun and games with the street hooker tonight and then kill her if she wasn't dead already by the time he finished with her. He had it planned out. He would enjoy her once more, then choke her to death, wrap her in the blue tarp, duct tape the tarp together, and find an obscure dumpster somewhere and dispose of her body. Traffic was light and he arrived at the Motor Lodge only fifteen minutes after leaving his apartment. He parked and approached the door. He placed his key in the dead bolt and turned it, but it was unlocked. He was sure he had locked it. At least he was almost sure he had. But he guessed it was remotely possible that he had not. He knew he shouldn't have been so careless. He made a mental note to be more careful next time. He turned the knob, opened the door, hit the light switch, and peeked into the room. He saw nothing right off that alerted him, so he stepped into the room and closed the door. He moved directly to the closet and opened the door. She was gone. Had she escaped? Surely not. He was certain that she couldn't even walk at this point. He had stopped feeding her or giving her water two days ago. He wanted her weak at the end. It had made him feel most dominant and powerful. She was a toy that he could toss around however he pleased. He couldn't make sense of it. The staff at the Lodge wouldn't have entered. He had requested privacy. They were fine with that. His room wouldn't be cleaned until he departed, and he said he'd come to the office and get towels or toilet paper if he needed more. This request wasn't out of the ordinary for the Motor Lodge, so there was no reason for them to enter the unit. He was angry. He was looking forward to his last night with the street hooker. He had been thinking about it throughout the evening. He had gotten very horny when he fantasized about their final encounter. But something told him that he should get out of there. He looked around to see if there was anything incriminating. He remembered the handcuffs and the key. He opened the drawer on the nightstand. The key was missing. He needed to get out of there. And he knew exactly where he would go.

# 41

JOEY CARRIED THE WOMAN into the emergency room. A nurse brought a gurney out and he set her on it. They wheeled her into an exam room. Joey tagged along. He had come up with a more complete story than Reid had suggested. He told the nurse and the attending physician that he and a friend were planning to dine at The Colonnade and noticed a woman stumbling naked from a lot near the restaurant as they were pulling in. She was stricken and disoriented and she looked to be bleeding and abused. They dressed her in some spare clothes from the car and brought her in. They looked at him evenly as he told his story and then asked him to wait in the waiting room.

About forty-five minutes later, the nurse came out and spoke with him. She said that the woman was coming around and was marginally coherent now, but still a bit confused about her circumstances. They had given her IV fluids and were controlling her pain. She told them her name was Liza, and that she had asked if the man who carried her in was still here. She had requested to speak with him; she claimed to have no family or friends to contact.

Joey waited another fifteen minutes and then the nurse took him back to a curtained area where Liza was receiving treatment. When Joey approached, she slowly looked towards him and reached her hand out. He looked at the nurse and she nodded.

Joey took Liza's hand and she whispered, "Thank you."

It was barely audible. The nurse fiddled with the IVs and checked the monitors Liza was hooked up to and then left to attend to other patients. Joey stood there and held her hand. She didn't speak again, but she would occasionally open her eyes a little and smile weakly at him. He left her side only once to locate a stool so that he could sit with her. She had no one apparently. He decided that he would not abandon her. He looked at her while she rested. What he had seen in the room where she had been held captive was brutality at its worst. He was stunned at the unspeakable horrors that people could inflict on their fellow humans. This woman had been through an ordeal that no one should ever have to endure. She would recover physically he guessed, but it would be a long road to mental and emotional recovery for her. The hospital staff had done a decent job of cleaning her up. The vile smell that had been on her when they found her was no longer noticeable. They had treated her cuts with some sort of antibiotic, he guessed, and had dressed the more severe wounds. Her brown hair was dirty and oily, but they had cleaned it up some and pulled it back and off her face. He thought that under better circumstances that she might actually be kind of pretty. Her nose was straight and proportioned well on her face. She had the beginnings of lines around her mouth that suggested street life and the few open sores were certainly unattractive, but they would heal. Her lips were chapped and cracked, but they were full lips that formed a mouth a bit like a cupid's. She had seemed about average height for a woman, perhaps slightly taller. When she had opened her eyes on those few occasions, he noticed that they were big and brown; pretty eyes that were soft and kind, despite what she'd been through. Joey had felt an outpouring of compassion and sympathy for this woman. This was a feeling previously foreign to him. He realized, sitting here now with this abused woman in the emergency room of a city hospital, that he'd always thought mostly of himself. A sense of shame and regret washed over him. Maybe the experience with Sarah dying in his home had changed him, deepened him somehow. He thought back to the previous Friday. He'd thrown on slick clothes and jewelry. He had stuffed his wallet with money to pay a woman to treat him like a king and provide sexual favors to him. He had a depraved night out with a fair-weather friend, thinking he was hip and cool. He had drunk top-shelf alcohol and thrown weed and coke around to his friends like he was some kind of big shot. And now, all of that seemed unimportant to him. He realized for the first time in his life that he had the capacity to be something better than all of that. It had taken a dead prostitute and an abused and tortured woman who had been lost and forgotten to teach him this.

# 42

REID CHANGED INTO A BLACK NYLON SHIRT and black cargo pants. He holstered his Glock 17 and a long knife with a serrated edge to his ankle. He placed black leather gloves in his pants and carried a black skullcap in his hand. He left his condo and jumped into the Accord. He checked his tracking app and saw that Klaus was back at the Motor Lodge. He hadn't expected this. This made things a little trickier. He could chase him there, but that wasn't ideal for several reasons. He believed that Klaus would not hang around the Motor Lodge once he realized that his prey was gone anyway. Why would he? He'd be shaken up and confused about how she escaped and whether he was being sought. He would want to get away from there in a hurry. Reid figured that Klaus would head back to his apartment or possibly to Club Utopia. Reid thought he might drive to Club Utopia himself. He could keep an eye out for Klaus in case he showed up there to consult his boss. And perhaps his boss would come in or out that back door at some point. He'd nose around and try to locate the Flex and maybe this time he could get a tag number.

Reid drove straight down PIB to Utopia. He circled the lot and saw the Flex parked in the big lot between the sports bar and the strip club, but on the opposite side from where Reid had parked much earlier that morning. It was maybe thirty feet from the back door where he'd seen Klaus enter and exit less than twenty-four hours ago. He was almost certain that the Flex was the same one he'd seen very early that morning. He supposed it was possible that there were two exact same model Fords that were the same dark-blue color, but he doubted it. He backed the Accord in behind the Flex, but a few spaces over, closer to the sports bar. He wrote down the tag: 637 ALE. He sat and watched the back door for a few minutes and then checked his detection app for the Tundra. Klaus was on the move again, heading north on 85. He tracked him for a moment and was surprised when Klaus took the North Druid Hills exit instead of continuing north on 85. Maybe he was coming to Utopia after all and cutting over to Peachtree instead of using the interstate. It was reasonable, he supposed, in light evening traffic.

Reid's phone rang.

"Yes?" he answered.

There was momentary silence, and then a female voice that Reid thought was perhaps a black woman said, "Salem Reid? You called me."

"Lara?" he asked.

There was another pause. "This is Salem Reid?" she asked.

"Yes. Thanks for calling me back. I think you might be able to help me. Could we meet?" he inquired.

"How did you get my number?" she asked.

"It fell out of a book that Sarah had been reading. I went to her apartment with her mom," he explained. He asked again, "Can we meet?"

The pause again. This time a long one.

"Okay. Tomorrow. Meet me at Starbucks by the Regal Cinema at Perimeter Pointe. It's off of Mt. Vernon. 2 pm. Come alone and sit in the back of the store. Find a table and order two Grande coffees. Have them in front of you. I'll find you," she said, and hung up before he could thank her.

She was scared. He thought now he knew of whom she was scared, and why she was frightened.

———

Millicent was dead tired. She had stayed late to cover for another manager who had left earlier in the evening because of a migraine headache. She thought she might be getting a migraine headache of her own. Her throat was a little scratchy too; she had felt a little rundown all day. The ARC closed at ten on Wednesdays, so she figured she would escape by 10:15. She had considered calling Reid earlier in the day to see if he had a few free hours tonight, but now she didn't think she would be very good company. Besides, if she was getting a cold, she didn't want to pass it on to him. Shortly after ten, she closed up her office and said good night to the few remaining people inside of the facility; mostly custodial people who would clean and secure the building before locking it up for the night.

———

Reid checked the app again and saw that the Tundra had not continued down Peachtree as he'd expected. Klaus was tracked at Ashford Dunwoody Road. He was at the ARC.

Reid located the contacts in his phone and called Millicent. She didn't answer. He wasn't sure of her schedule. He searched in Safari for the ARC website and found the main number. The call went immediately to an after-hours auto attendant. Salem Reid sped out of the parking lot and headed west on 285 towards Ashford Dunwoody Road.

———

Millicent exited the building and walked like a zombie to her car. She could hardly keep her eyes open and she knew as soon as her head hit the pillow that she'd be asleep. As she approached her car, she popped the locks with her key fob. She opened her door and as she leaned to get in her car, she was pushed roughly so that she fell sideways across the console and into the car. She made an effort to pop up but as she did, that monster, Klaus, was on top of her, pinning her right arm down with his left. Then he plunged his huge right fist into her face, connecting with her cheekbone and temple, and knocking her completely silly. He flipped her onto her front side and used duct tape to bind her hands behind her. Then he flipped her over on her back, and suddenly and with great force, shoved a towel into her mouth and quickly secured it with duct tape. He shoved her onto the floorboard as best he could. She was dazed and in an awkward position that made it difficult for her to move. Her head dangled between the seat and the console. She was out of view from a casual glance through the window. It was dark and the traffic was light, so he saw little risk in his plan. He climbed into the driver's seat and fired up the Honda. He left the ARC parking lot and headed north on Ashford Dunwoody Road towards the Perimeter. He took 285 East where he unwittingly passed Salem Reid on the westbound Perimeter just after Chamblee Dunwoody Road.

———

Reid had to be careful not to drive too fast. It would be the worst possible time to be pulled over. He was chasing after a madman who was potentially chasing after his girl, and he was in a car with swapped plates. He kept his speed around seventy as he drove the Perimeter west towards Ashford Dunwoody Road. He exited the interstate and drove inside the Perimeter towards the ARC. Traffic was okay, but he got caught at several lights. He got through the last one at the Marist School where Harts Mill Road dumped into Ashford Dunwoody and then he sped to the ARC. He spotted the Tundra right away and went straight for it. He jumped out and rushed to it, drawing his weapon as he moved. The Tundra cab was empty. A big blue tarp, the kind that you could get at any hardware store, was in the back of his truck. Reid looked around. There were several cars in the lot, but none were Millicent's black Honda Civic. He pulled his phone and triggered the app. He located her car almost instantly. It was heading south on 85 just north of Chamblee Tucker Road. The worst was happening. He got back in the Accord and drove as fast as the car would go. He didn't care about the cops now. They could follow him straight to Klaus's apartment for all he cared.

———

Klaus exited Chamblee Tucker, moved west past 85, and then north on the DeKalb Tech Parkway over to Chestnut towards his apartment. The girl was still dazed and sat motionless on the floorboard of her car as he pulled up to his apartment. He jumped out and locked the door. He ran into his apartment and returned with the second blue tarp. He looked around and saw activity at the far end of his apartment building. There were three Mexican guys talking some trash to each other in Spanish. They were posing and laughing and carrying on together. Klaus threw the tarp in the back seat and got inside the car. He waited them out. A few minutes later they slapped some skin and one of the Mexicans went inside of the bottom end unit and the other two jumped into a Chevy Silverado and took off.

———

Klaus glanced down at Millicent. She was slowly stirring. He grabbed the tarp and got her wrapped up in it. He used the duct tape to secure the ends. He went to the passenger door and hefted her out. She was moving a little bit now, so he would need to hurry. He got her up the stairs and into his apartment just before she started squirming noticeably. He pulled the duct tape free and rolled her out onto his grubby apartment floor. He leered down at her and grinned. He began rubbing himself through his pants and chuckling at her. She looked up at him and although one eye was puffy from the blow he had landed to her face, he could see through the slit well enough to recognize total fright. He reached for her and she tried to kick him—much like the street hooker had done at first, but he had remedied that with her and he would with this one too. He picked up the rope he had lying on the floor and tied it to one of her legs. He tied the other end off around the foot of his sofa. He repeated the process with her other leg as he positioned her facing him on the sofa. He then went behind the sofa and raised her bound arms over the back of the sofa and then taped her down. She was now practically immobile.

He cackled when he saw her reaction to the machete he wielded. She was wearing shorts and a tank top and tennis shoes. He tore off her tank top with the machete, making a small cut on her skin that drew a bead of blood. Then he reached down and yanked off her strapless bra. Her eyes bulged as she saw his erection straining against his jeans. He ran the machete over her breasts very lightly. She held her breath, praying he wouldn't cut her. To her relief, he pulled the machete off her and backed up a step. He set the machete on the floor. Then to her horror, he did something she hadn't expected. He removed his clothes. He was completely hard and he began slowly stroking himself.

# 43

LIZA WAS VACILLATING IN AND OUT of sleep. When she would wake, she would look for Joey with frightened eyes. They would calm when she saw him and she had understood that he had stayed by her side. He would take her hand and soothe her by stroking her forehead at the hairline, and she would eventually return to sleep. On one occasion when she had awakened, she had spoken.

"Wuz you name?" she asked in barely a whisper.

"Joey," he said.

She repeated it and smiled. "Joey," she said. She had a sweet, southern accent. Then she drifted off again.

The nurse came by and nodded her approval at Joey. He wasn't sure about the protocol for being in the emergency room, especially with someone he didn't even know, but the staff seemed to want him here. He wanted to be here. So he continued to stay by her side and hold her hand. The nurse had brought ice chips in a cup. When Liza would wake, he would try to get her to take some. She had taken a little at first, but now seemed uninterested. Her skin felt cooler to the touch now, but she was still feverish. He wondered how bad her infection was, but figured until she was lucid and gave the staff permission to talk to him, they would not say much.

She had awakened again and called out Joey's name.

He took her hand firmly and hovered over her, saying, "I'm here, Liza. It's okay now. You can sleep."

And she did.

She awoke a little later, but didn't say anything. She looked at Joey and gave him another weak smile. Then she groaned and moved a hand between her legs. Joey called for the nurse, who gave Liza more pain meds through her IV. Then she slept.

# 44

REID GOT TO CHAMBLEE TUCKER ROAD in less than ten minutes. He wound his way over to Chestnut and didn't bother with parking at the food mart this time. He could take no chances. Time meant everything. He pulled into the complex and drove straight to Klaus's building. The area around the building was dimly lit. There was no foot traffic this time of night, and the car traffic was quiet in this section of the complex. He spotted Millicent's black Honda parked directly in front of Klaus's building. He parked two spaces over directly in front of the stairs. He gloved up quickly and added the dark skullcap. He drew his Glock as he exited the Accord and took a quick peak into her car. It was empty. He quietly crept up the stairs to the small porch area. He could see soft yellow light coming through the drapes, but the curtains were drawn tight and he could not see inside of the apartment. He guessed the layout would be similar to older apartments like this one. It would probably enter into the living room, with a dining room or breakfast area behind it. He guessed a kitchen would be in the rear, walled off from the living area. A hall would lead down to the left with a couple of bedrooms.

He wasn't sure where Klaus had taken her, so he listened. He heard muffled sounds, but could make out no more than that. He figured that if his guess was correct about the layout, that Klaus had Millicent in the living room, probably tied up and gagged like the woman in the Motor Lodge. He was thinking through every option and plan of attack, but then he heard a muffled shriek; and then another. It was time to act.

———

Klaus stood over Millicent with his genitals just inches from her face. He was groping himself with his left hand and laughing at her. He had the machete in his right hand. She could smell him. He was foul. He smelled like a wild animal that had just devoured its prey. His eyes were crazed and he had a sheen of sweat covering his pockmarked, muscle-bound body. His cock was throbbing and she could see the sticky, clear pre-cum oozing from the head of his penis. He bent and wiped his ooze along her leg. It left a warm, wet trail. She thought she might hurl and choke to death on her own vomit. The gag in her mouth would see to that. She heaved, but managed to keep the contents of her stomach down. Klaus stood back up and then placed the tip of the machete on one of her breasts again. He slid it over her chest and let the tip toy with her other breast. Then he trailed the blade down her stomach and over her navel to the edge of her shorts. Then suddenly he reached with his other hand and ripped her shorts down her legs and then followed with her thong.

"My, my, Milly," he whispered.

She tried to scream, but the sound was muffled by the gag.

He placed the point of the machete at the top of her pubic hair and whispered again, "You're a little wooly, Milly. I think I'll give you a shave."

Then he pushed the tip of the machete into her skin just enough to cut her slightly and draw another bead of blood. This time she shrieked, then shrieked again. Then the front door flew off the doorframe.

———

Reid stepped back as he heard the second shriek and placed a swift and hard front kick, using the ball of his foot, just above and slightly to the right of the doorknob. The door was heavy and strong, but the frame was not. The door and most of the frame flew in and Reid followed. He saw that he had an immediate tactical problem. Klaus had turned abruptly upon the intrusion, and Millicent was strapped crudely to the sofa almost directly behind him. Reid had his gun out in front of him and aimed at Klaus's torso. It was a considerable risk shooting a handgun in close quarters like this. Not only was Millicent directly behind Klaus, but one could never be sure about ricochet. If he shot Klaus through the chest or head, the bullet would likely exit his body. With Millicent directly behind Klaus, she could be inadvertently shot too; a risk he didn't want to take. He attempted to maneuver to his right in an effort to get Millicent out of the line of fire, but it was an exercise in futility. Klaus charged him. He swung the machete on a straight horizontal plane. Reid stepped back with his right foot and pivoted his left foot while bending and extending his leg and turning to the right. He lowered his body in a forty-five degree angle with his head back safely away from the swing of the machete. The blade hissed viciously as it passed over his back. Reid had positioned his chin on his shoulder, so that he saw everything clearly. He was almost instantly moving. He stepped behind and past his extended left leg with his right, spun, and placed a crushing right elbow into Klaus's ribcage, just as the big freak was attempting to slice Reid in two with a vertical swing from over his head. The swing just missed him, but Reid had cracked three of Klaus's ribs. Klaus was bent at the back with the tip of the machete on the ground in front of him. Reid looked over his left shoulder and spun back to the right. He brought the side of his right hand down at the base of Klaus's head and sent him sprawling to his knees. Klaus's grasp of the machete was lost and it fell to the floor. Reid swooped and picked it up with a two-handed grip. Klaus raised his head to find Reid and when their eyes met, Klaus sprung like a human rocket at Reid. Klaus should have lowered his head like a charging bull, but he did not. Reid threw his weight back on his right foot like an exaggerated "load" for a baseball player preparing to start his swing. And just like he'd been taught by every hitting coach he'd ever had playing baseball, Reid brought his hands through first. He kept his hands inside the target, rotated his hips violently, and brought the barrel of the blade through with vicious velocity, severing Klaus's head at the neck. Blood spewed as Klaus's body crumpled and the head flopped to the ground and rolled. The dead man's head landed upright against a wall, staring wide eyed at the man who had just taken his life.

———

Reid tossed the machete to the ground and went to Millicent. She was screaming, but it was almost totally muted by the gag.

"Millicent, you can't scream when I take this off. You have to be very quiet. Do you understand?" he asked her.

She nodded violently.

He produced his knife and cut the duct tape just as he'd done hours before for the woman at the Motor Lodge. Millicent sobbed audibly. He cut the rope at her feet, leaving the knotted anklet tied at her shins for now. He moved behind the sofa and removed the tape and rope from her wrists. She stood and pulled her thong and shorts up, ignoring the trickle of blood running down her pubic area. Reid tossed her bra to her and shoved her torn shirt in his pocket. He looked for her keys, but didn't see them right away.

Then he saw Klaus's jeans lying on the floor. He grabbed them and searched the pockets. He located Millicent's keys, grabbed her by the arm, and moved her to the door.

"We have to call the police, Salem," she said.

"No," he said and added, "don't make any noise."

She stared at him incredulously but did as he instructed.

He glanced out the door. He had been fortunate. There had been little noise—no gunfire had been a really good thing. The night was quiet, no one was about. He pulled the door and part of the frame up and motioned Millicent outside. She complied and he quickly affixed the door to the space as best he could. Perhaps no one would notice anything until the morning. He grabbed her arm and pulled her down the stairs. He got her into her car and went over to the Accord and set the keys on the rear passenger tire. Then he jumped into her car and fired up her Civic. He drove at a normal speed out of the complex and wound his way to Chamblee Tucker Road.

He took it across Buford Highway towards his condo. He glanced at her. "Do you need medical attention?" he asked.

"No. I'm okay."

Then she shook and started crying. He had to pull over into a gas station about a mile past Buford Highway so she could puke. He held her and stroked her back as she did. He took her torn shirt out of his pocket and handed it to her so she could wipe her mouth.

While she was recovering, he called Ian. He would have liked to have done this out of earshot of Millicent, but he thought now he had no choice. She would need to be briefed. He hadn't expected her to be present when he took out Klaus. That hadn't been the plan; just the reality.

Ian answered on the first ring. "Salem."

"I need you to go to the Chestnut location. Park at the food mart as before. If it all possible, I need you to recover the Accord. Klaus won't bother anyone ever again. If you can't recover the car, let it go. Don't take any chances, Ian. If it's not clear, don't do it. But chances are good if you go now. The rest I'll explain later," Reid said.

"Where do I take the car?" Ian asked.

"Take it to Petey's and call me when you arrive. I'll get you back to your car," he told him.

They disconnected. Millicent was wiping her mouth. She was still crying and shaking, but now she was staring at him strangely. He said nothing else, and drove to his condo. He got her inside the condo and checked her wounds. They were not too bad. He told her to shower thoroughly and then he would clean and disinfect her cuts.

She emerged from the shower after twenty minutes and he thoroughly cleaned her wounds with alcohol. Then he spread an antibiotic ointment on them. He gave her some boxers and one of his tee shirts. She curled into him as she had done numerous times during the past five days. He held her and she cried again. When the tears ceased, she gently pushed him back and looked directly into his eyes.

"I have some questions," she said simply.

"I know. I have many things to tell you, but just a few tonight. Then you sleep. I'll tell you everything in the morning. I promise," he said.

"How did you find me?" she asked.

"I'll elaborate on that tomorrow. But I'll tell you this. I had my eye on Klaus. He was connected to some things that ended up involving me and my past," he said.

"Who did you call? Did you say you drove an Accord?" she asked.

"A friend who does some work for me. The Accord I borrowed from another friend."

"Your friend is going over there? Really?" she asked.

"I'd like to recover the car," he told her.

"Who are you, Salem Reid?" she asked and the strange look returned to her eyes.

He smiled at her and said, "I'm just a guy, Millicent. I care for you. I hope you know that," he added.

"Okay. Thank you for saving my life. But you tell me everything tomorrow," she said, and curled into him again.

Ian called and told him that he had recovered the vehicle, and Petey would drive him to his car, and return the Challenger to Reid.

He told Ian that in the morning when the parking lot at the ARC began to fill up, that he should locate the Tundra and remove the tracking device. It would be too risky to try to move the truck. They would just leave it there.

Reid thanked him and was grateful to Petey. He wanted to stay with Millicent and hold her through the night. He wasn't sure what tomorrow would bring.

# 45

REID AND MILLICENT SLEPT IN HIS BED together; she lay with her head on his chest through most of the night until dawn. Then she rolled onto her side, but stayed close to him as he began to stir. She realized her phone was still in her car; she had not brought it in during the confusion of the evening. She would need to call the ARC and let them know she would not be coming in today. She had a black eye, and wanted to sort through the events of Wednesday night before she returned to work. She wasn't due in until 10, but she wanted to find someone to cover her shift that ran 10 am to 7 pm.

She poked Reid.

"Hey, can I use your phone? Mine is in the car still."

He woke and kissed her on the forehead. She had a nice shiner on her eye. He grabbed his phone from the port on the nightstand, where he charged it, and handed it to her. He moved to the kitchen to give her privacy, and he took the time to make some coffee. He grabbed some ice and Ibuprofen from the kitchen and gave them both to her when he returned.

"I took the day off. I don't want to explain this," she said, and pointed to her eye and gingerly placed the ice bag on it.

They moved to the kitchen and Reid scrambled some eggs and made buttered toast. They ate and drank some apple juice. When they were finished and sitting at the table sipping their coffee, she looked at him again with that strange stare.

"How did you find me?" she asked.

"Tracking device," he told her.

"Tracking device!" she said in disbelief. "You were spying on me?"

"After I learned more about Klaus, I feared for your safety. I wasn't spying on you. I have no idea where your car went until last night," he said.

"When did you install it?"

"Monday morning."

She furrowed her brow thinking, and then the light bulb went off. "Dropping Chap Stick under my car was uncharacteristically clumsy. You did it then," she said.

"You are very smart."

"Don't placate me, Salem." She was visibly angry with him. "And I was thinking that was a very special morning."

"It was a special morning, Millicent. I've enjoyed every minute I've been with you."

He didn't add the obvious exception of Wednesday night.

"You deceived me," she said.

He didn't respond.

She sipped her coffee and glared at him.

She changed course.

"You killed a man last night."

He remained quiet. He knew she would eventually think this through and see that he had no choice.

"Do you like it?" she asked very quietly.

"Like what?" he asked.

"Killing people," she clarified.

"No."

"You've killed others," she said, more as a statement than a question.

He gave her a slight nod but stayed silent.

"Violence follows you," she stated.

He shrugged.

"You told me last night that Klaus was connected to your past. What does that mean?"

"It turns out he murdered a woman whom I knew many years ago," he said.

"How do you know this?" she asked.

"It started with a phone call I received on Saturday right after we had breakfast at the IHOP," he told her.

And then, as best he could, in his usual laconic manner, he told her almost everything. He told her about Joey, how they'd been friends and teammates in high school. He told her about Sarah. He left out details about her sexual appetite; he thought maybe she would figure that out as the story unfolded. But otherwise, he let Millicent get a sense of her personality, and the effect Sarah had had on him. He explained how she had become a dancer and a prostitute, and how this had all been news to him since they'd had no contact in fifteen years. He filled her in on the reaction from the police; how they'd written Sarah's death off as an accidental overdose and had dismissed many of Joey's claims. Reid explained how he'd taken Mrs. Lindstrom to Sarah's apartment to go through her things, but he carefully omitted details of the visit as they pertained to him. He told her about Sarah's parents and the funeral.

Then he told her about tracking Klaus and what they'd discovered from video footage that he and Joey had run down; how they knew he was involved in Sarah's death. He told her about the woman at the Motor Lodge and what Klaus had done to her. Reid explained to Millicent how he was chasing Klaus at the time she had been abducted.

He let her draw her own conclusions about the tracking device on her car. She was smart; she would figure it out.

He would have never told her all of these things in a million years. But because she was now involved and had witnessed him slaying the monster, she would need to know how to play this. She was in the middle of it. He had tried to avoid her being involved like this. He could have coerced her into looking for Klaus's address just like she'd found his, but he wouldn't do that. He had tried hard to protect her, and to keep her out of it. But now she would need to see that she couldn't speak of this to anyone without jeopardizing both of them as well as the other people involved. Ultimately, she would need to understand that he planned to finish the job. He could see that she was beginning to realize how convoluted this all was. He thought now that maybe she would see that he'd had little choice in how he had proceeded.

She gulped and her demeanor noticeably softened.

"Did you love her?" she whispered.

He shrugged.

"I'm not sure what it was. I was impacted by her for sure, Millicent."

"Did she love you?" she asked.

"Maybe she did. I really don't know," he told her.

She stood up and went to him. She sat on his lap and hugged him tightly and then the tears came again. They sat in this position for a long time and he simply held her.

"I've never met anyone quite like you, Salem Reid," she said when she finally stopped crying and spoke. "I forgive you for tracking my car. I will never be able to repay you for what you did for me last night. You saved my life. I'm certain of it now. You make my heart flutter and my nose tingle." She laughed a little at this and it turned into a cough. When she recovered she continued, "But the violence bothers me. I know it is part of who you are. I'm not sure if I can live with that, though. I have a lot to sort through. I hope you understand."

Reid said nothing. There was nothing for him to say. She would need time to think this all through.

"I'll take a leave of absence from work. I'll go home to Huntsville for a spell. I'll visit with Mom and Daddy. I'll leave this afternoon."

He thought that was maybe the best idea. The police would eventually link the Tundra parked at the ARC to the decapitated body at the Chestnut Drive apartment. They would have questions. It would be better for another ARC manager to handle the inquiries. He would be better off riding solo as he pursued the others complicit in Sarah's murder.

And then, just like she had done at her house off Keswick Drive, she slipped out of the boxers and tee shirt. They made love at his kitchen table. They took it slow. It was sad and sweet and wonderful and awful all at the same time for both of them. Afterwards, he carried her to his bedroom and they slept together for a bit. Reid roused first; he saw that it was almost noon. He jumped in the shower while she continued to doze. He was dressed and brushing his teeth when she passed him and got into the shower. He located his tightest pair of shorts and his smallest tee shirt and set them on the toilet seat for her to wear when she was finished showering. He walked her to her car and removed the tracking device. Then he followed her to her house near Keswick Park and helped her pack her bags.

"Text or call me when you get to Huntsville. Okay?" he asked.

She smiled and touched his cheek.

"Okay."

He placed her bags in the trunk and kissed her goodbye, and Millicent Ivey headed off to Alabama.

# 46

JOEY STAYED WITH LIZA all through the night. Around 2 am she had awakened in pain again, and the nurse had come and provided more meds. At 7 am she was groggy, but tolerating the pain moderately well. They had moved her to a room. A doctor and social services had popped in to check on her. She was fairly lucid and responsive and gave the medical personnel permission to speak with Joey about her treatment. Liza had suffered from anal abscesses, and they had been surgically drained when she had first arrived in the emergency room. They were treating her with broad-spectrum antibiotics, and she was responding well to the treatment. They had cleaned the area thoroughly, but she was raw and torn. That had been a major contributor to her pain. It would take a while to heal. She was being given morphine regularly, but they hoped to get her to an oral narcotic within twenty-four hours. Surprisingly, she had tested negative for all other sexually transmitted diseases. They were giving her fluids for dehydration. She said she would be agreeable to making an attempt to eat also. The staff brought in breakfast for her, and they had left it to Joey to try to get her to eat.

Joey opened the container. "Yum, they gave you Jell-O and apple-sauce! Do you have a preference?" he asked her.

"Applesauce," she said, and tried to smile at him, but she didn't quite accomplish it.

He took the spoon and dipped it into the tray. He held it to her lips and she took it. She struggled to swallow, but she was a trooper and tried for a second bite. It went down a little easier.

"Not bad," she said, followed by a sputtering cough. He took a paper napkin that was provided with the meal and wiped her mouth.

Her lips looked better than they did just twelve hours ago. He thought the two skin lesions on her face may have gotten a touch smaller too, but he couldn't be sure. At least they hadn't gotten worse. She took a few more small spoonfuls and then shook her head.

"You did great, Liza!" Joey told her, and this time she managed a weak smile.

He handed her some ice water, and she took a few small sips and pushed it away.

A nurse came in a few minutes later and asked Liza if she was up for a sponge bath. She told her that she could probably get her hair washed too. Liza told the nurse that she would like that and seemed to perk up a little at the prospect of being bathed.

"Look, Liza," Joey said, "why don't you get cleaned up? I need to get some food and make some calls. I'll be back in a bit."

She looked frightened again. "You'll come back?"

"Of course I'm coming back. Can I bring you anything?" he asked.

"No."

"I'm coming back, Liza. I promise."

Joey left the two women and located a cab outside that took him to the Motor Lodge. He retrieved his car and returned to the hospital. He parked and re-entered the hospital where he quickly got breakfast and some surprisingly decent coffee. He called Reid to fill him in but the call went to voicemail so he hung up. He also called his neighbor,

Walt, to have him check on Herschel. He went to a gift store in the hospital and bought a cheap vase and some moderately priced flowers. He also purchased a tube of toothpaste, two toothbrushes, and some mouthwash. He went to the bathroom and cleaned himself up, took care of his oral hygiene, and found the billing administration office. He located an accounts person and squared away the billing arrangements for Liza. Since she had no income or insurance, much of her treatment would be covered. He guessed by Medicaid. There were some aspects of her treatment that would not be covered. He told them to send him the bills, and he covered a small co-payment for her current treatment with his credit card.

He returned to the room, and stood at the door with the flowers and vase behind his back. Liza looked completely different. Her hair had been washed and blown dry and combed out. She had straight brown hair that fell past her shoulders, and looked significantly more luxurious then it had when it was oily and damp. She had been given a sponge bath and clean garments along with some little hospital slippers that were sitting at the edge of the bed. She had pushed the blanket off and the nurse was trying to shave her legs. She had about a six-day growth on her legs; the nurse had finished with her armpits prior to Joey's return.

"Wow!" he said. "You're looking great!"

He produced the vase of flowers, and he could tell she was delighted as much by his return as she had been to receive the flowers. He set the vase on the nightstand and she held her hand out to him.

"I didn't think you'd come back," she said, as a tear rolled down her cheek.

"I told you I would," he said, and took her outstretched hand.

The nurse finished, winked at Joey, and left the room.

He sat down next to her and held her hand. "How are you feeling?" he asked her.

"I feel much better after bathing," she said. "I'm really tired, though."

"I bought us both a toothbrush and some mouthwash. Maybe you'll want them later," he said.

"I'll take some mouthwash now, Joey," she said, and he got a pan for her to spit in.

She rinsed and spat into the pan, and he gave her some water and she spat again. Then she took two healthy gulps of water.

"Much better," she said, and then she laid back and closed her eyes.

She was out in a flash. Joey Mac watched her sleep and never left her side.

# 47

REID HAD ABOUT THIRTY MINUTES before he needed to be at the Starbucks at Perimeter Pointe to meet Lara Brooks. He called Raymond Strickland.

"Well hello, Salem," Ray said as he answered his mobile on the second ring. "To what do I owe this unexpected pleasure? I'm sure you're just calling to say hi, right?"

"I need you to run a couple more plates, Ray," Reid told him.

"Hmmm. Just like that, huh? No foreplay?" Ray asked.

Reid read off the numbers and the vehicle makes and models, ignoring Ray's other remarks. Then he added, "Thanks for your previous work. It was helpful."

"Two, huh? You'll be taking me to Bone's for this one, Salem."

Bone's was one of Atlanta's finest steakhouses, just a few blocks from the Buckhead Diner where they had met before.

"Okay. How fast can you get them?" Reid asked.

"Probably by the end of the day, Salem. Or tomorrow by noon at the latest."

"That's great, Ray. Thanks," Reid said, and clicked off before Ray could prattle on about how indebted Reid was to him.

———

Salem Reid drove down Johnson Ferry where it merged with Ashford Dunwoody and continued outside the Perimeter. He turned left on Perimeter Center West and wheeled in to the big parking lot at Perimeter Pointe. He parked, locked his car, and walked to the Starbucks. He was a few minutes early, so he had time to buy the coffee and be in place before Lara Brooks arrived. He ordered two Grande-sized coffees and found a table in the back as instructed. Then he sat and waited.

About ten minutes passed and then Reid saw a tall, thin, attractive black woman enter the Starbucks. She sported dark-blue women's moclav pants that looked to be a size too big; the kind you can get at most sporting goods outlets. She had on a blue long-sleeve cotton tee shirt that was also a size too large. She wore a dark-blue baseball cap pulled down so that the bill hid some of her face. She had long, straight, black hair pulled into a ponytail that was threaded through the hole in the snapback. She wore dark Nike running shoes and black Ray Bans. She had worn absolutely no jewelry and little or no makeup. She didn't need it; she was very pretty and had great skin. She was dark and had sharp features and full lips. She had tried to look as nondescript as possible, but she looked more like a Hollywood movie star trying to hide in public.

Lara Brooks walked directly to the table where Reid sat with his back to the wall. She did not sit down across from Reid, but came to the far side of the table. Reid had been sitting in the aisle chair, so he moved to his left and she sat down next to him. He caught a faint whiff of scented soap as she slid into the chair he had just vacated. She picked up one of the coffees and removed the top. She inspected the steaming brew that apparently met her requirements, and took a small sip. Then she took another.

"Thanks for coming," he said.

She turned and looked at him for a long moment and said, "Wow. The long-lost Salem Reid." She paused and added, "I want to help. I'm scared, but I'm more angry than scared. These are bad people you're tangling with, Salem."

Lara Brooks had a pleasant voice and she sounded educated and refined. More so than she had sounded on the phone.

"Bad people for sure," he said, holding her gaze.

She took another sip of her coffee and said, "Great coffee. I like Starbucks."

Reid liked Starbucks okay, but he usually bought Dunkin' Donuts coffee. He preferred it, but he didn't mention this to her. Instead he said, "You were close with Sarah, I take it."

"Yes. I wanted to be at her service, but there was no way," she said, and shook her head. "Did you go?"

"Yes. I saw Janice Cooley there and spoke with her. She is frightened too," Reid said to her.

"Yeah. I guess so," Lara replied.

"What can you tell me about a Latin guy who drives a Ford Flex and hangs out at Utopia?" he asked.

She appraised him severely. "You've been to the club?"

"Not inside yet. Who is he, Lara?"

She exhaled audibly. He figured that she realized that once she spoke, there was no going back. But she had called him back and now she had met him. Her decision had already been made.

"Oscar. He runs Utopia, the Slick Kitty, and maybe some club south of town…down by the airport," she said.

"What's his last name?" he asked.

She glanced over at him. "No one knows. Look, Salem, he's not officially the boss. All these clubs have managers and assistant managers that run things. Some of the bouncers have some authority too. But everyone answers to Oscar. He's in charge. People who question his authority get hurt."

"He hurt you?" he inquired.

"He tried to cut my tit off in his lounge. He cut me bad, though. Fourteen stitches and I had an infection. I'm left with a pretty big scar on my right breast. I'm damaged goods for an upscale club like Utopia. He robbed me of my earning power, Salem. He's a bad guy," she said.

"Why'd he do it...other than being a bad guy?"

"He sells dope: weed, coke, meth, heroin, pills. He attempts to get the girls hooked on heroin; he controls them then. They won't leave. He gets them to roll guys—married guys who won't do anything about it usually—in hotels or their homes after tricking with them. He gets the loot and they get a fix. Or maybe they just don't get their tits cut off as a reward. Anyway, I wouldn't use heroin. I've smoked some weed and done some coke, sure, but I wouldn't let him get me on heroin. I don't trick either. He likes to make extra money off his girls. I wouldn't help him. I stood up to him and he cut me. I think he might have kept cutting me, but I got a finger in his eye, escaped the lounge, and then bolted."

She held up a long index finger and poked it to demonstrate her retaliation on Oscar, then she continued, "I've been running ever since. He will kill me if he finds me. I know it."

"When did this happen?" he asked her.

"Towards the end of May," she said, and he figured that would be her answer.

"But Sarah stayed, why?" he asked.

"She wouldn't do smack either, Salem. But she badly sprained an ankle and chipped a bone trying out a new dance move. We have a medical staff of sorts, and they injected her with a pain medication. She realized later that they had used heroin and gotten her hooked on it. She got really pissed when she figured out what they'd done to her. She asked for treatment. Oscar hinted that he would get her some help, but of course, he wasn't going to. To my knowledge, she never even injected the stuff herself. They killed her, Salem, she had become baggage to them," she said, confirming what he'd believed all along.

He looked at her admiringly. She was pretty sharp.

"Why didn't you go to the police?" he asked.

"When he cut me? It's like the guy doesn't exist, Salem. He fades away when the heat is on. No one knows his last name or where he lives. He's not on record at Utopia. What would be the point? I'm sure when he cut me he laid low for a week or so. Sarah or the other girls I talked to didn't see him until ten days after it happened."

"Had Sarah rolled guys before?" he asked.

"Not that I'm aware of, but after the drugs got ahold of her, who knows? She tricked. She liked the money; she made good money as a prostitute. I'm sorry if that bothers you; I know all about y'all. She talked about you sometimes."

"Do you know a guy named Klaus?" Reid asked.

"Oh gross, yes. You have been busy, Salem." She looked at him with new admiration. He had figured some things out. "He's a bouncer at Slick Kitty, but I started seeing him at Utopia sometimes the last few months I was there. Nasty man. He's involved with Oscar. Does things for him. Maybe he's involved with Sarah's death. I really don't know. He's one of his guys. I'd watch out for him," she added.

"What about Janice?" he said.

"She's my friend; I'm afraid for her. I don't think she's on dope. At least she's not on the hard stuff. Like Sarah, she'll turn tricks, but she hasn't rolled anyone to my knowledge," she answered.

"She ran from me when I asked her questions at the service, Lara. She insists that Sarah overdosed, but I can tell she doesn't believe it.

She's afraid," he told her. "If you talk to her, try to get her to leave. She can call me if she needs help. Okay?"

"Okay. Maybe I'll try to talk to her, but I don't know."

"I'm almost finished," he said. "Do you know a blonde who drives a white Lexus?"

She laughed and it made her even prettier. "Alexis Lexus."

"Is Alexis her real name or dance name?" he asked.

She laughed again. "Dance. I don't know her real name. We aren't close. I thought I heard someone call her Betty once, but that can't be right."

"Is that all you know about her?"

"Why? How do you know her, anyway?"

"She was at the service," he told her.

"Really? You are kidding me, right?" she said.

"She was there with Janice and a girl with black hair. Only Janice came to the reception at the church, but Alexis followed her out of the parking lot when she left after the reception."

"Weird," Lara Brooks said, and shrugged. "She hardly knew Sarah. Alexis wasn't one of our girls."

"You disliked her?" he asked.

She thought for a moment. "Look, Salem, this may sound strange coming from a stripper, but we thought something was just wrong about Alexis. Sarah, Janice, and I all thought so. I'm surprised she was there with Janice."

"What's wrong about her?" he asked.

"She just seemed underhanded, not trustworthy. She seemed like one of those chicks who would stab you in the back. We avoided her is all," she answered.

"Lara, you've helped a lot. Is there anything I can do for you?"

She shrugged. "I'm not sure what you can do, period, but I'm hanging in there," she said.

"Do you have a place to stay? Money?" he asked.

"I'm fine, Salem. Really," she said, "I'm just scared."

"Okay. Here's my card. If you need anything from me, just call. Janice too. I can get you in a safe place if needed. Don't be afraid to ask," he said, and stood up. "Thanks."

She stayed seated. "I'm going to finish my coffee. Maybe I'll see you again sometime, Salem. Thanks for caring about Sarah...even after all these years."

Reid nodded and left Lara Brooks sitting alone at the Starbucks.

# 48

REID SAT IN HIS CAR going through his mental notes. He had learned a lot from Lara Brooks. She was a smart, brave woman. He had been impressed by her. Now he had a name for the stocky Latin guy who drove the Flex. He also had some information on how the guy operated that fit his theory flawlessly about what went down at Joey Mac's house Saturday morning. He had learned more about Sarah too. She had likely been tricked into heroin addiction. Maybe at some point he could pass that information to Patsy Lindstrom. He checked his GPS on his phone and entered the address he had for Consuelo Valdez. He thought he'd check on her.

———

Consuelo Valdez had an apartment off of Satellite Boulevard, a little south of Pleasant Hill in Duluth. It was a two bedroom that she kept clean and well maintained. Well, mostly so. Her spare bedroom had evolved into a storage closet for her cleaning supplies, mops, and vacuum cleaners she used on her job. Her complex had a mix of whites, blacks, and Hispanics, but the apartments had become more and more Hispanic over the past several years that she had lived there. She was okay with both whites and blacks; she cleaned the homes of both races. But she was most comfortable around her own people. She could speak Spanish and relax, knowing that she wasn't being judged too harshly.

She had returned home to secure some supplies for her final afternoon job of the day. It was for a wealthy family who had a home in Johns Creek where she usually made a little extra by pocketing some of the spare change that was in just about every room of the spacious home. Then she would come home, clean up, and begin preparations for some chile relleno. She would make her special batch and take some to Oscar on Saturday night when she would go to his home for at least part of the evening. She knew that the way to a man's heart was through his stomach…and maybe a few other parts of his anatomy as well. She giggled a bit when she thought of that. He had told her to come by at 6 pm on Saturday, and she said that she would cook for him. He had seemed pleased. She would do most anything for this man, she figured. She was confident that he was her meal ticket. She was playing this through her mind while she was loading supplies into her Honda CR-V and was totally clueless to the man watching her from a distance in the parking area in front of the building, sitting catty corner from hers. As she pulled out of her space, the man did not follow her as she drove out of her complex onto Satellite and drove north towards Pleasant Hill Road. Instead, he sat calmly and patiently waited.

---

Reid sat in his Challenger for about twenty minutes, then exited his car, and walked to the door he'd seen Consuelo exit. He removed his picks and got to work. This one was easy; it took him less than ninety seconds and he was inside her apartment. The space was clean and neat, but the carpet was old and a little worn. The walls could have used some paint and the furniture was a hodgepodge of odds and ends. But she had made it homey and comfortable. There was a sliding glass door that led to a little porch and then a steep drop off; maybe down into a creek or ravine of some sort. The kitchen was neat, but dated and worn like the living area. The appliances looked old, outdated, and a little tired. She had decorated sparingly, but a picture of a mariachi band playing on a crowded street was resplendent in color and gave the kitchen some life. He opened some drawers and cabinets but noticed only the normal things people kept in their kitchens. Her cupboard was filled with food, much of it Mexican fare like rice and beans and tortillas. Her refrigerator held milk and cheese and meats and peppers. There were sauces and spreads and a six-pack of Corona Light with all of the bottles intact near the back of the fridge. He opened what he guessed were utility drawers. They also contained the usual things people kept in such places: scissors, rubber bands, chip clips, AA batteries, small tools, etc.

He wasted no more time in her kitchen. He moved down the hallway that led towards the two bedrooms. There was a bathroom off the hall on the left that connected to what appeared to be a spare bedroom. The bathroom was clean, neat, and tidy. It looked little used. The door leading to the room from the bathroom to the spare was closed. He opened it and peeked in. It was mostly storage for her cleaning supplies, but it also contained a desk that was pushed to a corner of the room near the window on the back wall. He guessed she used the desk for the clerical aspects of her business. She had an older computer and printer sitting on the desk. The monitor was on and had a screen saver that displayed fish swimming in calm ocean waters.

He decided to check her supply room last. He closed the door and moved to the master. She had a full-size bed, neatly made. A dresser with a mirror attached to it covered most of the adjacent wall. A fairly new thirty-two-inch TV sat on the corner, and a DVD player sat underneath it. She had a simple nightstand with two drawers. A few uninteresting prints were on the wall; maybe something she had picked up at Target or Wal-Mart in an effort to spruce up the otherwise dull space. Her top dresser drawer was filled with underwear and a number of lacy thongs. Reid had watched her from a distance, but based on the way she moved, he guessed that she was between twenty-five and forty. Perhaps his search would narrow those parameters. If not, he would consult Joey. The lacy thongs and stylish undergarments suggested youth, but in reality he was sure that many middle-aged women wore thongs at times. He pushed around her garments and noticed nothing unusual. He checked her other drawers. She had some simple jewelry in the other top drawer; nothing that looked expensive, though, so he continued on. She had mostly clothing in the bigger sections: short pants and tee shirts, socks and some nightgowns. One bottom drawer was a catch-all or junk drawer. The place people threw the things they felt they shouldn't discard, but weren't really sure what to do with them: old photo albums, birthday cards, and letters. There was a deck of playing cards that looked unused, a brochure from Stone Mountain Park, and an atlas.

Reid moved to her nightstand. She had some boxer shorts in the top drawer that he guessed were made for women to sleep or traipse around the house in. There were some eye drops and a few Spanish magazines that looked like something a younger woman might be interested in. A box of Kleenex and a couple of coasters were also in the drawer.

The bottom drawer was more personal. There was a box of condoms, some lubricant, and a moderate-sized purple vibrator. He was a little surprised to see that she had two porn DVD videos at the back of the drawer. There were a couple of clean white towels in there as well.

He closed the drawer and looked under her bed. He saw only a spare pillow in a plastic zippered bag and a spare comforter in a larger plastic bag. He moved to the closet, but he saw only skirts, pants, shirts, blouses, a few decent dresses, and shoes mostly. The skirts were similar and he guessed she wore them during the warmer months of the year on the job.

Her bathroom consisted of the usual products that women use: soaps, shampoos, perfumes, and sprays. Her medicine cabinet contained Tylenol, Advil, and other OTC drugs that were perfectly ordinary in any bathroom. He saw no birth control pills. Maybe she kept them in her purse, used some type of device, or perhaps relied solely on the condoms she had in her nightstand.

He exited her bedroom and went into the spare. He went to her desk and touched the external mouse. The computer screen came to life. He examined her desktop. She had maybe a dozen or so icons on it. The third one down was an accounting program he recognized. He clicked it. He tabbed through several screens until he found a database of what appeared to be her customers. He scrolled down to the M's and found Joey's name and address. He scrolled to the bottom and realized that she had well over a hundred entries on this spreadsheet. He would not have time to sit and read them all now. He needed to finish up and get out of there. He'd already been in there over twenty minutes; he guessed based on the items he saw her pack in her Honda that she would be gone for at least a couple of hours. But he figured anything over thirty minutes ran the risk of him being present when she returned exponentially higher. He selected the print option. Nothing happened. He glanced over at the printer and saw that it was turned off. He turned it on and it kicked into life. The printer spat out six or seven pages, and he was glad to see that it was formatted so that it printed all of the data within the margins on the portrait setting. He would not need to spend extra time and fool with various settings to get his printouts. He turned the printer off and exited the program. He pocketed the printed sheets. He would like to have searched other components of her computer, but he wanted to check the little closet; there wasn't time to do both.

He opened the closet. There were some zippered sweatshirts and hoodies hanging in the closet along with a heavier winter down jacket. A clear plastic container on the shelf above held gloves, hats, and scarves. On the floor was a larger black plastic container. He removed the top. It looked like a treasure chest of sorts. There was loose change; lots of it. There were coin rolls; both full and unused. There were loose bills as well as paper money in stacks that had rubber bands wrapped around them. Sticky notes were attached to them. The yellow notes all had the number 100 written on them except for one. The number 50 was written on it and it was half the size of the others. He guessed that she had over $1,000 in cash in the container. Maybe another $200 in change. There were a few decent-looking pieces of jewelry in the container too. He closed the container and the closet, and looked around her storage room. He returned to the desk and opened the drawers. Mostly it was storage for paper, and other office essentials like paper clips, envelopes, and Scotch tape. He looked around the space once more to confirm that it was exactly how he'd found it. He moved to the hallway and into the living room. He went to the door and locked it from the inside, then proceeded to the sliding glass door. He unlocked it and slipped out onto the little porch. He closed the sliding glass door, and then moved down the incline, and then back up it on the far end of the building. He moved onto a sidewalk between Consuelo's building and the one adjacent. Two young black girls were using colored chalk to make a hopscotch grid on the sidewalk. They stopped and stared at him as he moved towards them. Reid smiled and moved off the walk onto the grass to avoid interfering in their game. They resumed as he passed. He did not turn around to look at them, and he continued walking past his vehicle when he reached it. He strolled around the side of the next building and saw no signs of the girls, so he backtracked to his car and got in. He exited the complex by driving away from Consuelo's building and circling around two more buildings before finding the main drive that would lead him back to Satellite Boulevard. He saw no signs of the little girls as he drove away.

---

Reid drove south on Satellite to Beaver Ruin Road, then went west towards downtown Norcross. Afternoon traffic was heavy but it was moving. Reid turned south at Buford Highway and continued through Doraville and into Chamblee. He took Chamblee Tucker over to Peachtree Road, then turned on Malone towards his condo. He parked and pulled out his iPhone. It was just before 5 pm and he felt fortunate that he had beaten the worst of Atlanta's rush-hour traffic. There was a text from Millicent at 4:40 pm: "I made it home to Huntsville. Talk soon."

There were no smiley faces or emoticons in her text.

He texted back: "Glad you're safe." He left it at that.

He saw he had a missed call from Joey, so he dialed him up. Joey answered on the fourth ring.

"Hey, Salem," he said. "Our girl is doing much better. Her name is Liza. She's scared, but sweet; I'm still at the hospital with her. I think they may release her tomorrow if her infection will respond to oral antibiotics."

"That's good, Joey. Have the police talked to her?" Reid asked.

"Yes. But she just told them she was raped at the Motor Lodge and that I saved her. She's not clear on everything that happened. I don't think she remembers much about last night. She was pretty much out of it. She gave only sketchy details about the guy who did it. She said he was just some big, ugly guy in a room there. Then she said she was tired. So they left her alone and took off."

"Okay. They will probably check out the room," Reid said.

"Yeah. They talked to me some, but I told them I really didn't know anything more than she told them. I slipped out and got my Expedition, so everything is cool. I think you have been left out of it, best I can tell."

"Okay. Good."

"How old is your maid, Consuelo Valdez?" Reid asked.

"Consuelo? I don't know. Thirty maybe," Joey said. "I told her I didn't need the house cleaned for a while. She used a hide-a-key to get in and I removed it. I plan to get the locks changed this week-end," he added.

"Okay. Let me know if you need anything, Joey. It sounds like you got it covered," he said, and disconnected.

Reid texted Ray: "I'm home. Come by when you get a chance this evening."

Then he climbed the stairs to his condo. He figured he'd make some food, grab a beer, and start on the list he printed at Consuelo's before Ray showed up.

Reid popped open one of the Sam Adams beers that Millicent brought over the previous Friday. He started an omelet and then called Ian.

"Salem," Ian said, answering on the first ring.

"How'd it go with the device?" Reid asked.

"I've got it. No problem," Ian said.

"How'd the job go last night? Did you keep the girls from ripping off Vance's V-neck?" Reid asked. Vance Fite was known for wearing V-neck tee shirts on stage. Teenage girls often decided they should have the V-necks for themselves.

"We kept the girls away from him and the jealous boyfriends too." Ian laughed. "It went real smooth."

"Great. Can you swing by in an hour? I will fill you in on every-thing," Reid told him.

"It might be closer to two…maybe an hour and a half if I'm lucky. Will that be okay?" Ian asked.

"Sure," Reid responded, and clicked off.

———

Reid ate his omelet and cleaned up. He was sitting down to look over the printed spreadsheet that contained Consuelo's customers when there was a tap on the door.

"Hi, Salem, thanks for inviting me up…finally!" Raymond Strickland said as he walked through the door Reid held for him.

He was carrying a moderately sized soft leather briefcase. He sat down at the kitchen table and extracted several folders. Then he looked around.

"Wow, Salem, you have a great place here. Very nice!" Ray seemed genuinely impressed.

"Can I get you a beer, Ray? I have Blue Moon or Sam Adams."

Ray considered that for a moment. "I'll have a Blue Moon."

Reid got Ray his beer, popped the top, and placed it in front of him. Ray looked at the bottle as if someone had just thrown a mutilated dead opossum next to him.

"May I have a glass…please, Salem?"

Reid brought him a glass and set it down, and Ray looked up at him patiently. Reid took the hint and poured Ray's beer for him.

"Anything else, Ray, or can we get started?" Reid asked.

"Okay. Sit down and I'll show you what I have."

Reid sat and Ray pulled a few papers from the first folder. "The Ford Flex is registered to Worldwide Entertainment. They are based in New Jersey. They own strip clubs, adult novelty stores, and have a stake in a casino in Atlantic City. They also operate online porn sites and run a few high-end escort services. That's their legitimate business…shady, but legit," he said. "They are rumored to be involved in drugs and prostitution…big surprise!"

"Is there an individual name you can tie to it?" Reid asked.

"No. I'm sorry. Doesn't tell you much, huh?" Ray asked.

"Some," Reid answered. "Did you get a VIN number?"

"Yes. It's in the package."

"Great. That may help."

"The Lexus is registered to a Bethany Lauren Bertrand. She is twenty-six years old. She grew up in Baton Rouge, Louisiana. She graduated high school and spent one year at LSU before dropping out. She then moved to Atlanta and has been employed by various strip clubs as an entertainer since arrival. The last two years at Club Utopia," Ray told him, and read off a Roswell address on Holcomb Bridge Road.

Lara had told Reid that she thought she'd heard someone call Alexis Lexus, "Betty," but said that couldn't be right. Bethany was very close. He was pretty sure he had her identity.

"Any arrests for Bethany?" Reid asked.

"Why yes, Salem. She was arrested in college for solicitation charges. She paid a fine and got a year of probation," Ray said. "She also was arrested for conspiracy to commit fraud, but I don't have any details. The charges were eventually dropped," he finished.

Reid thought about this. He was concerned for Janice Cooley. Lara had said that Alexis Lexus was not a friend; someone that the three girls had not cared for. But she had shown up at Sarah's service and then waited and followed Janice from the lot. She would be worth looking into; he had a bad feeling about this girl, and she had seen Reid and Janice in the parking lot talking and witnessed the confrontation that followed. Another concern that Reid had was about Klaus. Oscar would soon realize that his lackey was out of the picture; this would put him on alert and make tracking the guy more difficult.

Reid thanked Ray and whisked him out of his condo. He thought he'd at least go over a couple pages of the spreadsheet before Ian showed up. The list was alphabetical, so he started at the top and thoroughly combed over the names and addresses. It looked like she mailed invoices to most of her clients. He occasionally came across an entry that only listed a name; no address or phone number. In the space where the address normally was recorded, it simply said CASH. Reid reasoned that these clients likely left cash on site, and did not receive a bill. Therefore, there was no reason to enter an address into the spreadsheet for mailing. He guessed she had either a notebook or smartphone where she kept all of the addresses where she cleaned. Reid refined his search and checked only the cash entries. When he got to the last page near the bottom, he spotted it. Oscar Villanueva was entered as the penultimate client. There was no address for Oscar. It simply said CASH.

Oscar was a reasonably common Latin name. It could be coincidence, but the fact that he was a CASH customer was fitting with what Reid had learned about him. And now he possibly had a last name for the guy. He wasn't sure it would help, but it sure didn't hurt. Salem Reid would have a busy Thursday night.

# 49

OSCAR VILLANUEVA DID NOT LIKE that Klaus was not answering his calls. He wanted him for another job, and the window of opportunity was slim. If Klaus did not return his call soon, he would be very displeased. He had made excellent money using the big bouncer, and did not relish the thought of breaking in someone new. He had a few candidates on the back burner, but the process would cost him time and money. The more he considered the problem, however, he thought that perhaps Klaus had possibly found some kind of trouble. In the time they had worked together, the big man had never once failed him. Klaus was making very good money doing these jobs for him too. It was simply not in Klaus's interest to be unresponsive.

So something was not right, he decided, and when these situations arose, he had learned to lie low. He could afford to do so, certainly. His drug and prostitution sales were running near an all-time high. His looting business had exceeded his wildest dreams. Maybe he could spend a little time on the Southside at his club on Stewart Avenue. Perhaps he could also enjoy that juicy Mexican girl, Consuelo, a little more often. He usually did not mix business with pleasure, but with her, it might not turn out so bad. Of course, should she get out of line, she would be easy to straighten out. That was rarely a problem for him; he had straightened out many young women.

He had another concern as well. He had sent one of his dancers, Alexis, who had been a reliable ally and supporter of his for a few years to Velvet's funeral. He wanted her friend, Janice Cooley, watched. Janice, or Destiny, was a good moneymaker as a dancer and prostitute, but she had been close to Velvet. He was sure that she had some suspicions of him in regards to Velvet's death. He believed that little would come of it; he knew that the dancers feared him, but he could never be absolutely certain that they wouldn't talk. He was reasonably well insulated, but he knew to be careful nonetheless. But Janice had gone to the service, the reception, and then home. Alexis had reported that she had been involved in a heated discussion with a guy in the parking lot who had attended the funeral. He appeared to be a family friend or relative. He was a big and imposing figure who seemed to be pumping Janice for information, but it appeared to Alexis as if Janice had resisted. She had also seemed frightened. Alexis had done well, though. She had gotten a fairly decent shot of the guy on her phone and texted it to him. Oscar would be on the lookout for this guy should he come sniffing around, whoever he was. He was unsettled that someone was possibly making inquiries about Velvet's death.

Lara Brooks was a thorn in his side too. She was in the wind. He had been trying to locate her for months, but had been unsuccessful. No crazy bitch was going to poke him in the eye and get away with it. The pain had been significant, and he had temporarily lost sight in his eye. Because of that, she had escaped. But he would find her eventually and she would be eliminated...slowly and painfully for what she had done to him. He had wondered too, if she would possibly show up to the service. He had seriously doubted that she would attend. He turned out to be correct, Lara had not come to her friend's funeral. He had gone to her Sandy Springs apartment a number of times looking for her, but it had been abandoned. He had leaned heavily on Janice, but she claimed to have lost contact with her. He had thought that possible too. It made sense that if Lara Brooks were to survive Oscar, she would not be able to have contact with her old friends; at least not very easily. But he would find her one day, and she would pay.

# 50

REID CALLED PETEY WARD and arranged for another car. Petey told him he had a six-year-old, dark-blue Nissan Maxima with tinted windows. He also told Reid that he had the other items he had requested too. Reid would pick up the car and drops, then he wanted to return to the apartment of Consuelo Valdez. He would wait until after 11 pm to go to her home. Then he'd park his loaner in the parking lot at Utopia and keep his eye out for the Flex and Alexis's Lexus.

Ian showed up a little past 8 pm. He came in and dropped the tracking device he had removed from the Tundra on Reid's kitchen counter.

"Local news is running a story you might want to hear, Salem."

Reid turned on his television in the living room and flipped channels until he found a local newscast. A local anchor was on the set with a "breaking news story."

Ronald Klausen Vormer of Doraville was found dead in his apartment off Chestnut Drive today. Police were alerted to Vormer's unit late this afternoon when a neighbor noticed the door was awkwardly leaning against the frame. The police arrived and found

Vormer naked and decapitated in his living room. Police say that a machete found on the floor was possibly used in the violence and that rope had been tied to the sofa in what appeared to be restraints. Police have refrained from speculating on what occurred in the apartment at this time, but investigators are currently combing the property for more details surrounding the death.

Reid turned off the TV and nodded at Ian. "Thanks for bringing the device."

Reid filled Ian in on all the details he had since they had last spoken. "Meet me at Utopia tonight around midnight. Oscar will know by then that somebody's after him. Let's turn up the heat. I'm heading to Petey's soon."

Ian left and Reid called Lara Brooks. She answered on the second ring. "Salem?" she asked.

"Yeah. I need to get in touch with Janice," Reid said.

"What's wrong?" she asked in a nervous voice.

"I'm even more concerned for her safety now than I was yesterday," he said. "She could be in trouble."

"I haven't contacted her since May; I can't, Salem, it would put us both in danger," she said.

"Will you give me her number?" he asked.

She hesitated, then finally replied, "Okay. I'll send you her contact info."

"Do you think she works tonight?" he asked.

"I don't know; she probably does, but I can't say for sure," she answered.

"Okay. Thanks, Lara. I'll try to locate her and see what I can do," he said, and clicked off.

Janice's contact information arrived as a text message within minutes. He called her. The call went to a personalized voicemail and it was definitely her voice.

"Hi. It's Janice. I can't take your call, so leave a message or send me a text. Bye!" the message said.

He clicked off and texted her: "Call me. It's important. Reid."

Then he got dressed in black cargos and a long-sleeve black nylon shirt. He put on the Yankees hat and gathered all the gear together that he would need for the evening, including the tracking device, and placed it in his duffel. He called Petey and said he could meet him at his place at 10 pm.

Reid flipped through the news channels while he waited. He had another forty-five minutes before he would need to leave. He saw a report on a different channel that was similar to the one before, but nothing new had been revealed by the police. He decided to leave a bit early to swing by the ARC and check to see if the Tundra was still parked in the lot. He drove north on Ashford Dunwoody and pulled into the parking lot of the ARC. He drove through the parking lot and saw the Tundra not too far from where he'd seen it parked almost a week before. It looked as inconspicuous as any other vehicle parked there. He guessed it might take several days before the ARC personnel noticed that it had sat several nights in the lot without being moved. Then they might have it towed or possibly call the police. He suspected that the police would begin looking for it soon, though. Perhaps they had already begun the search. The ARC and the apartment complex on Chestnut were both in DeKalb County, but the apartments were in the city of Doraville and the ARC was in newly incorporated Brookhaven. He knew that law enforcement had databases to share information and it was likely available in real time, but if different forces were involved it could possibly create some delays.

Reid exited the ARC parking lot and took Ashford Dunwoody over to Peachtree where it dumped in near Patterson's Funeral Home. He wheeled through Brookhaven and took North Druid Hills over to Buford Highway. He arrived just after 10 pm and met Petey inside in his office. Petey handed him two S&W 22 compacts wrapped in cloth that were not traceable. Reid gloved up and placed one in his hip holster and then strapped the other to his ankle. Petey walked him through the dimly lit parking lot to the six-year-old Maxima. Petey had his mechanic check the car thoroughly, and he assured Reid that it was in great shape and ready to go. It had almost a full tank of fuel. As they stood outside, Reid briefed Petey on the events of the past twenty-four hours. He trusted this man completely, just as he trusted Ian.

Petey spoke, "I'm in on this tonight, Salem. You and Ian could use another hand. I just don't like fuckers like these guys...abusing women, stealing shit from people, selling hard drugs, and generally fucking people over! So I'm in," he repeated.

Reid didn't speak at first. Petey was a big, tough guy, there was no question about it. But he was in his mid-fifties and had gotten a little heavy over the past few years. He had a lot of muscle, but was adding some fat on top of that muscle. It could slow him down if things got tight. On the other hand, Petey could be very useful. And he had offered, after all.

"Okay, Petey. Thanks. Just ride with me then," Reid said. "I need to check on the maid first and see what she's up to. You ready?"

"Give me a few minutes to lock up and set the alarm," he said, and headed back into the building.

Reid transferred his duffel and a few other items to the Maxima, got in and fired it up. The car idled smoothly. It would work just fine. He adjusted the seats, mirrors, and AC. He was familiarizing himself with the car's features as Petey came out and climbed in the passenger seat. They drove north on Buford Highway through the southeastern part of Chamblee, to Doraville, and continued outside of the Perimeter into Gwinnett County. They entered Norcross and turned east at Beaver Ruin Road. They went north at Satellite Boulevard and cruised into Consuelo's complex. There was a little activity in one of the front buildings. A group of young Latinos and

Latinas were starting the weekend early and having a little party that had spilled out onto a couple of porches and the surrounding grassy areas. There were maybe a dozen or so people outside, but they weren't too loud or rowdy, yet.

Reid parked near where he had parked last time, and he and Petey sat for about fifteen minutes watching the area around her building. He had spotted the maid's Honda CR-V when they had driven through the parking lot in front of her building when they had first approached. He figured she was likely in her unit, but he supposed she could possibly be partying with the group in the front of the complex. He considered going around the back of her unit, down the incline on the far side of her building, and then back up near her porch to see if her unit was lit, but ultimately decided against it. If she were out on foot in the complex, he would just have to risk it. He would just need to be quick. He waited for the occupants of a car that had pulled up to the building across from hers to exit the vehicle and go into their apartment, but the couple stayed inside the car for a bit. When they exited he saw what he thought was a young white guy with a black girl about the same age get out of the car. They embraced and kissed for a moment, but then he heard some raised voices and what probably was the girl's father appear in gym shorts and a tee shirt. He was yelling at his daughter and then started in on the kid. The dad was a big, beefy guy and was apparently unhappy that his daughter had been kept out past her 10 pm curfew. The dad whisked his daughter into the apartment and turned to have a few words with the kid. Reid could tell that the kid was intimidated, but he stood and listened to what the man had to say. The dad seemed to be fighting to control himself, but he eventually placed a hand on the kid's shoulder and the kid started nodding. Then the dad gave him a couple of pats on the shoulder and pointed to the car. Reid was relieved that it was only a concerned parent looking after his daughter and that any kind of altercation was avoided. He didn't want a patrol car coming through the complex. The man walked back to his apartment and the kid got into his car and drove away. It got quiet then, but Reid gave it another ten minutes before he moved.

Reid exited the Maxima and headed for Consuelo's vehicle. He moved smoothly through the lot and when he reached her car, he moved in between it and an old Chevy van that had been converted to a work vehicle of some sort. There were long PVC pipes strapped to the top of the van; he guessed that the van was a work truck for some sort of irrigation company that installed lawn sprinklers. The van was good cover from that side. He took one last look around, then slipped quickly under the Honda and attached the device. He was in and out in no time. Just before he started to slip out between the vehicles, he noticed a car slowly cruising through the lot towards him. He moved to the front of the van and knelt between the van and a sickly row of shrubs that sat just beyond the curb separating it and the cracked cement walk that ran in front of the building. As the car approached, Reid saw that it was a Gwinnett County patrol car. He stayed low and still just behind the right tire of the van. He hoped that he was not visible from the apartments. His dark clothing and the neglected shrubbery probably gave him enough cover during the dark hours, but he would have trouble if the car stopped and an officer spotted him. The patrol car stopped, but Reid didn't move and then it slowly rolled forward and stopped again about three spaces beyond the van. Reid listened for a car door opening, but heard nothing. Then the police car drove off and out of sight. Reid waited for another five minutes and then moved slowly along the shrubs and the curb away from the van and back towards the Maxima where Petey waited inside the car. But the car was gone. Reid moved into the shadow of a building to try to decipher what was happening and where Petey had gone. Perhaps when he spotted the cops, he was spooked sitting in a car with stolen plates. Maybe he took off and would return when he felt the coast was clear. Or worse, the cops had Petey and were questioning him. He checked his phone, but hadn't expected a text. Guys like Petey who were in their mid-fifties and owned body shops didn't do a lot of texting. He set his phone from silent to vibrate, thinking it possible Petey would call. He didn't, but within several minutes the Maxima slowly pulled through the lot and Reid walked out of the shadows and met him close to where they had parked. Reid slid into the passenger seat and Petey drove off.

"I saw the police and figured I better not be sitting around in this car; I parked catty-corner at the Shell station across the street. When I saw them leave, I gave it a couple minutes and came back. Sorry, Salem, I didn't know what else to do," Petey said.

"It's all you could do, Petey. We're good."

Reid glanced at his watch and saw it was nearing midnight. He texted Ian: "Running a few minutes behind."

They took Beaver Ruin west and went through downtown Norcross, passing Mojito's where he'd dined with Millicent just a few nights ago. Now it seemed like forever. They took Holcomb Bridge up to PIB and went south towards Utopia. The nighttime traffic was light and they arrived at Utopia a few minutes after midnight. They cruised the entire parking lot, but didn't see the Flex. They did, however, spot the white Lexus owned by Alexis Lexus, or Bethany Bertrand. Janice's baby Benz was in the lot too, Reid had never gotten a response from her, so he was relieved that he now had her located. They did not spot Ian, but Reid knew he was there. He called Ian, and he answered on the first ring.

"Salem."

"We are in a dark-blue Maxima with tinted windows," Reid told him. "We will sit in the lot and observe for a while and then go inside. Petey is with me."

"I see the Lexus and the Benz, Salem," Ian told him.

"Good. Petey and I will get an angle on the other side of the building along the street where we can see the back door should the Flex pull up. He could still be inside, though. Let's not discount him just because we don't see his vehicle," Reid said.

They disconnected and waited. The evening was about to get interesting.

# 51

OSCAR KNEW HE NEEDED TO STAY AWAY from Utopia for a few days; maybe even a little longer. He sensed that someone was looking for him, but he wanted to figure out who it was. He had been hunted many times before so he knew the feeling well. Janice's demeanor and what Alexis Lexus had witnessed following the funeral concerned him. The guy in the picture Alexis had taken looked like a cop. Maybe he was. Oscar would get more information from Janice—or Destiny, as he usually referred to her—even if he had to beat it out of her. He had learned about Klaus's untimely demise as well. He wondered if the guy asking questions at the funeral had something to do with it. He would find out.

He had arrived at the club at 10:30 pm and met in his lounge with a client who distributed "product" for him. They had made the quick exchange of cash and drugs, and the client had departed immediately out the back door. He did not store drugs in his lounge; he kept them at his house in Norcross or in the storage facility that he rented. But it was safest to meet his business partners in the lounge at Utopia where his privacy was respected. He had parked his Ford Flex across the street in the hardware store lot. A bouncer whom he relied on had picked him up from the lot and brought him over, where he had entered through the back door. After meeting with his client, he had enjoyed a few drinks, a little food from the kitchen, and had been orally serviced by one of the dancers. Now he was watching the *Tonight Show* and considering how he would deal with Destiny. The crowd was starting to thin a bit, and he figured soon he would have someone bring her back for a little chat. He needed to get to the bottom of this and soon. He had every intention of accomplishing that goal early this Friday morning.

———

Reid glanced at his watch and saw that it was 1:15 am. He called Ian.

"Let's head in. Pay the cover like normal customers. Order a drink. Then we will see what happens."

The three men convened at the entrance and strolled in. The big guy at the door looked tired and grumpy; he wasn't pleased to see three guys walking in as most of the guys were heading out. He tried to discourage it.

"Ten dollar cover and we close in forty-five," he said, and was surprised when all three men handed over the cash and walked past him as he placed the money in his pocket.

There were maybe twenty guys hanging out watching the last few dances. There were perhaps six girls working the stage and floor. He spotted Bethany Bertrand right away. She was working the main stage, and was completely naked. She had a stack of bills in her garter, and when she turned and shook her backside, he got a glimpse of the Lexus symbol tattooed on her left hip. She was working a couple of guys who must have been in their early twenties, but looked eighteen, for the last few bucks of the evening. The trio of men sat on stools at the back of the club, so he didn't think she would recognize him. She had seen him once in a suit, and now he was in casual clothes with a cap pulled low.

He thought as long as he kept his distance that his identity would not be revealed. He wanted it that way for now.

The waitress came by and tried to be cheerful, but she couldn't quite pull it off.

"What can I get you guys?" she asked, as she threw down three cocktail napkins.

The men all ordered Budweiser in a bottle. The waitress gave them a weak nod and left them to get their beers. Reid scanned the room for Janice, but didn't see her. Her Benz had been parked in the lot when they entered, so he thought it very likely that she was still in the club. Their beers came just as Alexis was finishing with the young guys. She glanced over at the three men and Reid tapped Ian. As Alexis was making her way to the table, Ian stood up and intercepted her halfway. He got her turned around and paid her for a table dance. He tipped her generously as the song continued and then offered to buy her a drink as it finished. Reid glanced at his watch again. It was 1:45.

———

Janice felt like vomiting when a bouncer took her by the arm as she exited the VIP room into the hall and told her that Oscar wanted a word with her. She had been in the room with an older married guy who came to the club regularly, and she had no idea that Reid and his entourage had entered the club. She put on her best poker face and tried on a smile as she entered Oscar's lounge. Oscar was sitting on the sofa with his feet propped on his coffee table watching late night TV when Janice entered.

"Lock the door," he told her, and she did as instructed. She didn't relish the idea of sex with this man, but if that was all he wanted she would just go with it.

She locked the door and turned back to him; he stared at her for a long moment. Then he finally spoke.

"Sit," he commanded her as if she were a dog, much the way he had spoken to Velvet. She sat on the opposite end of the couch from him.

He glanced back at the TV for several minutes and then turned his gaze back on her. He gave her a vicious and evil grin and said, "Take off all of your clothes."

Again she did as instructed.

She tried another smile hoping still that all he wanted from her was sex.

"Spread your legs wide and hold your ankles up in the air."

Again she complied.

And then before she realized what was happening, he was on her. In the blink of an eye, he had wielded his knife and moved down the sofa next to her. He had the blade on the outer lip of her vagina as he held the inside with his thumb. She felt the sharp, cold steel against her sensitive skin. She wanted to scream, but she made no sound and held perfectly still.

"I have some questions for you, and you will answer every one of them or I will slice your pretty pussy into shreds," he said.

––––––––

Right at 2 am the bouncers walked the floor and encouraged the patrons to find their way to the exit. The dancers said their goodbyes to the men they had been entertaining, and moved to their lounge and dressing area as the last song of the night faded out. But Reid and his two partners sat at the table in the back corner of the emptying room sipping their beers. They made no move to leave.

A big, muscular guy who was probably six feet, three inches and weighed about 260 ambled over and curtly said to Reid, "Club's closed. Exit the building."

"No," Reid said.

The big bouncer looked at him like he had two heads. For a moment, he didn't seem to know how to respond, then he moved in close to Reid and grabbed his left arm thinking he would help Reid to the door. But before the bouncer had a firm grip, Reid rotated the guy's wrist so that his thumb was pointing out and slightly up. Then Reid brought the heel of his right hand down hard on the guy's arm, just centimeters above his elbow. The loud pop was quickly muted by the guy's shriek. Reid utilized the bouncer's downward momentum and rode him to the ground. But now, two more big men were scurrying across the room to aid their buddy.

Bouncer types look very imposing. That's why they are used in clubs; to intimidate the masses and keep them in line. But guys like these are rarely skilled fighters. For one, they have usually been big and imposing all their lives, so the average person would avoid getting into an altercation with them. Consequently, they have rarely been in fights other than to bully smaller people who defer to their size. They lack experience. Also, they lack flexibility. They spend hours in the weight room bulking up. They are strong, but often slow and inept at controlling a skilled opponent because their movement is limited due to sheer mass. These two muscle heads charging across the club were no exception. Reid threw a pair of plasticuffs to Petey as the bouncers approached.

"Cuff that guy and find Janice," Reid told Petey.

Petey quickly put the restraints on the bouncer who screamed again when his arm was pulled behind him.

Ian had stepped in front of Reid to intercept the first attacker. Usually, a guy as big as the second bouncer will throw a wild haymaker. Ian was anticipating it. But the guy surprised Ian by stepping in and throwing a straight right at Ian's head. Ian stepped slightly to his left, and caught the guy's wrist as it was sizzling past his head. Ian used his left hand to cup the back of the guy's head and drove a hard bony knee straight into his gut. All the air went out of bouncer number two and he bent forward at the waist. Ian didn't release his grip on the man's head but did release the grip on his arm. He clasped both hands at the base of the guy's neck and pulled his face downward as he simultaneously brought his knee up again, this time straight into the bouncer's nose. Then he grabbed the guy's scruffy hair and pushed his head to the side, exposing his jawline. He directed a precise chop onto the guy's jaw just beyond the ear that knocked him out cold.

Reid was busy with bouncer number three. The guy had taken a few wild swings at Reid and then had tried for a bear hug. Reid ducked and slid deftly behind number three and in the same movement brought his left arm around the guy's neck. Reid grabbed his own right bicep with his other hand and placed his right hand on the back of the guy's head. He squeezed his elbows together while keeping his body snug against the bouncer's. The rear naked choke worked flawlessly in fewer than ten seconds. The guy was dazed and sputtering. Reid flipped him over with some effort and cuffed him.

———

After cuffing the first bouncer, Petey Ward had drifted down the hallway behind and beyond the main stage. He peeked into the dancers' lounge and asked a black-haired girl with pale skin and a lot of ink if she could identify Janice Cooley for him. She told him that Janice wasn't in the dressing area, and that he was not permitted back there either. Petey apologized and moved down the hall. There were a number of doors on both sides of the hallway leading to the back door. He opened the first door on the right and it appeared to be what he guessed was the VIP room. He saw some faux leather sofas and a table in the corner where a dimly lit lamp sat. There was an opening at the far end covered only by a curtain. He guessed that was likely the entrance from the main floor into the VIP room. He moved to a door on the left. He quietly opened the door and saw a surprisingly nice office, but it too was empty. The third door he tried was on the right side of the hall and was some sort of storage space. He quietly approached the last door on the left and tried the handle. It was locked. He listened and could hear what he believed was a menacing male voice, but he could not make out the words.

Then he heard a shriek and a female voice scream, "OH MY GOD! PLEASE! NOOOOOOO!"

———

Janice Cooley knew she was in trouble. She had considered leaving Atlanta ever since her friend, Sarah Lindstrom, had wound up dead. Her gut had told her to get away from Oscar and Utopia and move elsewhere. She had thought about Miami or Los Angeles. The problem was that she absolutely loved Atlanta. Prior to last May when all of this craziness began, she had truly enjoyed her job. She liked dancing and she even enjoyed having sex with men and getting paid to do it. She understood the risks, of course, but she liked it nonetheless. But then Lara had run away and Sarah had changed; she guessed it was the injury and the drugs that did her in. And then Oscar had been leaning on her for information, and now he was demanding it. And he had a sharp knife on her genitals to prove he meant business.

"Who is the guy from the funeral?" Oscar asked her.

"Reid is his name. Salem Reid," she answered.

"A friend, brother, cousin…what?"

"Sarah's boyfriend from high school."

"What did he want?" he asked.

Janice coughed and sputtered and started to cry, and Oscar added pressure to the knife that was beginning to cut into her labia. She held her breath and tried not to move. She pulled herself together and forced the tears to stop.

"He was asking questions about Sarah," she said.

"What questions?"

"I don't know," she sniffled.

"Yes, you do know!" he thundered, and increased the pressure enough to draw blood. That was when she screamed.

———

Reid told Ian to check the parking lot for the Lexus and the Benz and meet him outside at the back door. A couple of Hispanic men came through the kitchen wearing aprons and looked at Reid. Then they eyed the bouncers bound and gagged on the floor. They glanced back at Reid.

"It's okay. I won't bother you. You can finish your work and leave," he told the two guys. They nodded and returned to the kitchen. Reid started down the hall to find Petey.

Petey stepped back and threw his shoulder into the door. Petey was a big man and the door swung open and dangled from the hinges. He immediately knew the man with the knife was Oscar. The girl he wasn't sure about, but he guessed it was probably Janice Cooley. Oscar had the knife on her vagina and there was a trail of blood running from her shaved pubic area. Petey immediately charged the smaller man, and that may have been what saved Janice Cooley's life. Oscar turned quickly and planted the knife into Petey's ample belly. Janice screamed again, but was on her feet and quickly past them as she ran from the room and down the hall towards the stage area of the club. As she exited the hall past the main stage and turned towards the exit, the naked and bleeding Janice Cooley ran straight into Salem Reid.

"Oscar! He has a knife. He just stabbed some big guy," she screamed at Reid.

Reid pulled one of the drops Petey had given him and rushed down the hallway. The first thing he saw was that the back door had been opened and was slowly closing as the pneumatic arm was gently guiding the door back in place. He rushed to the lounge and saw Petey lying on his side on the floor. His grimacing face and the handle of the knife protruding from his stomach told the story. He went to Petey and he was conscious but his breathing was labored.

"Get the fucker, Salem. He went out the back, I think," Petey hissed.

"Sssshhhh," Reid whispered.

He heard a noise behind him and turned quickly. Janice Cooley stood there, still naked. "Can I help him?" she asked.

He looked at her crotch. The bleeding wasn't too bad. He figured she was okay; maybe in shock a bit.

"Find some towels, and apply gentle pressure to the wound. Leave the knife in him. Put your clothes on," he told her, and moved fast past her and out the back door.

He saw Ian coming from the left and checked ahead of him. That's when he saw Oscar sprinting through the dark. He was maybe 200 yards away in the hardware store parking lot across the street. He was almost to his Flex. Reid knew his firearm was useless at that distance, and their vehicles were too far away to give chase. He also knew Petey needed immediate attention.

"Petey's been stabbed. We have to get him out of here now," Reid said. Then he added, "Pull your car around here and I'll bring him out. I'll meet you at the hospital."

Reid returned to the lounge and saw the black-haired girl with all the ink helping Janice with Petey. Janice had done well. She had covered herself with her skimpy clothing that had been on the floor, and was helping Petey as best she could. The black-haired girl helped Reid and Janice get Petey up and out the back door. Ian was there and had the back door to his Suburban open for Petey. They got him in and closed the door and Ian took off towards Northside Hospital.

"Janice. You are coming with me. No argument. Let's go get all of your belongings."

"What about my car?" she asked.

"Later," he said.

He took her by the arm and led her back into the club. He pulled his firearm in case the bouncers had been cut out of their restraints. She fetched her belongings and stayed close to Reid's side. He got her out of there and into the Maxima within a few minutes. Besides the Benz, he counted six cars in the lot. He figured three belonged to the bouncers and the other three to the dancers who had yet to depart. One of which was the black-haired girl with all the ink. He guessed she was a friend of Janice's. He wasn't sure if she was the same girl from the service or not. He had only seen her from a distance.

Reid drove the Maxima out onto PIB and headed south to the Perimeter. He took 285 west to Peachtree Dunwoody and made the short jog to Northside Hospital.

"How bad are you cut?" he asked her. "We can get you checked out if you like."

She had used Reid's first aid kit that he had pulled out of his duffel and cleaned herself with sterile gauze and antiseptic.

"I think I'm okay. I'm still bleeding a bit, but not too badly. I'll check myself out in a bathroom when we arrive at the hospital."

Reid wheeled into the hospital and parked the Maxima. Janice took a few packs of the sterile gauze and some alcohol swabs from the first aid kit and placed them in her bag. The bag was cumbersome and heavy because she had taken everything she possibly could that belonged to her from the club. They entered the emergency room area and found Ian.

"Petey went back as soon as we arrived…maybe ten minutes ago. I haven't heard anything."

"Okay." He turned to Janice. "Let's find somewhere to clean you up," he said.

He took her down a few corridors and they found a women's restroom. She went in and Reid stood outside the door. He took out his phone and called Lara Brooks.

The call went to voicemail. "Call me right away. I have Janice." Then he clicked off and texted the very same message to her. About ninety seconds passed and then his phone buzzed.

He saw it was her. "Lara."

"Salem, you woke me up. What the hell's going on?" she asked.

He told her, "We are at Northside Hospital. Janice needs you. She's okay physically I think, but she could use a friend."

"What? Janice is injured?" she asked. "What happened?"

"Get here quick. Come to the emergency room. I'll explain then."

"Okay." She paused. "Okay," she said again. "I can be there in fifteen minutes."

They disconnected. He wanted Janice and Lara together and with him. But he realized he would have to find a safe place for them. His home wouldn't do when he wasn't with them, but he figured they could go there and sleep a bit once he got news on Petey.

He waited another ten minutes outside the women's restroom and then Janice emerged. She seemed better.

Reid looked at her. She had put on some shorts, a polo shirt, and some sandals. She was no longer dressed like a stripper.

"I'm okay. The cut is deeper than I'd hoped, but it will probably heal just fine. I got the bleeding stopped mostly. I had a pad in my bag, so I am using it over the gauze. It will help. I think I got it disinfected too. The alcohol burned like hell, Salem." She gave a weak laugh and then started to cry.

He put his arm around her and she curled into him. She smelled of perfume, antiseptic, and anxiety.

She cried for several minutes and then pulled her head up and said, "What am I going to do?"

"I got some of that worked out. Let's get back to the waiting room," he told her, and kept his arm around her as they walked the corridor.

# 52

JUST AS THEY WALKED into the waiting room, he saw Lara Brooks stride through the entrance. Janice stopped dead in her tracks, made a small noise, broke free from Reid, and ran to her old friend.

"Oh my God, Lara!" she shouted, and hugged her friend fiercely.

Reid kept them in sight, but he walked out of earshot and gave the women a chance to speak alone.

He sat next to Ian but they didn't talk. They were both good at waiting and being silent. He watched the women and after a bit, they were laughing and smiling a little, two girls gossiping about whatever. He was glad. He hoped that Janice could forget, at least temporarily, the awful violence she had experienced just an hour ago.

They waited another half hour and then a doctor came out. He told them that Petey had been stabilized, but that his stomach had been pierced and he was bleeding internally. He was in surgery, but his chance of survival was good.

"Salem, why don't you get the girls settled? I'll stay here with Petey. I'll text you when he's out of surgery," Ian said.

Northside Hospital was located just inside the Perimeter in Sandy Springs. Reid's condo was only seven or eight minutes away at this time of night. He could get the ladies comfortable in the spare and be back to the hospital quickly whenever Ian contacted him.

"Okay. Call me as soon as he's out." He nodded his thanks to his friend.

Reid walked over to the girls and told them about Petey. Janice seemed relieved. She didn't even know the guy, but she understood that he was instrumental not only in her rescue, but limiting her physical suffering that would have hospitalized her instead of him had he not interceded.

"Can I come back with you when Ian calls?" she asked.

He thought that would be okay. "Sure. I bet Petey would like that."

He turned to Lara. "Why don't you stay with Janice at my place tonight? She needs her friend. I'll bring you back to your car when Petey comes around."

Lara and Janice exchanged a look. "Okay. I can do that. I have a bag in my car," Lara said.

When they got to Reid's condo, it was 4 am. He set the girls up in the spare. He had offered to take the sofa in the living room, so that one of them could have his bed, but they declined. They were happy to bunk together in the spare. He filled Lara in on the details of the evening while Janice showered. She had gotten much of it from Janice at the hospital, so there was little to add.

Lara smiled at Reid. "Thanks for what you're doing; for Janice and me, but especially for Sarah."

He nodded slightly but said nothing. She took his hands and reached up and kissed him on the cheek. He smiled and nodded again.

"Sarah was right about you," she said, and left him in the kitchen.

———

Reid checked the tracking app and saw that Consuelo's car was where he expected it to be. He figured her day would start around seven. He would keep an eye on her then.

He went into his bedroom and got into his bed. He set his phone alarm for seven. He figured there would be news on Petey by then. He closed his eyes and slept for three hours.

# 53

REID AWOKE ABOUT TEN MINUTES BEFORE his alarm was set to go off. He checked his phone. There was nothing from Ian, so he went into the kitchen and made a full pot of coffee. He took a shower and dressed in jeans and a polo shirt. He threw on his Cole Haan shoes and returned to the kitchen for coffee. Lara Brooks was sitting at the table; she had poured two cups.

"Thanks," he said, and sat down across from her.

He checked his tracking app and saw that Consuelo was stationary at a location in St. Ives in Johns Creek. He located the printout and circled the name once he matched the address. It was off by a couple of houses, but close enough he figured. The last name was Strauss. He recorded the date and time next to their name on the printout. He placed the printout in his pocket. He would be using it all day long he figured.

"Good coffee, Salem," she said. "What kind?"

"Gevalia," he said. "How'd you sleep?"

"Good. I felt safe for a change. Thanks for that!" she answered.

His phone buzzed. "Yes?" he said.

It was Ian.

"Salem, the doctor just came out and talked to me. Petey is in recovery. He got out of surgery about an hour ago. He's in and out. I wanted to let you know."

"Okay. I'm on the way. Janice is still asleep. Let's see him together first and I'll come back to get the girls later," he said, and glanced up at Lara. She nodded.

He clicked off and looked at Lara for a long moment. "I'm going to arm the security system, so stay inside…don't even use the balcony. Don't let anyone in and don't let Janice go out. I'll be back soon enough and I'll get Janice over to see Petey. I'm gonna work on a place for y'all to stay too. Here's not safe long term. You shouldn't go back to wherever you've been staying either. If you need to gather some things from your place, I'll take you later. Call me right away if you have problems."

"I will, Salem. We will be just fine for a few hours."

"Help yourselves to anything you want to eat," he told her.

He brushed his teeth and rinsed, gathered the things he would need for the day, and left his condo. He drove his Explorer to Northside Hospital. The traffic was brutal and it took him twenty-five minutes to get there. He found a parking space and went to check on his old friend, Petey Ward.

Petey was out of recovery and in a private room. Ian had called Petey's daughter, and she was planning to arrive by Friday evening. Ian met Reid on the third floor and they headed to Petey's room.

"The surgeon said all went well with the surgery. Infection is always a risk, but so far so good," Ian told Reid.

"Good. Petey is tough," Reid said.

Petey was awake but groggy when they entered his room. They had him on a morphine drip for the pain.

"Hey, Petey," Reid said, as he moved towards the bed.

Petey Ward held his hand out and Reid took it. "Hey, kid. I guess I'm gonna make it," Petey said.

"You're going to be fine, Petey. I'm sorry I got you into this," Reid told him.

"No. I'm in. I told you. Just get that fucker for me…and for the girls too," Petey instructed.

"Janice wants to come by and thank you. Will that be okay?" Reid asked.

"Oh hell yeah, son. You bring Petey some pretty girls to cheer him up," Petey replied, and then coughed and grimaced. Reid couldn't help the smile that spread across his face.

"I will. You get some sleep and I'll come back with them in a bit. Stella will be in later tonight too, Petey," Reid told him.

"Ah, y'all shouldn't have called her," Petey said, but Reid thought Petey was glad his daughter was flying in from St. Louis.

Reid and Ian stayed until Petey fell asleep and started snoring.

"Get some sleep, Ian. I'll call you if I locate Oscar," Reid said to his friend.

———

Reid dialed Lara Brooks and she answered on the third ring. "Salem, how's Petey?" she asked.

"He's gonna make it, Lara. He's in a room and talking up a storm. He said to bring the pretty girls," Reid said.

"Well, the pretty girls have to eat first. We're making breakfast. Hurry up and get here, so it doesn't get cold," Lara said.

Reid took Johnson Ferry Road from the hospital all the way into Chamblee and went north on PIB to his condo. He smelled the food the girls were making as he came through the door. They had cooked scrambled eggs with cheese, made some toast, and started another pot of coffee. They had found some premium brand ham in the refrigerator and were frying it as he came into the kitchen.

"Hi, Salem," Janice said as he sat down at the table.

"Did you sleep okay?" he asked.

"Pretty good. Just not long enough," she replied.

He wanted to ask about her wound, but the mood was surprisingly cheerful; he thought he'd try to keep it that way.

The girls brought the food to the table; it looked a little over-cooked, but he dug in heartily and told them it was delicious. They both seemed pleased that he liked the breakfast they had prepared. The girls sat at the table and nibbled; neither eating much. Reid indulged in seconds and Janice and Lara beamed at him. He forced it down like a trooper, poured another cup of coffee for all of them, and then got down to business.

"I've got y'all set up in a hotel in Buckhead. It's not far from my place of business. Ian and I can check in on you frequently if needed," he told them, and they both nodded.

Janice spoke up, "I'd like to forget last night, but there is something I need to tell you, Salem. Oscar has your name. He forced me to tell. I was so scared," she said, and sniffled. "He knows about you and Sarah."

"It's okay. But we need to get you out of here. The sooner the better," he said. "He knew about me from the funeral?"

She nodded, sniffled, and began to cry again. Lara reached over and took her hand.

Reid knew Alexis Lexus had filled Oscar in on the events after the funeral. She had fled quickly last night too. He wondered if she'd be back tonight.

"Alexis told him, Janice. That's why she came to the funeral. Who was the black-haired girl at the service? Was she the one helping you last night?"

"That bitch, Alexis?" she said. "How did you know?"

"She followed you out of the funeral home lot," he told her. "She probably took pictures."

"Bitch," she said again.

"The black-haired girl?" Reid asked again.

262

"Taylor. She's okay, I think," she said.

"Don't take calls from anyone you work with until this is over. Nobody!" he said. "Taylor may be okay, but we can't take any chances."

Reid cleaned up his kitchen while the girls packed up all of their belongings, and then they piled into his Explorer and headed back to the hospital to see Petey Ward.

# 54

ELIZABETH HARRIGAN WAS IN THE BATHROOM of her hospital room taking a monkey bath and cleaning up the best she could. She was being released in about an hour pending the doctor's visit scheduled within the next thirty minutes. Joey had bought her some new clothes and some other essential items she would need. He would take her to the drugstore after they left and figure out where she would go from there. He had some ideas—some rather bold ideas—but he had yet to discuss them with Liza. He didn't want her going back to the Piedmont Arms. He had learned a little about her recent life and had made some guesses about some other things she'd maybe gotten herself into.

While he was waiting for her, he was flipping through the channels on the TV in her room when he caught a news report on the local ABC affiliate. Joey had not watched TV or heard any news reports since Wednesday when he arrived at Piedmont Hospital with Liza. The report repeated the earlier one from Thursday about Klaus, but now it was learned that his truck had been discovered at the Ashford Dunwoody ARC. The police were baffled as to how Vormer had gotten to his apartment in Doraville when his truck was in Brookhaven. The staff at the ARC was being interviewed and it had been discovered that Vormer was a club member, but that he hadn't been seen at the facility for close to a week. The investigation was continuing....

Joey thought it through. He knew Reid believed that Klaus was responsible for Sarah's death. Joey was certain of it too. Then Klaus had raped and tortured Liza in a seedy hotel on Cheshire Bridge. He was a bad guy. Klaus could have crossed paths with other bad people who had violently decapitated him, but Joey thought it likely that his old friend and teammate was responsible. He felt the need to talk to Reid, but wondered if he would ever know the truth.

Liza came out of the bathroom and Joey clicked off the TV. "What's wrong?" she asked him.

"Nothing," he said, and she gave him a long look but she didn't push it.

She looked much better. She had applied some makeup and the spots on her face were faint. Her lips looked better too; she had glossed them a little with some product one of the nurses had given her. She was dressed in gym shorts and a tee shirt and running shoes. She moved gingerly, but more from her injuries than from weakness and fatigue. Her arm was a little discolored and bruised from the IV they had removed earlier in the morning, but that was not uncommon.

The doctor arrived and stood looking at her chart. Then he would glance at Liza and then at Joey. He scribbled some notes in her chart and then handed Liza several prescriptions. One was an oral antibiotic that she was to stay on for ten days, another was for Vicodin, and the last was an ointment she was to use on her rectum that would help speed healing. He departed without a word.

They dealt with the discharge and financial paperwork and Joey carried her bags to his Expedition. He threw them in the back and helped her into the vehicle. They drove to a pharmacy in Buckhead and dropped off her prescriptions. He told her to browse the store for any items she felt she needed, so she added some sundry items, nail polish, and makeup. They waited about fifteen minutes for the pharmacist to call them and then made the purchases. They returned to the car and as Joey wheeled out on to Peachtree, he noticed that Liza was crying.

"What is it?" he asked her.

"I'm broke, Joey. I don't have a place to live. I can't even afford the Piedmont Arms at $185 a week," she answered.

"Good," he told her, and she looked at him with a hurt expression. Then he added, "You don't need to go back there anyway. Let me help. I need to help."

"How?" she asked still crying.

"I have plenty of space. You can use a spare bedroom at my house for a while, Liza. Herschel will love you."

"Herschel?" she asked.

"My dog," he told her.

"I don't know what to say, Joey. That's incredibly kind of you!" she said.

"Say yes, then," he said.

"Yes, then," she said, and her smile warmed his heart.

Joey navigated the morning traffic through Brookhaven and Chamblee, then sped up as they moved outside the Perimeter. Joey didn't glance at Utopia as they passed it, nor the Peachtree Suites a little farther north. He decided to give Liza the prettiest view of Peachtree Corners by moving past Peachtree Corners Circle and Jimmy Carter Boulevard and taking the left fork onto Peachtree Parkway. It was a beautiful late summer morning and the crepe myrtles in the median looked especially beautiful, their pink flowers glistening with the morning dew. The northeast Atlanta Hilton stood regally on the hill like a castle, and the shops and buildings along the way were mostly new and clean looking. They drove past Technology Park—a large area of high-end, low-rise buildings that employed thousands. He passed Spalding Drive and Peachtree Corners Circle, then turned left into the heart of the Forum.

"So, if you need some clothes, shoes, a new purse, or whatever, this is where we will come to get it for you," he told her.

"I've never been up here. This is a beautiful area. Do you live near here?" she asked.

"Practically walking distance…maybe a mile and a half down Spalding. Perhaps we can come up here later and walk around if you feel up to it. Plenty of great restaurants here too for when your appetite improves," he said.

"It sounds wonderful, Joey," she said, and it looked like she might cry again.

He reached over and took her hand. "Let's get you home to meet Herschel," he said, trying to lighten the mood.

"Okay. Let's go see Herschel," she said.

As they pulled into Joey's driveway, Liza exclaimed, "WOW, JOEY! What a nice place!"

He was proud of his home, but he was mostly pleased to see her happy; pleased that he could offer something special to someone in need.

He took her inside and immediately went to the basement door to let Herschel into the living area. Herschel came scrambling in, shaking his backside and yapping. He licked Joey and yapped some more, then turned his attention to Liza. She had never had a dog in the house growing up. Her mom had liked cats, but Liza had been indifferent to her mom's pets. Herschel approached her and sniffed her. She held out her hand to accommodate him, and soon he was wagging his tail in approval. Herschel had decided that Liza was okay.

"Hey, boy," she said, and rubbed him behind the ears.

"Let me show you your room, Liza," Joey said, as he led her down the hallway carrying her bags. Herschel followed right behind Liza.

He took her into the larger spare bedroom that was equipped with a queen bed, dresser, chest of drawers and a nightstand. He set her bag down on the bed and showed her the bathroom. It was a Jack and Jill that connected to the other spare bedroom.

"Make yourself at home," he said. "I need to check the mail and swing by and thank my neighbor, Walt, for helping me out with Herschel for the last few days. I'll be right back. Get Herschel to show you around the house."

Joey left Liza and Herschel and went out the garage door. Liza sat on the bed and the big Lab sat on the floor next to her. She bent down and hugged him and he licked her neck. She giggled and sat up, but continued to rub his head behind his ears. She stayed in the room with the dog until Joey returned and then he showed her around his home. When they came up from the basement, he thought she looked tired, so he suggested that she sleep some and maybe they'd go eat and do some shopping later in the afternoon. She agreed and laid down on the bed. Herschel stayed with her and curled up on the floor just beneath her. She thought that this was perhaps the most comfortable bed she'd ever been in. She wondered if she was in a dream and then she drifted off to sleep.

# 55

MILLICENT IVEY SAT AT HER PARENTS' kitchen table alone that Friday morning pondering not only the past week of her life, but also the call she had received early that morning from Jill Cramer. Her parents had left before dawn to go to work while she was still asleep in her old bedroom. Jill had jangled her phone just as the rising sun was bringing a new day through the blinds of her childhood bedroom.

"Hey, Mil, it's me," Jill said in an unusually quiet voice.

"Jill? What's going on?" she asked.

"The police, Mil. That's what's going on. That guy, Klaus, who assaulted you…well, they found him dead and his car is parked here," she said.

"Oh crud," was all that she could manage.

"Yeah. Crud is putting it mildly, Mil."

"Did you talk to them?" asked Millicent.

"I confirmed that he worked out here. That was all I said. I wanted to talk to you first," she replied.

"Have you said anything to anyone about what happened last Friday?" Millicent asked her.

"No," Jill said.

"Good. Please don't," Millicent added.

Jill was quiet for a long moment. "Are you okay?" she finally asked. "It's not like you to just take off like you did. What's up, Mil?"

"Jill, there are some things I just can't tell you right now. Please don't say anything about Friday. I'll explain when I return home."

"When is that going to be?" Jill asked her.

"I will probably come home Tuesday. I'll be back to work on Wednesday. Okay?" Millicent said.

Jill softened. "Okay, honey. Anything you need me to do?"

"Nothing else, Jill. Just keep my confidence. Okay?"

"Okay, I will, but I'm damn curious. You know that, bestie," Jill said.

Millicent laughed at her friend, but it sounded hollow. "I know. I'll fill you in on what I can when I return," she said, and they disconnected.

———

And now she sat in her parents' kitchen sipping coffee, and trying to work it all out. She had known Salem Reid for exactly one week, and had become terribly infatuated with him in a matter of days. She'd had, without question, the greatest sex of her life with him, and then witnessed him decapitating a sick and evil monster while saving her life. And she could discuss it with no one. She had run away to recover from her ordeal and seek solace at her parents' home. She had found comfort just being with them. They loved her dearly and her father doted on her. She could do no wrong in his eyes. But she could not ask for their help this time; she would need to work this out herself. Part of her wished that Salem Reid had simply run off with her, but she knew he wasn't built like that. She understood that he needed to finish what others had pulled him into. He was that kind of guy. But she wanted no part of it.

She understood intellectually that Reid had been given no choice in his actions. He was defending her and himself from attack. She kept telling herself that. The thing she kept coming back to, however, was how cool and controlled he'd been in action. It appeared to her that taking off Klaus's head had been a simple matter of routine for him, much like taking out the garbage or doing a load of laundry. He showed no signs of anxiety, fear, or regret for his actions. It seemed commonplace for him to have executed a man. This is what troubled her immensely. She knew that his reactions were not normal for the average guy. And then she would ask herself if what she wanted was an average guy. And around and around she'd go.

She missed him too. She had picked up her phone to call or text him a number of times in the past eighteen hours. But ultimately, she had not made the contact. She knew she would need to give it more time. And then the call from Jill had been terribly unsettling. She would protect Reid, especially since his actions had been on her behalf. But also because of her feelings for him and her understanding that he'd been righteous. But the law didn't usually consider what was righteous; the law considered the law. And she and Reid had fled the scene and not reported it. They could not undo that. So, she would need to do some serious soul-searching and determine if she could live with a man like that, or if she could bear to live without him. She simply did not know.

# 56

AFTER OSCAR HAD SPED AWAY from Utopia early Friday morning, narrowly escaping the "gang" of Salem Reid, he had fled to a
hotel off Clairmont Road in northeast Atlanta. He felt that his home
was safe. No one knew where he lived; he had been very careful
about that, but he could not be certain that he wasn't followed.
So, he stayed overnight in the hotel. He had parked his Flex where
he could see it from the window on the third story. He sat at the
window and watched his car for over an hour after checking into
the hotel, but no one came for him. He was concerned, however,
that his SUV might still be a target. He had seen two men standing
outside of the door he always used for both entry and exit, as he
had driven away from the scene at the club. Despite the darkness, he
thought it possible that they at least knew the make of his vehicle.
He would need to avoid driving his Flex anywhere near the club
until he could sort through this mess. He would certainly not return
to the club in any capacity until the entire matter had been resolved.

He checked out of the hotel and shopped for provisions at a nearby
grocery store, and then carefully drove to his Norcross home off Beaver

Ruin Road. He took a circuitous route and watched his rearview mirror, and was satisfied that he had not been followed. He parked his Flex inside of his garage, and checked his house thoroughly. Everything seemed normal, so he removed his provisions from the Flex and ate a little something to tide him over. He had slept little since the previous evening, so he decided that he would spend most of the afternoon in bed catching up on his sleep. Then he would figure out what to do about Salem Reid.

———

Reid took the girls to Northside to see Petey. Janice wanted to stop and get Petey a stuffed animal from the gift shop. She picked up some flowers for him too. They rode the elevator to the third floor and walked down the long corridor to his room. They poked their heads in the room and saw that a nurse was checking the dressing around Petey's wound, so they hung outside in the hallway to let her finish. Reid checked the tracking app and saw that Consuelo had left the St. Ives home and was now at a location just east of the Chattahoochee River in Duluth. Sweet Bottom Plantation was a quaint and charming upscale riverside neighborhood where homes ranged from half a million dollars to about one and a half million. It looked to Reid like Consuelo had a busy morning cleaning for the rich folk of North Atlanta.

He pocketed his phone just as the nurse emerged from Petey's room, and Reid and the girls filed in. Petey looked a little uncomfortable; probably from being probed during the recent visit from the nurse.

"Petey!" Janice exclaimed and moved to his bedside so she could present the stuffed animal and flowers to him. Reid and Lara hung back a bit while Janice did her thing.

"Ah hell, honey, you didn't need to get me anything. But thanks, that's very sweet of you."

She placed the small stuffed kitten she had purchased for him next to him on the bed. "She'll keep you company, Petey. Isn't she cute?"

"She sure is, Janice. But when I was thinking about a little pussy, that's not exactly what I had in mind," he added.

That got both girls laughing and even Reid smiled a bit at Petey's clever joke.

It also earned Petey a gentle poke from Janice. "You're awful," she told him, but she was still smiling.

"No really, thank you, honey. I do appreciate you thinking about me. Why don't you set the flowers on the table under the TV so I can look at them?" he told her.

She put the flowers on the table and pulled Lara over. "This is my friend, Lara," she said.

"Nice to meet you, Lara. I usually look better than this," he said.

Lara smiled at him and said, "Thanks for saving Janice last night. You were very brave, Petey."

He waved the compliment away. "I'm glad everybody is okay. I'll be fine in a few days, I'm sure," he said.

Reid came over and took Petey's hand in his and placed the other on his shoulder. He simply patted his shoulder, but said nothing.

The girls chatted with Petey for another five minutes, and then Reid noticed he was looking tired. He was likely experiencing some pain too, so they said their goodbyes and Reid whisked the girls from the room and down the hall into the elevator. They exited the hospital and Reid drove them to Buckhead, where his office manager, Julie, had reserved a suite for the girls under her name. They rode the elevator up to the tenth floor of the luxury hotel and located their suite.

"Y'all should be safe here, but if anything is suspicious, call me right away," he said. "Stay inside the hotel. There is a pool, spa, gym, and a few shops. You can read, watch TV, and order room service…whatever. Pay with cash. Don't use credit cards. Understand?"

They both nodded and he knew he had done all he could for them. As long as they didn't do anything stupid, they would be okay.

Reid left the hotel and hopped on 400 and took it north to Holcomb Bridge Road in Roswell. He went east less than a mile, found the upscale apartment complex where Alexis Lexus lived, and turned in. The complex was gated, but it didn't take a lot of ingenuity to get inside. Reid pulled up to the digital monitor and glanced at his watch. It was almost noon. He scrolled through and found Bertrand at the address Ray had given him. She was in building four with an address of 4104. He assumed that she lived on the first floor in apartment 104. He scrolled back and found building three and pressed the number for apartment 3205. It rang but there was no answer. He tried 3206. Again there was no answer. He pressed 3204 and after five rings what sounded like a young man who had maybe stayed out partying too late answered.

"Lo?" the sleepy voice said.

"Subway Sam delivery," Reid said indifferently.

"I didn't order a sub, man," the voice said.

"Is this 2204?" Reid asked.

"Right apartment, wrong building, dude," the voice said.

"Darn. I got a line of cars behind me, bud. Can you let me in, so I don't have to hold these people up?" Reid asked.

"Sure," said the voice, and the gate began to open.

Reid drove in and located building four. The complex had twelve buildings. Buildings one through four were in the front of the complex separated by a big, beautiful pool with cabanas and huts spaced throughout. It had a walkway through the middle, cutting the pool in two. One side appeared to be for the active residents who wanted to hit the small water slide, play water volleyball, or splash around in the cool water and throw a football or tennis ball in the pool. The other side was for the residents who wanted to lie on rafts and floats and simply chill during their leisure time. Buildings five through eight were beyond the pool. Reid reasoned that buildings nine through twelve were in the back. There were probably tennis courts separating the last two rows of buildings. Building four was at the far end from the entrance on the east side. Each building had four stories of apartments that sat on top of the parking area. Both stairs and elevators offered access from the parking area to the individual units. Reid drove into the parking lot under building four. He spotted the Lexus parked near the stairwell, so he thought it likely that Alexis was home. He drove to the visitor section of the parking area, but spotted no other familiar vehicles. He parked his Explorer in the lot and took the elevator up to the second floor above the parking lot. He got off the elevator and followed the signs to the left. He found unit 4204 in the back overlooking some fashionable landscaping beyond the iron fence that enclosed the pool. Unit 4204 was in the back far corner of the building. Reid knew that 4104 would be directly below it, and that Alexis Lexus was probably in the unit sleeping or just awakening after a busy night dancing. Each unit had a wraparound balcony; he had noticed this when he entered the building, and he could see that the second row of buildings across the pool had the exact same balconies. It was quiet back here. Looking from the back breezeway, he could see a few young people sunning themselves at the pool, a few maintenance people roaming the grounds below, and the occasional dog walker. There was no activity on the breezeway.

Reid pounded on the door of unit 4204. He waited about thirty seconds and pounded again. He listened for sounds from the unit. Then he stepped across the breezeway and listened for noises from the neighbor's unit. He heard nothing. He removed his picks and got to work on 4204. It took him almost two minutes, but he got it unlocked. He wasn't sure if there was an alarm system or not. He opened the door quickly, stepped in, and closed the door. He heard a single beep, and noticed an unarmed alarm keypad next to the light switch just inside the door. The apartment was empty. There was some debris here and there and a few scuffs on the bare walls. He could see indentations on the carpet where furniture had recently been removed. He quickly scanned the unit. It was a two bedroom. The master was larger and had the pool view and a balcony that extended from the living room. It had a spacious bathroom with a garden tub and a walk-in shower. The second bedroom also had a bathroom, but it was a standard use bathroom that had entrances from the hallway and the bedroom. The living space was open with the dining area and kitchen on the far side of the living room from the balcony. He scanned the area outside. He walked into the master and opened the sliding glass door. He edged out and moved around the corner, so that he was only visible from the treelined eastern view. He leaned out over the porch and saw Alexis's porch and balcony. She had a table with a hole in the middle from which an umbrella extended. Four chairs surrounded the table. The furniture looked new. An ashtray with a few cigarette butts in it was the only item on the table.

He scanned the landscaping along the eastern border of the property. There was a narrow sodded area below; it was maybe five or six feet wide. It had a few shrubs and small crepe myrtles in a little island covered with pine straw. Beyond the narrow landscaping was a retaining wall that separated the property from pines that fronted a wooded area. It was very secluded on this side of the complex. Reid estimated the drop from the balcony where he stood was about twenty-four feet. It would be a twelve-foot drop from Alexis's porch. It would be even less of a drop if he were to pull himself over, and then dangle before dropping.

Reid stood perfectly still and listened. There were no sounds below, but he continued to listen. He waited over twenty minutes and then he heard a woman's voice speaking faintly. He heard the sliding glass door open beneath him and then the voice got louder. Alexis Lexus came out on her balcony talking on her phone. She was animated and seemed agitated. She sat at her outdoor table and lit a cigarette.

"Are you fucking kidding me?" Reid heard her say.

There was a long pause. He could smell the cigarette smoke from below.

"I know I'm scheduled, Bruce!" she yelled. "But what if they come back tonight?"

Another pause while she listened to his response.

"Oh? Just like you protected me last night, huh? They beat the shit out of y'all."

A shorter pause, then she said, "Right, Bruce." She added a cynical laugh.

Reid listened to the silence for a long moment and then she sighed heavily and said, "Fine. I'll be there at five. You better watch out for me."

She clicked off and finished her smoke, and then she entered the apartment. Reid listened for a bit and heard nothing. After about ten minutes, he heard a faint hissing. He listened carefully and wondered if he was hearing running water. He moved into the master bathroom and listened. She was in the bathroom, he thought. He heard a door close, so he guessed she'd gotten in the shower. He moved back to the balcony and climbed over the rail at the post and shimmied down onto Alexis's porch using the post to shield him from the western view. He moved quickly to the sliding glass door. It hadn't closed completely when she had re-entered her apartment, so he cracked it a little wider and slid into her unit. He glanced around and saw her phone on the corner of the bar surrounding the kitchen. He checked her pictures, and sure enough, he saw several of himself in the funeral home parking lot. There were several of him and Janice together. He exited and found her text messages. He thought she might have deleted any messages she may have sent to Oscar, but surprisingly she had not. He found a caption that read "O," which he opened and saw a message reading, "Family friend? Talkin to Dest." He saw a picture of himself holding Janice's arm, then another picture that caught his face. He hadn't been wearing sunglasses. He clicked on "O" and then pressed "contact." Now he had Oscar's number. He took a picture of it with his phone. He wasn't sure it would do him much good. He had a friend at the DMV, but not at the phone company. Besides, the number Alexis had could be a throwaway for all he knew. That he had proved another one of his theories, however, was gratifying. In addition, he had scoped out her place. He had also discovered that the apartment above hers was vacant and currently unlocked. He wanted to canvas her entire apartment, but heard the shower stop in the bathroom. He moved quickly through the sliding glass door and onto the balcony. He moved to the rail and pulled himself over. He dangled briefly from the bottom of the railing and dropped himself easily to the ground below. He walked purposefully around the building to the front and entered the parking area. He located her Lexus and attached the second tracking device. Then he walked to his Explorer, got in, and drove out of the complex.

# 57

JOEY REALIZED HE WAS TIRED TOO. He had gotten a bit of an adrenaline rush from having Liza in his house, and for how she and Herschel had taken to each other. He had crashed a bit afterward, though, and he knew he could use a nap. He couldn't stop thinking about Liza, and he was having a little trouble falling asleep. He felt very much attached to her, but it wasn't just that. He had hurt for her when he and Reid had discovered her in the hotel room. He had wanted to remove her pain. He had wanted to make her terrible experience disappear, but he felt helpless to do so. He had heard people talk about having a soul mate; he had always dismissed such talk as foolishness and nonsense. But he had only known this woman for a few days, yet he felt a connection to her like he had never known with another human being. She brought out the best in him. He liked himself better when he was with her. And the truth was he hadn't liked himself much lately. He was almost certain that she understood this on some level, and that she was experiencing the same thing. He could see it in her eyes; it was as if she could see right through him, and it didn't bother him. He didn't want to hide.

Joey had finally drifted off to sleep, and he dozed for several hours. When he awoke, it was afternoon. He was a bit groggy, but he felt a little rested from his nap. He took a shower, shaved, and brushed his teeth. He put on some shorts and a polo and loafers. He realized he was hungry and wondered if Liza was too. When he came into the great room, he saw her in the kitchen browsing the cabinets, refrigerator, and pantry. She was familiarizing herself with his kitchen; he was pleased to see her making herself at home. Herschel was lying on the floor and came to Joey as he entered his kitchen.

He reached to pet the dog and said to Liza, "You hungry?"

She looked at him and scrunched up her face; she was smiling a bit too when she said, "Yeah. I found some pretzels and cookies. There's some raman noodles too...*yum!*"

Joey laughed. She was showing a little spunk, which made him happy.

"How about I take you to J Alexander's for a late lunch? We can do some shopping at the Forum and then we can go to the grocery."

"Sounds good. Give me a few minutes to clean up," she said.

She was still wearing the casual clothes he had gotten her earlier, but he figured that it would be okay.

She took about fifteen minutes to get ready. Joey let Herschel out and then secured him in the basement while Liza was in the bathroom, and then they took the Expedition to the Forum.

They got a table at J Alexander's. It was early enough that the restaurant was only half full. The popular eatery would fill up quickly after 6, and then it could be close to an hour's wait for the remainder of the evening. Liza ordered water and an Alex's salad, and Joey got the half rotisserie chicken and sweet tea. While they waited, Joey brought up a topic that was a little uncomfortable for him, but he thought that they needed to discuss it.

"Look, Liza, I have something I want to say, but I don't want to upset you. I just think it should be discussed," he told her.

"What is it, Joey?" she asked, a concerned look on her face.

"Well…uh, I wanted to ask you if you needed any kind of treatment for everything you've been through," he said. They had spoken a little during her hospital stay about issues with drug addiction.

"You mean the drugs?" she asked, and looked down at her hands.

"Not just the drugs, but any kind of counseling. I'm not telling you what to do. You do what you want. I just want you to know I'll help you with any of that if you require it."

"I truly don't know yet, Joey. I don't want to do drugs anymore, but I do think about it…often, to be honest."

"Sure. I get that. There are places you can go around here that do outpatient treatment. You have people you can talk to and such."

"Okay. Let's see how it goes for a few days and I'll let you know," she said, and looked down at her hands again. She added, "The other stuff…well, you and Herschel are helping me there." A tear rolled down her cheek and she reached across the table and grabbed his hand.

He squeezed her hand and smiled at her. "Okay then. Enough of all that. Let's enjoy the day."

And they did. The food came and they dug in. The salad Liza ordered was much larger than she expected, and she could only eat half. Joey demolished his chicken and the spuds that came with it.

They shopped at Belk's and he bought Liza some shorts, blouses, and a few pairs of shoes. He purchased a nice handbag for her too. She wanted to toss her old one. Then they went to Old Navy and she picked out several pairs of jeans, a few gym shorts, some sweats, and some long-sleeve tee shirts. Then he took her into Brighton and let her pick out a chain and some earrings. After that, they left the Forum and drove down Peachtree Parkway to Target, and he bought her an assortment of underwear, socks, and other small items she needed.

They popped into the supermarket and loaded up on groceries. Joey pushed the buggy and Liza placed items into the cart that she felt she could put to good use. He was glad to see her take charge. She loaded very few pre-packaged items, but instead placed steaks, chicken, eggs, bacon, breads, fruits, and vegetables into the cart. She found some brown rice, pasta, cheese, and milk and added those items to the buggy as well. Joey grabbed some bottled water and some diet soft drinks from the shelf and they headed to the checkout.

Liza thought she was a decent cook. She aimed to prove it to Joey. She wanted to carry her weight at the house, and she thought that preparing meals for Joey would be a good start. She needed to stay busy too. She was still a little fatigued and tired easily, but she figured that would only last a few more days. Then what would she do? So she had already started planning to occupy herself with as many positive activities as she could think of. She was determined to turn her life around, and she was thrilled to have Joey's support.

They headed home, and together they unloaded the groceries and the items from their shopping spree. Joey looked at Liza and she still seemed energized. He was glad to see it. It was after 7 pm and the weather was perfect for an evening stroll.

"Do you want to take Herschel for a walk, Liza?" Joey asked.

Her face lit up. "That would be great!" she said.

So Joey grabbed the leash, collar, and baggies, and they ventured out into a beautiful late summer evening. The sun was beginning to set in the west and it colored the sky pink and purple on the horizon. It was a stunning evening. Joey walked on the outside and Liza held Herschel's leash with her right hand on the inside track. As they walked, Liza reached over and took Joey's hand in her free one. He noticed that her hand was pleasantly warm and a bit balmy. His heart skipped a beat. It had been a spectacular day.

# 58

OSCAR AWOKE EARLY FRIDAY EVENING and got to thinking. He wanted to find this Salem Reid. He had been ambushed by him and his gang last night, and he had been fortunate to escape. But he knew before he could take him down, he would have to change from defense to offense. He already had people looking into where Reid worked and lived; that could possibly be very useful, but he knew Reid would be on high alert. Oscar had also realized that his vehicle was likely compromised. His home could be next. He thought he was still solid on that front, but that may change since he was being sought. He decided that he would need to move soon. The house off Beaver Ruin had been furnished when he'd begun living there some time back, so he needn't worry about the furniture. His possessions could fit inside his SUV with room to spare. He decided that by early next week, he would move closer to town and find one of those extended stay suites to live in until he could figure out something more permanent. By Tuesday, he'd be gone. Then he would see about replacing his vehicle before settling in a new home. After that, he'd focus on Reid. He would need to be eliminated. He was becoming a pest. Oscar realized that he had underestimated Reid; he would need to be very careful in his movements, and even more careful about where he drove his vehicle. His plan for tonight hadn't changed. He would ride down to his club on Stewart Avenue on the south side of town, do a little business there, and head back in the wee hours of the morning. He would access 85 by heading north on Beaver Ruin and then go south towards the airport. It would be a circuitous route to the interstate, but worth the few extra miles. He wanted to steer clear of Utopia. He showered and shaved. Then he threw on some nice slacks and a silk shirt. He wore a pair of expensive woven oxfords and a fine leather belt purchased at a local department store. He wore the gold Rolex that had been looted from the UGA star's home. He really loved the beautiful timepiece and more and more he felt that he would keep it for himself and not sell it. He didn't need the cash; he had stolen close to $100,000 and made over $30,000 in his drug and prostitution ring in the past thirty days. So he sprayed himself liberally with cologne, combed his hair carefully, and left his home just after dark and headed out cautiously into the evening.

———

Salem Reid had tracked Consuelo throughout the day, but there was nothing that alerted him. She had cleaned the St. Ives home in the morning, and then gone to Sweet Bottom Plantation in Duluth later. Her final job had been in the Riverview neighborhood just south of the river in Peachtree Corners. He had located all the addresses on the spreadsheet he'd printed at her house and none of them had anything to do with Oscar Villanueva as far as he could tell. After the Riverview job, she had stopped at a grocery store in Duluth, and then continued to her apartment. He believed that she would at least have a couple of jobs on Saturday, so he would follow her movements again then. The sun was setting in the west, and he had nothing pressing for the evening, so he decided he would swing by the hotel in Buckhead to check on Janice and Lara. Maybe he would entertain them for dinner. He thought the more time he spent around them, the safer they would be. At least he relaxed a little more in regards to their well-being when he could keep an eye on them. He phoned Lara.

"Hi, Salem. What's up?" she said.

"Have y'all eaten?" he asked.

"We were about to order room service," she said.

"Hold off on that. I'll swing by and take the two of you to the hotel restaurant. I don't want you to be total prisoners. Give me about twenty minutes," he said.

"Sounds great," she said, and disconnected.

Just as he set his phone down it rang.

"Yes?" he answered.

"Reid," Tenise Jackson said.

"Tenise."

"So I hear an abandoned gold Tundra has been located in an ARC parking lot in DeKalb County, and the owner was found dead in Doraville," she said.

"How unfortunate," Reid said.

"Reid, what the hell are you up to?"

Reid said nothing.

Tenise endured the silence for a bit and said, "You're involved in this. I know it, Reid."

Reid remained silent.

"He's a bad guy. We know that, but I'm worried for you my friend. I can't protect you. I hope you know that."

"I don't need protection, Tenise," he told her.

"Yeah. Okay. You scare me, man. You know that?" she said.

He didn't respond.

"Reid, be very careful out there. Don't do anything stupid, especially in Gwinnett County. You hear?" she added.

"I hear you, Tenise. Is that all?" he said.

"Yeah. That's all. Take good care, my old friend," she said, and clicked off.

Reid drove to Buckhead in the Explorer and found a parking spot in the hotel lot without having to use the valet. He entered the hotel and rode the elevator to the tenth floor and knocked on the door.

"It's Reid," he announced, and the door opened a crack. He could see the chain still attached. Lara Brooks peeked through the crack and smiled.

"Hey, Salem," she said cheerily, "come on in."

Lara was dressed in her dark workout clothes, and she still donned her hat. Janice wore tight jeans that advertised her shapely hips and a V-neck that showed a lot of cleavage. He wondered how the tight jeans affected the tenderness in her groin area. She sported stiletto heels that made her three inches taller than normal. She looked good, but she looked a little more provocative than he would have liked for the occasion. Lara seemed to understand that a low profile was desired, but Janice seemed to want to show off her attributes despite what the situation called for. He shrugged it off and gave them both a warm smile.

"Hi, ladies. I hope you're hungry. I walked past the dining room. It smells great," he told them.

Janice smiled seductively at Reid and took his arm in hers as they walked out the door and down the hallway. Lara tried not to grin at Reid but raised her eyebrows at her friend's behavior. But Janice was having fun, and after her ordeal the previous evening Lara didn't want to burst Janice's bubble. Besides, they had been cooped up in the suite all day and both girls had been excited about the prospect of getting out of the room. Even if it was just to go down to the hotel restaurant, it was a relief to get a change of scenery. Other than visiting the hotel clothing shop to get Janice something to wear, they had not been out of the room. Reid regarded the situation similarly. He felt awkward with Janice flirting with him, but he realized that it had been a whirlwind twenty-four hours for her, and she was probably just trying to cope the best way she knew how.

They took a booth in the corner of the semi-crowded restaurant that served the normal fare for such places. A variety of steaks, fish, chicken, and pasta dishes were offered. The lighting was dim and a guy in a tuxedo sat at a piano and played familiar tunes. It was pleasant and cheerful enough. The bar had big flat-screen TVs at each end, and the Braves were playing. They were close enough to the bar that Reid could keep track of the score as they dined. He sat on one side of the booth and the girls on the other. Janice sat directly across from him.

The girls both ordered cocktails. Reid ordered a Miller Lite. Lara had chicken that came with rice pilaf and buttered carrots, and Janice had trout with the rice pilaf and a vegetable medley. Reid ordered the eight-ounce filet and a baked potato. They sipped their drinks and he listened to the girls talk about their shopping spree at the hotel clothing store. That topic segued into a discussion about fashion and then into what celebrities and movie stars were wearing. Finally, it ended with a discussion of the Kardashians and the relative sizes of their butts, and if Kim and Kanye would last. Reid stayed quiet and let the girls talk. He actually enjoyed their banter, if not the topic, and was pleased to see them temporarily removed from their predicament.

Their dinners arrived and they sampled each other's dishes. Reid thought the trout was excellent, the steak very good, but the chicken a little dry. He shared about a third of his steak with Lara because he thought maybe she had the same opinion of the chicken that he did. She ate all of her carrots and rice, so he felt like she had gotten plenty to eat. She seemed happy, so he was satisfied that she enjoyed her meal well enough. Janice ate all of her trout and vegetable medley, but wasn't big on the rice, so Reid polished it off and she ate a little of his baked potato. They ordered a second round of drinks. Janice slugged hers and was getting a little tipsy, but Reid nursed his beer and Lara paced herself with her drink. Janice ordered a third and got a little giggly and even flirtier. Reid wasn't totally unprepared when she ran her foot up inside his leg underneath the table. She was a gorgeous woman, no doubt. They both were and he was happy to be in their company, but Janice's advances were making him uncomfortable. He didn't mind that the girls were having a few drinks either, but getting drunk would be a bad idea.

Reid glanced at Lara, but she just shrugged. Then Lara polished off her drink and excused herself. She had decided that she'd return to the room, and watch a little TV and then crash for the night. He wondered if Janice had planned something like this with her friend in order to get him alone.

"Okay. Text when you're safely in the room. Don't put the chain on though. We will be up shortly," he told her.

He watched her go and saw her get on the elevator. Within a minute, she texted that she was locked in the room on the tenth floor.

Janice continued her probing with her foot on Reid's leg. She grinned, displaying a mouth full of perfect white teeth. "Thanks for everything you've done for me, Salem. How can I ever repay you?"

"You can stay alive and healthy, Janice. That's all you need to do," he said.

She took another big slug of her drink and ran her foot farther up his leg past his knee. She giggled again and he wondered if she was becoming Destiny, the dancer.

"Are you sure there's nothing I can do for you, Salem?" she said, and ran her foot towards the middle of his thigh.

He gently removed her foot with his hand and said, "Maybe we should be getting up to the room. I'm not crazy about the two of you being separated."

"You think I need some looking after, Salem?" she said, still flirting with him. "Why don't you stay the night and look after me?"

He ignored her suggestive comment and took out a hundred and fifty dollars from his wallet to pay the bill the waitress had just dropped on the table. He wanted to get her to the room in case she started a scene.

"Let's get up to the suite and have a nightcap," he suggested.

He was relieved to see that she thought this was a grand idea. He went to the bar and got her another drink and a third beer for himself. He carried the drinks up to the suite and she used a key card to open the door. She was surprisingly steady, but he figured she had a lot of practice being this tipsy and still graceful when she moved. He handed her cocktail to her as they entered the room. She took a big sip, and he set his untouched beer on the coffee table and went to the windows. He closed the drapes and the room darkened from being shut off from the bright city lights. The dim light from a floor lamp in the far corner of the living room was the only lighting.

She took another sip and then set her drink down. She took his arm and pulled him into her bedroom. She pushed the door shut, and led him deeper into the room.

She held him close and kissed his neck. "You are really hot, Salem," she whispered, as she ran her hands down along his waist to his thighs.

He felt himself stir and knew he needed to escape soon, or he'd be in big trouble. He pushed her back and could tell that she was surprised. He was sure it was a rare event for her to have her advances rebuffed.

"Janice, you're lovely, but we can't do this. I have a girl," he said.

She smiled alluringly and tried to pull him into her.

"No," he said, and held her back. "No," he repeated.

She bowed her head so that her hair hung in her face and she sat down on the edge of the bed. He wondered if she would cry. She didn't.

Instead, she looked up at him with a resigned look and said, "You don't like strippers, I guess."

"I like you," he told her, "but we're not doing this."

She shook her head, "I don't know too many guys like you."

"I'm just a guy," he said for the second time in the past two days.

"No. You're not. Maybe that's why I'm so attracted to you, Salem. You're special. I'm sorry for being such a slut, but I guess that's what I am."

Reid wasn't sure how to respond to this. There were plenty things worse than being a slut he thought, but he said nothing.

"Who's the lucky girl?" she asked.

"Her name is Millicent," he said.

"Pretty name. Is she?" she asked.

"Is she what?" he responded.

"Pretty?"

"Yes," was all that he could manage.

"Lucky her," she said, but she managed a short laugh.

Reid shrugged. He figured he was the lucky one.

"I better go, Janice. It was fun hanging out with you and Lara tonight. I'm glad you are both okay. Stay in here again tomorrow and call me if there are any problems," he told her.

She nodded resignedly. He bent down and kissed her forehead, touching her hair. "I'll talk to you guys tomorrow. Okay?"

She nodded again but didn't look up. Reid turned and exited into the living room. It was quiet in the suite. He wanted the door chained behind him when he left. He started for the other bedroom but before he reached it, Lara came out and smiled at him.

"I'll get the door. The walls are kind of thin around here, Salem. I was eavesdropping in case you're wondering," she said, and they both laughed a little. She reached up and kissed his cheek and walked him to the door.

"You're the best," she said, and chained the door behind him.

# 59

REID MADE IT HOME AROUND ELEVEN and took the stairs
to his condo. He knew sleep wouldn't come easily. He packed a
backpack with his gun and phone, and ran to Blackburn Park. He
thought about Janice as he ran. He wondered what he would have
done if he didn't have Millicent in his life. He knew it would be
the wrong thing to do even then, but he wasn't sure he would have
turned Janice down in that case. So he grappled with that notion as
he ran. Intellectually he knew that no good would come from trying
to have something meaningful with a stripper and prostitute. What
kind of a man would want a woman who was actively involved in
that lifestyle? Nevertheless, when she'd kissed his neck and rubbed
his thighs towards his crotch, he'd been sparked. He was still sparked
and he wasn't sure a vigorous run through the park would be enough
to settle him down. He'd wanted to have sex with her badly, and it
was offered up to him on a silver platter. But he had declined and
gotten away. He tried to tell himself that he took the high road. He
knew that he had, but it was little solace at the moment. His sexual
urges were still in charge, and he was sure it would be hours before

he would think straight in regard to what he had just experienced with Janice.

As he ran, he got to thinking about what drove people. He thought about desires and urges; whether it was for sex, money, power, celebrity, or even love. He thought of all the people he had encountered this past week. He knew there was pure evil in the world. He had seen that in Iraq, both during the war and later when the terrorists had come in droves. There was no question that Klaus had been an evil guy. The termination of his life had been nothing but a positive occurrence. He understood that Oscar was pure evil too, and he intended on hunting him down and bringing him to justice since the law had failed to do so.

He knew there had been very few true saints in the world. Most others fell somewhere in between, and he was certain that he fell somewhere in this group himself. But people fell on different points on that curve, and the curve was dynamic. It was easy to be nice, pleasant, and decent when things were going well. It was much more difficult to accomplish those same ideals when your back was flung against the wall by the obstacles, distractions, and setbacks of daily living. And when real tragedy occurred, it was even a bigger struggle.

He thought about Sarah. She had needed something from him fifteen years ago that he had been unable to provide. He still hadn't figured out what that was. He understood now that she had a hole in her somewhere that she had tried to fill up. At sixteen years old, she'd not known how to go about doing it, so she had searched for a way. The newspaper article he had read at Joey's had summed her up in a paragraph. She was an addict, thief, and whore. She had been these things to varying degrees he supposed, but she'd had goodness in her too. She had been a friend to Janice and Lara. She had worked hard and paved her own way in life; she hadn't counted on anyone else to provide for her. She had accumulated wealth and shared it with her family when they were in need. And he understood now that Sarah had truly possessed the capacity for love. He had seen the baseball clippings with the pink hearts she had drawn around him and his name. She had spoken to Janice and Lara about him. Sarah's mother had said, "A mother knows, Salem." She had lived quietly when she was away from her job. She had read romance novels, perhaps hoping one day she could find romance and true love. She had visited her sister and shared a Disney experience with her nephews.

But ultimately, she had done the hardest thing for the past fifteen years. She had let him be. She had not sought him at any point after the second trip to Statesboro during his freshman year at college. Maybe she hoped that one day Salem Reid would come for her, and whisk her off to a happy and normal life. But instead, he had found her dead on Joey Mac's sofa.

It wasn't just Sarah either. Joey Mac and Liza, Janice and Lara, and others involved on this journey were all flawed. But he knew deep down that these people were all struggling to find their way, and that they battled within themselves to do the right thing. Their traits were varied. They were people whose lives couldn't be summed up in a paragraph from the newspaper or a Facebook placard. They were both good and bad, right and wrong. They were many things to many people. They were worthy of grace, forgiveness, and understanding. They were, after all, human beings with doubts, fears, and anxieties. And these people were his friends. He would look out for them because now he could. He would pave a path for them and help them find their way because he could. He felt he had failed Sarah in this regard fifteen years ago, and wished now that he could have done something for her. But it hadn't happened that way. He wouldn't let it happen again. He would honor her memory. And he had work left to do to see that through.

Reid finished his run and returned to his condo. He still wasn't ready for sleep, but he had at least shaken off the spell Janice had cast over him. He punched his bags and did two hundred and fifty push-ups. He drank water and then showered. By the time he was out of the shower it was after 1 am. He got into bed and flipped through channels on TV, checking ESPN and the MLB Network for scores and news from Friday's games. Shortly, he began to doze and then he eventually drifted off into a dreamless sleep that lasted six hours.

# 60

LIZA WOKE WITH THE SUN on Saturday morning; she had slept better than she'd slept in years. She felt rested and energized. She had gotten in bed a little after 10 pm on Friday night, and gone right to sleep. Herschel slept on the floor at her side. Joey had brought the water bowl up from the basement, and as Liza got out of bed, Herschel began pacing. He needed to pee. And so did Liza. She relieved herself in the bathroom and then disarmed the security system, took Herschel to the basement, and let him out into the backyard. She came back to her room, brushed her teeth, washed her face, and put on a pair of shorts and a blouse that Joey had purchased for her yesterday. She put a pot of coffee on to brew, got out bacon, and started frying it in a skillet she found under the stove. She scrambled some eggs, added a little cheddar cheese, and started some toast. She cut some cantaloupe she had gotten at the grocery store and placed the melon on a plate on the kitchen table. Joey came out in a pair of gym shorts and a tee shirt and sporting a red Bulldogs hat with a big black G on the front. He smiled at Liza and touched her arm lightly as he passed her on his way to the garage door. He brought in the morning paper, grabbed a cup of coffee and a piece of the cantaloupe Liza had sliced, and went straight to the sports section. After beating Clemson in the home opener the previous weekend, the Dawgs were off in week two. So he scanned the paper deciding if he wanted to watch another SEC game later that afternoon. After checking the college football portion of the *AJC* Sports page, Joey examined the baseball scores. The divisional races were on, but the Braves were swooning. They had already blown the divisional lead, and were on pace to miss out on the wild card this year.

Liza set a plate in front of him. It smelled and looked great. He hadn't eaten a real breakfast at home since forever. He dug in and it tasted even better than it smelled. Damn if she wasn't a good cook.

"This is delicious, Liza," he told her. "Thanks for making me breakfast."

She smiled at him as he shoveled bacon, eggs, and toast into his mouth.

"Aren't you going to eat?" he said, as she sat down with a cup of coffee.

She plucked a piece of melon from the plate and nibbled on it. "I'll just have some fruit for now, Joey."

He noticed that she had been eating very lightly, and he wondered if she was concerned about using the bathroom. They talked about her recovery in general, but her injuries were of a very personal nature, so he had tried to be empathetic to her condition without asking too much. He had noticed that she had eaten only fruits and vegetables that were easy to digest. He thought that approach was probably an effort on her part to limit discomfort when she finally would need to go. Certainly understandable, but he guessed she simply did not wish to discuss it with him. So he let it go.

"What would you like to do today, Liza?" he asked her.

"After I clean up the kitchen, I'd like to shower and polish my nails. Is there a park nearby where we could take Herschel?" she asked.

"We can go to Jones Bridge Park by the river, or there is a nature trail where Johns Creek and Peachtree Corners come together. It's a more secluded trail along the river," he said.

"Let's go to the trail then, Joey."

He thought that a better choice. It was already getting warm and the nature trail was shaded.

They finished breakfast and she poured him more coffee as she began to clean up the breakfast dishes. He offered to help, but she insisted that he let her do it alone. He understood her desire to contribute, so he sat at the table and sipped coffee while she worked. He watched her as she moved around the kitchen. She was looking better each day. Her face was clearing up nicely and her lips were almost healed. Her brown hair looked nothing like the oily mess it had been when they'd found her. She had a good figure and nice legs. Sometimes when she looked at him with those big brown eyes and pouty lips, his heart melted. Beautiful was not a description he would use for her. Pretty or cute was more apt, and he found himself more attracted to her each day. He suspected that part of the attraction was because of her sweetness and almost melancholy demeanor. He liked the way she would cock her head and give him a half smile. She was very nuanced in her manner; something he had rarely noticed with other women. She caught him staring.

"What?" she asked, and gave him one of those half smiles that made him shiver.

"I was just watching you, Liza. You look very pretty this morning is all," he told her.

"Thank you, Joey. I feel better each day, but I don't feel very pretty."

"You're pretty. Case closed," he said.

She looked down at her hands. "You make me feel special, Joey. I don't deserve it, though. I'm a whore and a drug addict. I don't deserve you," she said.

He moved to her and embraced her.

"You're Liza. A pretty young woman who just made me a great break-fast, and I enjoy your company very much," he said.

He gently pushed her back to look at her face and added, "Look, Liza, I'm no prince. I've done some things recently that I regret. I regret not regretting it sooner too. I understand where you're coming from. I'm trying to leave some things behind also. We can do this together."

"I'd like that, Joey," she sniffled.

"We start today…actually, we started yesterday," he said and kissed her forehead.

# 61

REID CLIMBED OUT OF BED on Saturday morning and was a little sore from his vigorous run and workout late Friday evening. He put on some coffee and stretched for fifteen minutes, working out the stiffness that had built up in his muscles overnight. Then he moved to the kitchen and sipped coffee while he munched a few granola bars and some fruit. He pulled up the tracking app on his phone and saw that Consuelo was on the move. She was in the east Sandy Springs neighborhood of Spalding Lake cleaning a home of a client named Igor Johannsson. Reid found his name on the spreadsheet and scribbled a few notes, then went back to his coffee. He poured a second cup and turned on the TV. He checked the local and national news, but quickly changed it to sports before the usual garbage that filled the news made him cynical and jaded.

He finished his coffee, showered, brushed his teeth, and dressed for the day. He put on black cargos, a black tee shirt, and black Nikes. He gassed the Explorer and drove it to the Costco in Brookhaven where he did a lot of his shopping. As he pushed the cart around the store, he thought again about Janice. She was only a few miles down the road in Buckhead, probably sleeping off the vodka she had drunk too much of last night. He would need to call them in a bit to make sure they were okay, but he would avoid seeing them if possible. He didn't need a repeat of last night. He would dial Lara up, knowing she was the more stable of the two. She would be okay staying in the luxury hotel for a few more days, but he guessed Janice would get antsy soon, and she would want to get out of the room. He didn't need her tooling around Lenox Square or Phipps Plaza on a shopping excursion, or worse, drinking in some trendy Buckhead bar. He thought about putting Ian on them, but he had been carrying an extra load for Southeast Security while Reid had been chasing down Sarah's killers. He knew he could possibly need him at any time for more serious matters, so he didn't want to spread him too thin. He had also considered taking the girls to the hospital to visit Petey again. Petey's daughter, Stella, was there now so he didn't think she'd appreciate a couple of strippers hanging around her dad. Petey might like it, but Stella…not so much. Reid would need to make that trip alone.

He finished his shopping, returned home, and unloaded his groceries. He tracked Consuelo again, but she hadn't moved. He took the Maxima to Northside Hospital and rode the elevator to the third floor. When he entered the room, Stella was sitting in the chair across from the empty bed reading a book. She glanced up as he walked in and gave him a warm smile. Stella Ward Bellmaster had been a pleasingly plump, reasonably attractive girl when he had known her at Georgia Southern. She was now probably about thirty pounds overweight, but she had maintained some of the prettiness of her youth in her face. She had married an Anheuser-Busch executive right out of college and had lived in St. Louis for well over ten years. She had an eight-year-old daughter, and she spent most of her time carting the kid to school, violin lessons, and karate class. Stella had put the extra weight on during pregnancy, and had never been able to shed it. She hauled herself up from the chair and gave Reid a gripping hug.

"Salem, it sure is good to see you again. Dad is in the bathroom. He should be right out," she said.

"How's he doing today?" he asked, relieved that she was pleasant with him. She probably wasn't fully aware of what part he had played in getting Petey injured, but he was sure she had some suspicions.

"He's in some pain, but he insists on getting up to use the restroom. He won't use a bed pan," she told him. Then she added, "The doctor is concerned about the incision, but they haven't fought with him too much about it."

Reid nodded but said nothing. Silence filled the room for a few seconds, and then the bathroom door swung open and Petey wobbled out, pushing his IV apparatus.

"Salem! Good to see you, son," he said, and reached his hand out.

Reid grasped his hand and helped him back to the bed.

"Doctor thinks I can go home Monday, so I'm only stuck here another couple of days. Coulda been worse I expect," Petey said.

"You need anything?" Reid asked.

Petey glanced at Stella and was silent for a moment. "Nah," he finally said. Reid thought he wanted to say something more, but would have preferred his daughter out of earshot. Reid guessed he just wanted to ask about Janice and Lara.

They made some idle chitchat, mostly about Stella's daughter and her activities. Reid was not good at small talk, so he was happy to let Stella and Petey do the talking. He occasionally asked some questions about the daughter, but otherwise sat and listened. The nurse came in to check Petey's vitals, and Reid took the opportunity to say his goodbyes.

He rode the elevator down, jumped in the Maxima, and started the engine to cool the car. He checked on Consuelo yet again, but she was still at Spalding Lake. He dialed Lara.

"Salem," she said evenly.

"Hi, Lara, y'all doing okay?" he asked.

"I'm fine. Janice took off. She said she had to get out of here or go crazy. I tried to stop her, but she wouldn't listen. She's at Lenox Square," she told him, confirming his suspicions. "She shops there a lot, Salem. She drives all the way down here from Johns Creek about once a week to shop."

"How long has she been gone?" he asked.

"Maybe an hour…probably a little longer," she answered.

"Have you communicated with her since she left?" he asked.

"No," she responded. "Do you want me to text her?"

"Yes. Why don't you. Keep me posted, Lara," he said, and clicked off.

He called Ian and explained the situation. "Apparently she shops there a lot according to Lara. Oscar could look for her there, or send someone. I'm concerned," he said.

"I can get there a little later. Maybe a couple hours from now," he told Reid.

"Okay. I'll go there now. Meet me there in two unless you hear from me," he said, and clicked off.

Reid wanted to avoid texting Janice if possible, but he may not have a choice. He'd head to Lenox Square and decide when he arrived. Hopefully, he would hear back from Lara by then. He hopped on 400 from the hospital and made it to Lenox Square in under fifteen minutes. Saturday traffic was surprisingly cooperative, but it was still a bit early.

Reid wheeled into the parking lot of the mall and found a spot near an entrance. He thought that she might be shopping in a particular, popular department store, but it was just a random guess. He checked his phone and a text from Lara said she had gotten no response when she tried to contact her. He decided to text Janice himself: "I'm at Lenox. Tell me where you are and I'll find you."

He heard nothing in return. He threw on the Yankees hat and wore his sunglasses into the mall. He strolled through the department store, paying special attention to where shoes and fashionable clothing were sold. He repeated the process at the other large department stores. Nothing. He checked his texts again, but still had gotten no response.

Reid slowed down and thought. He'd been running around the stores trying to locate Janice with no success. He didn't know for certain that she was even in the mall, but he thought it was likely. He texted Lara: "Did Janice eat anything this morning?"

She responded immediately: "No. I ordered room service. She left before it arrived."

He headed to the food court. He found a spot with the greatest view of all traffic and waited. He sat for thirty minutes and did not see her at any restaurant. He texted Lara again, she had heard nothing from Janice. He sat and watched for another thirty minutes. Then he spotted Janice walking at the far end of the court from where he sat. She was carrying a large bag and strutting along in the same clothes she had worn last night. A number of guys she passed turned their heads to watch her as she shook her fine ass through the mall. She was in her element. She never saw the big bouncer from Utopia that Reid had choked out following about twenty yards behind her. But Reid did. The bouncer kept pace with her as she moved through the mall. She was heading towards the particular store where Reid had parked just outside of the western entrance. Reid casually fell in about twenty yards behind the bouncer. He figured this was Bruce, the guy whom Alexis Lexus had spoken to on the phone at her apartment.

Janice wandered into the store and stopped a few times to admire some clothing, but made no more purchases. The bouncer did an enviable job of being discreet for such a big guy, and she was completely unaware of his presence. But Reid was even better. He blended perfectly with the shoppers while keeping both Janice and the bouncer in view. Finally, she'd had enough and walked towards the exit. The bouncer closed to within fifteen yards as Janice left the building, and then he took out his phone, punched some buttons, and placed the phone to his ear. This meant trouble; the bouncer likely had a partner outside who would pull up next to Janice as the bouncer forced her into the vehicle. Reid exited the store and was about ten yards behind the bouncer who was still fifteen yards behind Janice as he saw the Lexus zooming through the lot. He wished now that he'd checked the tracker on her car while sitting in the food court, but it didn't matter now.

Janice walked towards the parking deck where she could take stairs that would allow her access to Lenox Road. The Lexus was circling around towards the deck and coming down a lane to cut Janice off as the bouncer moved within a few yards of her. Just as the Lexus stopped in front of Janice, the bouncer made his final reach for her. Reid was about five feet behind him now and shouted, "Hey, Bruce."

The bouncer and Janice turned simultaneously towards his voice just as Reid stepped in and unleashed a vicious side kick to the guy's leg, planting his heel just above the bouncer's right knee. There was a loud pop and the bouncer's leg twisted in a way nature never intended. He screamed like a little girl, and Janice stood motionless, stunned by what had just occurred. The Lexus, driven by Alexis, peeled away from the scene, leaving rubber on the asphalt parking lot. Reid glanced around and saw cars moving, but fortunately no pedestrian traffic. He grabbed the man and quickly pulled him under the parking deck along a retaining wall. The bouncer screamed in pain from the mangled leg that bounced and skipped awkwardly as Reid slid him out of view from passersby. Janice stood in place; she still hadn't moved since the confrontation began. The bouncer started to say something and Reid planted a fist firmly into his mouth. Blood sprayed from the man's busted lips and broken teeth. Reid hit him again...and again. Reid continued to pound the man's face with his fists. The bouncer's nose was no longer recognizable. His eyes were slits. He bled profusely from scalp wounds. He ceased movement. Reid glanced around and saw cars moving in the distance from several directions, but still no pedestrian traffic. Janice was standing behind him, her mouth agape. Reid viciously bounced the man's head off the pavement over and over until it no longer resembled a head. He reached into the man's pocket and took his phone. He took his wallet and keys from his other pockets. He snatched the bag from Janice, reached in, and removed a $90 blouse she had purchased, and wiped his bloody hands and face. His dark shirt had blood from the bouncer on it, but it was not very noticeable. Satisfied he had gotten most of the blood off his body, he placed the bloody garment back into the bag and handed it to Janice, who was shaking and crying. He took her arm and led her back towards the exit where they had all emerged just minutes ago, and moved quickly through the doors. They moved to the front of the department store and out through that exit. He led her to the Maxima, got her into the passenger seat, and moved around to the driver's side. He calmly started the vehicle and drove out to Peachtree Road and back to the hotel. Janice was still shaking, but the crying had stopped. He said nothing to her as they climbed from the SUV and entered the hotel. They took the elevator to the tenth floor and Reid texted Lara as they ascended that he had Janice and that he needed her to open the door to the suite.

Lara met them at the door. Reid pushed Janice into the suite and took the bag from her. She started to cry again and he ignored her.

"What happened?" Lara asked.

Reid ignored her too. He took the man's wallet from his cargo pants and looked through it. A Georgia driver's license showed a picture of a twenty-nine-year-old male who would never see his thirtieth birthday. His name was Anthony Bruce Geridino with an Atlanta address not far from where Reid had his office. He had a Visa credit card and a few other items in the sleeves. His wallet contained $320 in cash. He removed it from the wallet and placed it on the coffee table. He clicked the phone and checked the contacts. He found Alexis and Oscar both in the contacts. The number for Oscar was the same as the number Alexis had in her phone. He was sure it was a throwaway. The car keys were for a Toyota.

"Salem?" Lara said. "Please tell me what's going on."

"I located Janice," he said. "She's safe. See if you can keep her that way."

"Oh my God, Salem," Janice said to him. "What are we going to do?"

Reid was angry, mostly at Janice for her selfishness. He wanted to cool off before he said something that would just set her off again.

"Get her a drink, Lara. See if you can calm her down some," he said, and went into Janice's room and found the bathroom.

He removed his shirt and pants and cleaned himself thoroughly with a wet towel. He put his clothes back on and called Ian.

"I found her. We're good for now. I'll call you later," he said, and hung up before Ian responded.

Reid placed the bouncer's belongings in the shopping bag after removing the unsoiled clothing Janice had purchased at the mall. He left the $320 on the coffee table and looked at Janice. She was drinking straight vodka from the minibar.

"Do you understand that you can't leave here again?" he asked her.

"Yes," she said shakily.

"Stay in the room until I tell you it's safe," he told them both.

He gave the girls a long look and departed. He stood outside the door and listened until he heard the sound of the door being chained. He pulled his phone and checked the tracking app for Consuelo. She was at an apartment complex in Dunwoody now. He pulled the list from his pocket and matched the address to a Jennifer Renfro. Then he tracked the Lexus. It was at 400 and Holcomb Bridge Road in Roswell. It looked like Alexis was heading home.

# 62

CONSUELO VALDEZ HAD ONLY ONE HOUSE to clean on Saturday morning and an apartment in the early afternoon. She had both helpers today, so she hoped that she would not be too tired tonight to properly entertain Oscar at his home in Norcross. She had prepared all the food last night, and she would take it to his house to cook. It wouldn't take long; the preparation was the hard part. She had a late afternoon appointment to have her hair done, and she planned to visit a nail salon too. She had purchased a very short skirt and splurged on a skimpy thong from Victoria's Secret. She planned to pack a bag in hopes that he would ask her to spend the night again as he had done once before.

She finished at the apartment of the single woman who was an assistant principal at a private Catholic school in Forsyth County. She had several hours to finish unloading her equipment at her apartment, make her appointments, and finish cleaning up for her early evening date with Oscar. She arrived home and decided she would shower first, so that she wouldn't risk getting her hair wet after having it done at the parlor. She made her appointment on time, and then made the short drive to the nail salon. She was very happy with her hair, and almost as pleased with her nails upon completion. She was even happier that she still had an hour to perform all of her necessary hygiene, dress in her sexy outfit, and drive to Oscar's home. Her plans had come together nicely, and she considered it a good omen for the remainder of the evening.

————

Reid had gone straight home after leaving the girls at the hotel in Buckhead. He had disrobed completely and placed all of his clothing in the washer upon arrival. He washed his clothes on the hottest setting and jumped into the shower, scrubbing every inch of his body thoroughly. He washed his hair twice and then cleaned his body again. He dressed in another pair of dark cargo pants, a dark shirt, and donned the Yankees hat again. He packed all the items he would need for the evening and grabbed the keys to the Maxima. He sat at his kitchen table and inspected the phone of Bruce Geridino very carefully. Once he was satisfied that there was nothing else useful to him on the phone, he added it to the shopping bag he had confiscated from Janice. He started the washer again and washed the clothes on the hottest setting once more.

It was just after 6 pm when he checked the tracking app for the Lexus belonging to Alexis Lexus. She was at Utopia. Then he checked on Consuelo. She was at a location off Beaver Ruin Road. Did she have a Saturday night cleaning job? He wasn't sure exactly how many houses a maid would normally clean in a day. He did not have a feel for how long an average house would take to clean, or how late she would schedule a house cleaning either. Then he wondered about the location. The Beaver Ruin corridor in Norcross was a middle-class neighborhood. He didn't think many in that area would have maid service. He pulled out the paper and looked for the address. It wasn't listed. This meant one of two things: she was visiting a friend or she was cleaning one of the few homes that didn't list an address on the spreadsheet. He punched the location into his GPS and headed to the Maxima. He planned to detour over to Petey's place on Buford Highway to dispose of the contents of Janice's bag. Petey had a good-sized fire pit that was perfect for the job.

————

Alexis Lexus was not having a good night. Oscar had sent her and her sometimes boyfriend, Bruce, to several locations during the day to see if they could find Destiny. Destiny had always yapped about how she would go to Lenox or Phipps often during her leisure time to buy clothes at one of the upscale department stores. They had gone to Lenox first and had gotten lucky. Bruce had spotted her in the first hour and followed her as planned until she exited the building. Then it all ran backwards. The guy from the funeral she had taken pictures of, had attacked Bruce for the second time in two days and prevented them from capturing Destiny. Oscar would be displeased, and that was never a good thing. And worse, Bruce had not shown up for work. She knew what that likely meant and that scared her. She was much less concerned for Bruce than she was for herself. Truthfully, she could give a shit about Bruce. She was afraid that Reid would show up at Utopia and cause big problems, especially for her. It had distracted her from her performance tonight too. She had far fewer tips than normal and very few table or lap dances. Then there was Oscar. She hadn't spoken with him yet about their failure. She hadn't seen him tonight and hadn't expected to. She knew he was staying away from Utopia since the events of early Friday morning, but she knew she'd be dealing with him somewhere, somehow—and soon. This had added to her misery. And to make matters worse, Utopia had brought a couple of less experienced bouncers over from the Slick Kitty to stand in for the three that had been beaten by Reid and his gang. Bruce was missing, one of the others had a concussion and a broken jaw, and the third one had a broken arm that had required surgery. It had been an awful day.

———

Oscar had enjoyed better days. This mess with Salem Reid and Utopia was a thorn in his side. And to make matters worse, the business he had wanted to conduct on Friday evening at the Stewart Avenue location had fallen through. He would need to reschedule for this evening, but he couldn't go near Utopia. He had come up with an alternate plan, though. But in the meantime, he would enjoy this young maid of his for at least the early part of the evening. She had shown up about an hour ago and made a delicious meal of chile relleno for him. It had been quite good. She had worn seductive clothing for him too. He liked those short skirts she had been wearing, and she would bend over and give him a great view of her plump, ripe ass every chance she got. He enjoyed the show. So he decided that for the next few hours, he would enjoy Consuelo and then send her home a little later. Then he would get back to business.

He watched her clean his kitchen after he had stuffed himself with her fine meal. When she finished, he bent her over the kitchen table and pulled her thong down. She was very compliant. He screwed her from behind in his kitchen. He had discovered he liked sex with her better than the occasional service he received from the whores who worked for him. She excited him in ways that they did not.

After he came, he had her move around the kitchen naked. He told her to put on some coffee and bring him the dessert she had made. She again did as instructed and gave him a sheepish grin as she continued to wiggle her big ass in his face. He finished the coffee and dessert while she found a platter in the cupboard and carried two Coronas over to the table. He drank his beer and watched her, then he stayed seated at the table as she squatted down and rode him while he lounged in his chair. She made noises of approval and seemed to enjoy it when he would smack her ass from time to time. After she had satisfied him the second time, he took her into the bedroom and they both snoozed for a bit. When he awoke, he gave her one more whirl in his bed. When he finished with her, he got up without a word and got into the shower. She was naked and still lying in the bed when he returned to the bedroom and dressed. It was nearing 9 pm.

"I have business tonight, Consuelo. I must leave soon. You will have to leave, also," he said to her, as he put Joey's Rolex around his left wrist.

Consuelo was not happy about this, but she knew better than to complain. "Okay, Oscar. May I shower?" she asked.

"Yes. If you do it quickly. I have business," he repeated.

While she showered, Oscar called Utopia and issued instructions.

———

Reid had driven by the house off Beaver Ruin Road two times during the past two hours, but did not want to risk another. He had also driven down a road that spurred off the main artery of the neighborhood and ran behind the house that Consuelo was visiting. He could make out part of the house and backyard from the spur, but that had been before darkness had come. He doubted he would be able to see the house at all from the spur now. He sat at a strip mall at the corner of Beaver Ruin and the road where Consuelo was visiting. He waited and thought. He used his tracking app to keep tabs on her car and occasionally checked on the Lexus. Consuelo was parked at a nondescript house that was typical in the area. The two-story box of a home was probably less than two thousand square feet. It had vinyl siding on three sides and a brick facade in front. The yard looked like the owner kept the grass cut, but the landscaping was nothing special. A two-car garage was fronted by a solid white vinyl door, so the lack of windows eliminated a view into the garage to check its contents. Reid knew he would not be able to get close enough with the house occupied to see into the garage even if there had been windows. He speculated that she was visiting a friend or maybe a boyfriend, but he wanted to be sure, so he decided to sit and monitor her actions. He was good at waiting.

———

Consuelo exited the shower and dressed quickly because Oscar now seemed impatient. She packed the culinary items she had brought, but cleverly left the dish with the few uneaten chile rellenos in the refrigerator. She thought she might return either Sunday or Monday evening to retrieve the pan. Maybe she could repeat tonight's performance again for Oscar.

"I had fun with you, Oscar," she said, and came close to him.

He gave her a quick kiss and patted her ample rear. "Yes. I enjoyed our time too."

"I hope we can do it again soon," she said, and gave him a sheepish grin.

"Yes, yes. Of course. I will walk you to your car," he said, and took her firmly by the arm and moved her to the front door. He did not walk her to the car, but stood in the doorway as she moved to her vehicle parked in the driveway.

She opened her CR-V and placed her belongings in the vehicle. Then she turned and waved to him as she got into her car. As she backed from the driveway, he closed the door and went to finish his preparations. He went to the garage and removed numerous large bricks of heroin from the storage closet and placed them in a large duffel bag. He would net close to $25,000 for the deal tonight, but he was concerned that he could not make the deal at Utopia. He had given this plenty of thought. He did not want to drive his Flex anywhere near Utopia, and preferred to avoid driving it at all. So he needed a ride tonight, and he had arranged for that ride when he had phoned Utopia. He expected it to arrive anytime. He didn't like the idea of anyone affiliated with his business knowing where he lived, but he feared the alternative of driving the Flex to his meeting even more. Besides, he would be moving from this house in a matter of days. It was only a slight concern at this point.

———

Reid monitored Consuelo on his device as she left the house she had been visiting. He still sat at the strip mall and figured she would soon be pulling up to the intersection. In less than a minute, she arrived at the light and moved into the left turn lane. He could see that she was alone in the car. Was her night over? He wondered if she was going home. She didn't live far, so he would know within minutes.

She turned left out of the neighborhood onto Beaver Ruin. Satellite Boulevard, where she lived, was maybe a mile down the road. He watched her taillights as she sped away, and then suddenly he saw something that took him by complete surprise. A white Lexus driven by a woman with long blond hair made a left turn off Beaver Ruin into the neighborhood that Consuelo had just departed. He switched his tracking device to the Lexus, and sure enough, Alexis Lexus was making her way down into the neighborhood. There was only one place she could possibly be going. The night had become very interesting.

———

Alexis Lexus didn't think her day could get any worse, but she had been called to the phone at Utopia and Oscar was on the line. She was damn sure having a bad night, but she would much rather stay at Utopia than do what Oscar was asking of her. When he had inquired about the events of the afternoon, she had told him. He had gotten very quiet and then instructed her to a location in Norcross maybe seven or eight miles from the club. A place off Beaver Ruin Road. She had never been to that part of town. She was frightened, but she was even more frightened about what could happen if she disobeyed him. She had dressed quickly and exited the club with a fraction of the cash she normally made on a Saturday night and then drove to Norcross. She wasn't sure whether she was at the right house or not at first, but Oscar emerged from the house carrying a large bag. He motioned for her to pop the trunk, and he dropped his parcel in there, and slid into the passenger's seat.

"Drive to your apartment," he instructed her.

"What?" she said, and immediately regretted doing so when he gave her a hard head-smack that rocked her momentarily.

"Give me the address," he demanded.

She gave him her address, but said nothing else. They were still sitting in his driveway.

"DRIVE, BITCH!" he shouted, and she put the car in gear.

She drove out of his neighborhood and took a right at Beaver Ruin, oblivious to the dark Maxima that sat at the strip center as she passed. She navigated over to Buford Highway and went a short distance north to Langford and took it west where it merged with Medlock Bridge. She turned on Spalding and took it to Holcomb Bridge Road where she crossed the river into Roswell and headed towards her apartment.

———

Reid did not follow the Lexus as it turned right on Beaver Ruin Road. His knee-jerk reaction would be to chase down the car. He had seen Oscar in the passenger's seat and it had caused his blood to boil. This man was responsible for the death of Sarah, and for the terrible abuse of Janice, Lara, and Petey. All of whom were Reid's friends. He forced himself to remain calm and think. He checked the progress of the Lexus; they had gone west on Holcomb Bridge Road and were several miles beyond the Chattahoochee River. Time was on his side.

Reid pulled from the strip center and moved down into the neighborhood. He turned left at the spur and parked the Maxima on a curved part of the road between two houses that had a row of sickly cypress trees separating the yards. He secured the drop in his holster, and a knife to his ankle. He packed his picks and Maglite and exited the car. Reid had good cover as he walked through the dark along the cypress trees. They were brown and withered, but they stood about twelve feet tall and had been planted close together as a privacy hedge. And that was what they offered him—privacy. He scooted easily between the houses. A few homes had fenced yards, but the majority didn't, and he was able to quickly slip into the backyard of Oscar's house. He checked for signs of a security system as he got to the back door, but saw nothing that indicated that one was installed. The back porch was simply a slab of concrete that led to a single door. There was an old grill on the porch with a cover on it. The grill looked like it hadn't been used lately. There was a yellowish grime on the cover that was probably pollen from the springtime that even the summer rains had not been able to dispel. He wheeled the grill over so that it gave him partial cover from the houses behind him. Between the darkness, the various hedges along the backs of the yards and the positioning of the houses, Reid probably had adequate cover without the grill. But he took no chances. He kneeled and held the Maglite in his mouth as he worked the picks on the back door. It took him close to two minutes, but he was able to get the door unlocked. He drew his gun and stepped quietly into the dark house. He moved cautiously through the downstairs. The streetlights from the road in front of the house provided just enough light for him to avoid stumbling around as he made his way deeper into the home. He smelled the remnants of the dinner Consuelo had made. The main floor was a simple living room that was nicely furnished, a kitchen, and a breakfast room or small dining area were just off the kitchen. There was a hallway behind the stairs that went to the garage and laundry room. He checked the garage and saw the Flex parked in the near spot of the two-car garage. He moved from the garage back to the hallway. He cleared the downstairs and moved carefully up the stairway. There were three bedrooms upstairs. The smallest one was completely empty. The larger spare room had a full-size bed and a dresser in it, but it looked like it was never used. Reid moved down the hall to the master. It was very nicely furnished. A big credenza with a flat-screen TV inside of it sat across from the unmade king-size bed. There was a large dresser and two nightstands. A spacious, clean, and luxurious bathroom adjoined the master. A closet with double doors spanned the wall to the left of the room as you entered. Reid stopped his search temporarily and checked the tracker on the Lexus. The car appeared to be parked at the complex where Alexis Lexus lived off Holcomb Bridge Road. He had plenty of time.

He began with the nightstands. He found nothing interesting in them and moved to the dresser. He discovered nothing incriminating in the dresser either. He looked under the bed. There was nothing. He opened the closet. Clothing hung neatly and organized in the walk-in space. Oscar kept his pants, dress slacks, and jeans to the right and shirts and jackets to the left. He had about eight pairs of shoes ranging from dress shoes to loafers. He had placed little on the shelves; there were a few odds and ends, sweatshirts and hoodies, but that was it. Reid rifled through the shirts and when he did, a panel was exposed behind them. It had a padlock on a clasp that held the door closed and locked. The lock looked strong, but the clasp was vulnerable. Reid removed his knife and tried to work the clasp away from the panel. The wood was made of pine, so it was reasonably soft. Nevertheless, he spent ten minutes before he could pry the door open. The first thing he noticed was a stack of cash. He guessed it was close to $8,000. He removed the money stack and placed it in his cargo pants. There were a number of men's watches and timepieces in the compartment too. He took them out and placed them in his pockets. There were also five or six pieces of ladies' fine jewelry. They looked to be diamonds and sapphires in both white and yellow gold. He left them. He spotted a key with an orange plastic cylinder attached to it on a ring with a tab. The tab had a name of a public storage facility located in Norcross on it. Near the back of the compartment sat a cocktail glass with six or seven cards stuck in it. He pulled the glass out and dumped the cards into his gloved hand. They were business cards, and they were identical on the front. Reid flipped them over and shuffled them. They all had addresses written on the back. Two of them had four digits written on them below the address. One read 1613 and the other read 1980. The latter was Joey McIntosh's address. The other five cards had the word "none" written below the addresses, and a range of dates. He flipped one of the cards over to the front. He recognized the name on the card. He stared at it for a long moment. It was a person familiar to him, and now everything had become crystal clear.

He moved to the garage and climbed into the Flex. He opened the glove box and searched through it, and discovered more revealing information. He examined the console compartment and searched under the seats. He moved to the back and examined the entire vehicle. Then he searched the garage. He found twenty or so bricks of heroin in a big cardboard box that had an old rug thrown over it. He left the drugs. He moved back into the house and checked the tracking app. The Lexus was on the move. It was just west of the river near Nesbit Ferry Road. Reid sat down in the living room and waited.

# 63

OSCAR MET HIS VERY IMPORTANT CLIENT at the apartment of Alexis Lexus. He knew that she was less than thrilled about a drug deal of this magnitude going down in her apartment. The man Oscar had met was a big Russian guy with a pockmarked face and bad breath. He had an evil smile and when he laughed he made noises like a panting dog that sounded something like hey, hey, hey, hey, hey. And he laughed a lot. He had a bulge under his shirt too. A big guy with a big gun in her apartment was no comfort to Alexis either. She was very nervous. One moment was particularly tense when the big Russian placed his satchel of cash on her kitchen table and reached under his shirt and touched his gun. Oscar then opened his duffel and showed the man the drugs. The big Russian scanned through the drugs, keeping his hand on his gun the entire time. He told Oscar that one of the bricks looked too thin, and that he would need to withhold about $300 from the sale. The men bantered back and forth for several minutes, and then they finally agreed that the big Russian would pay the entire price for the product. But to compensate him for his concerns, Alexis Lexus would service him with a very special blow job. Thus Oscar was shorted no cash, and the big Russian got to enjoy himself at the expense of Alexis Lexus. She was certainly less than thrilled to be forced to fellate this big crud, but she knew to refuse would be worse.

Oscar carried the cash into the spare bedroom and waited. The big Russian pulled down his pants and withdrew the biggest cock Alexis had ever seen. To make matters worse, he was uncircumcised. He held his gun in his hand while she took his bulk into her mouth. She was skilled, and within five minutes he began panting like a dog again, but the noises were more like ee-ah, ee-ah, ee-ah this time. As he reached the point of climax, he grabbed the back of her head and held her, so that she would have no choice but to swallow his spunk. As revolting as it was, she managed to gulp down his entire load with only mild sputtering. He released her head and she stood up and tried to show that she was a pro and smiled at the guy. She just hoped that she wouldn't vomit before he departed.

The big Russian guy pulled up his pants, fastened and zipped them, and produced yet another one of his annoying chuckles. Alexis knocked on the spare bedroom door and Oscar emerged from the room.

"Was everything satisfactory?" Oscar asked the big Russian.

"Satisfactory, yes. We should do business many times, I think," the big Russian replied, and Oscar joined him in laughter.

The guy departed, and while Alexis washed her face, brushed her teeth, and gargled several times with mouthwash, Oscar counted his money a second time. The satchel contained $80,000. Twenty-five thousand of that was profit. He felt much better about the day. He glanced at Joey's Rolex and saw that it was approaching 11 pm.

"Take me home, Alexis. Then you can take the rest of the night off," he told her.

Oscar zipped the satchel of cash and the two of them headed for the Lexus parked below the building.

———

Reid kept an eye on the progress of the Lexus. When it turned onto Buford Highway, he turned off the lamp he had put on low to keep his eyes adjusted to light. It was three minutes later when the Lexus pulled into the drive.

———

Oscar had Alexis shut her car off and he took her keys. He went to the trunk of the car and removed the satchel. He closed the trunk and walked past the driver's side door and tossed the keys back to her through the open window. He said nothing to her and walked directly to his front door. He placed the key into the dead bolt and unlocked the door just as Alexis backed out of the driveway. He closed the front door and locked the dead bolt. He flicked on the light switch, which illuminated the room and as he turned he saw Salem Reid, sitting casually on his sofa.

Oscar didn't react at first. Reid had the 22 along his side in his gloved right hand.

"Salem Reid?" asked Oscar.

Reid said nothing and made no reaction, but he didn't take his eyes off of Oscar.

"You have broken into my house," Oscar said, overstating the obvious.

Reid remained silent.

Then Oscar sprung.

Reid fired off two shots that hit Oscar in the center of his chest, but it did not slow him down. He continued towards Reid. At the last possible moment, Reid propelled himself from the sofa and was up and sidestepping Oscar as he continued past him. As Oscar's hips passed Reid, he delivered a ferocious roundhouse kick to Oscar's buttocks. Oscar flew face first into his sofa, but quickly turned and somehow had produced a knife in his right hand. Oscar was breathing heavily and two small red dots had stained his shirt. He coughed and when he did Reid kicked the knife from his hand. It flew through the air and landed harmlessly on the floor behind the sofa. Oscar tried to get off the sofa and Reid kicked him in the head. Oscar fell back and stared at Reid.

"You have to answer for Sarah," he told Oscar, and then he shot him twice between the eyes.

Reid placed the gun inside Oscar's mouth and fired once again. Oscar's head flew backwards against the sofa. He would never harm another human being again.

Reid holstered the gun. He removed Joey Mac's Rolex from Oscar's wrist and placed it in his pocket with the other timepieces. He picked up the satchel and raced out the back door. He sprinted through the backyards at a torrid pace and was inside the Maxima within thirty seconds. He started the car and drove out of the neighborhood. He went through downtown Norcross and drove the speed limit. He jumped on Holcomb Bridge and took it up to Peachtree Industrial Boulevard where he stopped for a red light. He checked on the Lexus and saw that Alexis was at home. She had not returned to Utopia.

Reid took Holcomb Bridge Road all the way to the apartment complex where Alexis lived. There was significant traffic coming in and out of the complex as midnight approached, so he simply followed someone into the property. Reid parked close to where he had before and located the Lexus. He removed the tracking device and placed it in his cargo pants. He took the stairs to the second floor and found that 4204 was still unlocked, just as he had left it. He moved noiselessly through the apartment and very carefully slid the balcony door open. He stepped onto the porch and looked out into the surrounding area. At the far end of the pool, a young couple was necking on a lounge and oblivious to the world around them. He waited for a car to move out of the middle lot and watched it as it took the main artery towards the exit. He peeked down into the apartment below, and saw Alexis sitting alone and smoking as she looked out towards the pool. She was pushing buttons on her phone; probably texting or using social media. Reid climbed over the railing and quickly and silently shimmied down onto her balcony. She never saw him approach and he had his hand over her mouth instantly, as he shuffled her through the open sliding glass door into her apartment. He slid the door closed with his foot and pushed her down on the sofa. He had the gun in her mouth before she could utter a sound.

"You take nice pictures, Bethany," he said.

Her eyes widened and Reid knew she was terrified.

"Do you want to live?" he asked her.

She nodded vigorously.

"Good. Listen carefully. You are going to leave here in the next fifteen minutes. You will drive I-20 into Alabama. You will never return to Georgia. It's my state, and you can't be in my state. I'm going to take the gun out of your mouth. You say nothing. No questions. If you talk or disobey, I'll kill you. Do you understand?" he asked her.

She nodded again, and he slid the gun from her mouth. Bethany Bertrand packed her essential items quickly. Reid took the keys to her apartment from her, and walked her to her car. She placed several pieces of luggage into her trunk and took off. Reid followed her until she got on I-20 going west. He got on I-20 east, went through downtown, and took the connector north to 85. He exited at North Druid Hills. He turned north on Buford Highway and was at Petey's place within minutes. He exited the car, punched the code for the gate, and drove the Maxima into the lot. He parked it in the middle of the yard, exited, removed all his belongings from the vehicle, and placed them in the Challenger. He drove his car to his home in Chamblee, and sprinted up the stairs to his unit, toting the duffel and the satchel stuffed with cash. He got safely inside, locked and bolted his door, showered and climbed into bed. He slept for ten hours.

# 64

REID AWOKE AFTER NOON. It was the latest he'd slept in years. He had needed the rest. But he knew he had another busy day in front of him. He called Lara.

"Hi, Salem," she said cautiously.

"Hi, Lara. Are you two okay?" he asked.

"Bored, but okay," she said.

"I'll be there in thirty minutes. We'll have lunch and then I'll get you both to your cars, so you can go home."

"Salem, it's over?" she asked hopefully.

"I'll tell you in person. Thirty minutes," he said, and clicked off.

Reid showered, brushed his teeth, and rinsed with mouthwash. He dressed quickly and made it to Buckhead in ten minutes. He rode the elevator to the tenth floor and knocked on the door to the suite. Janice answered. She was dressed in shorts, pumps, and a sleeveless white blouse that showed off her tanned and toned arms. Her wavy brown hair was clean and shiny. Her blue eyes danced.

"Hi, Salem!" she said with a cheery smile.

She gently took his hand and led him into the suite. He did not see Lara.

"I hear we can go home. Is that right?" she asked.

"You can. Everything will be okay," he said.

She smiled. "I'm sorry for yesterday. I'm very grateful to you also. I hope you know how much Lara and I appreciate what you did for us," she said, and touched his arm.

She looked as if she wanted to say something else, and then thought better of it.

"Hungry?" he asked. "Do you like Houston's?"

"I love Houston's. And we're buying," Janice said.

Lara walked into the room, still dressed in the dark sports gear that had become her look. Despite the loose fit of the clothing, she still looked great.

They piled in Reid's car. Janice hopped in front and Lara in back. They made the short drive to Houston's and luckily found the last available parking space behind the restaurant. They surprisingly got seated at a corner booth in a matter of minutes, and they were quiet for a spell as they scanned the menus. Lara sat across from Reid and Janice. Reid ordered a full rack of ribs and fries. The ladies both got salads with grilled chicken. All three decided on iced tea to drink.

After the drinks arrived, Lara looked at Reid. "What can you tell us, Salem?" she said in a low voice.

He didn't answer right away. He squeezed lemon into his tea and added a little sugar. He took a sip and looked at the ladies. "You will never see Oscar again," he said softly.

"Like Bruce?" Janice whispered, her eyes wide.

Reid said nothing, but gave the slightest nod of his head. He didn't want to talk about it, but he knew that they would never rest easy unless they knew Oscar had been eliminated.

No one said anything for a few moments. It had been an ugly week for Janice and an awful summer for Lara. But now they could move on with their lives. They wouldn't have to live in fear. He watched them as the reality dawned on them. Suddenly Lara's chest began to heave, and she began to cry. Reid sat there in awkward discomfort, but Janice took her friend's hand and smiled. Lara had been a pillar of strength throughout the entire ordeal, but the feelings of relief and finality had overcome her and shattered the wall of toughness. She was like a little girl who had been lost in the grocery store, only to be rescued and then crying tears of joy and relief at being discovered. Reid excused himself and brought some paper napkins back from the bar. He handed her the whole stack. Lara laughed and snot blew out her nose.

"Oh, gross!" she laughed again, and wiped her nose and face.

She wadded up the napkin and used another to dry her eyes. She blew her nose again into another napkin and Janice decided to be funny.

"Eeeewwwww, like nasty gross, Lara," she said, and then they were all laughing.

Lara jumped up. "I think I'll go to the restroom and pull my nasty, gross self together," she said, smiling.

She left Janice and Reid in the booth together. Janice moved her hand from her lap reflexively and placed it on Reid's leg. He squirmed a bit, and she laughed and raised both hands in the air.

"Sorry, sorry, sorry. You're just so damn cute," she told him, and pinched his cheek.

He laughed in spite of himself, but felt more relaxed when Lara returned. They ate their lunches, and shared with each other just as they had done on Friday evening. Lara tried one of Reid's ribs, and raved about how good it tasted. After she finished gnawing the meat to the bone, both Reid and Janice leaned forward, squinted, and examined Lara's face around her mouth.

"What?" Lara asked, looking at them like they both had two heads.

"I think you have barbecue sauce on your face, but I can't be sure on yo black skin," Janice said the last part with a black accent, and this caused Reid to chuckle.

"Racist fuckers," Lara said to them both, and they all started laughing again.

Lara wiped the sauce from her mouth trying not to smile at her friends, and shook her head.

"Are you gonna need some more napkins, Lara?" Janice snickered.

"Fuck you!" Lara mouthed inaudibly, but the smile she had previously tried to conceal spread over her face.

Janice stuck her tongue out at her friend and Lara just shook her head again. They finished their meals and, as promised, the girls paid the tab.

Reid drove through Brookhaven and Chamblee and outside the Perimeter. He pulled into Utopia. The sports bar was busy, but Utopia would be slow until later. Janice's Benz was parked right where she had left it, but there was a big scratch along the driver's side door where she had been keyed.

"Shit!" she said, as they pulled alongside of it.

Reid and Janice got out of the car, but Lara stayed put. Reid examined the scratch; it was pretty nasty.

"Bring it to Petey next week," he told her.

"Okay," she said, and looked at Reid and smiled. "So this is goodbye?" she asked.

"I'm around, Janice, you know that," he told her.

She twisted her mouth into a smirk. "Do I get a hug?" she asked.

"Sure," he told her.

She moved into his arms and put her head on his chest. Then she raised her head and looked at him seriously.

"You're the best, Salem Reid. I'll never forget you. We used to laugh at Sarah when she talked about you...all romantic and stuff. But now I see what she saw in you. I get it. I'm here for you too, you know?"

He nodded. He had a lump in his throat. He wasn't sure how many more heavy moments he could have with this woman and escape unscathed.

She reached up and kissed him on the lips. It was a nice kiss. He gently pushed her back, but held her arms for a second longer.

"I'll see you around, Janice," he said, and knew it sounded lame.

He held the door for her and she got into the Benz. She started her car, gave him one more electric smile, and drove off. He exhaled audibly and climbed into the Challenger. Lara was still in the back seat.

"I'm your chauffeur, now?" he asked, "Why don't you climb up front?"

"Hmmmm. Is the seat wet? The way she acts around you, it wouldn't surprise me," she said, and started laughing.

"Come on. Let's get out of here," he said.

Lara climbed into the front after making a display of scrutinizing the seat that Janice had just vacated. He drove to the hospital and pulled into a spot two cars over from hers. Neither of them made a move to exit the car. Reid reached into his pocket and pulled out the $8,000 that he had taken from Oscar's hidden compartment in his closet. He handed it to Lara.

"What's this?" she asked.

"Back pay," was all he said.

She stared at him, then she looked at the stack of cash and rifled through it. Finally, she nodded and stuffed the cash in her bag.

"Thank you. I can use it," she said.

"What will you do, Lara?"

She shrugged. "I don't know. I could still dance somewhere, but I won't make what I'm accustomed to making. I don't think I want to, though. I'm tired of the life."

"I might have something for you. Probably pay well, and you can keep your clothes on," he said.

"What?" she asked.

"I'll call you later this week. Hang in there, okay?"

"Okay," she said.

They got out of the car and he placed her bags in her trunk. She hugged him fiercely, and it felt nice. He knew that Lara Brooks was his friend, and he was glad.

"Thanks for everything, Salem," she said.

Lara climbed into her car, started the engine, and drove away. She stuck her hand out of the window and waved as she rolled through the lot and out towards the exit.

Reid briefly considered visiting with Petey, but dismissed the notion. He had a lot left to do. He needed to visit Joey. He dialed his friend.

Joey answered on the third ring. "Hey, Salem, what's up?"

"Are you at home?" Reid asked.

"Yes. Liza is here too. She's staying with me."

"Good," Reid said. He was pleased with the altruism of his old friend.

"I'm dropping in on you for a bit. I'll be there in under an hour," he said and disconnected.

# 65

REID DROVE HOME AND TOOK THE SATCHEL from his closet.
He removed $15,000 and placed it in his safe. He took the remaining
money and the Rolex and left his condo. He drove to Joey Mac's in
Peachtree Corners and pulled around back. He removed the satchel and
went through the open garage door and knocked on the door leading
into the kitchen. He didn't recognize the pretty woman who let him
inside the house at first. He could not believe it was the same person he
and Joey had pulled from the seedy hotel room four days earlier.

"Hi," he said. "Liza, right?"

"Yes. And you're Salem Reid," she said as if she were taking an oral
exam in school and was certain of the answer.

"Wow. You clean up real well," he told her, and she gave him a half
smile that made her even prettier.

"I'm sorry I don't remember you, but Joey told me what you did for
me," she said. "Thank you." She held out her hand and he took it. It
was warm and balmy.

Reid stared at her for a second longer, and she looked down at
her hands. Then Herschel came running into the kitchen, and broke

the awkward silence as he greeted Reid enthusiastically. Joey came in behind him.

"Hey, Salem," Joey said, as he entered the kitchen. The two men shook hands, and Joey put his left arm around Salem in a half hug.

"What's in the bag?" Joey asked Reid.

Reid didn't respond. He glanced at Liza and then at Joey again. He wasn't sure what Joey had told Liza about everything. Liza caught the drift, and announced that she needed to take Herschel for a walk. Before she departed, she asked both men if she could get them a beverage, and both declined. She threw on some flip-flops, grabbed Herschel's leash and baggies, and took him out through the garage.

"She looks spectacular," Reid said. "You've taken good care of her, Joey."

Joey waved him off. "So, what's up?"

Reid opened the satchel and removed Joey's Rolex. He handed it to him. Then he unzipped the satchel as far as it would go, and showed Joey the cash. Joey stood with his mouth wide open.

"Before you changed your code, what was it, Joey?" Reid asked.

"Huh? My old code? It was 1980, the year Georgia won the National Championship. Salem, where did you find my stuff?" Joey asked, stunned.

"Put the money up in a safe place and let's go out back," Reid said.

"Salem, I don't know what to say. I never thought I'd get this stuff back."

"There are a few other timepieces in there too. If they don't belong to you, then let me have them back," Reid said.

"Sure, sure. Thanks, man. This is terrific. I'll put the stuff away," Joey told Reid.

He returned in less than a minute and they moved through the garage and into the backyard. They walked down towards the cypress trees and stopped. Joey handed Reid the watches.

"None of those are mine," he said.

Reid looked around. They were alone. He told him the story. He was only vague in regard to how Klaus and Oscar met their demise, but Joey put two and two together easily. He would need to figure out a way to let Liza know that the monster who had tortured her had been brought to justice, but he knew he'd come up with something.

Joey listened and marveled at his friend as Reid explained the delicate issue that would still need attention. He explained in great detail what it was he wanted to do, and how they would go about doing it.

"I'm returning to work tomorrow," Joey decided.

"I think that's a great idea, Joey," Reid told him.

"Liza is doing an outpatient program for a few weeks at Peachford Hospital. It's from 10 am until 3 pm, Monday through Friday. I'll need to drop her off and pick her up, but otherwise I'll be at the dealership."

"Sounds good. Let me know if you need some help getting her where she needs to be. I'm going back to work myself this week, but it will be Tuesday for me."

Joey changed the subject. "Let's watch some football on the Red Zone. Liza's a great cook. I bet she'll make us something when she returns. Sound good?" Joey said.

Reid thought that was a splendid idea. "Sounds great, Joey. Let's do it."

# 66

REID ENDED UP SPENDING MUCH OF SUNDAY afternoon with Liza and Joey. She had whipped up some kind of chicken pasta with pistachios in it. The meal was remarkably good, and she was pleased with the amount of food the guys put away. Reid enjoyed a few beers while Liza and Joey stuck with water. They watched the games on Red Zone and talked football through the afternoon. Liza surprised them with a decent knowledge of the game, and hung out with them as they watched. Reid departed shortly before sundown, and went home. When he arrived at his house, he snatched $1,000 of the spoils from Oscar's house and took the stairs down two flights. He banged on Ray's door. Ray answered wearing a kimono of all things. Reid tried hard not to laugh, but didn't quite succeed. He entered Ray's condo and closed the door.

"Salem Reid, don't you laugh at me. I paid over $100 for this garment. You need to appreciate it. Here, feel how smooth it is," Ray told him.

Reid held up both hands, palms out. "That's okay, Ray. I just wanted to come by and thank you for all your help."

He took ten $100 bills from his pocket and handed them to Ray.

"Ewe-wee," Ray said. "That is very nice of you, Salem."

"No problem, Ray," he said.

"So tell me," Ray said, "who were those two lovely women spending the night with you Friday? Vanilla and chocolate, Salem. You are quite the Renaissance man!" Ray exclaimed, and then cackled.

Reid shook his head at Ray and chuckled. "It's not what you think, Ray. Anyway, buy yourself another kimono," he said, and pointed to the cash.

"I may just do that, Salem. And thank you for your generous contribution," Ray said.

"Sure thing, Ray. Goodnight," Reid said, and headed up to the fourth floor.

Reid watched a bit of the Sunday Night Football game, but was dozing by halftime. He had another busy day tomorrow.

———

Reid awoke early Monday morning and made coffee. He trekked down to the IHOP in Chamblee Plaza where he and Millicent had their brunch together nine days ago. He ordered the harvest grain pancakes, fruit, and bacon, just as he'd done before. He drank coffee and considered the day ahead. As he sat there finishing his breakfast, his phone rang. It was Stella.

"Hi, Salem," she said. "Dad checked out of the hospital early this morning. I'm at his house now, but I leave for the airport in about an hour. Do you think you could swing by sometime today and check on him?"

"I was planning on doing just that, Stella. No problem," he told her.

"It was nice seeing you again, Salem. You take care of yourself. And take care of Dad too," she said.

"I'll do it, Stella. You have a good flight home," he said, and disconnected.

Petey lived in an unincorporated area of DeKalb County called Toco Hills. It was located a little east of 85 along North Druid Hills Road.

He had a sprawling brick ranch house with a nicely landscaped yard. The house was built in the fifties and sat on over an acre of land. Petey had lived there for over twenty years. Reid pulled into his driveway a little after 10 am. Petey met him at the door and didn't look too bad. He didn't look particularly good either. He moved slowly and his color was a little gray, but being stabbed in the gut and lying around a hospital for several days would do that to you.

They got themselves seated in the living room, and Reid tossed the stack of cash he had allocated for Petey. It was $7,000.

"What's this for, son? I ain't no hired gun," Petey said.

"Use it for your deductibles and co-payments, Petey," Reid said. "Maybe you can pay for Stella's airline costs."

"Nah, fuck it. I don't want your money," Petey said.

But when Reid explained how he had procured it, Petey had a change of heart.

"Hot damn, son! I knew you'd get that SOB. In that case, I'll gladly take it," Petey said, and laughed until a coughing fit overtook him.

Reid detailed the events of Friday and Saturday. He knew he could talk openly with Petey, but he was still vague and concise when it came to the actual conquests. It was just something not worth discussing in Reid's estimation. Then Reid returned the two drops to Petey. He would let the older man decide whether to keep the one he'd used or destroy it. It was up to Petey.

Reid asked Petey if he needed anything, but he said he'd be fine. He told Reid that he planned to be back at the shop by Thursday.

Petey inquired about the girls.

"How are Lara and Janice doing?

"They're doing real well considering. Lara is a brave soul. She's smart and goodhearted too, Petey."

"That Janice is some looker, Salem. I think she's got a flag in your ass, son," he said. "She's all googly-eyed over you."

Reid shrugged and tried not to laugh at the older man's crudeness. But he reckoned he was right. He was having difficulty getting her off his mind.

"Yeah? Maybe so, Petey," he replied.

Reid listened to Petey talk his talk for a bit, and when he seemed to tire some, he stood up and took out his keys.

"Petey, you call me if you need anything, okay? You're no kid anymore, don't try to do too much," Reid said.

Petey walked him to the door and they embraced. They had been friends for many years, and that friendship would last a lifetime. They had been down the river together on more than one occasion. The bonds were strong. These men understood each other without a lot of explanation, and they both realized what a precious gift it was to have a friendship like this. They also both understood that Reid would not allow Petey in on the "fight" again. Those days were over. It could easily end up costing Petey his life. He would not ask again, and he wondered if Petey was relieved, but he figured conflicted was a more accurate description. He guessed, however, that Petey knew it was best.

As Reid left Toco Hills, the Monday lunch traffic was brutal. It was especially congested near 85, so it took Reid over thirty minutes to get back to his condo in Chamblee. When he got inside his home, he called Joey.

"Salem," Joey said.

"How's the first day back at work?" Reid asked.

"So far, so good, Salem," Joey responded.

"How about 1 pm? Does that work for you?" Reid asked.

"It does, Salem. I'm ready to go," Joey said, and Reid noted the conviction in his voice.

"I'll see you at 1, Joey," Reid said, and clicked off.

———

Reid showered and shaved. He brushed his teeth and rinsed, then he put on some faded Levi's and a black tee shirt. He wore a long-sleeve shirt from Old Navy unbuttoned over the tee, and stepped into a pair of black Skechers. He attached his gun and holster to his belt, and grabbed the remaining $7,000 he had taken from Oscar and placed it in his pocket. He drove in the rain north on Peachtree Industrial Boulevard to McIntosh Ford. He parked in the visitor lot and walked quickly into the showroom. He ignored the salesman who approached him as he came through the door, and walked directly to Joey's office. Joey sat at his desk wearing a white oxford dress shirt, black slacks, and a red and black tie. He was looking at his computer screen and scribbling some notes. Reid nodded to his friend and closed the door. Joey motioned him to the other side of the desk where Reid could see the computer screen. Joey pointed out a few entries to Reid. Salem Reid nodded as Joey navigated the program. There were no surprises, just confirmation of what Reid already knew.

The two men exited Joey's office and walked down a hallway and up a flight of stairs. They entered the office of Michael McIntosh. He had a great spot. It was a secluded corner office with a window overlooking PIB and a portion of the new car lot. They stepped in and closed the door. Michael looked up and removed a pair of reading glasses. He was surprised to have visitors in his office. The big window behind Michael was covered by the closed blinds. He hadn't wanted to look out on the gray, rainy, and depressing Monday.

"Joey?" he asked. "Is there a problem?"

He glanced at Reid. He had met him a few times over the years, and he recognized him but didn't remember his name. He wasn't sure why this guy was in his office with Joey either.

"There is Michael," he said, as he sat down across from his brother.

Reid remained standing. He was at the side of Michael's desk, perhaps five feet from the man. Michael McIntosh glanced nervously at Reid, and then he looked past him at the closed door. He looked back at Joey.

"What's going on?" he asked.

"You sold me out, Michael. You're a disgusting piece of shit," Joey said. "A woman is dead because of you."

"What the heck are you talking about, Joey?" Michael gave a nervous laugh and shook his head.

"You sold a Flex a few years ago to an Oscar Villanueva through Worldwide Entertainment. I checked the system. You gave him an incredible deal."

"So?" Michael said, and again glanced around nervously.

"I don't know if he leaned on you or what, but he got you in his grips one way or another. You fed him information that gave him access to homes that he looted. My house was a big score for the man, and I imagine for you too. You ripped off your own brother," Joey said.

"Get out of my office, Joey. And take this man, whoever he is, with you!" Michael yelled.

Michael McIntosh didn't even see Reid move, but he was on him in a flash. Michael was a decent-sized man. He wasn't as big as Joey, but he was over six feet and weighed north of two hundred pounds. Reid had stepped in and hit the man flush on the side of his head with a powerful blow. It knocked him out of his chair and he lay dazed and bleeding on his plush carpeting. He tried to get up, but Reid kicked him in the ribs hard enough to cause an audible pop. Reid shoved his Glock into Michael McIntosh's mouth, and hauled him up onto his desktop.

Joey continued. "No, Michael. We are not leaving. We have much to discuss."

Reid produced the business cards he found at Oscar's, and held them in front of Michael's face. Joey resumed talking.

"Recognize these, Michael? You knew my code, and it's written on the back of your business card with my address. This is your handwriting too. Then I did more research. You've been pushing the Cobra alarm system that's linked to people's homes. It doesn't sell all that well. Alarms are a pain in the ass, and a lot of people forgo them because they go off when they shouldn't. So when you talk to people that purchase vehicles here, you sometimes discover who doesn't have alarm systems in their homes. You passed that on to Oscar."

Reid shuffled the business cards in front of Michael's face, and Joey kept talking.

"Every one of these addresses matches up with a vehicle purchased here, Michael. You are a sorry piece of shit," he reminded him.

Michael McIntosh began to sob. Reid tossed him back into his chair.

"How are you going to fix this, Michael?" Joey asked.

There was a long silence. Michael continued to sob.

Finally he spoke. "I don't know how to fix it," he whined.

"Well I do, Michael," Reid said. "Listen very carefully," he added, and began outlining the plan.

———

McIntosh Ford would start and fund a new charity. It would be called "The Sarah Fund" and it would benefit women desperate to leave the life of prostitution and the men who had coerced them into that lifestyle. The charity would provide temporary housing, medical care, drug and alcohol treatment, and protection from those who might do them harm. Five percent of the profit of each vehicle sold from the dealership would go to the charity. Michael McIntosh would personally fund the first $50,000, but would otherwise be uninvolved in running the charity. He would maintain his position as McIntosh Ford's general manager, but for the next twelve month's he would receive only 40 percent of the remaining company profits, and Joey would get 60 percent in order to compensate the younger brother for the injustice he had endured.

The Sarah Fund would maintain and operate an office on the premises of McIntosh Ford at no expense to the charity, and would be run by two employees who had been pre-selected by Reid and Joey. The employees, pending their acceptance of the job offer, would be nicely compensated at $75,000 per year.

———

After listening to the conditions he would have to meet, Michael McIntosh had gone pale. He would no longer be able to live the lavish lifestyle he had become accustomed to. Of course, he would still be far better off than most people, but that was no comfort to him.

"What if I refuse?" he asked weakly.

Reid placed his gun firmly in Michael's eye socket. "You won't refuse. And we have a number of people keeping their eyes on you. Don't be foolish. You've been given an out."

"Okay," he said. It was little more than a whisper.

Reid backed away and Joey took his place next to his brother.

"Stand up, Michael," Joey instructed, and the older sibling did as he was told.

When Michael stood, Joey hit him as hard as he could directly in the mouth. Michael's mouth spewed blood and he spat out at least one tooth as he held himself up using both hands on the desk.

"You'll need to get the blood out of the carpet or replace it, Michael," Joey told him. "I want this office in excellent condition when The Sarah Fund takes it over next week. You can find some space on the first floor."

Reid and Joey left the office, walked down the stairs, through the long hallway, and back to Joey's office. Reid handed Joey the $7,000.

"For The Sarah Fund," he said.

Joey smiled big and said, "For The Sarah Fund."

Joey locked the cash in his safe and walked Reid out into the showroom.

"How about food?" Joey said cheerfully. "I'm hungry all of a sudden."

"Sounds great, Joey," Reid said, and they ventured out into the rainy Monday afternoon for lunch.

# 67

REID RETURNED TO WORK EARLY on Tuesday. He arrived at 6:30 am in hopes of getting a jump on emails, voicemails, and going through all the paperwork that had piled up on his desk during his sabbatical. The rain continued through the morning and it put him in a somber mood. He persisted through the morning at the mundane tasks of office work and by noon he was almost caught up. He took some calls and arranged a few security details for the weekend and for the following week. He tried to put aside thoughts about the detour his life had taken the past ten days, but he kept coming back to it. He felt a loss deep within himself. He regretted not ever making contact with Sarah now. He felt a longing for her. It was like a piece of his life had been snatched from him that he could never replace. But he knew it was his own fault. He could now forgive her for the way she was and for the things she had done. He hoped that she had forgiven him. He wanted to believe so. Based on everything he had learned over the past ten days, he thought it likely. He knew that was the best he could do with it, but it gnawed at him nonetheless.

Janice had been on his mind too. He could tell himself that she was a stripper and a hooker, and that having her in his life would bring nothing but misery. It was probably the truth. But she was a stunningly beautiful woman who desired him. It was hard to overlook that. It would be for any man.

And then there was Millicent. She had become leery of him because of his propensity for violence. She had identified something he had always known about himself, though. He did not seek violence or wish harm upon others, but violence always seemed to find him. He had been unable to avoid it since he was young. Had she not run off to visit her parents, and stayed in Atlanta throughout this ordeal, she would have possibly been aware of the worst of the violence during this entire affair. He was sure she wouldn't have stayed with him then. So what did the future hold? Would she contact him when she returned? He had wanted to call her, but he had restrained himself. Besides, how would he respond when she would say, "What have you been up to?"

"Oh, not too much. I've just been hanging out with a couple of strippers and taking violence to the extreme while you've been gone."

But she was the complete package to him. She was kind, smart, compassionate, and absolutely gorgeous. He knew that she shared his feelings too. She was struggling with the right thing to do; he just hoped he was the right thing.

His thoughts were interrupted by Julie. "Salem, you have a call on line one," she told him over the intercom.

It was a call from a pro basketball player from the West Coast. He was coming to Atlanta in a few weeks for a wedding ceremony. He planned to stay a few extra days and do a little partying in the Peach State. He wanted to know if he could secure Reid's services for a limo and a bodyguard for two nights in late September. Reid assured him that they could do that and sent him back to Julie for scheduling.

He glanced at his watch and it was nearing 1 pm. He was hungry and he had gotten a lot accomplished, so he decided to get some food. He called Lara Brooks.

"Hey, Salem!" She sounded excited to hear from him.

"I need to grab some lunch. Do you want to join me? I have something to ask you," he said.

"Hmm. Mysterious," she said. "I'd love to, Salem."

"Okay. Where are you?" he asked.

"Sandy Springs. I came back home," she said. "I had been living in an extended stay in Vinings. I've been renting two places for three months."

"How about Ruth's Chris Steakhouse on Roswell Road at the Perimeter?" he asked.

"Absolutely!" she said.

"Okay. Meet me there in fifteen minutes," he said, and clicked off.

When Reid walked in the restaurant, Lara was waiting for him, but he didn't recognize her at first. She wore an elegant pair of blue-and-white striped shorts that showed off a pair off shapely, smooth ebony legs. She sported a bright yellow, half-sleeved blouse that flattered her well-proportioned chest. Her hair was out of the baseball cap and her long, flowing black locks looked lovely. He had thought her quite attractive, but now he considered her a knockout. She wore makeup and jewelry and held a Kate Spade handbag at her side. She saw Reid, smiled, and waved as she moved towards him. When they embraced, she smelled wonderful.

She stepped back from him and he stared at her. He was speechless. She decided to tease him a bit, so she cocked her head and twirled for him, then cocked her head to the other side. He finally broke out of the trance, and grinned from ear to ear.

"Wow!" was all he could manage.

"I'm hungry and it smells marvelous in here. Take me to lunch, Salem," she said, and hooked her arm in his.

They were seated and placed drink orders. They both had water with lemon.

"So what did you want to ask me, Salem?" she asked with a coy smile.

"How would you like to be president of a newly founded charity organization called The Sarah Fund?" he asked. "It has been started by McIntosh Ford and would pay you a starting salary of $75,000 a year."

She stared at him. "Are you kidding me?"

"No, I'm not kidding," he said, and explained what it was and what the charity would do. He went on to describe roughly what her role would be.

"Salem, I'm flattered, but I don't have the skills to run a charity organization…as much as I would love to do it," she said.

"Sure you do. You're smart, savvy, tough, and kindhearted all at the same time. And you have experience in the field. You're perfect for it."

"I don't have great clerical skills," she said doubtfully.

"We have that covered," he said. "You will be the person raising funds. You'll meet with people. You can dress just like you are now and woo the hell out of them. You'll raise more money for this cause than ten strippers on the main stage," he told her, feeling like a salesman himself.

She laughed. "Do you really think so?" she asked, and he knew he had her.

"I know so. Are you in?" he asked.

She smiled and nodded. "I'm in!"

They celebrated with a fine lunch and splurged on a bottle of red wine. Reid wasn't a big wine drinker, but he ended up enjoying the one glass he drank. Lara had two glasses and she seemed to be really enjoying her freedom and the prospects of her new position.

They finished their meals and Reid paid the bill. He walked her to her car, and hugged her goodbye.

"Are you good to start on Monday?" he asked her.

"Yes. I'll be ready," she said.

He watched her get into her late-model Mazda. She zoomed out of the parking lot, waving as she left.

Reid climbed into his car and pulled into traffic on Roswell Road. As he wheeled south towards Buckhead, he realized yet another beautiful woman was making his head spin.

# 68

CONSUELO VALDEZ HAD HOPED that Oscar would call her for another evening together after spending time with him on Saturday night. He had not and she was disappointed. But on Wednesday morning, she put on a cute, low-cut maid's uniform and went to his home for the regular cleaning. Normally, he was home when she cleaned and she hoped he would be there this time. But when she rang the doorbell, he did not answer. She used her key and entered. She immediately knew something was amiss. Black flies swarmed the house and the stench was unbearable. She spotted the corpse on the sofa in seconds and ran from the house and vomited in the bushes outside. She used her cell phone to call the police, and waited inside her car for them to arrive.

She was questioned and detained for several hours. She explained that she was the maid, and had come to perform her regularly scheduled cleaning of the home. Then the parade of detectives and forensic people arrived. The heroin in the garage was discovered, and they found the back door unlocked. A paneled compartment in the master closet had been pried open, but items of value remained. The police discovered a key to a storage warehouse that conveniently had a tab with the storage facility's address on it. At the storage facility, the police found close to $750,000 in cash, and a large display of jewelry, coins, and other valuables. The detectives were confused as to why the panel in the master was broken, but items of value remained. Large quantities of drugs remained on the premises as well. Had the intruder been looking for specific items, or was the main goal of the intrusion to murder a man who appeared to be a thief and drug dealer? These questions plagued the detectives, but ultimately they released Consuelo after attaining her address and license plate number. Consuelo Valdez left Oscar's home without her pan of chile rellenos. She no longer wanted it back.

———

Millicent Ivey sat in her office at the ARC. Much like Reid, she was trying to catch up on email, paperwork, and the assortment of items that were left unattended in her absence. She was glad to be back to work. She had enjoyed being home in Huntsville at first, but she had gotten bored and ended up having too much time on her hands. Her thoughts would drift. Mostly she thought about Salem Reid. She was infatuated with him. She knew it and she knew he knew it too. She had arrived home late Tuesday, and had wanted nothing more than to run to his condo and hug and squeeze him. She longed for his touch. She knew if she saw him she would melt and be unable to pull herself away from him. She didn't want that. She needed more time to think. She also wanted to consult Jill. She had told Jill some things, but she had left a lot out too. She had let Jill draw some of her own conclusions, but Jill wasn't stupid. She would figure it out over time, and that may bring more questions. But for now, she had let it be.

Millicent had a busy work schedule through the weekend. She would have little time to socialize as she got back into the daily grind. She had a busy fall program beginning soon, and she needed to work out all the details on scheduling. On top of that she had a cheerleading camp this weekend comprised of middle school girls aspiring to be high school cheerleaders over the next few years. She had aerobics classes to lead every day this week, but that was okay. She got some relief from the tough physical workouts, and it helped with the anxiety of her current emotional state. At least for a while. So she plunged into her work and tried to fight the confusion of what direction her romantic life was heading. She wondered if she should get a dog, but then dismissed the idea. She simply didn't have the time for a pet.

———

Liza had been getting better every day. It had been a week since Reid and Joey had rescued her and taken her to the hospital. She had energy and a new enthusiasm for life. When she had looked in the mirror over the past few days, she had seen some resemblance to the pretty cheerleader she had been in high school. It had been over a week now since she had taken drugs; she estimated nine or ten days. She was coping. The outpatient treatment program was helping her. She had completed three days. There were classes and meetings and doctors' lectures and she enjoyed them all. She hadn't been sure what to expect, but it had not been a grind at all. She felt as if she was recovering. She understood that her recovery was fragile and in the early stages, but with Joey's support and Herschel's love, she was finding her way.

She was getting some exercise too. She had pulled an elliptical and a treadmill out from the corner of Joey's basement and dusted them off. Since Monday, she had worked out every morning before outpatient on the elliptical for twenty minutes. Then when she arrived home, she ran on the treadmill for two miles at six miles per hour. After her treadmill run, she would take Herschel for a one-mile walk. Her diet still consisted mostly of water, fruits, and vegetables, but she had eaten a little pasta and some whole wheat bread recently. Her visits to the bathroom were tolerable the last two occasions as well. She knew she had reason to be grateful. Joey had been wonderful to her. He was patient, understanding, and very supportive. She was physically attracted to him also. He was handsome and had a nice smile. He was big and strong, but always very gentle in his manner with her. She felt safe and protected with him. She wondered if she was falling in love with the guy. He'd been a rock for her. The problem was that she wasn't completely sure how he felt. He hadn't come to her bedroom in the night or made any suggestive comments at all during the time she'd been in his house. She had never been involved with any man who hadn't been aggressive with her sexually. He had told her that she was pretty, but she wondered if he was just being nice. Was he different or was he just not interested in her that way? She was afraid to ask, but it was the elephant in the room for her. She hadn't really thought about it much until the last couple of days. She had been so preoccupied with both her mental and physical health that romantic notions had not even entered her mind. She had relied on Joey for moral strength and support. But now her feelings were evolving. It was exciting to her, but also scary. And now he was sitting in the living room having just showered while she was cooking dinner. Prior to his shower, he had completed a three-mile run on the treadmill. He had jumped on it both yesterday and today after he'd come home from work. He was looking at her and smiling like he did sometimes. It filled her with excitement when he did this, but it embarrassed her too.

"What?" she asked and gave him her half smile. He noticed her cheeks were a little flushed also.

"What are you cooking? It smells great!"

"Chicken and rice with some broccoli in it," she said.

He got up and moved to the kitchen. "I have something to ask you."

"What is it, Joey?"

He explained how McIntosh Ford had started The Sarah Fund, what it was, and how it would work. She listened attentively, but paid close attention to the food she was cooking too.

Finally, he said, "Would you like a job? Maybe part-time to begin and then closer to thirty-five hours a week after you complete the out-patient program. You would work with a woman named Lara Brooks. She's a smart, competent woman who has agreed to run the charity."

"Oh Joey, that is so nice, but I don't think I'm qualified," she said. "I wish I was. I would love to do it."

"You are qualified. Lara would be the person to do speaking engagements and try to solicit donors. But she lacks the clerical experience that you have. It would be a perfect fit," he said.

"You really think so?" she asked, and he could see the excitement in her eyes.

"Yes. I really think so. The pay starts at $75,000 per year," he said.

Her big eyes bulged. "Did I hear you correctly? $75,000 a year?" She was incredulous.

"That's right," he answered.

"Joey, I don't know what to say," she said.

"Say yes!"

"Yes, then!" she said, and he took her in his arms.

———

After dinner, Joey helped Liza clean up, and then he retired to his bedroom. He watched a little baseball and then turned the lights off. Liza was in her room with Herschel at her side. She couldn't sleep. She was very excited about going back to work at a real job. And the money. She had never made anything close to that. But she was mostly excited about being with Joey and Herschel in this great home. She wondered if Joey was awake and what he was thinking. She lay in bed for another hour, tossing and turning. Sleep wouldn't come. She wondered again what he was thinking about. She got out of bed. She decided she would go and ask him.

# 69

SALEM REID HAD SPENT THE LAST two weeks immersing himself in his work. He had landed several good-paying security jobs, and the limo service was riding high too. September was shaping up to be a very profitable month. He had also gotten back into the routine of training with Ian on the mats in the warehouse area of his business. They had sparred and grappled two nights ago and he was still sore. He had a nice bruise where Ian had nailed him pretty good on the chest with a spinning back kick. He had made several trips to the shooting range in Sandy Springs over the past week also. He ran eight miles every other evening, and did push-ups, crunches, and hit the bags on the nights he didn't run.

Earlier in the week, he had taken time to drive out to Embry Hills and visit Sarah's mom. He was able to relay some of the things he had learned about Sarah in regards to the drugs to her mom without saying too much about anything else. He had basically referred to Lara as a reliable source and had let Mrs. Lindstrom know that Sarah had been duped into drug addiction through an injury she had sustained at work. Patsy Lindstrom seemed relieved. He also told her about The

Sarah Fund, and what they were doing to help girls who wanted out of the life to succeed in that effort. They had a nice visit and she asked him to stay in touch. He promised to keep her posted on the progress of the charity, and said he would visit again soon.

Reid had spoken with Janice once. She had called him a week ago and asked about arrangements to get her car fixed. He had set her up with Petey, and asked her if she needed to borrow a car. She had declined the car, but asked if she could borrow him for the night. He, of course, declined.

She laughed and said, "You can't blame a girl for trying."

He saw Lara, Liza, and Joey several times over the past two weeks. He'd met them all for lunch just yesterday in Brookhaven, and was glad to have them in his life. They had become good friends to him; he discovered he laughed a great deal when he was with them. It felt good to laugh. Lara had gotten the charity off the ground in good fashion. Aside from the original funding of $57,000, she had accumulated an additional $20,000 in donations and they had added another $2,000 from the dealership contribution. In two short weeks, the charity had raised almost $80,000. Lara and Liza worked well together. They each had talents where the other was deficient. It was the classic yin and yang. Reid was certain that they would be successful, and help many young women along the way.

Autumn had arrived in Atlanta, but it was still warm, and probably would be into early October. Reid glanced at his watch and decided he would polish off a few emails and some paperwork in the next thirty minutes, and then call it quits for the day. It was almost 6 pm, so if he knuckled down he'd escape soon enough. He got to work clicking and clacking. He had responded to three emails, and was making some entries into a spreadsheet when a shadow passed his door. He didn't look up right away; he figured it was Julie or one of the limo drivers moving down the hall to the warehouse. But then he saw movement again and glanced up.

Millicent Ivey stood in his doorway. She was wearing tight blue shorts and a tighter red tank top. She had running shoes on her delicate feet. Her black hair was loose and hung just below her shoulders. Her green eyes sparkled from across the room. She had a big smile on her face. She was breathtaking. She held two Braves tickets in her hand and waved them as she moved forward. She walked around his desk and plopped down onto his lap and hugged him fiercely. She pulled his face up and kissed him passionately.

When she came up for air, she said, "I've missed you terribly, Salem Reid."

She fanned the tickets in front of him once more and said, "It's been a while since we talked baseball. We can make the first inning if we leave right away."

He pulled her close and kissed her again. Then they jumped up together and headed downtown to Turner Field. The Braves had folded in September. They had played awful baseball, and had been eliminated from any playoff hopes. But Salem Reid had never been more excited to attend an Atlanta Braves baseball game.

To learn more about Patrick Brown and his other novels,
visit www.patrickbrownnovels.com

# ACKNOWLEDGMENTS

I am deeply grateful to Jeff Hopeck for guiding me into this process. Your wisdom and insight are without peer.

To Susan Brown and Paul Swanson for believing in me, and giving me the gentle nudge to take this step.

To Emory Potter for your valuable service and keen eye.

To Jordan Agolli for your constant encouragement, optimism, compassion, and friendship. The sky is the limit for you, my young friend.

To Bethany Brown of the Cadence Group for your dedication and prompt professionalism.

To Gwyn Snider for bringing the book to life.

To Katie Ingraham Hopeck and Vance Fite, you both are just awesome people. Your never-ending support and friendship mean everything.

To Pharoe Hickson for your artistic contribution and great hair.

To Logan Brown for your photographic assistance and constant support. You are a fine son, and a great pal.

To Madison Brown for making dad laugh. You are the funniest person I know.

To my mother, Julie Brown, for her love, support, and for never missing a ballgame.

To my long-time friend, Arnold Vickers, for going down the "river" with me on numerous occasions. Your laughter and sense of humor have brightened some dreary days.

A special thank you to the Uchida clan, Brendan Dumont, and the Taido Family for constant inspiration, encouragement, and support. Thanks for reminding me to "never give up" and to live the dream every day.